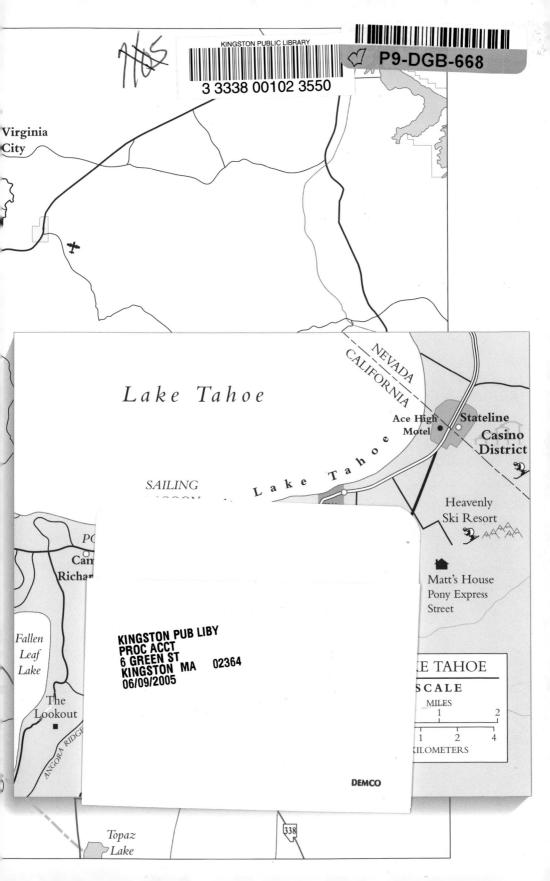

P9-DGB-668

Virginia
City

NEVADA

CALIFORNIA

Lake Tahoe

Ace High
Motel

Stateline

Casino
District

Lake Tahoe

SAILING

Heavenly
Ski Resort

Matt's House
Pony Express
Street

P

Ca

Richa

Fallen
Leaf
Lake

The
Lookout

ANGORA RIDGE

E TAHOE

SCALE

MILES
1   2

1   2   4
KILOMETERS

DEMCO

Topaz
Lake

338

CASE OF LIES

PERRI O'SHAUGHNESSY

CASE
OF
LIES

DELACORTE PRESS

CASE OF LIES
A Delacorte Book / July 2005

Published by
Bantam Dell
A Division of Random House, Inc.
New York, New York

Book design by Glen Edelstein

Delacorte Press is a registered trademark of Random House, Inc.,
and the colophon is a trademark of Random House, Inc.

Library of Congress Cataloging-in-Publication Data
O'Shaughnessy, Perri.
Case of lies/Perri O'Shaughnessy
p. cm.
ISBN 0-385-33795-7
1. Reilly, Nina (Fictitious character)—Fiction. 2. Women lawyers—Fiction. 3. Tahoe,
Lake, Region (Calif. and Nev.)—Fiction. I. Title.

PS3565.S542 C37 2005   2005047026
813/.54 22

Manufactured in the United States of America
Published simultaneously in Canada

10 9 8 7 6 5 4 3 2 1
BVG

To our brother, Patrick.
He helped thousands of California workers in his law practice, and in his private life he loved fully.

CASE OF LIES

PART ONE

The behavior of fundamental particles is essentially random.

—HEISENBERG

Chapter 1

Nina Reilly lay on her stomach, her eyes closed, a white washcloth draped over her backside. The endless mental lists had fled from her head, lulled by Chelsi's electronic ambient music and her soothing hands on Nina's back. Now Nina kept slipping into a snooze, the kind where you disappear and then snap back your head as your senses return.

Let's see, she had dreamed a little dream about an old woman approaching, babbling something. This apparition had a dreadful aspect, as though if Nina ran away she would become gigantic and even more frightening. She kept coming closer, the hideous old witch, whispering so low Nina couldn't quite—then she understood, and deep dream relief came over her.

All the old lady wanted was a piggyback ride, then she'd go away. Nina crouched and the old lady hopped on—

"Lots of my clients take naps," Chelsi said as the snap thing happened and Nina's eyes jerked open.

"And miss the whole massage? No way," Nina said.

"Your body will remember."

"Big deal. This is too good to spend asleep."

"We could talk a little if you want. Some people just like to relax." She was stroking Nina's sides, almost lifting her up from the table, her hands strong and the points of her fingernails digging in now and then. Chelsi was a tall ponytailed girl in her early twenties, and the smile she always wore seemed to be for real.

"You talk," Nina said. "I'll just moan here and there."

"All right. Let's see. Well, last week when I worked on you for the first time, I thought, She's somebody. I even thought you might have used a fake name. That would have been fine, by the way. LeAnn Rimes came here when she was appearing at Caesars last year and wrote down that she was somebody named Ms. Exter. It's not an insurance situation, so who cares what you want to call yourself?"

Chelsi waited, but her hands kept working and Nina didn't respond.

"Dr. Whittaker sends me all his headaches. He says ninety percent of the time it's tension and he says I have good hands. He comes to me himself. Oops, I'm not supposed to say that. Anyway, my dad says I got the curious gene. He says I ought to be a detective. Wow, you are so tight around the neck."

"Mmm."

"For instance," Chelsi said, then pressed hard, her hands making tiny squeezing motions on the back of Nina's neck. She was using kukui-nut oil to baste her. One could die at the beginning of the hour and Chelsi would never know it until her chime went off. "I'm gonna say you're a swimmer."

"Whenever I can," Nina managed to say.

Chelsi laughed in delight. "I knew because you have these excellent muscles in your shoulders, square shoulders and a tiny waist. A swimmer's back. I am so good. Now, your neck, I've seen that a lot with people with big pressures at work. Last week when I did that scalp massage you practically melted. It's definitely the cause of your headaches. That or your eyes. I'll work on them in a minute.

"And then there's this." Chelsi's finger delicately traced the scar along Nina's side, still sore after almost three years. "You don't have to tell me or anything. I'm putting oil on it because you may not have incorporated that place back into your body and you need to have it witnessed. It's part of you and it's nice and neat—"

"It's ugly, come on." Nina's voice came out harsh.

"Never mind, I'll move on, just let me touch it again next week, okay?"

"It's an exit-wound scar," Nina said. "From a thirty-two-caliber pistol fired by a woman in a courtroom."

"I knew. I just knew it. You're a policewoman!"

"What if I said I'm a bank robber?"

Chelsi's hands paused. "I don't believe that. It wouldn't bother me if it was true, though, I have to admit. I had a guy from Vegas in here who told me about how he embezzled from his boss at a credit agency. Even hustlers suffer from stress and hold it in their muscles. But you're not a bank robber. Your haircut is too primo. Long layers, really nice, no spray. And you don't wear much makeup. Your style is all wrong for a bank robber."

Nina didn't answer. She imagined Chelsi's big-haired mama of a bank robber.

"Let's work on your neck some more." She dug her fingers under Nina's skull at the back. It should have hurt. Instead, it was a catharsis, a stream of accumulated tension breaking up and flowing away. "You *are* kidding me, right? Although you don't work at Tahoe long before you realize we're all running some kind of hustle. Look at all the rich people who rent a garage on the Nevada side and claim they're Nevada residents so they won't have to pay state income tax in California. I hustle a little myself. You're paying me on the cash-discount basis, right? It's a tax-free zone up here. The showgirls make so much money outside the shows doing entertaining, you wouldn't believe it. No offense, but I also know you're not a showgirl."

"Because?"

"Too petite. And, you know, not in your twenties anymore. So what do you really do?"

"Law. I'm a lawyer." The hands stopped, and Nina wondered if Chelsi would slide out of her cheerful mood. Confessing her profession at a cocktail party often resulted in a step back and eyes averted from hers, as though she'd admitted she was a hooker.

Both necessary evils, she said to herself.

But Chelsi took no offense. "Right! Nina Reilly. I read about you in the paper. You do murder trials. Keep your head down. Relax."

"I do all kinds of law work. Whatever comes through the door. Not just murder trials."

"Well, that might explain your neck. Is that where the head-aches start?"

"Actually, they start right in my temples, even when I haven't been reading," Nina said.

"Let me try something," Chelsi told her. She rolled Nina over and began massaging her face, starting with her forehead and temples, circling the eye sockets with expert fingers, prod-ding under her jaw. "It's a Tibetan technique. Kum Nye." Again, the relief was both subtle and intense. Nina felt her jaw go slack for maybe the first time since childhood.

"You poor thing. You need to come in at least once a week for a couple of months. I can do more for you than those pills you were prescribed. You have stored-up tension everywhere."

"It's a deal," Nina muttered.

There was a long silence while Chelsi did some acupressure

on Nina's cheekbones and around her sinuses, then did that dainty pressing around her eyes again. "I'm sorry you got shot," she volunteered finally.

Nobody had ever said that to Nina at the hospital or afterward. Her brother, Matt, had been furious with her for taking the murder case in the first place. Her son, Bob, had been inarticulate with shock. She had been given flowers, kudos for catching a killer, but not a lot of sympathy. In fact, looking back, there had been a tinge of "you asked for it" in the reactions of the courtroom personnel. You take murder cases, you take your chances, was the attitude.

Nina realized that she still felt resentful about that, but even as the realization came, the resentment was going away, in waves accompanying the long strokes of Chelsi's hands.

So it was true, you did hold emotions in your muscles.

Chelsi was as healing in her speech as in her hands. She was working Nina's jaw hinges again. "Whenever you start to feel tense, yawn. Do you like what you do?"

"When I win. When I do good work."

They lapsed back into silence for some time while Nina's shoulders and biceps got a final workout, Chelsi leaning over Nina from above like an angel of mercy.

"Let's give you a foot rub. Are you good at it?"

"At what?"

"Your work."

"Yes."

"Now, see, I ask women that, and hardly ever do they say yes. The guys never hesitate. They say, 'Sure.' You're awesome to have that kind of confidence. What is it really like? I mean, really?" She oiled Nina's foot and started tweaking and pulling on her toes, as if they had muscles too.

"Practicing law? Well, a case starts with an immediate problem. Your client is in jail, or your client's about to be evicted, or your client's marriage is falling apart. You try to organize this real-life chaos into a theory or story that calms things down and will resolve the problem in a fair and orderly way. You get all the information and you try to work the system so your client has the outcome he or she deserves."

"How do you come up with this theory?"

"You read other legal cases and try to organize the facts so that your client comes out the hero, not the villain. Then you try to convince the judge that your version is the best version. Because the other guy always has a good story, too."

"You don't try to get the client what they want?"

"Sometimes they don't know. Sometimes they are unrealistic. Sometimes the system can't give them what they deserve. All the system can really do is lock people up or transfer money around. It can't bring back a loved one, for instance, and sometimes that's all the client wants. What's the matter?" Chelsi's hands had faltered, and she sighed.

"You make me think of a loved one I lost," she said.

The chime rang.

"That darn thing," Chelsi said. She gave Nina's feet one final squeeze and said, "You take as long as you need to get dressed." The door shut behind her, the soft New Age chords switched off abruptly, and Nina, deposited back into rude reality, blinked open her eyes to a shelf of unguents and towels and strong mountain sun filtering through the pines outside Chelsi's window.

She sat up reluctantly and slid off the table. While she dressed, she thought about Chelsi. She pulled on her blue silk jacket last and brushed her hair in the mirror above the sink, then consulted her watch. Court in thirty minutes.

She opened the door.

In the cubbyhole office, Chelsi hung up the phone and said, "Feeling better?"

"Much better. There's one thing I wanted to ask you. For

about two minutes, when you were working on my face, I suddenly got the most splitting headache. Then it disappeared like air, and now I'm fine."

"That was your headache quota for the week. It let go all at once. You'll have a good week."

"Thanks. Really. I'm glad I found you. What do I owe you today?"

"Nothing."

"Excuse me?"

"Not a thing. And nothing next week, either." Chelsi folded her arms over the flowers embroidered on her smock. "I'd like to ask you a favor instead. My uncle Dave has—he needs—he has a legal thing. Would you talk to him?"

Nina put on her sunglasses and laid her business card and fifty dollars on the desk. "Like I said, Chelsi, anything that comes through the door. The first consultation is free."

"It's urgent. My dad and I have been trying to help him find a lawyer fast." *Fast* usually meant *too late.* Nina grimaced. "He's charged with a crime?"

"No! No! He was a victim. He and my aunt Sarah. Two years ago. There was a robbery in a motel they were staying at near Prize's and—and my aunt Sarah was shot." Chelsi gave Nina's body a look and Nina could almost feel her curious fingers on the scar again. "The South Lake Tahoe police couldn't find the shooter. Uncle Dave went to a lawyer who helped him file a suit against the motel. For—for—"

"Negligent security?"

"Right. Something like that. And he put in a bunch of John Does like the lawyer said, so when he found out who the robber was he could do a—"

"Substitute in the robber as a defendant," Nina said. "There must be a wrongful-death cause of action too."

"That sounds right. Even if the police didn't feel they had

enough evidence to arrest the robber, Uncle Dave could still sue him for damages. But now there's a court deadline or something where the motel is going to have the suit thrown out. Uncle Dave drinks too much, you know? He's broke and he's broken. My dad and I can put in some money to help, but—anyway, would you talk to him and look at his papers? For two massages?" She handed Nina her money back.

"I'll be getting the better of the barter," Nina said. "Have your uncle Dave call my office and set up a time with Sandy, my secretary."

"Great! My aunt Sarah was such a good person. It can't happen that the universe could let her die and not punish anyone. She was only thirty-eight, and here's the worst, it still makes me choke up to talk about it, she was pregnant. Their first baby. They had been trying so long. It makes me so sad and mad. My mother left us when I was three, and Aunt Sarah was always there for me. Anyway, I appreciate it."

"I'll see you next week, then."

"We won't talk about it during your next massage. It's bad for relaxation."

"I'm sorry about your aunt, Chelsi," Nina said.

Chelsi gave her a pained smile.

"Thanks. I can tell you mean it. I know you can't bring her back, but—anyway, thank you. Now here's your assignment for the week. Yawn whenever you feel tense," Chelsi said.

Chapter 2

Two days later, a fresh mug of Italian espresso in hand, stockinged heels riding the edge of her desk, Nina stole a moment to reflect.

The long workday had begun. On the drive down Pioneer Trail that morning toward the office, Nina had watched the bicyclists and joggers with even more than her usual envy. They were out grabbing the last glories of fall, so damn happy, smelling the fresh tang of high snows and watching fluttering dry leaves while she contemplated her day, the bitter child-custody battle coming up, along with two grisly settlement conferences, all to be conducted in the windowless courtroom of the irascible Judge Flaherty.

Long ago, when law began, the advocates and judges must have met in tree-shaded glades, toga-clad, birdsong the accompaniment to their work, courtesy and dignity their style, and—

—And of course, as a woman, she would have been pouring the wine from the ewer, not arguing the case. But one could fantasize at 7:45 in the morning while watching birds and squirrels chase around the autumnal marsh that rolled out toward a distant, twinkling Lake Tahoe.

After several months in Monterey, she and her teenage son, Bob, had returned to Tahoe. Sandy Whitefeather had returned to her domain in Nina's office in the Starlake Building and was drumming up business before Nina had time to put down her cup on the desk. The young woman lawyer who had been handling Nina's cases found a law job in Reno, and left open files and a busy calendar of court appearances.

In spite of the time crunch, Nina found just enough space in the morning to pour Hitchcock's kibble and Bob's cereal, and to enjoy the short trip up Pioneer Trail to her law office.

When evening came, after she and Sandy locked up, Nina would drive home through the forest to the cabin on Kulow Street, noting the hints of winter to come she perceived in the dry pines and parched streams. The cabin still basked in early-evening sun. Inside, she would kick off her shoes and pour herself a glass of Clos du Bois and watch the world news, make dinner, and nag Bob into finishing his homework. Once a week she called her father, and once or twice a week she and Bob went to her brother Matt's house for dinner.

September and October passed in a flurry while she re-established her routines. The fees rolled in and she paid off her debts.

The judges accepted her back. She had a pretty good working relationship with most of the local lawyers, and she finally knew what she was doing.

The small office suite in the Starlake Building on Lake Tahoe Boulevard, right in the heart of town and less than five miles from the Nevada state line, now felt like home, but some part of her was still restless. She had gone from Carmel to San Francisco to Tahoe and back to Carmel and then back to Tahoe again in the past few years. She was starting to ask herself, uncomfortably, if she would ever settle down. Bob deserved stability, and she was going to have to stay put for a while.

She wasn't even sure why she had returned to Tahoe. She might just as well have stayed in Carmel and joined the Pohlmann firm, which had made her a very good offer.

And she had made one other uncomfortable discovery since returning to Tahoe.

Her ex-lover, Paul van Wagoner, and his new flame, Susan Misumi, had quickly moved in together down in Carmel. Fair enough, since Nina had ended it with Paul. The choice of Susan Misumi, with her black bangs, her humorlessness, escaped Nina, but it wasn't her business anymore. Nina and Paul still checked in on each other. They managed to stay friendly because they had been friends before they became lovers.

Nina had moved on. She went out, danced, ate good food, had a few unexpectedly intimate conversations. But she had discovered that she didn't expect much from men anymore. She didn't want to try for love.

That feeling had been growing in her for a long time, and she sometimes wondered if it had something to do with the breakup with Paul. Finding a partner seemed impossible, based on her experiences, so she put it out of her mind.

Men and places. Still, the restlessness would come over her, and she'd feel a need for another place and another man. Other people followed their lifelines. She careened along, too fast, not able to see her own.

But she would always have two constants to ground her: Bob, and her work.

Today, we persevere, she thought. With the last gulp of coffee, she threw two ibuprofen down her throat.

★   ★   ★

The phone buzzed. Nina swung her legs down, sighed, and picked up the phone. Sandy must have come in. Her desk was only ten feet away, through the closed door, but Sandy didn't like getting up.

"He's here, and so's she. Your eight o'clocks," Sandy said.

"And a fine morning it is."

"Hmph. You have half an hour."

The man stood with his back to her, hands in his pockets, looking at one of Sandy's decorations, a Washoe Indian basket on the shelf. He wore a green-and-black plaid lumberjack shirt tucked into a well-broken-in pair of jeans. The belt, a leathercraft affair, must have dated from the sixties. Work boots, a body used to physical work.

A conservative local, Nina thought, pegging him almost before he turned around. Nice wrinkled tan face. Grim expression. Plenty of gray-brown hair on both head and chin. A belly, that was a surprise.

Behind him, pretty Chelsi nodded. She was taller than her uncle. She wore her hair down today and it fell straight and satiny. Something had turned off the smile.

"Hi. I'm Nina Reilly," Nina said, looking the man in the eye, holding out her hand.

"David Hanna."

"Please come in." After ushering Chelsi in, too, Nina glanced toward Sandy, who, resplendent this morning in a heavy turquoise necklace and a denim jumper, seemed to be writing something in the appointment book. Sandy gave Nina a swift look back, one eyebrow cocked.

Look out.

Now, that was an interesting take, since Uncle Dave looked harmless, but Sandy's first impressions had to be taken seriously.

Sandy knew where clients hid their guns and buck knives; she knew if the Rolex was real or faux; a few words to her in the reception area revealed if a new client was resentful, desperate, or suicidal. Recently they had installed an emergency button hooked up to the local police under her desk, and the golf club propped behind her desk only doubled as a decoration.

Such is solo law office life in a gambling town. Prepare for Uzis, Sandy frequently said.

Nina closed the door and Hanna pulled an orange chair away from the wide desk. He sat, crossing one leg at the ankle, stroking his beard, looking out the window behind her desk toward the steel gray lake, but not focusing, just gazing. Chelsi sat in the chair next to his, back straight.

Nina took her time getting comfortable, arranging a few papers on her desk, adjusting her chair. Let them get used to her.

"I don't know why I'm here," David Hanna said finally.

"Because you need to be," Chelsi said.

"I'm not working much. Money's tight. Chelsi and her dad, they've offered to pay for your services, but I just don't know. It doesn't seem right. I hear Chelsi's already told you about the case."

"A little," Nina said.

"Rog was Sarah's brother. I know he can't help wanting to do something. What I can't figure out, what I haven't been able to get my head around all along, is what good it does, suing someone. My wife is gone."

"What's your brother-in-law's name again?"

"Roger Freeman." While Nina made a note on her yellow pad, Hanna watched, squinting. The tops of his ears were red and his nose looked sunburned, too. Either he spent a lot of time outside, or, as Chelsi had suggested, less healthy indoor pursuits heightened his natural color. "What's your usual line of work, Mr. Hanna?"

"I'm a carpenter. Used to be a firefighter."

Nina looked at her client-interview sheet. "Placerville's a great town."

"It's a long drive up Fifty to get here. I don't come up the Hill much anymore since it happened. Chelsi said this conversation right now isn't going to cost us anything?"

"Free consultation," Nina said. "We have half an hour and you came a long way, so how can I help you?"

Hanna shrugged and said, "That's the point. I haven't got a fucking clue."

When Nina didn't bridle at that, he added, "Like I said, talk won't bring her back."

"But you're already involved in a lawsuit. Isn't that right?"

"I had a lawyer in Placerville named Bruce Bennett. Two years ago, after Sarah died, Roger contacted him and had this lawyer file a civil suit against the motel where it all happened. I wasn't sure about the whole thing, but Bennett got us in his office and oh, he talked it up, how much money we were going to hit them up for, how they were negligent. They let the bastard onto the property. No video camera and the clerk off somewhere. The lawyer talked us into suing the motel. Why, he practically had us convinced that the motel owner, who by the way wasn't even around that night, did the shooting."

"Sounds like he was trying to put on a very aggressive case on your behalf."

"I guess." He shook his head. "It never sat right with me, blaming the motel, but Roger was so gung ho. We used up some of Sarah's life insurance to pay Bennett, but when the money ran out he filed a substitution-of-attorney form and left us flat."

"I guess that didn't leave you with a very high opinion of lawyers. I know Bruce. The lawsuit stayed active?"

He shook his head. "I really don't know where things stand with it."

"You couldn't pay Bruce Bennett, so he quit?"

"Basically."

"I would think carpenters were in big demand around here. I can never get anyone to come out and fix my porch," Nina said.

"I don't work much lately." He sighed. "I have problems."

"Problems?"

He chewed on a thumb, as if the question demanded arduous consideration that was beyond him. Scanning the room as if he might locate a swift escape route that wouldn't require him to pass Sandy, his eyes landed on Chelsi.

"Uncle Dave's been sick," Chelsi said, taking her cue.

"Hmm," Nina said. "Well, I understand you were going to bring me the court papers to look at," she went on neutrally.

"Right." He reached inside his wool shirt and pulled out a battered envelope. He set it on the desk, the hand revealing a slight tremor. Nina looked at him carefully, noting the thin burst of broken capillaries in his ruddy cheeks, the tangle of red veins around the edges of his eyes.

He hasn't had the hair of the dog this morning, she thought, and he misses it. No wonder Sandy had given her a warning eyebrow. Sandy didn't like drinkers.

On the other hand, wasn't it a positive sign that he had held off to talk with her? Maybe there was still hope for him.

She opened the envelope and pulled out several legal documents in the Wrongful Death and Negligence case of *Hanna v. Ace High Lodge and Does I-X*.

The complaint Bruce Bennett had drafted was on top, followed by some unserved summonses, an answer filed by the Ace High Lodge, and a set of pleadings filed recently by the Lodge's attorney, Betty Jo Puckett of South Lake Tahoe. While Nina skimmed through the pleadings, Dave Hanna slumped in his chair, never taking his eyes off her.

Chelsi had displayed a good grasp of her uncle's legal situation. He was about to have his case dismissed on the motion of the Ace High Lodge, because he had done nothing to bring the matter to trial for almost two years.

Bennett had done a workmanlike job laying out the facts in the complaint. The Hannas had been celebrating their tenth wedding anniversary by spending the weekend at Lake Tahoe at the Ace High Lodge, one block from Harveys and the other Stateline casinos. They had gone to a show at Prize's and walked back, then stepped out to the second-floor balcony of their room.

There, according to the dry legalese of the complaint, "they observed an armed robbery in progress." And, in what seemed to be a case of being in the wrong place at the wrong time, at thirty-eight, third-grade teacher Sarah Hanna had been shot once through the heart. She was three months pregnant.

There were few traces of the gunman or other witnesses. The motel clerk, Meredith Assawaroj, had heard the shots from an adjoining property. She had missed seeing the killer but had provided the South Lake Tahoe police with a fair description of the three motel guests who had been held up, young people who had packed up and left before the police arrived.

The clerk's descriptions of these three led nowhere. The gun hadn't been left at the scene. The witnesses had paid in cash and the description provided had been inadequate to find them. Nina made a note to find out more about that.

Now the Ace High Lodge wanted out of Hanna's lawsuit, which alleged that its clerk should have been in the office, that the motel security should have been better, and so on and so on. Hanna might have had some sort of case on the merits if he had pursued it, but leaving it to languish for so long had exposed him to Betty Jo Puckett's Motion to Dismiss.

Puckett's work looked good. Her law was solid. Statutory limits restricted the ability of plaintiffs to file a lawsuit and then do nothing, as Dave Hanna had done.

Puckett had apparently advised the motel owner well—to lay

low for as long as possible and then attack Hanna for failure to prosecute. Nina hadn't met the lawyer, but the courtroom grapevine said she had an effective style.

She looked up. Hanna's cheeks flamed, but his eyes were sunken into the sockets. He looked like a big, healthy man who had developed some wasting disease that was ruining him. Nina wondered how long he had been drinking way too much. At least he was sober at eight in the morning. She found it painful to imagine what he'd gone through, how bitter he must feel now.

She cleared her throat. Setting down the motion to dismiss, she said, "Your wife seems to have been the classic innocent bystander."

"Did you know she was expecting?"

"Yes."

He shifted in his chair, like the seat hurt him.

"What do you plan to do now?" Nina asked him.

"Slink away, I guess."

"The Lodge wants attorney's fees."

"I might get socked with their lawyer fees?"

"Perhaps."

Dave Hanna put his hand on his heart and said, "Let me get this straight. They want *me* to pay them? How much money are we talking about?"

"I don't know. I could guess, from the amount of work I see here, possibly several thousand dollars."

"If I do nothing, what will happen?"

"You'll probably have to pay their fees."

During a long silence Hanna deliberated about whether to— what? Confide in her? Walk out on her?

"Well?" he asked finally.

Nina raised her eyebrows.

"What do you think?"

"It isn't hopeless," Nina said.

"There isn't a damn thing I can do to stop them, is there?"

"You can fight the motion. The Code of Civil Procedure does require that a suit like yours be dismissed two years after service on the defendant with no action. But it hasn't been quite two years. It's still in the discretion of the court."

Hanna blurted, "Look, lady. I understand you need to drum up business. Maybe you hope we've got a stash of dough hidden away. I hate to say this, but we don't. Bennett demanded a hundred fifty dollars an hour and five thousand up front, and called himself cheap. I don't want to bankrupt Roger and Chelsi. And I'm broke, like I keep telling you."

"We'll take care of the money, Uncle Dave," Chelsi said.

"I will need a retainer," Nina said, thinking of Sandy, who would hold her accountable. She came up with the lowest amount she could manage. "Two thousand, billed against my hours. I also charge a hundred fifty an hour. There may be expenses. If we manage to keep the case going, those expenses could mount up fast."

"Done," Chelsi said, whipping out her checkbook. Hanna bowed his head, looked at the rug. "It's not for revenge," Chelsi said. "It's not for money. It's for my aunt. You know?"

Nina nodded. She pushed the button as though Sandy hadn't left the door open a crack and been listening the whole time.

After Hanna had signed an agreement and left with Chelsi, Nina adjusted her suit coat and hung her new briefcase over her shoulder.

"You think we can make money on this?" Sandy said. She reposed like a Buddha in her Aeron chair, detached, hands folded calmly on the desk over Nina's notes.

"I do. Fast money. That's if we can get past this motion to dismiss. The motel clerk should have been in the office. The area should have been less of an ambush invitation. There may have been other incidents—this kind of crime occurs in clusters. Maybe the motel should have been on notice."

"The client's unreliable."

"Yes. But his relatives seem to have him in line. I think some money might help him, Sandy. Rehab. Grief counseling. Whatever. I trust Chelsi to steer him right."

"Where do you want to start?"

"Let's get the police reports and check to see if there were similar crimes reported in the area over the past ten years. File a notice that I'm in as Hanna's attorney and send a copy of the notice to Betty Jo Puckett. She represents the Ace High Lodge."

"Betty Jo Puckett?"

"You know her?"

"I met her. She has a problem in the tact department."

Nina smiled, saying, "Report anything else you hear."

"Before you go, what else do you need?"

"Get the file made up. I'll get going on drafting the Response to the Motion to Dismiss after court. There is a long line of precedents regarding innkeeper liability for inadequate security. Sandy, remember Connie Francis?"

"The singer? Nineteen-sixties. 'Lipstick on Your Collar.' That wasn't even her biggest hit. But even now it strikes a chord with me." Sandy's husband, Joe, and she had broken up for many years and only recently remarried.

"She won an early motel-security case. The damages award was in the seven figures. I don't think it was in California, though. The trial took place in the mid-seventies. See if you can locate the case on Lexis."

"She was robbed?"

"She was raped. While staying in a hotel room. It was brutal. I think it almost ended her career."

Neither woman spoke for a moment. Nina was thinking that

people don't get over violence like that. They may carry on, but they are changed forever. Finally Sandy said, her voice tight, "So some turkey fired off a wild one during a stickup and killed a pregnant third-grade teacher. Do we go looking for him, or just nick the motel?"

"We go looking."

"Good."

"We get started, at least."

"Shall I call Paul?"

"He's tied up."

"You'll need an investigator, and he's the best."

But for many reasons, Nina did not want Paul van Wagoner involved. She did not wish to see his confident face, his flirty manner, his sexual vibrations. She was over him, at least for the moment. Someday, Paul could reenter her life neutered into a professional associate. Until then, he needed to stay filed in the Great Memory file.

She said with emphasis, "Do not call Paul."

"Okay, okay. I heard about another good investigator who might be available."

"Good. See what you can do." Nina trotted down the hall and climbed into her old Bronco. Five minutes until court. She bumped off the curb into the street.

There's an advantage to small-town law. She would make it to court right on time.

Chapter 3

Two DAYS LATER, JUST AFTER FIVE, Nina drove north on the Nevada side of the road that circled Lake Tahoe.

Her response had been filed with the court that morning, and opposing attorney Betty Jo Puckett was nothing if not decisive. She had called Nina within an hour of the faxed service to her office and invited Nina to have a drink with her at her home in Incline Village, on the North Shore.

In all her time practicing law at Tahoe, Nina had never been invited to the home of another lawyer. A talk like this would ordinarily occur in a paneled office where computers clicked and whirred just outside the door. The reason, she had long ago decided, was that she was one of the few women lawyers in town. Men could meet after work, but a meeting with a woman lawyer caused gossip and trouble at home.

She hoped Ms. Puckett would be reasonable. Maybe she'd even be a congenial person, a new friend. Nina snorted at herself as she waited at the Stateline light. A new friend! The woman was a lawyer on the other side of a case, for Pete's sake!

At least she'd enjoy the forty-five-minute drive.

Rush hour does not exactly exist on the twenty-five-mile stretch between the south and north shores of Lake Tahoe. Traffic may be slowed by gawkers, by people pulling over to park at the nude beaches, by the construction projects that last all summer, but the population for a real traffic jam just isn't there.

Just barely over the Nevada state line, extending for a few blocks along Highway 50 on the South Shore, the gaming industry reigned supreme. "Gaming" had a much nicer ring than "gambling." "Gaming" implied ingenuity, and Nina did admit poker and blackjack to a realm where gambling could ascend into skill. Most people played the slots, though, and everyone knew that slots were the main source of casino revenue.

The casino district's face-lift was almost complete, down to a new gondola gliding up the slopes of the Heavenly ski resort. Old Cecil's Liquors with its narrow aisles and products piled to the ceiling had been replaced by the new Cecil's, twice as expensive, a neon sign advertising its new location, too brightly lit, too neatly stocked.

Cecil's also had new, twenty-first-century neighbors: a bookstore, a Starbucks. The Village Center—brand-new, built with a heavy hand from fieldstone—held a hotel and expensive shops. On her left, the unregenerate originals, the T-shirt shops and tchotchke vendors, stuck it out behind shabby storefronts, still fielding plenty of customers. Raley's Supermarket had been gussied up into chalet style. As she passed that corner, Nina searched for the lone tree in the parking lot, which had once figured in a murder case she had handled.

No tree. Progress had leveled trees, crime scenes, and favorite haunts with the same dispassion.

At Prize's, with its house-sized treasure-chest logo looming overhead, she saw that Sammy Hagar's Cabo Wabo Cantina had started up. Caesars, the class act of the district, had the Reno Philharmonic playing *Carmina Burana,* but for the regulars, DJ Jazzy Jeff was spinning CDs at Club Nero. *X—An Erotic Adventure* would be getting playful on Friday night at Harveys. Tall, forest-green Harrah's looked down its nose across the boulevard from humble Bill's, which didn't monkey with erotica, magic, or expensive music acts, but got right to the point. Its neon marquee simply promised "Loose Slots."

She hit another light at the end of the row, near the Lakeside Inn, the locals' casino, the last casino before the forest crept back in. To her left now was Kahle Drive, where the casino workers lived in mobile homes and cottages facing an undeveloped meadow. A young woman with long bleached hair, a leopard-print blouse, and jeans walked her big, wild-looking mastiff, fitting symbols of the transition from civilization back to the wooded mountains.

The forest closed in, olive and brown, the sky blindingly clear and the lake on her left filtering its blue-grays now and then through the firs. With air so dry and at an altitude of over six thousand feet, everything was high-focus, almost too clear.

Off Cave Rock, a white cabin cruiser trailed dark blue waterlines. The lake looked as enormous as an inland sea. Sometimes waterlines appeared by themselves out there, sinuous ridges that had given rise to the Tahoe Tessie legend.

Just after the Carson City turnoff, the road wound up high above the lake and the Bronco passed an unmarked gated trail to the left. Nina knew from Sandy that this led down to Skunk Harbor, where the Washoe Indians had been granted an exclusive right to camp, hunt, and fish. The cove was invisible, but she could see from her high seat the untouched meadows and forests below. A couple of hikers toiled up the trail.

Fifteen minutes later she came to the North Shore, the water suddenly close and sparkling on her left, down a hundred feet of steady-sloping granite and dirt to the nude beaches. Nina could see a few plumes of smoke on the distant West Shore—prescribed burning even this late in the year. The mountains over there were a deeper blue frosted with white from early snowfall.

She was alone on the road, Sand Harbor's shallow, bright water just ahead. Swinging the wheel, she continued around the curve past the old Ponderosa Ranch and took a right at Country Club Drive, the street name that told her, in several ways, that she had entered Incline Village.

The Bronco labored up the mountain. Just off Mount Rose Highway she came to Champagne Way and turned down the long, winding street, marveling at the chateaus with their mile-high views of the lake basin. She had heard of this street. Local gossip said that a very well-known singer, songwriter, and record producer had a home here. The neighbors didn't exactly look poverty-stricken, either.

At the end of the street she arrived at a large stucco hacienda with a green-tiled roof surrounded by walls with fir-tree borders. The house was built on a promontory of the mountain. Nina slowed down to take in the view, but then Betty Jo Puckett appeared in the flagged driveway and the Bronco plowed toward her.

Betty Jo practically dragged Nina out of her seat. "I've been wanting to meet you," she said. A tall, rugged, gray-haired woman in her fifties; her jeans and white shirt encased a rangy body. Her face, sawed into a hundred lines and angles, exhibited every second of wear, and she had let dark eyebrows grow in thick. She looked a little like Judge Milne, in fact.

"Let's go inside." They passed through a tall entry with saltillo tiles underfoot and a lot of plants into a high-ceilinged living room with a flagstone fireplace next to a bar at the far end.

A little old man stood behind the bar, pouring from a bottle of vodka. "Heh," he said.

"That's Hector, my husband. He doesn't talk too well these days, but he loves company. What would you like to drink? Here, set down."

Nina chose a leather chair near the fire. "Tea?"

"Tea?" Hector growled almost incoherently, obviously peeved.

"Tea," Nina said firmly.

He took a flowered teapot from below the bar and flicked the lever of a spigot over the sink. Steaming water filled the pot. He measured quantities of tea from a silver tin, dunked a big silver tea ball into the pot, and set a timer. He said something Nina couldn't catch.

"Four minutes," Betty Jo translated.

They chatted while they waited and Nina looked around. Picture windows, French doors, whitewashed beams, a lot of expensive furniture. Precisely four minutes later, Hector removed the tea ball, poured liquid into a mug for Nina, and shuffled over to her.

"Thanks." Close up, she saw he wore a silk ascot. His teeth were blindingly white and perfectly regular. The tea sloshed dangerously as he handed it to her.

"Heh." Back behind the bar he began sipping something of his own. Betty Jo sat on the long white leather couch opposite Nina's chair, picked up a beer mug from the Noguchi coffee table, and said, "*Salud!*"

"Heh!"

"*Salud.*"

They all drank. Nina took a sniff, then a taste. The tea tasted delicate, perfumed with flowers and something like popcorn, quite a change from the supermarket stuff she was used to drinking. "What is this? It's great."

"Is that the stuff from China we got last year, doll?"

Hector nodded his hoary head. He was very old, in his eighties, Nina decided.

"Shoot. I forget the name. Hector, what's it called?"

He examined an ornately decorated canister and answered her.

"Right," Betty Jo said, nodding. "How'd I forget that?"

Nina, who had not understood him, sipped some more, wanting to know but not enough to ask again.

"Oh, here's Jimmy." Betty Jo got up to greet a man who had entered the room. She took him by the hand and brought him in for a hug, then led him toward Nina. "Jimmy Bova, Nina Reilly."

Bova shook Nina's hand.

"I'm the owner of the Ace High," he said. "You know—the motel." Bova wore a red sweater, which clung like silk to his well-defined upper body. He had fleshy lips, a long Roman nose, the kind that drops straight from the forehead, and unusual, light-colored eyes set off nicely by the even tan a tanning booth provides. He looked like a man who took his exercise inside a gym, wearing really nice sweats, rather than the typical Tahoe man, who got it outside at the woodchopping block.

"Glad to meet you," Nina said. "I didn't know you'd be here." Betty Jo had sprung a surprise, inviting her client along. Bova smiled. It was a warm smile, and Nina gave him one back, always ready to give the benefit of a doubt. If he hadn't been on the opposite side, she might not have described him to herself quite so harshly. He actually had a dash of Sylvester Stallone when he smiled.

"I hope you don't mind," Betty Jo said innocently. "I always reckon people should talk, get to know each other. Didn't figure

Mr. Hanna was ready to join us, though. He's hell to talk to. I'm glad you're in the case, Nina."

Nina set her cup down and decided to play along with Betty Jo. They were all friends here, with no sticky clients like Nina's around to mess the place up. "Your house is superb. Spanish style isn't common up here."

"Hector and I couldn't resist when we saw it. We're from Modesto. Only been up here a couple of years."

"Happy practicing law at Tahoe?" Nina asked her.

"Oh, yeah. Love it."

Bova, roving the room as if searching for a comfortable landing site, made no attempt to enter the conversation. Walking over to the fireplace, he picked up a poker, which he used to make a perfect pyramid of the burning logs. Then he turned to look at her, and Nina felt a shiver in spite of the warmth from the fire. She had been a little startled by how attractive Betty Jo's client was. He did not resemble the mean-spirited innkeeper of her imagination. His amber eyes glowed in the dimly lit room like the fire behind him.

Betty Jo launched into a story about meeting Sandy at the grocery store. "She walked by me and I noticed one of the buttons on her blouse had popped. It happens to us big gals, so I kind of whispered as I passed, 'Look down in front. Your button.' So she looked down and she fixed it. Our carts passed and she never said a word. Then at the checkout she came up behind me and she whispered, 'Look behind you. Your butt.'"

And at that, illustrating for them, Betty Jo turned her back on them, bent over, rolled her neck so that she could see her backside, and jiggled it.

When nobody said anything, she jiggled again. She was not to be denied.

Nina and Bova, equally astonished at this display, looked at each other and broke out laughing.

"Sandy doesn't take kindly to being corrected," Nina said when she recovered herself.

"Well, I'm sure she's a fine legal secretary in spite of that big honking mouth of hers," Betty Jo said, sitting down again on the couch. "And she's observant. I do have a big ass, which Hector considers a major asset, don't you, Hector?"

Studying Betty Jo there on the couch, taking it all in—the invitation, the fire, the down-home way of talking, the drinks, the little old husband, the alert eyes—Nina suddenly realized what this foolishness was all about. Betty Jo wanted Nina unguarded. She wanted her friendly. She wanted Nina to underestimate her enemy. A little joke at her own expense was far cheaper in the long run than a big settlement. Legal strategy, country-style.

"Now, I also hear that you recently came back to Tahoe and set up again. That right?" Betty Jo was saying.

"I tried something else out for a few months, but I'm back for good now."

"Glad to hear it. The more women we get up here, the less cussin' and fightin' there'll be in court." A Chihuahua skidded into the room, followed by a large gray cat. They both jumped into Betty Jo's lap. Her strong hand settled the sudden squabble as they vied for position.

Nina said, "How about you?"

"Oh, I was living in the same little place I'd had for thirty years down there in the Central Valley, doing a little divorce work here and some personal-injury there. And what should pop up one fine morning but a great big injury case with a deep-pockets insurer. I had to litigate it. By the start of trial I was in hock to my kids, my friends, plus the devil. Three weeks we went to court every day, me palpitating and my poor old client on his last legs. Then the jury came in and gave us fifteen million bucks." She laughed. "You believe it? Like winning at Lotto. Impossible odds."

"Congratulations."

"I always thought I would hit a big one. Thirty years was a long time to wait, though. Anyway, Hector and I fell in love and got married and decided to spend our best years someplace beautiful. So we came here. You married?"

"No."

"Divorced?"

"Divorced and widowed." Nina felt rather than saw Bova absorbing the information. He cruised over, close to her chair, shifted on his feet, and leaned in.

"And still so young," he said.

She couldn't believe it. He was flirting with her. And this wasn't the first time since she had returned to Tahoe she had been hit on in ridiculous circumstances. Could it be some kind of single-female pheromone she put out now that she was no longer with Paul?

If so, she didn't mind too much, because she liked male attention, always had. Lately, maybe, she had started to wonder if she had come to rely on it a little too much. That didn't mean she trusted Bova. She drew away from him, attempting to use body language to send him an unmistakable friendly nonverbal signal to get lost. Businesslike, aloof, and polite: She went for that effect, and it worked. Bova stepped away and resumed his examination of the objects in the room as if nothing had happened. Nina picked a few grapes from a bowl on the immaculate glass coffee table and ate them, giving herself a moment to slip back into lawyer mode. "Shall we talk about the Hanna case? I'm afraid I'll have to get back soon."

Betty Jo said, "I know you're busy. Yet you came to see me right away and didn't put us off. I like that."

"I consider this situation urgent. You're fighting to have David Hanna's case thrown out and I can't let you do that."

"In a nutshell. Yes, in a nutshell. Here Jimmy and I thought we were in the home stretch and then you galloped up from behind. Your responsive papers are good, and that worries me. Understand, Jimmy didn't do anything wrong. You can't put up an electrified fence around a motel with a guard gate to prevent robberies, especially right around the corner from a casino district. You could just as well have sued the cops for not showing up and preventing the incident."

"You don't need me to tell you the law," Nina said, "so I know I don't have to remind you that places of public accommodation have duties to their customers that are completely different from the duties of the police."

"Jimmy's a nice guy." Betty Jo continued to talk as if Bova weren't there, ears cocked to take in every word. "The motel's all he's got."

Nina took a long sip of tea. "No offense, but Mr. Hanna lost everything he held dear when he lost his wife."

"He's only suing me because he can't find the guy who killed his wife," Bova interrupted. "I'm sorry about that woman. I heard she was pregnant. Is that true?"

Nina nodded, watching him touch the smooth brown skin on his forehead.

"It's a shame. You think I don't wish every day this hadn't happened? But I'm not responsible."

"You have a proposal?" Nina said, on firm ground with him at last. "Do you want to settle this case and have peace of mind? Because I'm sure Betty Jo has told you, we can do that. We can settle with you and keep looking for the killer."

"We can come up with something," Betty Jo said before he could respond, "but I'm afraid your client won't want to take what's on offer, because we're the only money around, and he thinks we should pay for everything."

"Surely the motel's liability insurance covers this situation," Nina said.

"The company said no for a long time. But in the last two days they offered to make a payout."

"What is the policy limit?"

"They offered twenty-five thousand. And we'll drop our claim for attorney's fees."

"I see," Nina said.

Hector brought over another bottle of beer for his wife. She gave him a pat. She had not touched the first beer after the initial toast. Her mug now stood on the coffee table like warnings to Nina not to relax too much. "It's all standard stuff," Betty Jo said to Nina.

"Standard? One, you won't tell me their limit, and two, the offer's a pittance." Ah, she loved this tea. What in the world was in it to create an effect so relaxing yet so exciting? She felt a sneaky sympathy for Betty Jo, who was doing her damnedest to settle the case for a miserly amount of money, and who would not succeed unless she found more. For a moment, she wondered if Hector would go so far as to spike her tea somehow.

No. It was just wonderful tea.

Betty Jo looked at Jimmy Bova, now sitting beside her on the sofa. He shrugged. Then he turned his yellow eyes toward Nina. They now held nothing personal.

"Jimmy's just getting by. But he can put a little in too, from his personal account. Now, let me explain something about the way I practice law. I really think the way the men do it, with all the dicking—excuse me, I mean dickering, around, and the hee-hawing and trying to score points, is a waste of energy. What I do is this. I make my last and final offer the first time around. And I stick to it. It never goes up, because I've already put out everything I can.

"A good attorney on the other side, she's going to appreciate how efficient that is. It takes a little trust to work. I know I haven't got my reputation established up here in the mountains.

All I can tell you is, I'm about to make you a last and final offer from the Ace High Lodge, and your client has two days to decide whether to accept it. After that, we incur a bunch of expenses getting ready for trial, and we withdraw the offer."

This practiced-sounding speech had a lot of appeal. Implicit in the offer was an assumption that the motel would lose its motion to dismiss. If Nina heard right, then Betty Jo was making a concession lawyers weren't supposed to make, in addition to offering an authentic settlement.

"I don't know how much you're offering yet, but I appreciate your frankness," she answered.

"Jimmy can scrape together another twenty-five thousand. That's absolutely all he can spare and keep going. He feels terrible about what happened at his motel and he's willing to dig deep. But these fringe places are strung out on the profit end, Nina. He's not a rich man. We're prepared to show you his income-tax returns to reassure you that he's not hiding money and that this constitutes a real sacrifice. So, fifty thousand dollars to the bereaved husband, and you can still go after the killer."

"I'll talk to my client," Nina said. "But I can't advise him to take your offer. I'll advise him to request the policy limits, which are going to be quite a bit more."

"The insurance company won't go for that. You think I haven't tried?" Betty Jo said.

"Maybe losing the motion will convince them."

"It won't. They already factored that in. Even if a jury finds the motel negligent, it's only contributory negligence. They'll decide that the motel is about ten percent responsible and the killer's responsible for the rest. So even if you get a half-million judgment, we're still only going to have to pay the same old fifty thousand. Last and final, Nina."

"I understand," Nina said. She stood up. "Nice to meet you, Hector. That is some amazingly delicious tea."

"Heh. Heh."

"He's delighted you liked it," Betty Jo said cheerfully.

"Nice to meet you, Mr. Bova."

Bova said, "I'm sure we can work something out." The words were basically formulaic, but Nina thought he really did want out, and that there wasn't any more money. How would Dave Hanna react to the offer? Nina followed Betty Jo's broad backside outside.

At the Bronco, Betty Jo said, "I forgot to mention one teeny thing, which is a possibility based on complete speculation and not a scintilla of evidence, that Jimmy might have a line on one of the witnesses. The tourist kids with the fake IDs."

Nina stiffened. "What's that?"

"He'll be glad to tell you when we settle."

"You can't do that. You'll be getting my interrogatories tomorrow, and he'd better answer the questions."

"He doesn't have to provide complete speculation to your client."

"He'll be in court if he—"

"Let's part friends," Betty Jo said gaily. "Okay? Let's just think on it. We'll talk again. Meantime, I like your style, Nina. You're a cool customer."

Nina smiled. "Okay. We'll talk. I appreciate your straightness, too. I'm with you on the negotiating business. I also prefer to lay what I have on the table."

"We'll have lunch sometime. I'd like to hear some juicy legal gossip."

"Sure. Nice having you up here, Betty Jo. The winters must be knocking your socks off after Modesto."

"My love bunny keeps me warm."

"Hector—he's retired?"

"Oh, yes. He had a bad accident and crushed his larynx and suffered a little brain damage. But he's fit as a fiddle in other respects. In all the ways that count." She smiled. "He was as broke as me when we tried his case, and we both got rich at the end."

"He was your *client?*"

"Yeah, he got ten million and I got five, and we decided what the hay, let's put the whole shebang together." Betty Jo put her hand on Nina's shoulder and said, "I wouldn't have done it if he wasn't a world-class lay. Life's short, and you better pay attention to that, sister."

Nina got into her vehicle, and Betty Jo closed the door after her. "Jimmy and I look forward to hearing from you."

Nina started up the engine and waved. Betty Jo had seen it all, engineered every nuance of the evening, this canny, middle-aged lady from Modesto. Driving away with her windows open to the night, loving the way the cool air lifted the hair on her arms like the brush of a hand, Nina thought, Life's short. She's got that right.

Chapter 4

ELLIOTT WAKEFIELD WENT TO WORK AT Caesars casino-hotel on Lake Tahoe Boulevard at 10:00 P.M. on Friday night, dressed as usual in baggy khaki shorts and Vans sneakers from his MIT days. The night had a flat, metallic smell to it. The stream of light along both sides of the slow-moving line of cars could almost have passed for palaces and public buildings in some grand European metropolis that had missed being bombed in World War II.

But Stateline wasn't a real city, it was slow robbery in a mountain town dressed up with a lot of liquor and eyeliner, and those weren't palaces, they were casinos. November had arrived, and it was cold after dark. As he climbed out of the subcompact, handing the keys to a valet older than he was, a couple of very young hookers sashayed by in black leather minis. He walked across the portico, jammed his hands into his pockets, and ignored them.

He didn't like Tahoe, but he'd been flying here for years. He entered the imposing glass doors of the casino and the stark air-conditioning caught him.

Inside, people flowed in and out of the main gaming floor. Most were excited; some were drunk, and a few were thieves. Elliott was acutely conscious of being alone. Knock knock, who's there, Thelonius. Thelonius who? Thelonius boy in town.

At MIT, living in the tiny dorm room, eating at the Commons every day with the same people, Elliott had still always ended up alone. Now, living with his father in the small brick house on Vashon Island near Seattle, he sometimes felt the loneliness might kill him when the MS got Pop. He did it to himself. Even now he was wishing he were back on the island, sitting at his desk and working with his Mathematica program on the computer.

He loved Pop, and Pop was his only company. They ate dinner and watched TV together like an old married couple, and Pop didn't have a clue as to how Elliott paid the mortgage. They were happy, happy like a pair of trilobites embedded in a layer of shale, safe and stable.

Still, even if he had the misfortune of being a mathematician, he wasn't a priest. He had thought sometimes about paying for sex, since he seemed to be too picky and shy to pick up a regular girl. But hookers, no. They were phonies. He couldn't stand the fake smiles and arm squeezes, the self-conscious way they went about their business. Elliott wanted love, not a hustle. And sometimes they could be dangerous, and the danger quotient in his work had already proved high enough.

He took one more look at the girls entering the casino. Then he rubbed his pocket, where his stake was.

He couldn't help glancing upward as he moved into the gaming area. The Eyes in the Sky, video and live cams, were barely visible in the ceiling if you knew where to look. In spite of the marble columns and marble floors of the hotel section and the sumptuous look of the casino, it attracted exactly the same customers as anywhere else in Stateline. The out-of-towners, especially the Asians, dressed up. The locals and California week-enders wore the same clothes as Elliott, straight off the sale table at the Gap. He looked just like every other techie from Silicon Valley, getting ready to say adios to his paycheck after a hard week writing code in a windowless cubicle.

Elliott circled the blackjack tables, which were almost all full. He liked that, because it kept the pit bosses occupied. They might not notice him. Not that he was looking for a killing tonight without Silke or Raj or Carleen to act as a spotter. He only needed a few thousand, and he still had Saturday night coming up.

The minute he thought of Silke he wanted to call her, say, "Guess where I am?" just because he knew she would be shocked and angry that he was back at Tahoe. He was still heartsick enough over her to enjoy any kind of emotional reaction, even the negative ones. But she belonged with Raj, working like him on her doctorate, and he had no business bugging her.

He stopped suddenly at a twenty-five-dollar-minimum table where a First Base spot lay open. On the next seat, a girl with red streaks in her hair, spotty skin, and trendy glasses sat behind several stacks of chips.

Oh, shit, he thought. Carleen. What's she doing here? How coincidental was that, him thinking about her just a minute ago and her being here?

Well, it shouldn't surprise him. Once, they had traveled this route together.

He ought to leave; no telling how she would greet him, but driven by perverse curiosity, he slid in beside her. She looked up at him. After the first flash of disbelief, her expression turned firmly noncommittal. Only he would know the tense brow-pinching thing she did when she was truly angry. She looked up once more, just a glance, full of fire. Her eyes said, What the hell are you doing here, anyway?

He settled down in his seat. She didn't own the joint.

She slapped her chips into neat stacks. Okay, then I don't know you, her body language said, and you don't know me. He remembered her silent language well, and instantly perceived the virtue in not knowing her. Maybe they could play the old game together a few times and make a few bucks.

The shoe was a six-decker, and the dealer, a middle-aged woman who wore a lot of gold in her cleavage under the required white shirt, had only run through a couple of hands. Giving Elliott a sharp look, she exchanged two thousand for him. The black chips felt as substantial as marbles as he pulled them toward him. He put one dead center on his spot on the green felt and waited for the cards.

He pulled a thirteen and busted when he hit on it. Fine. He was only playing basic strategy right now, warming up, checking out the cards. He played a few more hands, going down three hundred dollars rapidly on his single-chip bets.

"You're too hot," Carleen told the dealer.

"Our luck turns just like yours does," said the dealer, who fielded complaints like this all night long. Carleen was winning most of the time in spite of her complaining. The other people at the table, who told everyone they had just arrived on a bus from Boise, Idaho, each set out a chip at a time, playing decently.

A couple of minutes later: "No, she's gonna come through for us," Elliott said, including everyone at the table in his optimism. They were two full decks into the shoe by now, with enough cards laid down for him to know the deck was ripe. He placed all the chips he had left onto the table, seventeen hundred dollars' worth, not an outrageous amount at a twenty-five-dollar minimum table.

Edging her bottom teeth with her finger, Carleen fidgeted

unhappily at his bet, but she pushed all of her remaining chips onto the playing area, too, thirty-seven hundred bucks and change. "I fly back to Seoul tomorrow," she said. "This better be good."

The dealer pulled a six after her hole card. Elliott checked his own ace in the hole with a seven showing, soft eighteen, a very good hand against the dealer's probable sixteen. But he scratched for another card. The card count told him the deck was very short on high-count cards.

A two. He had pulled a total of twenty. A thrill coursed through him.

Carleen was showing a ten card. Elliott bent around to catch a glimpse of her hole card when she turned up the corner to have a look, but she turned it over so they could all see.

Another ten.

"I'll split my tens," she said, pulling a wad of cash out of her wallet and handing it over, and now she was running two hands on the table. They were still barely under ten thousand in bets for the whole table, so the dealer didn't have to get approval to accept the bet.

The Boise couple couldn't believe she was splitting tens, a stupid mistake under basic strategy rules. The dealer laid down a card on each ten, face-down. Carleen picked up the edge of the new card over one of the tens, then scratched for another. The dealer flipped her a card and let her hand stay right there, ready to scoop up the busted hand, but Carleen hadn't busted yet.

"It's such a fun game," she said, uttering a totally uncharacteristic girlish giggle. "I wish my fiancé hadn't gone over to the Sports Book."

Elliott watched her check the new card over her other ten, and scratch again.

Standing pat, Carleen waved her hand negligently over the hands.

The rest of them went through their paces, and when they

had all finished the round, the dealer flipped over her hole card. Another six. Now she was showing a total of twelve and she had to hit again.

The dealer turned over a four this time. Sixteen. The rules required her to hit again, so she flipped herself one more card.

A third six. She'd busted. "Too bad we're not playing poker," said Third Base from Boise. "You'da wiped us out."

Starting with Elliott, the dealer went around the table turning over the hole cards. When she turned up his hole card, she looked surprised. "You got someone watching out for you," Boise said as they all stared at the three cards adding up to twenty. "You hit on a soft eighteen."

"I had a good feeling," Elliott said. The dealer turned over Carleen's two hole cards and they all had a look. She had taken another card on hard seventeens on both hands. Both those plays were also dead wrong against the dealer's original twelve, according to basic blackjack-playing strategy.

But she had won. She had pulled threes on each of her hands, winning both. The dealer pushed over their stacks of chips and the pit boss came over to check out the table and spread some glowers around.

Between the two of them, Elliott and Carleen had just won almost ten thousand dollars on a single bet. The pit boss, a short thin man in a dark suit, moved in to stand next to Elliott, hanging in close enough so that Elliott could smell the cigars on his breath. Then the boss motioned to the dealer to shuffle up, wheeled, and walked rapidly back to the podium in the pit where the phone was.

Elliott gathered up his chips, passing a couple over to the dealer as a tip. "I'm out," he said with a smile that hurt his chapped lips, it stretched them so wide. He felt eyes chasing him as he cashed in and hurried out the door.

Carleen followed him. Sitting on a bench alongside the drive-way, leaning against the wall, his eyes half-closed, he was waiting for his car.

"So, Wakefield. What's up? You following me?"

"You don't want to be seen talking to me here."

"You're the one who sat down by me."

"I mean because of the cameras."

"Screw them," she said, "any damage is done. I should have jumped up and left when you sat down."

"Why didn't you?"

"Maybe I foolishly imagined you would have more sense than to sit down beside me. Or come to Tahoe at all." She took off her useless glasses and tucked them into a shirt pocket. "You spot two security men who were following me when I left?"

"Why didn't your fiancé from the Sports Book take care of them? I'm sure he's a muscle-bound freak, just the way you like them."

She laughed. "Why, are you jealous at the thought?"

"Yeah, sure. I hate imaginary rivals. Is he from Korea, too?" They had a running disagreement about Carleen's disguises. She liked them conspicuous, like the nasty tricolored hair she wore tonight sticking up like a kid's paper crown, thinking that she was less likely to get made if she went bold. And she couldn't keep her mouth shut. She chatted up the dealers, compounding lies until nobody could keep track of the latest story.

"Why'd you bet so big? If you hadn't put up such a massive bet, we could have made the same money in three or four hands without anybody noticing. We could still be playing."

"You bet twice what I did."

"Well, hey, I had to, didn't I, after you spoiled any chance for anonymity. She was going to shuffle up for sure after you bet. The pit boss made us so fast after that."

"Ah, but it was kind of fun, wasn't it, Carleen? Like old times. So what was all that about flying to Korea?"

"I don't know. I just felt like saying it. God, it's cold tonight. Wakefield, really, are you nuts? What are you doing here? Are you here with Silke and . . ."

"I'm alone."

"She stayed on the East Coast after graduation, didn't she?"

He shrugged. "Don't know." Best not to feed her gossip about Silke.

"Don't know? Yeah, right. She still with Raj?"

"Challenge question." Dr. Braun used to come up with these quizzes on a regular basis. She would recognize the allusion. "Is the square root of two still one point four one two and change?"

"I thought so. So what else?"

"I wait for my car."

She shook her head impatiently. "Not until we talk." She looked away, toward a white-haired man in an aloha shirt who was climbing into a limo, but Elliott still felt the force of her nervousness and interest pouring over him like sticky goo. He looked at her, at her streaky hair and the triple piercings in her ears and the discontented expression, and thought, She keeps coming back to gamble just like me.

"I went back to Seattle after graduation," he said.

"Still living with your father, I bet."

"And?"

"Is he still driving you into mad ambition?"

"Not at all. He's infirm. He needs me." Elliott was well aware that he was minimizing his father's influence, but then, what did you say about your father to a girl who must hate you at times and who knows things you wished she didn't know?

"I guess he probably does. You can't just dump your family the way you can dump a lover. You're locked up into playing along with their psycho needs for life, aren't you?" She untucked the silk blouse she had been wearing and slouched down on the bench. "Hey, Elliott. Forget I said that. You know I'm not talking about your father."

She had her own family problems, a brother with troubles of his own. But Elliott didn't want to ask about her problems right now.

"So where are you working, Elliott?"

"Here, tonight."

"You were supposed to become a professor, but you still make your living counting cards at blackjack?"

"It pays the rent," Elliott said.

"How does your father like that?"

"He doesn't know."

"I never took you for the outlaw type," Carleen said. "I'm still in good old Boston. I'm making big bucks." She shifted a little and he felt her small breast brush his arm.

Pathetic, the fact that they were two hungry twenty-somethings in desperate need of human contact, the fact that he didn't like her but wanted to kiss her. He sat on the bench, unable to decide what to do. She seemed to want to stay with him, though he wasn't sure, she was so nervous, looking around like casino security might come outside for them.

"You are actually alone, aren't you?" he said.

She wet her lips and said "Yes," but Elliott thought maybe she was lying. Then—she was willing to walk out on her date?

But—now that he was calmer—he didn't want Carleen to join his lonely party. He was reacting to her just as he always had. She put his teeth on edge.

"I never thought I'd see you here," she said. "Not after the robbery and all. I thought you and Silke and Raj decided—"

"They don't know I'm here. I'm doing some checking."

"I was curious, since I was coming here for the gambling. I checked the *Tribune* archives and found out they haven't caught the guy. Is that what you're checking?"

"Yes. And the case that got filed afterward. By the husband. Why do you care? You weren't even there. You quit taking trips with us months before."

"Oh, I care, Wakefield. If you all got in trouble, do you think I wouldn't have been dragged in? MIT would have found a way to expel all of us. It would have been very public, and I wouldn't have gotten a good job. And if it comes out now, how we paid our tuition, all that, it will still cause me trouble."

"Relax, Carleen, you weren't a witness. You've graduated. The publicity might not hurt you at all."

"I thought you all agreed to stay out of it! It's too dangerous!" She looked really upset. Carleen always had an opinion on everything.

"It's bothering me that they still can't find the shooter," Elliott said.

"No. You can't be that stupid," Carleen said. "You can't be thinking of going to the police after all this time!"

He retreated into himself and said nothing. It was none of her business, but she knew all about it. The only way he knew how to deal with her incessant questioning was to be silent. Unfortunately, that made Carleen furious every time.

It had been bad luck, running into her. All thought of picking her up, getting laid—okay, that had been in his mind—fled. Where the hell was his car?

"Well?"

"Let's talk about something else."

"Yeah, calm down." She put her hand on his arm, but that wasn't working either, he could feel the crackle of her edgy energy even better that way. She licked her lips again.

"So," she said.

Elliott thought she was pissed off but still hoping. She really did want to go with him. He'd never understood Carleen, and he really didn't have the energy to start now. He was weary of her. "So."

"Still obsessed with predicting the primes?" Carleen said. "Still addicted to dreams of greatness? Got anywhere yet?"

"Got to go. Places." The Neon or Echo, or whatever the little blue car was, had rolled up. Finally! A chunky, red-faced valet got out and gave Elliott his keys.

Elliott handed him a few bucks.

"I could use a ride back to my hotel," Carleen said behind him.

"Sorry. In a rush. I'm going straight to the airport in Reno." He opened the car door and climbed inside.

For a minute she didn't move, absorbing the insult. Then she got up and stood by his open door and said, "That wasn't a pass, that was just me needing a ride somewhere."

"Next time," he said. He tried to pull the door closed, but she held on to it, eyes flashing.

"Silke would never have dumped Raj for you. The way you mooned around after her was disgusting, a real turn-off. I don't care how brilliant you think you are. You suck."

"I need to go, Carleen." He pulled again. She jerked the door back so that it was open. The valet, arms crossed, watched, wearing a slight smile.

"I have a boyfriend now, several boyfriends, and maybe this will surprise you, Robot, but I don't give a shit about you anymore."

He disliked the nickname. He hadn't heard it in so long, he had almost forgotten it.

"I wasn't hitting on you," she repeated. "Is that clear? Is it?"

The valet exchanged a sympathetic male glance with Elliott.

"You're very direct. It's admirable, in fact, how you state your mind," Elliott said.

"Fuck you! I hate you."

Elliott said, "I'm getting close to a proof." He couldn't help himself. He patted his chest, where he kept the notebook.

"God! Same old crap!" She made a guttural sound in her throat. "You don't have anybody else to tell, so you tell me! Screw you, Robot, you big loser." Her eyes filled with bright angry tears.

Elliott left Carleen standing behind the car with her fists clenched at her sides. He pulled into the neon boulevard with its miles of traffic.

She had got to him, talking that way about him and Silke. He had never mooned after Silke. In fact, he hadn't known that Carleen knew how much he . . .

What now? Elliott, who did not have to go to the airport yet, got off the main drag and drove down a dark winding road until he came to some subdivision where the streets were empty.

It was self-castigation time. He couldn't talk reasonably for five minutes with Carleen, after four years at college and many successful blackjack trips together. The craziest thing was that she had tried to pick him up, or something.

He was too lame to even drive her back to her room, a girl he knew and once loved. Well, okay, he made love to her, not the same as loving her but almost. He hadn't loved her, be honest.

Actually, he'd never made love to her either, now that he was telling himself the truth. But he could have, she would have let him. She had wanted him. She had been interested in his theories and she had been willing to listen. He'd even seen the glint in her eye when he said just now that he'd almost finished the proof.

She knew what that meant, and she was still interested no matter what she said.

But he'd found reasons to chase her away. As usual.

He'd never felt so lonely.

It was getting to be a mantra.

At a strip mall along the forested road he saw a Mexican restaurant with red and yellow and green pepper lights strung around the front. Fuck it, I'm hungry, he thought.

Inside, he almost thought better of it. Except for the cooks and the waiter, who scowled at him, the place was empty. When the waiter threw down Elliott's beer in front of him, Elliott said, "If you want to close up, just say so and I'll leave."

The waiter didn't answer; he just walked away and stood behind the counter, ignoring Elliott. Fingering the wad of cash in his pocket, Elliott drank his beer. His notebook nestled reassuringly in his pocket, and he thought of getting it out to review some figures, but he didn't. Pretty soon greasy chiles rellenos arrived on a plate with room-temperature rice and refried beans. Elliott ate until he thought he'd explode.

When he came outside, he saw a guy in a black leather jacket and baseball cap bending down, looking at the half-bald thirteen-inch wheels of the rental car with a flashlight. When the dude saw him, he gave Elliott a hard stare. Then he turned and left, leisurely, as if he knew Elliott wouldn't question him or follow him. The way he moved as he walked off into the night scared Elliott.

It couldn't be! He stepped back into the shelter of the restaurant and held on to the door, breathing hard.

So someone had been watching while he and Carleen wrangled.

"We're closed," the waiter said.

"Just—one second. I have to use the head." He wasn't ready to go out there yet. Locking himself into the bathroom, Elliott pulled out his cell phone and called Silke. "He's here," he said fast into the phone. "The guy who robbed us at Tahoe. The shooter. He followed me from a casino."

"Elliott? Do you know it's three in the morning? What's the matter?" came the sleepy voice with its accent that took the *r* way inside the mouth.

"You are probably aware that most of what happens on a daily basis follows a pattern, a predictable one," he said. "Today's unique. The ski-mask guy has found me."

"Hang on a minute." He heard a male sigh in the background, all the way from Boston. Raj, next pillow over. Then Silke got back on. "I have turned on the light," she said. "If this is one of your persecution delusions, I will never talk to you again."

"I'm giving you facts, nothing more. I made a few bucks and I got hungry so I stopped at this restaurant . . ."

"Are you playing blackjack again? I thought we agreed . . ."

"Just a hand or two."

"Just wait a minute. Back up. Elliott, where are you exactly? Vegas? Atlantic City?"

"Tahoe."

Silence on the other end of the line while she digested the information and passed it along to Raj. Well, he had wanted to shock her earlier, and now he had gotten his wish.

"Have you lost your mind?"

"It's been two years. I wanted to find out whether it was all over. It's been bothering me."

"I don't know what to say to you, Elliott. You promised you'd stay away from there."

"Yes, and that's not the only remarkable thing happening. I ran into Carleen earlier."

"Carleen?" Silke sounded confused. "She was with the robber?"

"No, no! She was playing cards. I left her at the casino and drove to another part of town. I'm coming out of this restaurant and some dude in a hat has got his hand on my wheel cover and he's bending down. He stands up and sees me and leaves. It's him."

"Did he say anything?"

"No."

"You got a good look at him?"

"It was dark. He wore a baseball cap this time. But it's him. Ski Mask."

"You say he followed you."

"I'm at Zephyr Cove in a tract where the locals live. It's midnight. There's nobody around but me and the people who work at the restaurant. And I come out to find this guy examining my car."

Silke said, "Remember how in junior year you thought a police siren was following you all the time and you had to stop driving...?"

"I'm not imagining this."

"How can you be sure you recognized him?"

Elliott hesitated. "I still couldn't tell you what his face looks like. But his right foot turns outward about eighteen degrees."

"Oh, no." She covered the phone and he heard muttering on the other end.

Raj got on the phone. "Hello, old man. Has he gone?"

"He left. I'm safe, I think. The car's right in front of the restaurant front door."

"Was it unlocked?"

"No, and the alarm was on. You think he was trying to steal it?"

"Maybe he saw you win. Maybe he wanted to steal your money. He robs people. You know that."

"He'd know my cash was on me. Damn, Raj. Could it be a coincidence? Do you think he remembered me? Maybe he planned to hide in the back seat and attack me..."

"Take it easy."

"No problem! Meanwhile, you lie peacefully in bed with a—a woman three thousand miles away. I'd better call the cops."

"Don't do that! Look, we've kept things controlled all this time. You say you're safe, and you might still be wrong about who he was."

"I recognized him!" Elliott said. He heard a pounding on the bathroom door and some Spanish expletives. "What should I do?"

"Go home to Seattle. Hurry. Can you manage that?"

"Okay."

"Call us then and we'll talk. And just to be sure, you might check the underside of the car before you leave."

"Oh, hell," Elliott said, and he couldn't control the tremor in his voice. "I shouldn't have come back. It was foolish, wasn't it?"

Raj, always the diplomat, cautious with Elliott's moods, said nothing.

"I'll check under the car," Elliott said. "I definitely will."

"Be careful. Call us the minute you get home."

The waiter followed him to the door, locking it pointedly behind him. It was only after the lights went out in the building and the dark closed in that Elliott realized the two rear tires on the rental had been slashed.

Frantic, examining the woods at the edge of the parking lot for a lurking figure, he pounded on the restaurant door, but nobody answered.

Elliott started to punch in 911, but before he could send the call, the waiter and a buddy walked around the corner into the parking lot, talking loudly. Elliott rushed over to them, wallet in hand. It cost a hundred bucks to get back to the hotel, but he got to ride in an old Trans Am. The whole way, Elliott watched out the back window, but nobody seemed to follow.

Once in his room, he bolted his door and left a message on the rental-car company's tape. He could take a shuttle to the airport. Let them deal with their vandalized car.

It's him, he kept thinking. He's letting me know. He wants me to shut up and go home.

Fingers shaking, he called downstairs for the shuttle number.

Chapter 5

SATURDAY, AN INDIAN-SUMMER DAY: NINA wore hiking shorts and a tank top to the office, with a light sweater in deference to the changeable season. At least she could pretend she wasn't working. And, indeed, she would be shopping at Costco at the foot of Spooner Pass that afternoon. With any luck, she and Bob could also take a quick hike around Spooner Lake late in the afternoon to take in what remained of any fall foliage.

Sandy had already come in and brought along Nina's new investigator. Wish Whitefeather, Sandy's son, stepped forward shyly, waiting for his hug.

"I heard you needed a real pro." He smiled, white teeth a bright contrast to the brown of his skin. At six-four, a hundred sixty pounds, Wish was all smile and big nose. He had gone back to his old ponytail and familiar denim shirt, but he had passed through the difficult late-teen years and now, entering his twenties, his face had toughened and his body, once so gangly, had knitted itself together. He had finally finished his criminal-justice program and, only a month earlier, received his license to work as a private investigator in California.

He was an old friend and Paul's assistant. Wish had worked down in Monterey with Paul for a few months but decided he missed the mountains and his family too much, so he had come home to roost and start his own business. Wish didn't have Paul's experience, but he was tireless and devoted. Paul, the master, had trained him well.

They sat down at the conference table, Paul's absence as active as a poltergeist in the room. But lovers break up, and they don't often work together afterward, and Nina had high hopes for Wish. She knew how important he considered the work, and how excited he was.

"Mom already gave me the files," Wish said. Sandy nodded. "I have some ideas."

"Go ahead," Nina said.

"Point one, the obvious thing, we find out who shot Sarah Hanna two years ago, locate the individual, and collect evidence against him. But at the moment, we don't have a description. We don't have anything on this individual. Our client doesn't seem to remember a thing about him."

"Except that he was masked."

"Right, even though this all happened in October, he wore the good old ski mask. Except at Tahoe it doesn't look totally crazy, even in early fall. People just think he's some skidoggy who rents helicopters to take him to the top of Job's Peak or some other ten-thousand-footer so he can keep skiing through spring and maybe even into summer."

"The shooting happened after midnight," Sandy reminded him. Sitting across the table from him, she took computer notes just in case something important was said. "It can get cold any time of the year."

"My point is that anyone seeing this individual on the street wouldn't automatically call 911, not up here in the mountains," Wish said.

"He entered the parking lot of the Ace High," Nina said, "and probably slipped on the mask then. The motel clerk was instant-messaging her boyfriend in Thailand from the cybercafe next door, so nobody saw him."

"Except the three individuals he proceeded to rob, who gave fake IDs to the motel to start with, and split in a hurry. I recommend we start with the witnesses."

"Be my guest," Nina said. "Book 'em, Danno."

"If the police couldn't find them, where do we start?" Sandy asked.

"First, we contact the authorities. Try Sergeant Fred Cheney of the South Lake Tahoe police," Nina told them. "He's worked with Paul."

The name hung like a cloud in the air for a moment, then dissipated. Sandy liked Paul, too, and while she was no doubt proud of her son, Nina knew she missed him.

Wish wrote the name down. "And reconnoiter the premises."

"You mean the Ace High?" Sandy asked.

"That's it, Mom. The premises. The crime scene, where the shooting occurred. I'll interview the clerk, Meredith Assa— Assawaroj."

"Go for it," Nina said, pleased at his careful attempt to pronounce the unfamiliar name. "Then I've got something special for you."

"Oh?" Wish said. "What's that?"

"I think the motel owner, James Bova, knows something about the witnesses," Nina said, "but he's represented by counsel. Now, I can't talk with him directly."

"Does that mean I shouldn't?" Wish asked.

"No ethical rule forbids you from talking to his wife or his drinking buddy. Or anybody else he might be inclined to unload on."

"Excellent," Wish said. "It's so useful, working for attorneys. You people know rules nobody else knows."

"Keeps you out of trouble," Sandy said.

The comment made them all smile. Wish had had his share of trouble. They all had.

Flipping through some papers, giving him a home address, Sandy said, "Maybe he talked to the motel clerk. The Meredith individual."

"See what you can find out," Nina agreed. "Also, these three young people—the witnesses—they were outside, evidently on their way back to their rooms. That means they had just returned from somewhere. This is harder, Wish, but if you can get decent descriptions from the clerk, you should check the casinos. It was too late for theaters and restaurants, after midnight."

"But if they were kickin' it at certain eating establishments earlier, someone might remember them. Because, who do you talk to at the casinos? There are a dozen of them, with all kinds of staff, and they're all on privacy patrol," Wish said.

Nina nodded. This made sense. "They had to eat somewhere, and it might have been close."

"So first we find the witnesses, and from those individuals we get the shooter's description so we can find him."

"Child's play," Sandy said, "for an individual of your vast potential."

"That is correct," Wish said. "I hope." He swiveled to eyeball his mother. "Are you teasing?"

"Far be it."

"Because if you are, now's not a good time. A woman died. I intend to help Nina find out how it happened."

Appearing chastened for the first time Nina had ever

witnessed, Sandy nodded. "I know you will, Willis." As quietly as the breeze floating through the pines outside the window, she added, "I hope you realize your dad and I are proud of you."

Wish sat up straight and firmed his jaw. He and Sandy looked away from each other.

"The court hearing on the motion to dismiss the lawsuit is set for Tuesday," Nina announced.

"Say no more," Wish said, getting up.

"How's the old brown van working these days?" It had been Paul's before he passed it on to Wish and bought himself a Mustang. It had been Paul's when she met him, and danced with him, and fell in love with him.

"Perfectly, as long as you fill the tank every five minutes."

"Well, good luck, Wish."

"Thanks, boss," Wish said, donning his sunglasses. "I'll check in on Monday."

Nina and Sandy worked through the morning. Finally, Nina said, "Enough. I have to pick up Bob."

Sandy squared up her file pile, asking, "What's he doing this fall? Besides high school?"

"Well, he started a business. He wants to make some money."

"What's he doing, yard work?"

"No," Nina said. "He collects hazardous waste all around Tahoe Paradise and takes it to the dump. He has a partner, Taylor Nordholm, his friend at school."

"Hazardous waste?"

"Paint, mostly."

"And how does he get it to the dump? He's only fourteen, right?"

"Taylor's father takes them in his pickup. But I think the neighbors are driving hard bargains. They ask the boys to take washing machines, car parts, all kinds of stuff that's hard to dispose of. And they want to pay later."

"I'll have a talk with Bob next time he comes in the office about getting paid and what's legal."

"Great. Uh, speaking of pay, I can't give you that raise for a couple more months. When some of the receivables come in."

"I should know. I cook the books."

"I'm sorry."

"No problem," Sandy said. She shut down the Macintosh and pushed her chair back, her earrings faintly tinkling. "Of course, you could give me a raise effective today and make a back payment when the checks come in."

"Good suggestion. I'll think about it. Well, got to get going," Nina said.

"Me, too."

"What are you up to on this beautiful Saturday afternoon?" Nina asked as she packed up her briefcase.

"Job interview," Sandy said. She checked her watch, her face serene.

"What?"

"Michael Stamp's office. His secretary quit to have twins. Very inconsiderate of her, he said. I hear the pay is good."

Nina snapped the briefcase shut. "Very funny. Stop kidding around, Sandy. You gave me a bad shock for a minute there."

"I never kid," Sandy said. She wiped a speck of dust off the telephone with her finger. Nina stared at the competent brown hand, the varnished fingernails, the silver ring with its three turquoises. Sandy bent down and blew on the phone receiver, inspected it critically, seemed satisfied. She picked up her tote.

Nina said, "Hang on. I'll walk out with you." She locked the door and they walked at Sandy's dignified pace down the hall to the exterior door of the Starlake Building, Nina deep in thought. The hell of it was, Sandy didn't kid, not much anyway.

"See you Monday," Sandy said.

"So what I'm thinking is, when some of the big checks come in, you'll get your raise retroactive to today," Nina said.

Sandy shaded her eyes and looked east toward the mountains.

"Okay?"

"I was just thinking I better get home right away. Clouds risin' up from the coast. Might storm. Joe's getting lazy. He needs to make sure the animals make it into the barn."

Late in the afternoon, just as Nina, Bob, and their dog, Hitchcock, reached the far side of Spooner Lake, the clouds did boil up and blow, offering them the choice to run for twenty minutes through the downpour or seek shelter. They decided to run for it, Bob recklessly crashing along the trail with its clutter of roots and pine cones, Hitchcock at his heels, running with his nose to the ground, Nina picking her way behind, the brim of her baseball cap pulled low. They jumped into the Bronco, laughing wildly, Hitchcock making a mess in the back seat.

Nina turned the key in the ignition, and stopped laughing. "Our truck appears to be dead," she said. Rain pounded on the roof, and she shivered and reached back for her emergency sweatshirt.

Bob scratched his head and leaned over. "It's in gear. It won't start in second gear, y'know, Mom."

"Of course I know. Did you put it in second for some reason?" She moved into park, started up, shifted to drive, and turned on the wipers. Bob found some paper towels in the glove compartment and dried his face. Hitchcock poked his furry head between them and Bob carefully wiped the dog's face too, saying, "That's it, blame me."

"Well, I didn't do it."

"You did it by accident. You're getting absentminded."

At fourteen, he thought the worst of her. "Not so. Why would I do such a thing?" She pulled onto the wet road.

"Why would I?"

She had no answer for that.

"Hey, do a rooster tail in the flooded part of the road there."

"I don't think so." But the water was so tempting. Pushing hard on the accelerator, getting up to forty, she angled through a foot of water and enjoyed spritzing the fir trees along the road.

Bob laughed heartily. Then he said, "Uh-oh. A guy was standing in the trees right there. I think we got him." Nina slowed.

"Too late now," Bob said. "Anyways, he was already wet."

"We'd better go back and apologize," Nina said, "or he'll go home and kick his cat. Bad karma will vibrate through the universe."

"Let's not and say we did," Bob said. "He looked funny."

"Funny?"

"I think he was wearing a ski mask. Like in a slasher movie. It was hard to see."

"It's raining."

"That's really going to keep the rain off, a knit ski mask." Nina thought, But you wouldn't call 911 because of it. The shooter in the Hanna case had worn a ski mask.

Don't think, she told herself. It's just a guy in the road.

But what was a man doing in the road in that downpour, in a ski mask?

"I say keep going. If you want to get punished, I can always spray you with the hose when we get home," Bob said.

Looking in her rearview mirror, Nina could see no sign of anyone. The rain came down like the sky really was falling, one of those autumn cloudbursts that come from nowhere and leave just as abruptly. The wipers had a hard time maintaining visibility.

They had lost him. "Okay, let's go."

When they reached the highway that circles Lake Tahoe, the rain stopped. It was almost six o'clock and wouldn't be dark for some time yet. "What shall we have for supper?"

"Pancakes."

"That's so inappropriate for dinner."

"You could have a burger. You don't have to eat pancakes. We're almost at Zephyr Cove. Are you pulling in or not?"

"Okay, okay."

The pancake house, an old wooden structure in the trees not far from the yellow beach, housed a motley collection of drenched tourists. Their table, just under a tall window, offered a good west-ward view as another cloudburst flitted across the lake. They sipped ice water, watching as sheets of rain fell here and there in the distance and evening slipped across the world. The mountains ringing the lake were only a shade or two of darker blue against sky above and water below.

"Uh-oh. Red alert. Look who's here," Bob said, pointing toward the window with his menu.

"Who?"

"I think maybe it's that guy in the woods you soaked."

"Where?" She felt a clutching in her chest.

Oh, yes. There was a figure a long way away, in the parking lot, near a beat-up white SUV . . .

"Hey, that's our Bronco!" Nina cried, sliding off the wooden bench.

"Wait for me!" Bob took the lead as they ran out the front door. Now, even across the lot, they could hear Hitchcock. Part malamute, mostly mutt, he seldom barked, but he was barking now, loudly and continuously. The man had disappeared.

They walked around the Bronco, trying the doors—locked, as they had left them.

"Mom!" Bob yelled. Nina ran around and saw Bob crouched on the ground by the right rear tire, holding something. He held it out and Nina saw that it was an air-valve cap. Bob jumped up and walked cautiously around the truck with her. The air plugs had been opened on all four of their plump, balding snow tires.

Bob twisted the caps back on. The tires looked soft but drivable. Hitchcock leaped against the window.

"Well, at least he didn't get in the car and steal our crummy radio," Nina said. There was plenty of open asphalt around them. He seemed to be gone.

"Hitchcock would've had to kill him."

Nina didn't want to disturb Bob any further. She said, "Let's get poor Hitchcock out and calm him down, then go back inside and eat. This guy's not coming back. Man, some people don't know how to take a little accident with good grace. Can you believe he would follow us just to pull a nasty trick like this . . ." She took out her keys and began to stick one into the driver's-side lock, but Bob's hand swooped out to stop her.

"Mom, wait a second. I have a bad feeling."

The paranoid professional self kicked in immediately. She clipped her keys to her bag and stepped back. "What's the matter, Bob?"

"Maybe those caps—you never know. Maybe he wanted to distract us." Bob apparently found that an adequate explanation.

"From what, exactly?"

But he had finished explaining. "Just wait, okay? Step away a long way from the vehicle." He said it playfully, but she sensed he was trying to protect her in his own way.

She stepped back, frowning, nervous and unhappy. Black clouds like the ones overhead clumped in her mind.

Methodically, moving with the practiced ease of an experienced Gulf Warrior, or at least like a kid who had played quite a few video combat games in his day, Bob slunk around the car, examining each inch of the exterior, then shimmied underneath.

"What are you doing? Don't do that." Nina kept the panic out of her voice with an effort.

"Looking."

She swallowed, watching Hitchcock hurl himself against the window. "Anything?" she asked when she could stand the suspense no longer.

"Well," Bob said, "yeah." He wriggled out from under the car, grabbed her by the arm, and pulled her farther away.

"What's the matter?"

"Come on! I hate to tell you, but it's bad."

"A tracker?" she asked. "GPS or something?"

"Worse!"

"What do you mean?"

"Mom, I think it's an explosive. Call the cops, Mom. You stay right here. I'll get Hitchcock out..."

"No! No! Stay away from it!" This time Nina did the pulling, and it took some lengthy argument and anguished begging to stop Bob from risking his life to save his pet.

Once she felt she could trust Bob to stay away from the Bronco, she called the police, all the time watching Hitchcock's liquid eyes, frightened for him and his big wet tongue. Oblivious, just wanting to get with the people he loved, he continued to assault the windows. Nina and Bob walked out of his line of sight so that he would stop.

Within minutes several police cars arrived. Six officers carefully evacuated the restaurant, filing people out one by one, keeping them as far away as possible from the parking lot. People from the restaurant, unable to leave without cars, were joined by a crowd of neighborhood people. Everybody stood bug-eyed behind yellow caution tape, rubbernecking, but still unable to see much.

"Our dog," Nina said to a policewoman. "Our dog!"

"We'll try to save him, ma'am."

Was that supposed to make her feel better, she wondered, succumbing to an anxious gush of tears. Bob, glitter-eyed but too old to cry, patted her on the back.

A bomb squad showed up in a white van. For another hour, they scurried back and forth between the parking lot and van. "What's going on?" she asked everyone she saw who looked official. "What about our dog?" She imagined him inside, confused by the strangers invading their territory, banging against the window, and although she tried to stop such thoughts, she imagined him dead, in pieces flung all over the parking lot.

In every scenario she had ever seen on TV, the car blew up. In this scenario, the police prodded spectators to move back, back, back. Everyone moved. They all heard the bass boom as the bomb detonated hundreds of yards away on a beach by Lake Tahoe, well away from the parking lot.

They were informed that their vehicle was now "good to go."

Bob walked up to their car and stuck his hand through an open window so that he could touch Hitchcock. "I guess we won't be doing any more rooster tails, Mom."

Back in the restaurant the newly returned, excited patrons plied her with questions, but Nina didn't know what to say, so she beelined back to their table and tracked down their server. "You saw what happened. Was anyone around here—watching us or anything?"

"There was a guy. He checked out your table after you left. I thought he might be hoping you ran out without your purse or something." The girl, no more than seventeen, held a steaming platter with at least four plates full of food in one hand.

"What did he look like?"

"About forty. Denim jacket, work boots. Dripping."

"Was he wearing a ski mask?"

"A floppy hat. Uncool people wear them to golf in, you know? I chased him off." She eyed the plates she was holding. The food was getting cold.

"Thanks," Nina said. She pulled a bill out of her wallet and put it in the girl's free hand.

"Oh, one other thing," the girl said, tucking the money into a pocket. "He walked funny."

"How funny? How did he walk?"

"Crooked, like the old guy on the old *The Real McCoys* show. Remember? Well, that was pretty exaggerated, the way he walked. This guy was bowlegged. Or maybe he just has a bad foot?"

Out in the lot the wind whipped through the trees. She spent some time with the cops. She told them about the ski mask in the Hanna case, and the floppy hat, and the bad leg. The officer did not seem impressed. "Ski mask on the road, no information as to his walk. Then floppy hat, bad leg. Different individual, probably," he said. "Too bad you didn't see the guy in the road take a few steps."

"Look. This was an attempted murder."

"More likely, ma'am, an attempt to frighten you. There wasn't enough explosive to kill you inside the passenger compartment. On the other hand, any explosive at all is terrifically dangerous around a gas tank. You were lucky."

"Please give your reports to Sergeant Cheney. It may be a link to the Hanna case."

"I will."

"Who else would try to blow us up? I don't have any enemies like that."

"How would this man even know you were in the case? And if he knew, why would he want to kill you?"

"Because—I don't know why."

"I'll talk to Cheney." They talked about her security system.

Bob waited for her in the truck, petting Hitchcock.

"Did you walk him?" she asked through the window.

"Yeah. He took a good long whiz. Must've smelled the explosive. He was heading for the beach."

"Tell me you didn't go there!"

"I stayed by the truck. The beach was roped off. They're still cleaning up."

She slammed the door and got in. "Whew! It's evil out there!" She unclipped her keys and they dropped onto the floor.

While she felt around for them, Bob said, "You don't have to worry anymore, Mom. This car's safer today than most days."

Finding them, she reached toward the back seat to give Hitchcock the opportunity to lick her wrist and hand.

"You were right about the bad karma," Bob said. "He followed us here. It's like, if you accidentally spill your soda on some kid, of course he turns out to be the meanest psycho kid in school, and waits for you after school, gets you back much worse. Know what I mean?"

"What did the police say to you?"

" 'What's he look like?' I told them."

"Bob, do you remember? Was the man in the parking lot wearing a ski mask? Or a floppy hat?"

Bob shrugged. "He was a ways away."

"Maybe. Bob—" Bob had his arms around Hitchcock's damp, furry neck, his eyes closed, his cheek pressed against the dog's ear. Hair pressed flat to his head, ears standing out, Bob looked a bit like a dog himself as he communed with Hitchcock. Nina caught herself thinking, If anything ever happens to that dog—and she knew she was really thinking about Bob. A sharp pain lanced through her right eye.

"Yeah, Mom?"

"How sure are you that the man by the Bronco was the same as the man in the ski mask on the road?"

"I just thought it must be him. I'm sorry, Mom. I just figured, you know. I couldn't see the man by the Bronco through the rain."

"It's okay, honey. I think you saved our lives."

"Yeah, Hitchie, we saved you." Bob hugged the dog some more. He did not seem particularly upset by the whole incident.

Nina said, "The world has—it's changed. It's not a safe place."

"It never was, Mom. That's why we buy good locks and use 'em."

That night, as Nina lay in her bed reading, Bob knocked and came in and sat down in the wicker chair. He usually stayed up much later than she did and slept as late as he could in the morning, but he asked her to wake him up if he slept through his alarm.

"But tomorrow's Sunday."

"The dump takes hazardous stuff on Sundays. We have some things under the house I need to get rid of. Taylor's garage is full, too. What are you reading?"

She struggled to remember. "A book about the Big Bang. New theories about what the universe looked like in the first few minutes after the explosion. Speaking of big bangs, is any of the material you have been collecting flammable? Or potentially explosive?"

"Only a little."

"I don't like the sound of that. Don't store anything like that under the house!"

"We charge twenty bucks per house to haul away old motor

oil, mostly, Mom. We have all the customers we can manage. We'll put it in the backyard under a tarp if you want."

"Why do you need money, Bob? You have a new bass. You like your skateboard, and you can't want new clothes after all the shopping we've been doing."

Bob dropped his eyes to Hitchcock, snoozing on the carpet, and nudged him with his stockinged foot. "I want to take a trip to see my dad."

Nina put her fingers to her temple, closed her eyes. "You saw him in Sweden a few months ago."

"I need to go again."

"You miss him so much?"

"Well, sure, I miss him, but the thing is, I talked to him a couple of weeks ago. He lost his job with the Stockholm Opera Company and he's back in Germany. He's having trouble with his hands."

Kurt Scott, Bob's father, was a concert pianist who had eked out a living touring Europe for most of Bob's life. He hadn't known about Bob's existence until a few years before, because Nina hadn't wanted him to know. He had left her, waiting for him, with no word, soon after she learned she was pregnant. That day had become a turning point in her life, and she had polished the memory, along with the grief and rage over being abandoned, for so many years, that even when she learned years later that Kurt had left her to save her life, she had not been able to change her feelings from that day. The memory was encysted in her, permanently, it seemed.

But Bob had no such memories. Since discovering each other, he and Kurt had seen each other several times and developed a close bond that didn't include her.

Nine felt a now-familiar tugging at her heart. She didn't want Bob to leave her. It wasn't Kurt's fault that his life was in

Europe or Bob's fault that he wanted to see him again, but she didn't want Bob to go, even for a few weeks. Her life, her routines, were built around Bob. She knew she feared that one day he might go and live with Kurt. Then what would she do? He was her companion, her fellow traveler.

All right, tell the truth. She didn't want to stay alone in the house, not right now.

She had barely seen Kurt in the years since Bob's birth. She trusted him with Bob, knew he cared for Bob and had been unfairly deprived of the chance to father him over the years, knew he needed to make up time. But she didn't see why he had to take Bob away right now, at the start of a new school year, when she had so many plans for them. Okay, she hadn't made many plans. But she would think some up, right now.

"Now isn't a good time," she said.

"I'm not asking you for a ticket or anything, Mom. I'll pay my own way."

"I'm thinking we should spend some time poking around the Gold Country on weekends," Nina said. "Take a car trip up to Idaho to ski. Maybe Uncle Matt and Aunt Andrea and Troy and Brianna would come with us."

"Troy and Brianna are in school. Like me. Aunt Andrea's busy with the new baby and Uncle Matt works twenty-four hours a day, seven days a week, winter and summer."

This was more or less true. Troy, her nephew, a few years younger than Bob, had been diagnosed with a learning disability and couldn't miss school, and her brother Matt's tow-truck business had started up the day parasailing got too cold on the lake. There would be no big happy family trip to Idaho.

Bob ran his hand through his dark hair. Like Kurt's, his eyes were a speckled green.

"Did your dad ask you to come?"

"No. But he'd like it."

Nina wanted to say, But I won't like it if you leave, but Bob didn't need any more burdens on him right now. "What's wrong with his hands?"

"I don't know."

"Let's talk more about it tomorrow night," she said. "It's been a hard day. I'll give your dad a call."

"Okay. Want to go to Wild Waters in Sparks tomorrow after I finish? They close next week."

"Sorry, honey. I have a meeting in Placerville."

"On Sunday afternoon?"

"Drive down with me."

"No, thanks. I'd rather hang around here with Taylor."

"Okay. Did you set the alarm?"

"An' checked the windows good. Are you scared, Mom? I don't see how he could know where we live, and the police are watching an' I'm watching. He got what he wanted. He made us afraid. That's the last of him."

"I guess so. I'll be fine. Love you. G'night."

"G'night."

She turned off the lamp and shut her eyes, seeing once again Hitchcock's frantic eyes as he lunged against the window of the Bronco.

Chapter 6

FOUR-ELEVEN IN THE AFTERNOON. ELLIOTT was just waking up. He crunched through two bowls of crispy cereal, standing at the kitchen counter, back safe at home on Vashon Island. He had gotten in very late from Tahoe and hadn't been able to sleep until morning because he couldn't stop thinking about the man in the ski mask.

In the dreary daylight, which highlighted the broken tiles near the toaster, he considered that he was now more than a thousand miles from Tahoe, an eighteen-hour drive. He was safe. Relatively safe.

He went through a box a day sometimes. Boxed cereal might look like pure junk, but actually, the vitamins added later, plus the fact that the cereal had once, a very long time ago, grown in a field and been alive, resulted in a substance that tasted good and also contained all minimum daily requirements. It took almost no time to pour cereal and milk into a bowl. All in all, he wouldn't eat anything else, except that Pop had surprised them both and turned into a master chef after his mother's death.

Through the door into the living room Elliott could see the back of his father's head, the silver hair shaking when he disagreed with the umpire or got excited about a play. The orange-leafed trees outside their picture window, and the fact that his college team was winning, made Pop forget about the MS. Sometimes he did get depressed, though. Then he'd say things like, "El, you'll be on your own someday."

But most of the time Pop seemed to feel fine. He ran the house from his wheelchair, he and Gloria the sexy housekeeper.

Someday Pop would be in trouble. Elliott was saving up for that, to make sure he'd have the best care.

Four-thirteen. "Get 'im!" Pop said. "Did you see that, El?"

They still lived in the brick house he'd been born in. For many years, Pop had ferried back and forth from Seattle, where he was a professor of linguistics at the university. He was also a Sanskrit scholar. Even now, those two words sent a shiver of excitement through Elliott. His father knew things nobody else knew, about ancient magical words.

Pop had seemed like the smartest man in the world when Elliott was a kid. Most nights after supper, between six and seven, they'd go into the den and shut the door. His father would pull down a volume of the *Encyclopaedia Britannica* from the shelf, and they would read an article together. They worked in alphabetical order, so one night it would be electromagnetism, and the next, elephants.

Then Elliott would finish his homework, which hardly took any time, because he was a bright one, so Pop said. He told Elliott about Sanskrit. Linguistics wasn't about languages, it was about logic. Pop showed him how to diagram Sanskrit grammar so the little x's and y's added up to a sentence, and Elliott enjoyed this a lot, even though the words themselves flitted from his mind.

Somehow his interest turned from the language to the x's and the y's. Subject plus verb plus direct object equals a sentence. In English, anyway. English moved like a number line, marching to the right. But there were other languages that put the direct object first, or even the verb. X stayed the subject, y still described the verb. Math described language; wow!

He had first discovered numbers when he was three or four. Someone gave him a set of magnetic numbers and letters that his mother put on the refrigerator for him, and he threw away the letters and kept the numbers, because he couldn't read, but he could add.

He was sure numbers were real. One was the Stick, a skinny black stick that got left behind all the time. Two was the Blue Policeman; Zero was the Crystal Ball, white and glowing like a ghost. Three was the Bully, red and angry. It turned all the numbers it could divide into a reddish color.

To him these four numbers were as real as rocks, more real, alive in some sense. But what were they? What was a number? Where did numbers come from? Had humans invented them or discovered them? Where did they go? He thought they followed a line toward some far infinity where a little breeze sprang up and supported them.

He never saw the integers as hard-edged; to him they were like clouds, with moving centers depending on what was pulling on them from either side. The clouds touched each other, even early on in the line of numbers, but as the numbers got bigger the clouds became a continuum, a long streak of cirrus.

But when he was young, he had little interest in the large

numbers; it was Zero, One, Two, Three, and the rest was just amplification.

"Yes, Elliott?" Mr. Pell said from the blackboard. Sharon, the girl in the desk next to him, grimaced, because Elliott was a pudgy pest who kept his hand raised all through class. He couldn't help it. Mr. Pell kept saying all these things that made no sense. The class had spent most of the year memorizing the multiplication tables, which Elliott already knew, and this month they were learning long division.

"Why is the answer zero when you multiply by zero?" Elliott asked.

"Because that's how the system works," Mr. Pell said. Then he sighed and said, "Zero times three equals zero plus zero plus zero. Think about it."

Elliott was supposed to be quiet now, but instead he argued, "But zero is nothing. It can't do anything to another number. Three times nothing can't change three."

"No, one is the number that doesn't change anything in multiplication," Mr. Pell said.

"Then zero and one must be the same number," Elliott told him. The class giggled, even Sharon, as if he had said something funny, but he felt a need to know, or maybe to be right, and it didn't stop him. "Ten times one, that's ten times itself, isn't it? Shouldn't that be a hundred? One should be a—a—"

"An exponent," Mr. Pell said. "You'll learn about them next year. Ten times itself is a hundred, true. But ten times one is ten."

"And ten times nothing is nothing?"

"Good. Right."

"Then what is ten divided by zero?"

Tall Mr. Pell looked at the big clock on the wall and finally said, "You can't divide by zero, Elliott. It's a rule."

"Why is it a rule?"

"Because the rest of arithmetic won't work otherwise. You just have to accept it."

"I thought math was supposed to be logical."

"It is."

"Then how come multiplying by nothing wipes out a number?"

"Talk to me after class."

Mr. Pell went back to the blackboard after the bell rang and the rest of the class ran out. He was awfully young to be a teacher. Elliott's father said Mr. Pell had been a PE major, but he'd minored in math and the school needed a math teacher more than a coach. He wore a bow tie and a short-sleeved blue shirt. He looked like Eddie Murphy, but without the funny stuff.

"Look. Division is based on multiplication, right? Twelve divided by zero equals x. Then zero times x would have to equal twelve, but that can't be. Zero times x equals zero, you already know that."

"But why?"

"Because," Mr. Pell said, "it works. A million math operations say it's true. Let's look at it this way. Let's take nine divided by three. If you have nine rocks, you can separate them into three groups of three. Got that?"

"Sure." In his mind they were reddish rocks, like on Mars.

"So let's look at nine divided by zero. How many groups of zero can you separate nine rocks into?" Mr. Pell smiled. "You see? You can't have a group made of nothing. It just doesn't make sense."

"That's an artifact of your definition," Elliott told him.

Mr. Pell dropped his chalk. "Who told you that?"

"It's logic."

The teacher gave Elliott a long look. He seemed excited. Elliott thought, I'm a bright one, and warm satisfaction spread through him. He couldn't wait to see what Mr. Pell would come up with next. Without noticing, he had clenched his fists and stood with his legs apart, chin out.

"This isn't a boxing match," Mr. Pell said. "You're pretty competitive, aren't you? All right, Elliott. Let's try looking at it this way. When you divide by a number, you expect the result to be a number. Got it?"

"Got it."

"Let's look at a sequence of numbers." He wrote some fractions on the board. One over two, one over three, one over four, one over eight . . .

"See how the numbers change in a regular pattern? Get it?"

"Got it."

"Know what happens if you keep on going this way?"

"They get smaller."

"Very good! That's right. The end result is something infinitely small. Approaching zero."

"Awesome! It ends at zero?"

"No, it never ends."

Elliott's mouth fell open.

"It goes on forever, approaching closer and closer to zero. Zero is sort of the end of infinity."

"So when it gets so small . . . when it's one over zero . . . that's infinity?"

"It's something we simply can't assign a number to at all. It's outside the system. I'll tell you why. You know what negative numbers are? Minus numbers?"

"Sure."

"Try following another sequence: One over minus two, one over minus four, and so on. What's at the end of the sequence?"

"Minus zero?"

"Good try. In fact, the answer is also zero. Because zero is zero. There cannot be a minus zero."

"Why?"

"It's not allowed. Don't ask why. Just accept that the answer is zero for both sequences. But you can't have the same answer for two different number sequences. Don't ask why. You can't. Since you can't, we say that dividing by zero doesn't result in a number."

Mr. Pell expected Elliott to ask why you couldn't have two separate answers, or why the second sequence was zero when it ought to be minus zero. He had a couple of slam-dunk sentences planned to put Elliott away, like "Don't ask."

But Elliott was way past that. "Yeah. That's right. I always thought there was something strange about zero. Now I understand," he said.

"Good." Job well done, Mr. Pell's face said.

"The number line must be a circle," Elliott said. "Like a clock."

"No. No." The bell rang again and the next class started coming in and sitting down while Mr. Pell was still shaking his head.

"The number line. It's really a circle. Like you said, the zero at both ends ties it together," Elliott said hurriedly.

"No. The number line is a line. By definition." But Mr. Pell rubbed his mouth and said, as if he were talking to himself, "... not bad. Sounds like elliptic geometry."

"What?"

"Just accept that it's a line, Elliott."

"But why? Who made it that way? God?" Now several other kids were listening in. Elliott didn't care. He needed a real answer, not an answer for a kid, an answer that worked for him, or else it might be that the nagging thought he sometimes had at night was true—that he wasn't a bright one after all, he was just the pudgy pest of the class, too stupid to understand what was obvious to Mr. Pell.

If he couldn't understand a simple thing like why you can't divide by zero, then he'd never understand anything. He felt like he was going to bust out crying. Why couldn't Mr. Pell answer the question in a way he could understand?

Elliott said loudly, "You don't know anything, I guess," to his teacher. He heard the laughing in the background again. Everybody thought he was a freak. It made him mad. "I know what an exponent is," he boasted. "I know what a square root is. What's the square root of minus one?"

"This is way beyond third-grade arithmetic," Mr. Pell said. "Who told you to ask me these questions?" He still had a peculiar look, like he was really interested, too, and this emboldened Elliott.

"Nobody. My pop. He's a Sanskrit scholar. What's the square root of minus one?"

"You know what? I bet your father already told you the answer, told you it's an imaginary number with its own number line."

"Egg-zackly. So if you can set up a brand-new number line for negative square roots, why can't you set up a new number line for one divided by zero?"

Mr. Pell looked down at him from the height of a mountain. He bent and picked up the chalk, and said in a low tone, close to Elliott's ear, "Listen to me, kid. I'm going to tell you a secret. You'll understand it better when you're older. Do not tell the rest of the kids about this. You cause enough trouble already. They'll get confused."

Elliott raised his eyebrows. He tried to look nonchalant.

"You can divide by zero, if you invent another arithmetic. This arithmetic you're learning—it's just the one that works best for things like building houses. There are all kinds of arithmetics and geometries."

Elliott understood immediately. His head swam. The relief was so overwhelming, he almost fell down. This arithmetic was a game, and *there were other games.*

"Got it?" Mr. Pell said. "Satisfied? Now beat it, would you? Please?"

On his tenth birthday, his father gave Elliott an old edition of Euclid's *Elements.* Winter had brought its cold wind to sweep down on the island. Elliott stayed up in his room for two weeks. When he came down he said, "I don't understand this at all."

"Let's have a look." They opened the book to Euclid's assumptions, the logical statements that are self-evident and are the basis of plane geometry.

"Two points make a line," the book said.

"Why?" Elliott said. "The line could stop halfway to the second point. Or the two points could be on top of each other, so it looks like one point. Or the line could be wavy."

"Oh, I quite agree. But you have to think like Euclid," his father said. He smoked Marlboros. The smell of math to Elliott forever more would be connected to the smell of burning tobacco. They were in Pop's warm den, piles of papers and books everywhere, the TV on a football game as usual. Elliott's mother was sitting on the chair under the window, reading a book, her brown hair lit by the lamp.

"Euclid developed a system that hangs together, that's the main thing. Let's try to make his sentence about points more accurate. He's saying that if you take any two points in the universe, the simplest relations between them is generally a directional arrow that we call a line."

"Okay. That makes sense. But why triangles? Angles and sides and all that. Why is a right triangle so important?"

Pop stubbed out one cigarette and fired up another one. "Because the Greeks discovered that they could say beautiful, simple, elegant things about right triangles. And because they could build houses using right triangles."

"Houses again! How come it's always about houses? Why not start with a—a cloud? Why not invent a formula for finding the volume of a cloud?"

"Too messy," his father said. "Euclid started with something easy and useful. In all fairness, he was fond of squares and circles too."

"Why did he get to make up his own rules? They're wrong!"

"The one about parallel lines may not always work. The others have stood up pretty well," Pop said mildly.

"But what about two points making a line? I could make a system where they don't, couldn't I?"

"Attack the system at your own risk. I'm going to tell you a story." Commercials had taken the place of football on the TV in the wall unit across from his father's desk. He muted the sound and said, "A long time ago there was a genius named Pythagoras. He was a genius because he made some discoveries about the integers that no one had ever made before. These discoveries were so elegant, so incredible, that numbers became a religion. The Pythagoreans believed, for instance, that the cosmos formed from a one. It split into the integers, which formed themselves into geometrical shapes, and finally became air, earth, fire, and water. All Nature, all Reality, grew from Number."

"Is it true?"

"I'm a linguist," Pop said, "so I wouldn't turn to Number. I suppose I could found a religion that said that in the beginning was the Word. Wait a minute, I'm already Episcopalian." Elliott's mother laughed.

"So the Pythagoreans were an important cult. The most important belief they held was that all Nature came from whole numbers, by which I mean integers and ratios of integers, what we call fractions today.

"Then one day something terrible happened. One of the Pythagoreans, maybe the Master himself, made a new discovery." The football game came back on, but Pop was rolling now and his eyes went to the screen but his voice stayed with the story.

"They had just discovered the formula for finding the hypotenuse of a right-angle triangle," he said. "A squared plus B squared equals C squared. Can you imagine how they must have felt, sitting in the shade on a summer's day, looking at each other when they found this wonderful formula?" Elliott thought of the bearded men in white robes, sitting on steps by white columns, clapping each other on the back. It must have felt like winning the Super Bowl.

"Then somebody said, 'Let's try that triangle out with a side that measures a single unit, a one,'" Pop said. "They tried it out. And a devil sprang out! Because one squared plus one squared equals two. Therefore the hypotenuse was the square root of two." He leaned toward Elliott and said in a chilling theatrical whisper, "And that number couldn't exist."

"Wow!" Elliott said.

"That thing, that square root of two, couldn't be described as an integer or as a ratio. It completely contradicted the beautiful universe the Pythagoreans had constructed. Now they had a choice—to accept this ugly thing into their system and work with it, or to try to suppress the fact that it existed. To lie about it, because the Pythagorean religion could not encompass something as ill-formed, as unlocatable as this."

"So what did they do?" Elliott's mother said.

"They swore the whole brotherhood to strict secrecy. This

secret made a mockery of their beliefs. Now their religion was based on a lie."

"What happened?" Elliott asked. He lay on the rug, his head propped in his hands, near the fireplace, the book forgotten. It was almost nine, but he wasn't feeling sleepy, he was all fired up.

"A young man named Hippasus leaked the secret," Pop said. "And you know what happened then?"

"What?"

"They killed him. Set fire to a ship he was on near Calabria. Sunk it."

"The Pythagoreans did that?" Elliott gasped.

"Never underestimate the passion of a mathematician," Pop said. "Of course, the secret was already out. Nowadays we call those ugly numbers the irrational numbers."

"We let those numbers in?"

"And even uglier things. The imaginary numbers. The transcendents. The transfinites."

"Poor Hippasus," his mother said. She dog-eared her page and went into the kitchen.

"Those numbers aren't real," Elliott said. "Not like One and Two."

"Prove they don't exist and I'll give you a canoe," his father said.

In this way Elliott learned that what his intuition told him was only acceptable to other people if he could show them a proof. Elliott became obsessed with mathematical proofs. He had found his own language, a language his father couldn't learn any more than Elliott could remember the conjugation of a Sanskrit verb.

The proofs of the main theorems of mathematics contained

absolute certainty, a certainty that existed nowhere else in his universe of home and school.

A fever overtook him. The proofs burned into his eyes late at night.

Proofs were the rewards of playing this particular game of arithmetic, but he never forgot that other, more difficult games waited in the murk of the future for him to discover.

"El," Pop called. Elliott put his memories aside, set his bowl into the stainless-steel sink, and went into the living room. Pop never went upstairs anymore; the muscles in his legs had become too weak. Pop was barefoot. His back had hunched in some indefinable way. How strange. He was growing old as well as sick.

As he looked at his father carefully taking out the ad supplements, then putting the newspaper back in order so he could read it in sequence, he felt again the burning pressure to work, to find, as quickly as possible. Pop was only fifty-five, but he had been ill for five years now and his sharp mind had changed in some way hard to describe. It was as though only small things mattered to him anymore, the Zeros, the Ones.

His mother's clock ticked on the mantel, next to a picture of his father shaking hands with Noam Chomsky at a podium somewhere.

"I don't know why, but I feel so cold," Pop said.

"How about a bath?"

"I need a little push." Elliott pushed his chair into the adjoining bedroom, pulled down the curtains, and got the water running in the tub. Pop had a special tub where you opened the waterproof door and stepped in and sat down on the bench. So far, he could manage.

"Think I'll go upstairs and do some work," Elliott said.

"You look tired. You haven't told me about the conference at Lake Tahoe."

"Well, lots of presentations that didn't interest me much. Nothing new, really," Elliott lied.

"Did you see any old friends?"

"I did see a couple of guys from MIT, but I didn't know them well."

"What are they doing these days?"

"One works at Lawrence Livermore Lab in California. The other one went to Los Alamos." He was used to lying about his activities, so the words came out very naturally.

"Oh. Physicists. That's nice."

"By the way, I got paid on the consulting work I did last spring. It'll keep us going until Christmas."

His father said, "You have found such an interesting career, all this flitting about, doing your consulting. It's wonderful that you can spend so much time with me."

"It's my home. I doubt I could work anywhere else. I wouldn't want to leave you, Pop. We get along."

"My good fortune, that you love it here so much."

"I do have to go to town for a couple of hours in the morning. Gloria will be here, though. Do you want anything special at the store if I leave before you're up?"

"How about some of those Paul Newman chocolate wafers. Those are so good."

"Cookies it is," Elliott said. He locked up, then went upstairs, to the scratched oak desk he had spread his papers over all his life, to the single bed with its heavy plaid comforter. The closet door was open; he pulled it shut, locked the bedroom door, and leaned out the window toward the gleam of Seattle across the sound. Cool air flowed in, and he breathed in deeply.

His thoughts went back to the man in the ski mask at Tahoe,

doing something to his car. He couldn't avoid thinking about it anymore. He went over the events of the night before again and tried to analyze them.

Two possibilities presented themselves: Either he was heading toward another psychotic break, or the Tahoe shooter had found him and still wanted something from him.

Both alternatives frightened him. It felt like his heart had turned to a sack of crushed ice. He slammed the window shut and checked the lock again, pulled the blinds.

Then peered through them one last time, but all he saw was darkness.

Chapter 7

PLACERVILLE USED TO BE A GOLD town back in the mid-eighteen hundreds. Today, gold still can be gathered, especially in the summer, from tourists on their way up Highway 50 from the San Francisco Bay Area toward Tahoe, 250 miles of not much happening until the steep peaks of the Sierra take over. First there is the Bay Bridge to get across, then the long traffic jam of the East Bay, then the new Carquinez Bridge where the Delta country begins.

Then there is nothing much—fields, heat, truck stops, military bases, Sacramento, factory outlets—for a couple of hundred miles. Then the uplift of the Sierra succeeds the hot valley behind as the SUVs and sedans labor up seven thousand feet of altitude to Echo Summit and Lake Tahoe just beyond.

But first, where the foothills begin, still seventy miles from Tahoe, the highway goes through Placerville, with its historic courthouse, quaint streets full of shops, and endless forest all around, and the culture begins to change with the climate. The idea of working ten hours a day in a Silicon Valley cubicle begins to seem suspect. The men want to stop for a beer, DUI laws be damned. The women want to wander down the street looking for a tiny piece of history to take home with them. It is freedom they are looking for, as if the flatlands have imprisoned them, and Placerville is the first town on the road where they can let loose.

Nina turned left and went up a short hill. Most of the homes were small and old, well-settled in their arbors of firs.

She drove until she saw a metal mailbox reading "Hanna." Cracked asphalt led to a red Ford 150 pickup, which took up a lot of the driveway, and another filthy old truck huddled in the carport. Nina parked behind the pickup and climbed out. The sun shone down; it was so quiet here she could hear the creak of the trees catching breezes high above.

Chelsi, in shorts and a shirt that showed her brown stomach, opened the screen door on the shady porch and came out to greet her. Behind her shambled a man who must have been her father, tall and athletic like her, big-handed and big-footed.

"Dad, this is Nina."

"Roger Freeman." He squeezed her hand and put his other hand lightly over the squeeze as if to apologize for the strength of the handshake. "Sarah's brother. Come on in, Dave's inside." He shot a quick glance at Chelsi. "He's not at his best this morning."

Dave Hanna sat in a La-Z-Boy in front of a recorded ball game on TV, the sound turned off, his eyes glued to the screen. He didn't get up and barely acknowledged Nina's greeting.

The small living room still held traces of Sarah Hanna—a white-framed wedding picture on the mantel of a smiling young couple, she seated quietly, big blue eyes hopeful, flowers held in her lap, he with his hand on her shoulder, making it clear how the marital dynamics would work even then. Sarah's auburn hair touched the shoulder of her ivory gown. Dave looked a lot younger in the picture. Nina knew from her notes they had been married for ten years before Sarah died. Dave had been thirty-two, Sarah twenty-eight when they married.

A white lace tablecloth on the dining-room table still looked as if it had received Sarah's touch, and the green upholstered chair and ottoman with its own reading lamp across the room had obviously been hers. The rest of the room had a shoddy, stained look, and smelled like somebody slept in it.

The wreck on the recliner pressed the remote control. The TV went black. Dave Hanna shifted around, saying, "This better be good."

"A settlement offer usually is," Nina said. "May I?" She took Sarah's chair. Roger pulled out a couple of straight chairs from the table, and he and Chelsi sat down. Now they had a sewing circle going, only Dave was clearly a stitch short today. Eyes downcast, he scratched his neck. Nina would bet he had already tossed down a couple of beers this morning.

She glanced again at the wedding picture. A traditional male, yes, but he had lost the woman most important in his life. Grief killed some people, she thought, along with: You take the client as you find him, unless he or she is too far gone to reach at all. Nina opened her briefcase.

"It's a formal offer, made in good faith, I think," she said. "But it isn't much to compensate you for the loss of your wife, Mr. Hanna. A total of fifty thousand dollars." She recapped her visit to the Puckett mansion and Bova's proposal to add to the insurance company's offer. "We have until Tuesday before court to accept or reject. Or counteroffer."

"Not enough," Roger said. "Obviously."

"It may be close to all they have to offer," Nina said. "Bova brought the Ace High out of bankruptcy three years ago. He has tax liens against him as an individual. His home in Incline is mortgaged heavily. The motel isn't exactly flying high as a business."

"But Aunt Sarah is dead and those people have got to take some responsibility for that!" Chelsi cried. She shook her head, her expression pained. "I don't think I told you enough about her. She was so great. Did you know she coached the girls' basketball team at the high school here? There were easily a hundred kids at her funeral."

"Crying," Roger Freeman added.

"I understand," Nina said. "No amount of money can compensate your family for losing her. But you have to remember the motel wasn't directly responsible. It was negligent at best. In other words, the motel legally won't have to bear the full burden of compensating you for your loss."

"If the clerk had been at the office watching out like she was supposed to, she could have called 911!" Chelsi argued.

"I agree," Nina said.

Roger said, "Maybe Bova had something to do with the shooting. Maybe the clerk did. Maybe the clerk had a friend who picked the motel because she'd conveniently go next door. We don't know anything yet."

"We're investigating," Nina said. "But we're starting so late, we're in a risky position. The judge may dismiss the case against the motel on Tuesday."

"How much did you say?" Dave Hanna said.

"Fifty thousand. Each side pays its own attorney's fees."

"How much would you get?"

"I'll add up my actual time and my investigator's time. A couple thousand dollars, I'd guess, would be the amount."

"That's very decent," Roger said. Chelsi nodded.

"The important thing you need to know is that if the motel was directly involved in the shooting in some way and we find that out, I believe we can sue them again on a different legal theory. This settlement would not release them from any direct involvement, only from a negligent involvement," Nina said.

"What do you think?" Hanna said.

"I would let the motel out, so long as Mr. Bova agrees to co-operate fully while we try to catch the shooter. And so long as the judge will let us keep the case against the shooter alive for a while longer."

"If it's going to end the case, I don't want to settle," Roger said.

"Rog, this isn't about you," Hanna said. "Sarah was my wife. This is my case."

"My name isn't on it, sure, but she was my sister."

"Why don't you butt out?" Hanna said. "Whatever happens, you won't get a dime. Sometimes I think you keep hammering at this suit to punish me."

"What are you talking about?"

The glaze of alcohol in Dave Hanna's eyes suddenly departed, to be replaced by simmering anger. "I was there and couldn't save her. You hate me for that."

"That's not so."

"Yeah, well, you don't give a damn about me, about how this has affected my life. You're chasing a ghost. You keep Sarah alive that way. For you, this lawsuit is really just a way to keep people thinking about her, isn't it? Sometimes I think if we ever found the guy who shot her, you still wouldn't believe it! What would you do for a hobby then, huh?"

"Dave, please."

"Meanwhile, I'm stuck in this goddamn chair with the god-damn TV on. I can't work. I can't do anything. We should take the money, shut our mouths, put flowers on her grave, and get the hell out of Dodge."

"This is not about money!" Roger cried. "Sarah was slaugh-tered, and for what? Being in the wrong place? It was so random. I want the bastard who killed her to be watching his back for the rest of his life, right up until the day he's arrested and thrown in jail."

Hanna turned to Nina. "I'll take the settlement offer. I want this thing over. I need that. I need to stop being sick at heart. I need to move on. We all do, Roger, you and Chelsi as much as me."

"Taking a settlement won't fix everything, Uncle Dave," Chelsi said. "You need more help than money can buy."

"If you two would just leave things alone. Isn't it enough, that we lost her? Isn't that enough punishment, that I'm alone and feel so guilty? I think back to that night—I think of what should have happened. Maybe I could have saved her. It all happened so fast."

"Of course you did what you could, Uncle Dave. We know that," Chelsi said.

He didn't seem to hear her. "For two years dinner conversation is all about her, all about justice, all about finding the killer. I don't even remember what normal life is like. You and your dad are making me sick with all this obsessing," Hanna mumbled. "You're the sick ones."

Chelsi looked stricken.

"Don't speak to her like that," Roger said sharply. "If you want to fight, you fight me." He sagged. "Ah, why do I talk to you? Why do I bother?"

"Nina," Chelsi said, "even if Uncle Dave takes the settlement, I want you to know our position. We want you to try to keep the lawsuit alive."

Roger agreed. "We want Sarah's killer found. Do whatever it takes to make that happen."

"Even if the case settles, the police will—" Nina started, but she didn't get a chance to finish.

"You stay the hell out of this!" Hanna said, rising from his chair like a hungry bear. "You feed off her memory, you stinking ghoul!" He raised his fists and threw a punch that Roger easily dodged. Roger put a widespread hand on Hanna's head and shoved him back into his chair.

"Everybody get out," Dave Hanna said. "Go."

Roger stomped out of the room, but Chelsi went over to him, putting her hand over where his lolled on the chair arm. "We understand how hard this is for you, Uncle Dave. We really do. Maybe the money will help you get a new start," she said.

"Sure, sure," he said, all the fight gone out of him. He picked up the remote control and turned the sound up on the television. Sighing, Chelsi left the room.

Nina thought, He's still got papers to sign, but I'm not staying in the house alone with him. She could hear Roger in the next room speaking softly to Chelsi.

"Dave," she said, "if you want the settlement, here's where you sign. Let's go over to the table." He went with her, casting looks through the open door toward the next room. Then he took the pen and signed where she indicated.

"You need to come to court on Tuesday morning," Nina told him. She wrote down the time and place and handed him the note with another of her cards. "My secretary will call and remind you."

"Another trip up there?" Hanna said. "Okay, let's get it over with."

Chelsi stood in the doorway. "We'll walk out with you," she told Nina. "Good-bye, Uncle Dave."

Hanna waved a hand, his eyes back on the TV screen.

Out on the driveway, Roger said, "He needs an intervention, a treatment program. Don't get the wrong idea. He wasn't like this until she died. So it's good that he has the money coming in. Is there any way to get a hold on it so he has to use it for medical purposes?"

"You'll have to talk to another lawyer about that, Roger," Nina said. "He's my client. I'm not comfortable talking about something like that without him present, and I think he'd probably object."

"Oh. Of course. Sorry."

"I understand." She not only understood, she agreed with him, but she was in no position to say so.

"He doesn't want to move on, you know," Chelsi said softly. "I believe he just wants to be left in peace to slowly kill himself. He misses her so much."

"I hope you'll continue to be patient with him," Roger said.

"Come on, Dad. Let's go home. Uncle Dave has definitely kicked us out. Thanks for doing all this, Nina. See you Thursday for your massage," Chelsi said.

"Wouldn't miss it for the world." Nina started up the Bronco, her briefcase on the seat beside her, relieved. The case would probably be over on Tuesday, and she had helped Hanna some.

He wasn't the most charming client she had ever had. She wouldn't miss him. She felt sorry for him, though. You can't blame a wounded dog for snapping.

She rejoined the line of cars winding up toward South Lake Tahoe. At twenty-five miles an hour, she thought it would be safe to make a cell-phone call. The German time zone was nine hours ahead of California, making it about 8:00 P.M. at Kurt Scott's home in Wiesbaden.

His number was in the phone memory. She hadn't spoken to Kurt since Bob's last trip to Europe, but if she was going to stamp out the idea of another trip she would have to do it before Bob made enough money for a ticket.

He answered immediately.

"It's Nina."

"I knew that." He had a deep voice. "Is Bob okay?"

"He's great."

"Good."

"How are you?" Nina said.

"Apparently you heard I'm back in Germany."

"Bob told me. Why'd you leave Sweden and go back there?"

"The doctor says I've pounded my fingers on piano keys so many millions of times that I wore them out. It feels like rheumatoid arthritis and the joints get swollen, but he says it's just a nasty tendonitis."

"You're taking time off from the Stockholm Opera Company?"

"It's permanent. I'm finished as a performer." He gave a self-deprecating laugh. "My hands were bugging me, so I dosed up on ibuprofen. Every day, maximum dose. One day, that didn't work anymore."

"Oh, Kurt, I'm sorry."

"I'm not crippled. The old hands work fine for most things, just not toccatas. Nina," he paused, "do you remember what I was doing for a living when we met?"

They had met at Tahoe fifteen years before and embarked upon a passionate romance that lasted three weeks. Then Kurt had gone away, not because he wanted to, but Nina hadn't heard the full story until years later. She had been angry when he left, so angry that she hadn't tried to find Kurt to tell him about her pregnancy. "Remember?" she asked. "I was camping in one of the cabins at Fallen Leaf Lake. You came around to warn me that bubonic plague had been found in the area. Of all things." She recalled her reaction. She had thought, What a line.

"I had to convince you to quit consorting with raccoons and squirrels."

"You were a park ranger."

"And you were an argumentative law student. Barefoot and beautiful, sitting on the rickety steps of that little place you had rented, painting your toenails, as I recall."

Embarrassed, Nina said, "Anyway."

"Anyway, I've missed the outdoors. I always regretted that a person can't play the piano outside. Meanwhile, I have some free time to consider my future. I thought I'd do some camping in the Taunus woods, not far from Wiesbaden. Then Bob called me and I thought, I'll take him along. I suppose he mentioned that?"

"He said he wanted to visit you. It's why I'm calling," Nina said. "He's worried about you."

"He thinks I'm lonely."

"Are you?"

"Now and then."

"I think he's concerned that your hands—that the changes coming up..."

"He's a good kid when he's not being a rascal. I'd send him a ticket, but I can't get at my money. Long tangle with the bank, which amounts to I'll get things straightened out eventually but meanwhile I haven't got the ready cash."

Nina felt worse and worse about the purpose of her call. "Kurt, listen. Bob's moved to Carmel and back in the last ten months and made a trip to Sweden to visit you," she said. "He's back in school now. He needs stability."

"You mean you do."

"What?"

"Bob told me you split up with Paul."

"It was inevitable. But that has nothing to do with..."

"Bob seems confused."

"You mean—because I took away his father substitute?" Nina said. "That's ridiculous. He never viewed Paul as a father."

"He liked Paul. They had a relationship, too."

Stung, Nina said, "I can't help that. I really can't. What's your point, Kurt?"

"Hey, just be honest about what's going on."

"I'm trying."

"Let him come, Nina. He can miss a week or two of school. He's a smart guy. He'll make it up. He can write a photo-essay about Germany."

"I just think that Bob—"

"Ah, it's so frustrating. I have no power in this situation, which makes me angry."

"Kurt, it's tough. You live half a world away. Okay, I do rely on him, maybe more than I should. And I don't want to keep him from you, but I don't like him putting his energy into schemes to get back to Europe all the time."

"You're used to having him all to yourself. Wait. I don't mean it that way."

"You can always make me feel guilty." She had kept Bob's existence a secret from Kurt for twelve years. Now he liked being in his son's life. Naturally.

"I'm not trying to bring up old business, Nina. Let's deal with this right now."

"Right now I feel like I'm in some kind of popularity contest with you that I might lose."

He laughed, easing some of the tension between them. "You're joking, right?"

The car in front of her came to an abrupt halt. Slamming on her brakes, she realized minutes had passed and she had no consciousness of driving. "I have to go."

"We aren't finished, Nina."

She knew that, and she knew they had reached an impasse.

"Give my love to the boy."

And the feeling in his voice almost changed her mind, but swerving left, distracted by a car broken down alongside the road, she kept her good-bye brief. They hung up. The Bronco toiled up the winding road along the American River with the other trucks and SUVs. Nina felt guilty, but Bob would stay home. He would understand when she explained it to him, and Kurt would support her. He had no choice.

Chapter 8

FOR SEVERAL DAYS IT RAINED STEADILY on the island. Elliott and his father had a thousand-piece picture puzzle to work on. Gloria brought in the groceries. Elliott spent a lot of time in his room, worrying about the man in the mask, thinking about the robbery two years before. He couldn't concentrate on working on the proof. He stared out the window at the new streams running down the steep ravine behind the house into the cove.

Elliott never had been able to prove that irrational numbers don't exist, but his father gave him a canoe anyway the day he turned twelve. That was when Elliott dropped out of school and started teaching himself, though his mother made him take piano lessons and volunteer at the library.

Not far from the house the woods gave way to a small, stony beach and a sheltered cove bounded by tumbled rocks. Elliott spent his teenage summers pulling rhythmically on the oars, circling the cove, mostly alone, thinking. His parents didn't bother him, and he had no friends, so he was free to think. Sometimes he thought about girls, but mostly he thought about calculus. He began carrying a spiral notebook with him to record his thoughts. When it filled, he would start a new one.

Numbers: the integers, the irrationals, the transcendents, the imaginaries; numbers that presented mysteries brighter and more challenging than the mysteries of religion, because they could be solved with logic, someday, by someone.

He had first met the greatest mystery of all, the mystery of the prime numbers, when he was ten years old.

How these building blocks of all numbers are distributed along the great number line has never been understood. They seem to occur at random—2, 3, 5, 7, 11, 13, 17—and so on and on forever to those regions of monstrous limitlessness where Elliott's little breeze blew. An integer was a prime number if you couldn't divide it by any other integer except itself and one. But no formula could predict the sequence of primes. No formula could find the factors of large numbers, except by the crude method of searching one by one along the number line.

Yet all the great minds in mathematics over all the centuries agreed on one thing: The primes could not be random. If they were random, the ground of the universe was random, and this could not be, not with planets revolving around stars, not with the soaring bridges and skyscrapers people have built, not with the human eye, which seeks and finds harmony everywhere.

No, the primes could not be randomly distributed. One day as he furiously rowed across the flat water, Elliott made up his mind to devote his life to the primes. If he introduced a new devil into the world, if he found a truth that added to chaos instead of harmony, he would hold his answer close and decide then what to do with it.

He read everything he could about the attempts to find a formula to predict the primes. The geniuses of mathematics, the smartest people who ever lived, had tried to understand the primes, and been defeated. Some had lived long, quiet lives, but many who flirted with the primes had fallen while very young: Gauss, who left math forever in his twenties; Ramanujan, the vegetarian Brahmin who died at thirty-two; Gödel, who starved himself to death; Nash, teetering on the edge of the void most of his life; Grothendieck, still alive, cloistered in a hut in the Pyrenees, obsessed with the devil; Turing, who killed himself at forty-one by eating a cyanide-laced apple.

And the greatest of them all, in Elliott's mind at least, Bernhard Riemann, who died in Italy at thirty-nine. Because of pleurisy, the books said, but Elliott figured he had died because the heat in him had died. Riemann had simply gone as far as he could. He had found a possible order in the primes and given the world a direction in the Riemann Hypothesis. It made sense to die then.

"The distribution of primes is linked to a mistake about what Zero and One actually are," he told his parents at dinner one day. "Zero and One are the same point. They are definitely not numbers."

"Prove it," his father said.

"I will. I am going to be a mathematician."

"Of course you are," his father said. "But you have to study hard so you can go to a great university."

Elliott scored a perfect 800 on his math SATs, but only 710

on the verbal side. The Massachusetts Institute of Technology offered him a scholarship anyway. He was eighteen when he got on the plane to Boston. His mother gave him two ham sandwiches so he wouldn't have to eat airplane food. His father gave him a silver-chased mechanical pencil. He wrote down his solutions with that pencil forever after.

MIT appeared to bustle with student life, but in fact it was a lonely place where a lot of young people like himself, wearing specs, walked around in the same pair of jeans for days and ate alone in cheap eateries, punching calculators and hunching under the weight of their backpacks. Elliott wasn't free to think anymore; he had to take classes in areas of knowledge that bored him, like English literature, and he spent a lot of time eating pizza and hiding out the first year. His dorm room, a high-rise on Memorial Drive, was always too hot from the central heating, and he shared the room with a social misfit from Minneapolis who talked even less than he did and dropped out during the second part of his sophomore year, leaving behind an empty bed and a starker silence.

Elliott tried out for crew, but confronted with the unfamiliar currents of the muddy Charles, he blew the tryouts. The broad shoulders he had developed rowing across the cove at home slumped and his neck was out most of the winter. He stayed through the winter break and caught a semipermanent cold from the foreign bugs of the East Coast. He missed his father and mother and wrote them endless E-mails.

His mother died suddenly. A heart attack. He spent the summer at home, trying to help his father cope.

It was so cold that second winter at MIT that Elliott almost gave up and went home. But then something happened that made weather and thoughts of home irrelevant.

At the Science Library one freezing January day, Elliott was working through some functions when Silke Kilmer, the most beautiful woman in his physics class, came up behind him and placed her divine soft cheek next to his. Startled, he gave her a push that almost knocked her over and jumped out of his chair.

"Sorry," she said, smiling. She had recovered like a cat, her hand barely touching the table to stabilize her.

"No. My fault. I'm sorry."

"Can I talk to you for a minute? I know you're working, but—just for a minute?"

"By all means," Elliott said, kicking himself mentally for sounding so pompous.

They sat down again, alone in the group of cubicles on the third floor where Elliott spent a lot of his evenings. Silke set down her heavy backpack and took off her navy pea coat, revealing a fuzzy white sweater with a turtleneck that gave her an exaggerated silhouette, the angles between her chest and ribs and stomach fascinatingly concave and convex.

Elliott tried not to stare at her. She had dark hair and red full lips, and olive skin as though she were Mediterranean, not from some little town in Germany whose name Elliott couldn't remember.

He knew that she was on scholarship, too, and that she sometimes answered questions in class he couldn't. She wanted to be a quantum physicist, they all did, all except Elliott, who wanted to be a mathematician. Of the three girls in the class, she was the one who came in late, who smiled, who would talk to any of them. The bet was that she would not return to Germany, that a big American university like Princeton would grab her. She had the smarts, but she was also gracious and sociable, which was not something you came across every day at MIT.

That she had sought him out brought a flush to his cheeks.

That her young and beautiful body exuded heat and perfume right next to his made him take a wadded-up handkerchief out of his shirt pocket and take off his glasses and wipe them thoroughly.

"What are you working on?" she asked. "I don't recognize your symbols, Wakefield." A pink nail, comma-shaped, perfect as a seashell, tapped his paper.

"My paper for number-theory class. On the Riemann Hypothesis. The zeta function."

"Of course." She smiled, and he understood what she meant: that it was just like him to choose the most difficult, abstruse subject possible.

She said, "My paper is also on the primes."

"You're kidding!"

"But I'm following a line based on the work of Michael Berry. I'm interested in the idea that the energy levels in heavy nuclei seem to be related to Hermitian matrices in the same way the primes are. I'm a double major in physics, did you know that?"

"I didn't know you had this interest," Elliott said. "But the Hermitian matrices correlations—they are just interesting correlations, until someone can explain the actual relationship, if there is one. Personally, I don't believe there's any connection between the primes and the real world, even the subatomic world. I used to think that, though. When I was a kid."

"You are wrong, Wakefield. The primes have a deep connection to the real world. I think maybe the primes *are* the real world, the real building blocks of the universe. Have you read Volovich's paper for CERN on that topic? Anyway, there's room for both of us, wouldn't you say?"

"Sure. It's just incredible that you are into the primes. Berry, that's pretty new stuff. He's in England, isn't he?"

Silke said, "*Ja,* it's new. That idiot Riemann. Saying his

hypothesis was probably true, but never giving us any part of a proof. I'll never forgive him."

"It wasn't his fault. After he died, his housekeeper threw out most of his papers."

"He should have had a better housekeeper." She smiled. "Why can't geniuses find decent housekeepers?"

"You should look at my work. I have brought in some of Ramanujan's work on partitions and factorization. The primes show that addition and multiplication aren't transparent vis-à-vis each other. It's going to be revolutionary."

"Oh, really? Ramanujan? I have a friend you ought to meet." That smile again. She had a dimple to the right of her chin when she smiled, showing small, even white teeth. Elliott wanted very badly to impress her.

He jabbered, "Riemann was trying to get past the discrete problem. The primes are deep indications that the discrete is an arbitrary convention. You know, One, Two, Three. Discrete numbers. The integers."

A silence followed this pronouncement. Elliott thought to himself, That is so elementary. If I get any more boring, no one will ever talk to me again.

But Silke finally said, "I love it. It sounds absolutely wild. I'd like to read your work."

He wanted to give it to her, give her anything she required, but there existed many reasons why he could not share his work. "When I have the proof," he said.

"What exactly will you be able to show with this proof?"

"More than Riemann." He stuck his chin out.

"What an ambitious boy you are. Math students are supposed to be modest and retiring, aren't they? 'More than Riemann'?" She cocked her head and gave him a look of such understanding, such sweet compassion, that he wanted to fall at her feet and hold her legs in the neat jeans and brown boots and bury his head in her lap. She was so smart, he wondered if she might be on a better track than his. He decided then and there to take more physics courses.

"My God, I can't believe we haven't talked before," he said.

"But what is this supposed to mean?" She was looking at his notebook. "This symbol looks like a little man with a long prick." Her efficient accent made it sound dry and academic. "So you are going to outshine Riemann? Are you going to go after the Clay prize?"

"What prize are you talking about?"

"You have to be kidding. You don't know about the Clay prize? It's a million dollars for the first person to prove the Riemann Hypothesis. It was first offered in 2000, and so far there are no takers."

"What about de Branges? He published a proof of it last year," Elliott said. "Didn't he apply for it?"

"Have you looked at his paper? People seem to think it won't stand up to peer review. You really didn't know about the Clay prize? I heard you came out of the Western woods, but how could you miss that?"

"Why are they offering money? It's a corruption—a commercialization of pure math. I just do my work. And that symbol at the bottom you're pointing at—that's just a doodle."

"Wakefield. Look at me." She still smiled, as though there was something amusing about him. He hoped he could somehow keep her amused. He didn't want her to leave. He had so much to share with her, and she was so gorgeous, and he was getting an erection—oh God, she had noticed—

"I—I can't just this minute," he said, and heard her silvery laugh. She put her long hand with its pink nails on his leg. He stared at it, cheeks flaming.

"You need money, don't you? I heard your mother died and you're still living in the dorms. Not too good for concentration, is it?"

"I'm doing okay." He wondered how Silke knew about his mother. Did the other students talk about him? The idea bothered him.

"I have a proposition for you, Wakefield."

"Okay, S-Silke." She was making him a—

"I'm going to help you make some money. Easily."

"Money?"

"You look so silly. Stop by my place tonight about eight." She gave him an address on Everett Street in Cambridge. He wrote it into his notebook. She patted him on the head like a dog and got up.

"Silke?"

"*Ja?*"

"Did you know I was working with primes before you talked to me?"

"I heard something about it."

"Is that why you . . . sat down?"

"No."

"Then, why me? Why did you talk to me?"

"Because you are the smartest SOB in the class," Silke said. "Of course."

Chapter 9

Looking back, Elliott believed that the air in Cambridge, Massachusetts, in January must be precisely equivalent to the air of Murmansk, Vorkhuta, or Nikel, Russia, in the same month; gulag bone-chilling. A wind sent from some cold hell whipped up the old cobblestones, sending trash flying into the dirty banks of snow. Icicles four feet long and six inches in diameter hung from the storm windows. The low white sky touched the rooftops. At night, ice formed along the sidewalk cracks and the yellow light of the lamps revealed high-water-content snow blown this way and that, born in the churning Atlantic.

The students came in September, when the grass was green and the boats slipped sedately along the Charles River. By the time they realized what they were in for, that the bucolic scenes of September wouldn't return until May, it was too late.

By now Elliott had found ways to avoid the weather, seldom leaving his room at MIT with its damp towels hung over the radiator except to go to class or the library. This survival strategy limited him to the company of the all-male denizens of his floor, however. Tonight, on this sortie to the Harvard gulag, he wore rubber-soled boots and a parka with a fake-fur hood pulled around his face, and carried a brown paper bag containing a bottle of Chianti cradled in his arms.

He wasn't exactly hopeful. But he was prepared.

The steps of the big house on Everett had been shoveled to allow an eighteen-inch-wide path to the door with its frozen mat. Christmas lights still hung unlit from the eaves, but behind the curtains of the windows flanking the porch he saw warm light and figures passing back and forth.

A party. His heart sank.

The door creaked open and the guy standing there looked at him without comment. He was an Asian Indian whom Elliott vaguely remembered from his class in set theory the previous semester.

"Hello, Wakefield."

"Hello."

"Raj."

"Right. Raj. Is Silke here?"

"Of course. She's waiting for you. Is that alcohol? Very good! Come in."

It was a student house, one of the mansions near Harvard that was rented to the children of the well-heeled. The entry floor was piled with grubby boots and hung with jackets. A runner with a practical brown pattern mounted the staircase.

"This way." They passed into the living room with its coffered ceilings and air of genteel decrepitude, where two girls were lounging on the couch, watching TV. Silke flicked it off with the remote in her hand and came over and stood under the shelter of Raj's arm and said, "Welcome." Reaching for the wine, she said, "Nice. You know Raj. And this is Carleen. She was in your class in set theory, too." Carleen didn't get up. With her legs curled under her, she looked like a punk kid of twelve or so.

"Hi" was all she said. Silke pointed to a chair and Elliott sat down and crossed his legs, which were now inches from Carleen's on the couch.

"So what's happening?" he said. Raj sat down across the coffee table from them and Silke came back into the room with a corkscrew, an extra bottle, and actual wineglasses. "*Prost,*" Silke said after their glasses were filled, and Elliott thought he wouldn't be able to stand their attentive eyes much longer. Obviously the evening would not go as he had hoped—Silke had joined Raj in the big easy chair and it was clear their intimacy was long-standing—and therefore he wanted to go home.

Silke smiled and Raj reached into his pocket and drew out a deck of cards.

"Ever played blackjack? Twenty-one?" he asked, casually flipping cards onto the table. It seemed that they were about to have a game.

"A few times. With my father."

"Let's try a hand." Carleen sat up and took a look at the face-down card she'd been handed. They each had a card face-down and one face-up.

"We already ate up the eights," she said. There were three eights showing on the table among the four of them. "Hit me." Raj dealt her a ten and she turned over her hole card in disgust. It had been a four. With the eight showing she had hit on twelve.

"How'd she do?" Raj asked Elliott.

"She lost."

"Silke?"

"Hit me."

Silke took a seven. With the six she already had showing, she now had thirteen points showing on the table, her hole card still hidden. "Hit me," she said again. Raj gave her a two this time. "I'll stay."

"Wakefield?" Elliott had a ten hole card and an eight showing. "Stay."

"Okay," Raj said. "So you lose."

"How do you know that? You haven't even dealt to yourself. You could bust."

"I'm going to get a ten, so I'll have total nineteen and beat your eighteen. See?" He dealt himself a card face-up. It was a ten. He turned up his hole card. An ace. With the first face-up card he had dealt himself, an eight, he had hard nineteen.

Since an ace could be one point or eleven, Raj had already had soft nineteen. He hadn't had to hit. In fact, it had been crazy to deal himself another card.

Therefore, he had known already what the card would be.

"Oh," Elliott said. "The deck is rigged. Fixed."

"You think so?" Raj said. He gathered up all the cards and began shuffling expertly. "Eight times I'm going to shuffle," he said. Silke drank her wine, her eyes bright.

Raj's hands moved expertly, but there was no doubt that he was fully shuffling the deck over and over. "Here we go," he said, and held the cards as if to deal them. "Ready?"

"For what?" Elliott said.

"For me to call the cards."

"You want me to tell you the trick?"

"I don't think you can tell me anything until I show you what I can do with these cards."

"You're gonna call them. You said so. You can probably remember a sequence of fifteen or twenty."

Raj smiled and started laying down cards. "Ten of spades," he said, and laid down a ten of spades. "Ace of hearts." He laid down an ace of hearts. "Three of hearts. I can actually tell you the whole deck of fifty-two. So you know what I can do, but how did I do it?"

"Eight shuffles," Elliott said. "I read about it someplace. If you already memorized the order of the deck, which you did, and you're good enough, you can divide the cards equally from both sides as you shuffle. After eight shuffles, you're back where you started from. Same old order."

Raj and Silke looked at each other, and Silke smiled again. She wore a soft blue sweater tonight with her jeans. Elliott was jealous of the way her hip touched Raj's hip so familiarly in their chair.

Raj said to Silke, "Not bad."

"It was me who recommended him," Carleen said. It was the first time she had spoken.

"Maybe you can tell me the next card," Raj said.

"An eight."

It was an eight. "There were three eights close to the top originally, and you hadn't altered the order. It was the best guess," Elliott said. He picked up his glass and let the liquid flow down his throat. He wasn't much of a drinker—he had just turned nineteen and it had been hard to get alcohol, even with his fake ID, earlier. He took another look at Raj. Raj was definitely a few years older than the rest of them, not because he looked older, but because he dressed older and possessed the air of confidence that comes from age and money. He had a thick gold wristwatch that had some long French name scrolled across the dial. He wore a white dress shirt, sleeves rolled up, and actual slacks, and he smiled a lot. A happy type, like Silke. Elliott could see why Silke would find him attractive.

"I like games," he said sourly, "but this feels like a test."

"Part of one," Raj said. "It remains to be seen whether you have the required nerve. I think you may pass that part of the test, too."

"So?"

"Have some more wine. Pour it for him, Silke. I'm going to tell you a story, my friend. It's about a team of people who play blackjack professionally."

"You? You three?" Elliott said, looking around. "You all go to MIT."

"We take a weekend off once a month," Carleen said.

"We bring back ten to fifteen thousand apiece each time," Silke said.

"Dollars? You mean dollars?"

"You have to practice for a couple of months. It takes a lot of concentration. We fly together and stay together. Sometimes Atlantic City, sometimes an Indian casino, sometimes Tahoe, sometimes Las Vegas." Silke was leaning forward. "It's fun, Wakefield."

"You count cards? Isn't that illegal?"

"If they catch you, they throw you out, but it isn't illegal. We did get thrown out last month from Caesars in Atlantic City. That's why you're here."

"I'm too conspicuous and they're starting to recognize me," Raj said. "We work as a team. Silke and Carleen are spotters. They go around the tables and play low bets until the cards get hot—lots of tens in the shoe. Then they signal me and I sit down and play big for a while. Then we move on."

"And that's why I'm here?" Elliott repeated slowly.

"We need another player. Another team member. We'll train you."

"I'm not sure I have time. I'm working on something, plus the classes are hard."

"Tell me about it," Raj said. His look was challenging. Elliott remembered him better now from class. He couldn't understand set theory. He kept asking stupid questions all through that class.

He would be easy to surpass. Elliott thought, I can get an A in this game. Plus maybe some money. Plus travel with Silke.

"I find this hard to believe," he said. "It's not some joke? Because I don't have much of a sense of humor."

"It's a business deal," Raj said. "The tuition at MIT is staggering, in case your family hasn't noticed."

"And we all get to be friends," Silke said.

It took three months before the team judged Elliott to be ready. He turned out to be a fast, accurate card counter. The calculations were nothing. He had no trouble concentrating, either.

Silke was still better. She had an eidetic memory, which meant she remembered every card played. She had a mental notebook where she jotted down everything she saw, and she could flip back a few pages in her mind and look at what she'd noted.

Carleen was fine as a spotter, but she got nervous and overbet. She seemed to like Elliott, and Silke and Raj kept throwing them together.

They held his first session at Circus Circus in Reno, Silke signaling him to an uncrowded table just past a set of progressive slots. A hundred-dollar minimum, and he had been provided with a stake of ten thousand dollars. He got to work.

The dealer, quick-handed and ready with a smile, dealt from a six-deck shoe that had already been played by Silke down to four decks.

She said from somewhere behind him, "I think I'll get something to eat, a bagel or something." The word *bagel* meant an extremely high number of ten pointers was left in the deck. He played five hundred, then a thousand a hand. Six minutes later he was up fifteen thousand, and the dealer shuffled. Elliott cashed in his chips, gave the dealer a couple of the hundred-dollar chips, then left the casino.

The rest of the team met him in the parking lot and they went somewhere—some other casino on the downtown Reno strip—to celebrate. Elliott got drunk and didn't play any more. He was drained like a marathoner, and had to be helped to his motel room.

The next night he played for a longer time, with less money, and made $12,500. Raj, playing at another table with Carleen looking on, picked up $18,000.

They flew home with $45,500 in cash, carried by Silke and Carleen in plastic bags under their jackets. Airport security scared Elliott, but apparently the Reno screeners were used to seeing large amounts of cash on money belts. To draw notice to a tourist's stash wouldn't be good for Reno.

The girls had no problem.

Elliott's share was $10,500 after expenses. He gave himself $500 for some books he needed and sent the rest to his father in Seattle, writing that he had been asked to do some consulting.

He went again in May and June, to the Mohawk casino in upstate New York, and to Loughlin, Nevada. Both times he came back with more than $10,000.

Raj became a friend. He was reliable and funny, impossible to dislike. Carleen hung around, sulky, right on the money with her job, though. The only problem was with Silke. He was in love for the first time in his life, and considering his personality, he thought maybe it would be the last time, too. But she and Raj were in love with each other, in a way he could only respect. Respect and suffer over.

Elliott picked up the phone again, wanting to hear Silke's voice. The rain flowed down his window, and the calculations in front of him looked as blurry as the view. But he didn't dare call her for the third time in three days. She'd be irritated. Raj would be irritated. They would be in touch when they had some information about the man in the mask.

Meantime, college had been over for two years, and Raj and Silke were still together. They would always be together, and Elliott's job as third wheel was to avoid being a pudgy pest.

Chapter 10

WISH SHOWED UP AT THE OFFICE on Monday afternoon, wearing his sunglasses and Paul's old leather jacket, as Nina was ushering out her four o'clock.

"Coffee first," Nina said. They went into the conference room next to her office and Wish pulled out his usual chair, next to where Paul used to sit. Sandy came in and shut the door. They all fixed espressos on the new machine standing in the corner. The windows streetside let in a fresh breeze and the sound of traffic stopping and starting at the light.

Wish passed out his report. He had his own new letterhead: "Whitefeather Investigations." Naturally, a white feather was drawn under the new firm's name.

"You're the first people to see it. What do you think, Mom?"

Sandy said, "I never thought I'd see the day." The side of her mouth twitched. She was thrilled.

"Are you going to rent an office?" Nina asked.

"I've been thinking about that," Wish said. "And you know,

you don't use this room much, and I'll be in the field a lot. So just as a temporary move I, er, put down your address." Now she saw it, just under the white feather.

Nina had to think about this. Wish wasn't presumptuous, so why had he jumped ahead like that? Then she thought, He's only twenty-five, he's just gotten his license, and he needs to stay close to us. This conference room was the only office Wish had ever worked in, except for Paul's in Carmel.

"You should have asked first," Sandy said.

"It's fine, Wish," Nina said. "We just have to stay at arm's length. We'll do a written rent agreement and I'll talk to the Starlake Building landlord."

"Great! How much shall I pay a month?"

"Sandy?" Nina said.

"Three-fifty," Sandy said. Nina's rent had recently gone up to twelve hundred dollars a month, not bad for a reception room, private office, and conference room in a small town.

"Let's start at two hundred," Nina said. "For the first six months." Wish's face broke into a big smile, and she saw how nervous he had been about his proposal.

"You're the best," he said. "And I'm going to give your work top priority. As soon as I get some other clients."

"I'll expect that. So—report."

"I talked to Sergeant Cheney, South Lake Tahoe Police Department, Sunday. He was surprised the civil case was still pending. He said to say hi. The police report, the autopsy report, the coroner's findings on the Hanna shooting are all attached."

"That'll help a lot. Did you notice anything of interest?"

"There's plenty in there. Ballistics stuff. It was ruled a homicide by persons unknown. Mrs. Hanna was three months pregnant at the time. The best stuff is witness descriptions. The clerk, Meredith Assawaroj, had checked in this group of students who were the ones robbed. See the witness statement, right here."

"Got it," Nina said, thumbing through the pages.

"Meredith indicated that there were three people who checked in. A couple and a young man. The couple had one room and the man had a separate room."

"Descriptions?"

"Pretty good ones. I think Meredith felt really bad about leaving her post at the desk that night. She still works at the Ace High, though."

Nina was already reviewing the clerk's description of the three witnesses.

"Sandy, let's get this on a separate sheet," she said. "The single one first. About five feet eleven, weight one-seventy, average build, blond hair, not too long, but hung in his eyes in front. No tattoos or piercings. White oxford shirt, jeans, hiking boots. Glasses. Backpack."

"Generic kind of guy," Sandy said. "Not conspicuous at all."

"Wait till we get to the other two," Wish said.

"She didn't talk to the girl or her boyfriend at all, but Meredith heard this individual say something to one of the others. She thinks he said, 'Professor Brown would love that.'"

"'Professor Brown would love that,'" Sandy repeated thoughtfully. "So she decided they were students."

"We'll get to that. The couple was pretty conspicuous. Good-looking. The boyfriend did all the talking for the group. He paid cash for the two rooms. Meredith asked for a driver's license and he gave her a fake ID. So did the other two. Meredith kept the copies and they're attached."

"It's a New York license. The name is Mukul Dev," Nina read. "Age is twenty-six. Address is—"

"Nonexistent," Wish said. "Sergeant Cheney had it checked."

"That's an Indian name. East Indian, I mean."

"We know what you mean," Sandy said.

"Sergeant Cheney says it's the name of a big star in Bollywood. The police checked him out, but he was in Mumbai working on the set of a musical that day."

"Mumbai?" Sandy said.

Wish said, "Bombay, Mom."

"Then why not say so?"

"But our fake Indian actually was from India. At least, he looked that way to Meredith. I doubt she's an expert."

"Medium height, full lips, dark eyes, long eyelashes. Hmm. Gray slacks, black loafers. Blue dress shirt. Smiled a lot. Sort of British accent. She didn't see his bag."

"Doesn't sound like a student to me," Sandy said. "Now that first one, yes."

"The Indian's a standout individual," Wish said. "He's going to lead us to the rest of them."

"And the girl?"

"On the next page. Five-five. Early twenties. Brown hair with a lot of curl. Not a lot of makeup. Trim shape. Wearing a pink tank top and jeans. High-heeled boots. And this one had a different accent," Nina said, reading.

"Indian?" Sandy asked.

Wish answered, "German. Meredith said they used to get a lot of German tourists in her hometown in Thailand, and she's pretty sure."

Nina said, shaking her head, "It's such a shame Dave Hanna let this drop. The three of them came to Tahoe two years ago. Somebody tried to rob them and they saw a woman get shot. Finding them isn't going to be easy. They could have come from anywhere. What about the rental car?"

"Same fake ID and cash," Wish said. "Dropped at the Reno airport Enterprise car-rental place at five A.M. There were several flights out early that morning and the sergeant checked the

passenger manifests. United had three last-minute passengers to
Logan Airport in Boston, Massachusetts, on its six A.M. flight that
morning with the same fake names."

"What were they up to?" Sandy said. "They sound like
crooks. Drug runners or something."

"They didn't want to be found after the shooting, that's for
sure," Wish said. "And nobody did find them. The trail went cold
in Boston."

"I bet airport security would have a film," Sandy said.

"The airport-security firm stonewalled the sergeant. He
couldn't even find out if there was a film."

"All right," Nina said. "You talked to the clerk?"

"Meredith. She really wanted to help. So she saw them when
they checked in, and she's told the police all she knows about
that. But—this is good—when she heard the shots—two quick
shots—she ran right out the door with the kid behind the
counter of the Internet cafe, and across the parking lot toward
the office. She said she never thought about getting shot herself."

"What happened then?"

"It's all in her statement. She heard yelling. Two of the students, the Indian and the girl, ran right past her, telling her to
watch out, toward their rooms. Then the third student came running in the same direction. She looked around the corner of the
office toward the vending machines and saw Dave Hanna coming down the steps yelling that his wife was shot. Up on the balcony of his room she saw a woman crumpled in a corner."

"Do we have photos of the crime scene?"

"The police report has copies of the photos taken. I also
went to the Ace High this weekend and took digital photos.
They're in my computer, and I'll have them printed for you by
tomorrow."

"And the shooter?"

"Gone," Wish said.

"The gun?"

"She never saw one, and the sergeant says the police haven't located one. But they have the casings and two bullets, including the one recovered from Sarah Hanna's body, so the ballistics are really together. It was thirty-eight caliber. That's it. There's no description of the shooter or really the robbery except what Mr. Hanna said."

"Or what the three witnesses could tell us."

"Correct. It comes back to them. Okay, Nina, you know we decided to check the restaurants. After two years, I was just looking for security films. That's going to take a while. It's harder than I thought. I don't have anything for you on that yet."

"Fair enough."

"And now we come to the big news."

"You have big news?" Nina said.

"You are talking to Whitefeather Investigations," Wish said. "Remember you asked me to check out the motel owner, James Bova, but not to try to talk to him? Well, I went out to his house at Incline Village this morning and jogged around there."

"Oh, so that's why you dug out those gym shorts this morning," Sandy said.

"And he wasn't there, but his housecleaner was. Her name is Esther. She cleans his house and his motel."

"You talked to her?"

"I told her I was investigating, and she seemed to think I was undercover or something." It was an old trick of Paul's. "She said I was the first officer to talk to her. I said it was about time. She said she read about the shooting at Mr. Bova's motel. And the next morning she came to clean the motel rooms the students had been in. She found a cash receipt in the room the single guy had stayed in. From a bookstore. She thought it might be important, so she gave it to Mr. Bova. And she hasn't seen it since."

Nina rubbed her temple. Sandy pulled at her lip.

Nina said, "If Bova didn't pass it on to Cheney, that's major."

"He didn't," Wish said. "It's not in the evidence list."

"Why wouldn't he tell the police?" Sandy asked.

"Maybe he was worried about a suit even then," Nina said. "I don't know. His lawyer hinted that he knew something."

"The receipt might tell us if they really did come from Boston," Sandy said. "Did she remember anything about the receipt?"

"She's sharp. She was curious because of the shooting. She remembers it was from Sierra Books and the receipt listed the book titles. Two math books, she said. And the receipt was dated from the day before the shooting."

"Sierra Books is the biggest bookstore on the South Shore," Nina said. "They're at the Y. Wish, I think they're open until six. I know the manager. I'm going to call her." She went into her office and called Gretchen Pike, who said she'd be willing to share her old records with Wish.

Wish and Sandy were waiting in the conference room.

"Better get going," she said. "Check what got sold and who paid and whatever you can figure out for the day before the shooting. Call me tonight if you learn anything. Maybe we'll get lucky."

"Court is at nine-thirty," Sandy reminded her.

"Right. Sandy, call Dave Hanna. Then call Chelsi Freeman. Make sure Hanna's got a ride up the Hill. If there's any problem, Wish, will you go down there early and bring him up?"

Wish nodded, pulled on the jacket, and left.

Sandy said, "Well, well. I had my doubts. His room at home still has his old penguin posters on the wall, and he still keeps his clothes on the closet floor."

Nina said, "He's grown up a lot. I've watched Wish for two years. He's very dedicated. And he was trained well."

"He always planned to be a cop."

"He could still do that someday."

"He'll be moving out soon. Find some girl."

"Yes, he will."

"The boys, they always move to wherever the girl's mother lives. My girls, they'll stick around."

"He'll find someone here."

"You know anybody?"

The question was rhetorical. But Nina thought of Chelsi.

Ten P.M. in the Reilly household, Bob in the living room watching a reality show, Nina blowing out her damp hair in the upstairs bathroom, wrapped in her green silk kimono.

"Bob?"

"Yeah!"

She unplugged the dryer and leaned over the railing. "I talked to your dad yesterday! Could you turn that down!"

"She's about to roll over in the kayak!"

"Turn it down!"

"What!"

"Your dad and I don't think a visit to Germany right now is a good idea!"

He turned it down and the silence bristled. She could see him sprawled on the couch with Hitchcock. His head turned toward her and he said, "It was all your idea, wasn't it? I know my dad wanted to see me."

"Of course he did, but he agreed that right now—"

"He's not doin' so good. I told you. Why can't I go?"

"Well, you've been doing a lot of moving around—"

"You mean you have, and you drag me along."

Stung, Nina said, "You sound like a punk. I don't like your tone."

Bob didn't answer this.

Nina considered her remark and realized she was out of line. But Bob had been, too. "I know you've been working hard. It's admirable, the way you and Taylor have gone around the neighborhood. I doubt I could have done that at fourteen."

"Okay, then." He sounded as though he had reconsidered, too. He didn't want to argue any more than she did.

"We'll talk about it some more in a few days. Meantime, speaking of removal of hazardous wastes, our recycling bin is overflowing."

"As soon as this show is over."

"Sure." They had passed through some sort of delicate and subtle negotiation, and they were still friends. She had extracted an okay from Bob. He still did as he was told. But she couldn't read him like before, as though his transparent heart were being infiltrated by the shadows and solids of coming adulthood.

Chapter 11

A BRIGHT MORNING AMID THE PINES, THE Springmeyer fountain actually spouting water for once in the courthouse
yard, a couple of police officers exiting the adjacent station with
coffee in their hands, stopping to watch the squirrels. Betty Jo
Puckett came marching up the trail with her client, wearing a
dark pantsuit and a diamond solitaire at her throat.

"Morning!" she called out. Nina stopped and shook hands.
Bova wore a wool sports jacket. His hand squeezed Nina's.

"It's all over, then?" he said.

"Your part in the case is. With a few caveats."

"I explained the conditions to Jimmy. We're willing to go
with those. You have the paperwork?" Betty Jo said.

"I'll give you copies as soon as we're inside, so you can look
them over before the case is called."

"Everything's hunky-dory, then. I assume Mr. Hanna will be
here?"

"Due any minute."

"Anything else we need to talk about?"

"A receipt," Nina said. They had paused in the shade just out-side the doors to court. Nina nodded to a lawyer she knew who was just going in.

"You're as good as they say," Betty Jo said. "How did you ever learn about it? We were going to give you that as soon as we had the file-stamped paperwork."

"I don't want it," Nina said. "I want to look at it but not touch it. Then I want Mr. Bova to deliver it to Sergeant Cheney with a full explanation."

"Absolutely. Jimmy, show it to her right now, okay?" Bova reached into his pocket and pulled out a small unsealed envelope. The Sierra Books receipt was inside.

"I still don't know if it belonged to the witnesses," he said. "Could have been the people in the motel room the day before." He held it out and Nina examined it. Then she reached into her briefcase and got out a copy of it. Wish had slipped it under her office door the night before.

"Yes, that's it," she said. "I'll be checking to make sure that goes into police evidence."

"Wow!" Betty Jo said. "I'm outclassed, no doubt about it. We didn't follow up, no need to since the case wasn't happening. But what did you learn? I'm as curious as hell."

"It was a cash purchase the day before the shooting," Nina said. "The clerk can't remember anything about the purchaser, not at this late date."

"How did you learn there was a receipt, though?"

"Good investigative work," Nina said briefly.

"I guess you're not violating anybody's privacy if it's a cash purchase," Betty Jo said as if to herself.

"Not at all," Nina said.

"Well, I'm sorry," Bova said. "I just didn't feel it was impor-tant. Betty Jo didn't hear about it until last week."

"I scolded the shit out of him," Betty Jo said. "He knows if you get any farther finding the shooter, he's going to have to testify about it. He's going to cooperate fully. So what books did the witnesses buy? Most bookstore receipts these days list the titles."

"They do."

"And?"

"That's no longer your concern," Nina said. "I'm letting you settle out of the case without making an issue out of this, but your client withheld evidence. I'm not in a position to share information I obtained in spite of his obstructive tactics."

"Oh, come on," Bova said. "Somebody bought a book. Big deal." He gave her one of those speculative looks again, looked her up and down as if she were a doll propped up for viewing. It was obscurely exciting, and for the moment it took to catch that flashing glance Nina thought, Why not? He wanted her, and that was almost enough.

A whiff of his cologne reached her. He was from a world where men wear cologne. Not aftershave, not good soap, but a perfumy, expensive spritzer from a department store. Was this where she was heading? For anybody who asked? It struck her that she wasn't looking for love anymore, that she had dropped out of that endeavor because it was just too hard.

Still. Not Bova. Not yet.

She looked away, toward the fountain, and Bova shrugged.

"Hush up, Jimmy. I understand, Nina. You're right. It's none of our business. Jimmy wants out, that's the main thing. Let's go in."

They had to wait almost an hour while Judge Flaherty disposed of more urgent matters. Nina sat in her hard chair up front, watching the parade of the wronged with their petitions and their lawyers. Dave Hanna finally arrived about twenty minutes into the court session and took a seat in back.

Judge Flaherty, fiftyish and florid, had adopted a more judicious attitude since his elevation to the superior-court bench. He processed the cases efficiently and at ten-twenty he pulled out a file and said, "*Hanna versus Ace High Lodge,* motion to dismiss."

"Good morning, Your Honor." Betty Jo introduced herself and her client. Nina did the same, and sat down with Hanna.

"We have a stipulation," Betty Jo said, "to dismiss the negligence case against the Ace High Lodge and James Bova as an individual and as an insured of his insurance company. Mr. Bova to continue to be available as required should the case proceed further as to other defendants. No admission of liability, limited release solely on the issue of negligent provision of security. In consideration for which a check in the amount of fifty thousand dollars to be paid by close of business today to Law Offices of Nina F. Reilly, made out to the plaintiff, David S. Hanna."

A mouthful like this took a few seconds for Judge Flaherty to digest. He thumbed through the case file and said, "Just a minute. I see the proposed stipulation has been filed and I have it here. Let me read it." He wiggled his glasses and got to work.

Flaherty had the power to refuse to accept the stipulation, and there were a couple of reasons he might do just that. Dave Hanna was sweating under the lights. He didn't look well, though he had found a shirt and tie to wear.

"Why don't I just dismiss the case?" Flaherty said eventually as he laid down the paperwork. "Ms. Reilly? There aren't any defendants left."

"There are still the John Does, Your Honor," Nina said, getting up fast.

"After two years, nobody else has been served in this case."

"The individual who killed Mr. Hanna's wife is still at large," Nina said.

"Sometimes we can't get full justice," Flaherty said directly to Hanna. "I'm sorry, sir, but this court can't hold your civil case open forever. There's no statute of limitations on murder, so if the person who shot Mrs. Hanna is ever apprehended by the police, you will have some justice in seeing him punished. But it doesn't appear that you will be able to maintain this case here before me right now. Because I'm going to dismiss it based on Code of Civil Procedure Section 583.420, providing for a discretionary dismissal after two years when the remaining defendants haven't been served."

"Your Honor," Nina said, "the Ace High has dropped its request for a full dismissal."

"This is on the court's motion. We can't go forward on this, so we'll have to end it."

"With respect," Nina said firmly, "this court does not have jurisdiction to do that."

The famous flush spread across Flaherty's cheeks. "Because?"

"Because it has not yet been two full years since the date the suit was filed."

Flaherty went back to the file while Nina stood behind the table, waiting for him to have another look.

"I see that we are two weeks shy of the two-year discretionary limit," he said finally. "You are correct, Counsel. May I ask if you expect to identify and serve another defendant in the next two weeks?"

"We hope to," Nina said. "We intend to move forward much more rapidly from now on."

"Well, give it your best shot," Flaherty said. "I'm going to take this matter under submission until"—he looked at his clerk, who gave him a date two weeks away—"November twenty-seventh. On that date I will look at this file again. And if the plaintiff hasn't found somebody else to sue I will dismiss the entire case at that time."

Now Betty Jo was on her feet. "There would be no reason for the court not to approve the settlement with the Ace High today."

"In the current state of the paperwork we have an all-or-nothing situation," Flaherty told her. "Your client hasn't made a move in two years, either. He can wait another two weeks, then we'll sort out the whole thing. You don't need to appear in court again. You'll get a minute order and that'll be that."

"But—" Nina and Betty Jo said together.

"If you don't like my decision, you can bring a different motion," Flaherty told the two lawyers. "Of course, that will take longer than two weeks. Anything else?"

"No, Your Honor."

"So ordered. The court will take its midmorning recess." He stepped down and the audience straggled out.

Betty Jo came over to Nina's table. "Sometimes I want to kick him right in the *cojones*," she said. She and Bova went out.

Dave Hanna said, "We're going nowhere fast, it seems. Why did he stop the settlement?"

"He postponed it. He doesn't like cases to hang on. It messes up his calendar. He wants to dispose of the suit."

"Why didn't we just agree to end the whole thing?"

"Because we have a line on the man who shot your wife."

Hanna looked startled. "We do? What are you talking about?"

"Let's go outside and I'll explain." They went downstairs and out the doors to the fountain and sat down on Nina's favorite concrete bench in the sunlight. Nina gave Hanna her copy of the bookstore receipt and said, "Dave, I think we can find at least one of the witnesses with this." She explained its history.

"So what?" Hanna said. "One of them bought some books, and one of them mentioned a Professor Brown, and they flew to Boston, but that might have been a ploy. You think that's enough to find them? I don't."

"Not just any books," Nina said. "Wish found out the names

of the books. They were texts in advanced mathematics. Now, I agree that there will be a number of Professor Browns on the East Coast. But there won't be too many teaching graduate-level math. And we have descriptions of the three witnesses. Dave, as soon as I have a list of the Browns, I'll call them. I think one of them will remember this trio. I think we can find them. I think we can give Judge Flaherty the name of one or more new defendants within two weeks."

"Even if you find the witnesses, that doesn't mean you have the man with the gun. The man who shot Sarah."

"Leave it to me," Nina said. "Did you drive up alone?"

"Yeah. Rog and Chelsi have gotten way too involved in this."

"Well, sorry about the check from the motel. It'll still be there in two weeks, though. Mr. Bova is going to want out even worse in two weeks, if we get lucky."

Hanna said, "I'll get going, then. Keep me posted."

"Stay strong," Nina said. She watched him walk down the path toward the side parking lot, sorry that he just didn't seem to care about anything anymore.

Back at the office, she held a deposition in a medical-malpractice case in her office. The doc didn't give an inch, and by the time she and Sandy slid into the booth at Margarita's across the street she felt like she'd had a full day.

Sandy slid a printout of a long list across the table to Nina. "Colleges within a twenty-mile circle around Boston," she said. "There's one on every block, like convenience stores. There are hundreds. Think of all those heads in the clouds."

"Good work! How'd you get this?"

"Off the Web. It took about five minutes. I'm going to look at the faculty listings this afternoon with Wish while you're back at court."

"That's going to take longer," Nina said. "Maybe we should prioritize."

"Maybe we should eat." The quesadillas had arrived and they took a break from talking. The little cantina was almost empty. The dark booth with its border of Christmas lights soothed Nina. She leaned back against the red vinyl and said, "The big universities first. Because they have the most professors."

"Like Harvard?"

"Harvard, Tufts, Boston University, UMass Boston, MIT, uh, I can't think of any more. But those are big places with graduate schools. Let's start there."

"Can Wish use your computer at your desk while you're out?"

"Sure."

"And all we know is Professor Brown. Why couldn't he have been named Professor Rastafarian or something?"

"Might be a she," Nina said. "Might be a high school. Might be the motel clerk remembered the wrong name. Let's be grateful for what we have."

"Hmph." Sandy put out a twenty on the table.

"That's way too much for your share."

"I'm treating today. In honor of my raise. Which I hope to see in my lifetime."

Sandy called Nina at the courthouse at four that afternoon. Nina was out in the hall, trying to set up a visitation schedule for another client, a father of twin toddlers whose estranged wife didn't want him to see them. "Excuse me," she told the client, and went into the bathroom.

"We found three Browns so far," she said. "Plus a B-r-a-u-n and a B-r-e-h-o-n. All teaching math courses. Just with the five places you wanted to start with. Should we keep going, or do you want to make a few calls?"

"It's already seven on the East Coast," Nina said. "Try to find a few more before you go home. I'll make some calls in the morning."

She went back out into the hall. Her client was sitting on the bench, head between his hands. "Sometimes I feel like killing her," he said to Nina. So she dealt with that, and didn't get home until after six.

Dinner, a walk, a bath. Then sweet, sweet bed.

PART TWO

God doesn't throw the dice.

—EINSTEIN

Chapter 12

I N THE FALL OF HIS JUNIOR year, Elliott tried to steal Silke away
from Raj. He calculated his odds at fifty-fifty. He attempted to
impose rationality on what was essentially an irrational urge, deciding to go for it and risk losing Silke, losing face, and losing
Raj's friendship.

He had recently undergone a sea change in his thinking. He
would be reading a paper from the Moscow Math Institute online and would lose his concentration, remembering how beautiful Silke looked when she sat at the blackjack tables, tossing back
watered-down booze and joshing around with naive tourists.

A girl he dated a few times when he was sixteen accused him
of never thinking about anything except math. He didn't correct
her, because it would have been rude, but he also thought about
sex. Sometimes both things churned around inside him simultaneously, good whiskey mixed with rich food.

And all good things converged in Silke.

Carleen had the flu, but the rest of them had just taken their first junket of the year to Atlantic City. During one enormous night at Harrah's, Elliott won seventeen thousand dollars. They flew back, drinks all around, euphoric, Silke squashed between Elliott and Raj on the plane.

At Logan Airport all three shared a cab back to Everett Street. Elliott went inside with the others, ostensibly to see how Carleen was doing and to have a drink of the Chivas that Silke always kept in the kitchen, but actually to plot moves.

Raj, unknowingly cooperative, yawned and excused himself. Silke checked on Carleen but found her sound asleep, "Snoring, poor thing," so she and Elliott hung around downstairs, laughing, carving equations into the pitted pine table. When she yawned for the second time, she looked in on Raj, and returned in her nightgown. "Raj crashed, but I could use one more tiny nightcap. How about you?"

"I should go." He played true to type to avoid warning her, scaring her off too soon. He didn't intend to go.

"Why don't you just stay over?"

Her blue eyes appeared to hold nothing but a friendly welcome. He wished, as always, that he saw more in them. "Your couch is hard." He had a new apartment across the river on Marlborough Street near the Esplanade, a new Jeep, and a new attitude, thanks to the change in his financial circumstances. It wasn't just the money, though—being around the others, being part of their group, gave him a confidence he had never had. He saw cracks between Silke and Raj—his family's dislike of her, her disdain of his extravagance, the arrogant way he had noticed that Raj treated her.

"On the other hand," he said, "it's not that late."

* * *

Silke wore her dark hair tamed into a braid tonight except for some shorter strands that brushed against her ears, shining like loose satin threads. Unable to resist the impulse, Elliott reached toward her and undid the braid. "That's better," he said, stroking it free. "Your hair's getting long."

She ran fingers through her curling hair, stretched, and shook her head, sighing with pleasure. "I forget how good it feels, letting it go," she said.

He admired how the line of her browbone extended in a curve at her temple beyond the delicate brows. She had no pretensions, no artifice. He loved these things about her. "What are you thinking, Silke?"

"About you, Wakefield."

"Why? Do I want to know?"

"Of course you do. I would have nothing but the most pleasant thoughts regarding you. In Heddesheim, where I grew up, a farmer lived outside town. He had a little boy named Kristof. This kid was so shy, he had a hard time at our little school. I think he was the unhappiest boy in the world, but he was so smart. I heard he went away to a private high school in Darmstadt and then, in the summer we were sixteen, I ran into him at a street market. He wasn't the same. He was really happy. Really happy, Wakefield."

"How come?" On his third whiskey since they had returned to Cambridge, Elliott did not feel intoxicated, just hot. Just a little aggressive.

Silke leaned forward. Her nightgown, basically a long T-shirt of gray cotton, tightened over her breasts. Elliott noted the outline of her nipples, that she was unconscious of her effect, and didn't mean to make him crazy. She wasn't coming on to him. She never did. She was so damn proper, loyal to her man, monogamous. As if Raj, with his family's millions, big houses in

India, and condo on Riverside Drive, would ever marry her. One fine day Raj's parents would introduce him to a nice girl from Madras with the dowry of a maharani's daughter. Silke would be history. How could this smart woman not realize that?

"Let me guess," he said. "Uh, your boy had found a girl-friend. She loved and respected him. He adored her. They stayed together, got married, took over the farm. Bought sturdy furniture. They have two kids, a boy and a girl, both excellent students. He's happy. Ecstatic. Is that what you want for me?"

"What do you want for yourself?"

He set his glass down carefully and thought. What to say? The truth? She already knew how he felt; why not come out with it? No, too aggressive, wait for the right time. He said, cravenly, "Immortality. Nothing else counts."

"Oh, Elliott." Her voice scolded him.

"You think there's something more important?"

"Love, of course."

"Oops. Forgot about that. Of course you're right."

"You're teasing me, Wakefield," she laughed. "You need a relationship. You deserve happiness. You're not unattractive, you know."

"Oh, don't push Carleen again," Elliott said, tracing his finger along the carving they had made, then he lifted his hand to her hair, as if to straighten it over her shoulders, stroking it. "We won't happen."

Silke didn't push his hand away. Two red spots appeared on her cheeks. "Too bad. She cares for you."

"Listen. I'm not attracted to her. I'd rather sleep with a Gila monster. She's fine as a friend, but stop pushing her on me."

Silke looked behind him, her eyebrows up high, so he turned around, sloshing the whiskey in his hand. Of course Carleen had come downstairs just at that instant. Her tartan robe was hanging open and she was wearing just underpants. Elliott's eyes went to her pale rib cage, her short, skinny legs; he couldn't help himself.

Carleen made a strangled sound and turned and ran. Rolling her eyes at him, Silke went after her.

Elliott drank down the whiskey. He would sleep on the lumpy couch and leave early. Silke did not come back down. It seemed his chance had fled, and just for a minute there, when he said, "Immortality," he could have said, "You," and Silke might still be talking to him. Now Carleen was mad and complications would ensue.

All external thoughts fled, and he fell gratefully into the rutted byways of his theories, like a junkie who knows it's dangerous but can't fight it anymore.

Back, back to Cantor's Continuum. The central difficulty lies at the intersection of linguistics and math analysis, he thought, the intersection of what is discrete, like the integers, and what is continuous, like infinity. What is that intersection? Where is that intersection?

The Greeks had such a horror of infinity, and it still afflicted number theory, this need to make the infinite finite, these tortured reciprocals, these sequences that lead to the infinitely small, this strange reversal of the kingly truth...

The primes are discrete, but extend into infinity like any set of integers. They are discrete in some qualitatively different way. The integers are at equal intervals from each other by definition. What if I make a number line putting the primes at equal intervals... how is that function constructed... no damn imaginary numbers, not even reciprocals to make the series converge, forget the zeta function, I'll invent my own...

"Wakefield!" Whiskey-tinged breath blew into his face. He lay on his back on the couch, his neck at an impossible angle. His eyes refused to open. It was very late, or maybe very early?

"You have to go home. Carleen can't see you here in the morning."

He reached up and around Silke's body, finding her waist. He drew her down to him.

"Wakefield, no . . ."

"It's you. It'll always be you."

"Stop!"

"You, not immortality." He squeezed tighter. He loved holding warm, soft Silke against him. He felt hot tears on his face. Hers or his? She stopped struggling and lay exhausted on top of him.

"Please," he said. "Just this once. I need you so much."

"Idiot," she said. "No."

"Then kiss me. That's all I ask. Silke, I need you more than he does. Please." His lips already lay against her cheek. She turned her head slightly and her mouth caught his. He drank her in.

His arms relaxed and she rolled off the couch onto the floor and went away. He turned onto his side and went back to sleep.

Sun came through the curtains. "Old man," Raj was saying, and shaking him none too gently. "Up you go."

"What time is it?" Elliott mumbled.

"Eight-thirty."

"I have class at nine."

"The bathroom is clear. The women are upstairs, but the atmosphere up there is what my mother would describe as overspiced. Get up."

Elliott borrowed Raj's toothbrush and splashed cold water on his face.

Raj awaited him in the kitchen. "Drink."

Elliott drank the hot coffee, Raj watching him curiously. "What happened last night?" Raj asked.

"Nothing. I dreamed about a function to factor large numbers. Over two hundred digits."

"Only God can do that."

"The discrete has to be made continuous first. Cantor was close. Grothendieck..."

"Later. You have your car keys?"

Elliott felt them jingle in his pocket.

"Go."

"I'm not sure I'll ever come back," Elliott said. "I think I'm going to lose all this."

After that Elliott worked on the Riemann Hypothesis, staying at his apartment.

He ate his cold cereal and drank a lot of coffee. He sat at his kitchen table twisting bits of paper into dough.

His father called claiming to be fine, always a bad sign. He only talked of his health when he'd had an episode, but Elliott's probing yielded no further information about any deterioration in his condition. Every few days Raj came by. Once he brought lentils and rice in a big pot. Elliott lived on that for a week, spooning portions into a bowl each night, no longer caring that it was cold food.

The problem with Raj was that he didn't love math enough, not like Elliott did. Raj didn't *need* math. As a result—his loss—he'd never be an immortal. And Silke... Elliott was glad now that she had rejected him; what a huge distraction.

With a few thousand in the bank, his tuition and rent paid, he closed the blinds. He stopped answering his phone.

Raj brought Professor Braun to see Elliott. Braun had contributed several original papers on differentiable manifolds before the age of twenty-two, and at the age of twenty-nine had been made the youngest full professor in the history of MIT. He taught the advanced number-theory course.

"You're wet," Elliott said as Raj and Braun took off their jackets and hung them on chairs.

"It's pouring outside," Braun said. "Didn't you notice?"

"Did you come to see my work? Because it's not ready yet. You know Erdős's proof that a prime can always be found between an integer and its double? It has to do with the number One. The Stick. One is an integer. I don't care if you won't call it a prime number, you have to admit it's an integer. Why doesn't the proof work with One? There is no prime between One and Two. How can it be said that Erdős proved anything? Have you thought about this problem?"

"We want to take you out to lunch," Raj said. "And Professor Braun wants you to return to class."

"Wait, I want you to think about it. The way there's no integer between One and Two, but where the prime should be, there is one-half. What does that remind you of, Raj?"

"Real part one-half," Raj said softly. "Riemann's critical line."

"Yes! Yes! The Riemann Hypothesis! There's a link, but I haven't been able to prove it. Shall we talk about that?"

"We'll talk about anything you want if you'll come have a meal with us," Dr. Braun said.

"Okay. I'm out of food anyway."

They walked out into the rain, to a grubby pizza place on Mass Avenue. Drinking beer fast, eating a large salad, Elliott talked about his new suspicion that the Riemann Hypothesis was undecidable, unprovable either way. He talked about Cantor, about the discrete integers and the continuum. He explained how he had tried the algebraic approach through finite fields; how he had used Cramer's model, treating it as a perturbation problem, trying to get a set of wobble frequencies. He talked about Sarnak and Wiles and Bump.

But mostly he talked about Cantor, the master of infinity. "I need a math that will operate with divergent series," he explained, "comfortable with infinity. That happens if you permit division by zero."

Raj groaned.

"Yeah, that again," Elliott said.

They pumped him, or did they? Maybe they were just curious. He couldn't tell. They wanted to know about his work on factoring large numbers, and he told them he had been trying a variation on the Pollard-Strassen method on his computer. He told them that Dixon's method using the quadratic sieve was inferior. He talked, because he hadn't talked for so long, he had no choice. He knew he had no perspective anymore, but drunk or not, he didn't go into detail.

He didn't talk about his new idea, for a function that seemed to predict the location of large primes. He had to work alone. The function had some flaw he couldn't find yet, some error in the calcs. If his idea got around the campus, it might be stolen, published half-baked in some journal under someone else's name.

He promised Dr. Braun that he would return to class the next morning. The professor gave him some class materials and said he'd pass Elliott if he turned in some work. Raj kept talking about eating better. The two of them and the other people in the restaurant seemed to be talking in some other universe, their minds occupied with all the wrong things.

"Carleen moved out of Everett Street," Raj announced. "She claims she's forgiven you, but she won't hang with us anymore."

"And Silke?"

"Did Silke have something to forgive you for?"

"Are you and Silke still taking trips?"

Raj cast a glance at Braun. "Sure," he said. "You're always welcome to join us again."

"When I finish my work."

"Do you sleep at night?" Professor Braun said, his blue eyes intent.

"I'll sleep when I'm dead."

"How old are you?"

"Twenty," Elliott said. "How old are you?"

"Forty-two."

"What have you discovered lately?"

"Don't," Raj said.

"You have to watch your health. I don't like the look in your eye," the professor went on.

"I don't give a shit about my health."

"Remember what happened to Cantor?"

Elliott thought of Cantor, alone in wartime at the asylum in Halle, begging his daughter to bring him home. She wouldn't. He had always wondered how she put it: "Sorry, Father, but you're too much trouble," she must have said. Cantor had died swiftly after that.

"Don't squander it," the professor repeated, pushing the last piece of pizza away from himself. "Wakefield, you have to pace yourself. It's a question of balance. You should see people. Your friends are worried."

"No, no," Elliott said, draining his mug. "Accomplishment requires sacrifice, even pain. You have to set priorities. Right now, my work comes first. Friends, family, romps in the park, children, lovers, these things have to wait." He stood up, carefully placing his chair under the table. "Thanks for the vitamins. I need to go." He felt pressure to flee from their slowness and their compromises before they infected him.

"See you tomorrow, then," said Dr. Braun.

"See you." He gave them a friendly wave. He could afford the ten seconds it took to make them happy.

He didn't go back to class the next day, or the next.

*   ★   ★   ★

A week later, at four in the morning, Elliott finally fell into sleep, or something like sleep. He had been taking No-Doz and drinking a lot of coffee and hadn't slept for a couple of days. He should have slept too hard for dreams to reach him.

But one did. It was early in the morning, he would remember later.

An angel appeared, her wings outspread, calling him to her and clasping him tight. He wasn't afraid; he felt that he was already dead, and nothing worse could happen to him. In a way, he felt that this was his reward for dying. Maybe the angel was his mother.

They flew to a place at the dim limits. Here he found waves, rhythms, measures he had never known existed. All answers were here.

The angel generated a zeta landscape, infinitely dense. Even so, the mountains they flew over were porous, one or two stretching up into infinity. Between the mountains he saw deep holes, the points spiraling inward. The beauty of it made him weep.

They moved down to sea level and flew along the cross-section. The angel pointed. Then he saw it breaking through below: a huge prime, lonely and beautiful, its gray back shiny with spray. It had lost its way and was moving away from the other primes, spuming and slapping their tails in the limitless distance.

They moved into higher densities, Elliott now carrying his black notebook to write it all down. This rolling sequence, which looked like a field in Wisconsin, converged on both zero and infinity at the same time.

He looked at the angel, and the angel nodded its blazing head.

He didn't really want to do it, but he felt he had to. He did the unthinkable. He divided by zero.

The white sky split and the rules gave way to random crime. The universe compressed into its basic reality, the four numbers surrounded by their clouds of probabilities. But Zero, staggering, was vanishing into the mist. One was a hard black branch beating the other integers. Two, the cop in blue, struggled to keep order, but it was outgunned by Three, red and bursting, rampaging all through the set.

The Three destroyed adelic space and time. Elliott, horrified, had to watch the gruesome factoring of the prime.

His angel faded away, leaving him to drift all alone in this disintegrating universe. It would all collapse into pure theory soon.

He became very frightened. Flying low across the sea, he found a hidden crater a few fathoms beneath: the square root of minus one, a geyser of fresh water rushing out of it into the saltiness.

He dove into the deep cold system.

Chapter 13

TOO MANY COLLEGES, TOO MANY BROWNS. Nina recalled a math instructor at Lake Tahoe Community College she had helped with a contract problem once, Mick McGregor. Mick had his math doctorate, but had lost his first job at UC Berkeley for reasons he had never told her. Luckily for her today, he had landed right around the corner.

High noon on Thursday at the LTCC campus, and the place wasn't exactly hopping although school was in session. Nina parked among shady pines and walked to the Administration Building. An art exhibit was going on inside, student sculptures propped amid the seats in the high-ceilinged reception area, paintings on the wall, but few students circulated. The building was brand-new and even the carpeting still looked fresh and welcoming.

At the registrar's window she was directed to McGregor's office, but she found him outside the building talking to a student.

"Uh-oh," he said when he recognized her. He might as well

have said, *Here comes trouble.* She often called forth that reaction, a hazard of her trade.

"Everything's fine," she assured him. "I've come to consult you about something I'm working on." The student wandered away and they entered McGregor's office, which was as neat as a marine's cot. Nina looked around approvingly at the orderly books and papers and photos of McGregor with his family and students.

"Long time," McGregor said. "I still wake up at night remembering how worried I was in those days that I'd lose the case. No offense, but you're always in the dreams."

"For Pete's sake, Mick. We won the case. Can't you rehabilitate me? I hate to think I'm part of somebody's nightmares." Nina was only half-joking.

"Let's start over," Mick said. "Let me think of you as a very pretty lady who dropped in on me unannounced for a chat about nothing much." He was still young, with reddish hair, wearing jeans and a purple shirt with a white undershirt showing at the neck, his hands freckled, his manner ironic.

"I'd like to ask you about some math students, at least I think they may be math students, who I need to locate. They may be in Boston."

"I was raised in Lawrence, Massachusetts. But you knew that."

"I did know that."

"What do you want to know?"

"I want to find them. I know three things: One or more has or had a professor named Brown; they flew from here to Boston; and one of them bought two books at Sierra Books here at Tahoe while they were visiting."

"The plane was flying at the rate of four hundred miles an hour, and the student read one-fourth of the first book on the flight. Elementary. Want me to write out the proof for you?"

Nina handed him the names of the books. "I want to know what kind of math this is, and what level."

McGregor read the names. "Ooh. Somebody's into the Riemann Hypothesis. And Cantor's Continuum Hypothesis. I've seen these books at Sierra Books gathering dust. It's a wonder they carried them."

"What can you tell me about these—these hypotheses?"

"Analytic number theory. A fancy word for arithmetic, but do not be misled. This is graduate-level stuff, very sexy math, very deep. Hardly anybody is working on it. The universities want combinatorics people and physicists and topologists these days. Students who read books on these topics on vacation are going to be obsessed with the hypotheses. For them it's the closest thing to fun."

"It sure doesn't sound like fun to me. So would you think this student was working on a graduate degree?"

"Could be an advanced undergraduate. These books concern the most famous problems in math. Some people think figuring out whether the Riemann Hypothesis is true or not is the biggest mystery in the universe, bar nothing. It has to do with the prime numbers. You know? Prime numbers?"

"I remember that they're the numbers that you can't divide anything into," Nina said. "Am I saying it right?"

"Sure. They're the basic building blocks all the other numbers consist of. But they have a devilish aspect. They appear randomly on the positive number line. There's no satisfactory algorithm that identifies them in sequence, and with large numbers it's almost impossible to find the factors and determine if the numbers are prime or not."

"So what?" Nina said.

"So what, you ask. Well, if we can't find a formula to predict such a basic and crucial number sequence, we look like clowns, and the whole orderly system of mathematics we've built up over twenty-five hundred years looks like a pile of shit," McGregor said. "It's the black hole at the center of this area of human knowledge. We don't even know what the fuck prime numbers are. Maybe they're aliens from outer space sent to drive us crazy."

"Oh. Aliens. Sure."

"Riemann gave us a big clue about the behavior of the primes a hundred fifty years ago, but nobody has managed to take full advantage of it. Until his hypothesis is proved, we're all a bunch of buffoons. Same with Cantor's work on infinity. Until we figure out what to do with series that diverge, we may as well admit our whole mathematics system is a joke."

"I see."

"We're screwed at the source. If my students had any idea how shaky math really is, they'd run screaming over to the English department."

"That would be pretty dire," Nina said. "May I ask, how are things with you?"

"My wife left me. I was thinking of coming to see you, then when you came here, I thought you must be representing her. I almost took off running, like I said. Reminds me of the old hermit mathematician who cracked open his door to some colleagues and said, 'Please come at another time and to another person.'"

"Well, I'm not here to harass you."

"And they're not renewing my contract here. I had an affair with a student." He had the grace to look embarrassed.

Nina gave him her card. "Any time," she said. "But right now, I need help on this case."

"Okay. Brown, Boston, Riemann." He turned to his computer and clicked a few times with his mouse.

"Brown University," he said. "Amherst. Northeastern. Brandeis. BU. MIT. The Big H. To name a few. Have some coffee and don't interrupt me." The thermos he pointed to was almost empty, but Nina took the last drop. McGregor clicked away, grunting occasionally to himself.

The campus was quiet. Occasionally a bird twittered, a squirrel chittered, or a student littered—no, muttered with another student, passing by. Not bad, acres of wooded park near a world-famous mountain lake, a state-of-the-art campus, friendly registrars—not her memory of college, but then, that was so long ago.

"Bingo," Mick said dourly. "Got him. Come around the desk." She jumped up and came around to where the sun made it hard to see the screen.

"Gottlieb Braun," he said. "I've even heard of him. He hangs with the giants at MIT. Massachusetts Institute of Technology." He sang to the tune of *The Mickey Mouse Club* song, "M-I-T, P-H-D, M-O-N-E-Y."

He added, "That's a song the envious folks at Caltech sing, by the way, not the one they sing at MIT. Well, okay, they sing it at MIT but the difference is, at MIT they think it's funny."

"How do you know it's the right Brown?"

"Come over here." She put her case on the ground and walked over to stand behind his chair. "Look," he said.

Focusing on the MIT site, they reviewed the research interests of the math faculty. Dr. Braun was listed as being interested in "Areas Bridging Discrete and Continuous Math, Riemann Hypothesis, Continuum Hypothesis, Continued Fractions."

"A number hound. A real throwback," Mick said. "None of the other colleges I checked with had Browns with these kinds of research interests. Ready for a conjecture? Your student is one of his. Or was."

"How sure are you?"

"What a question. I'm guessing, baby." He raised and lowered his eyebrows at her, shot a look at her legs, then cleared his throat to distract her from his crassness.

She pressed on. "Gottlieb, huh?"

"A lot of the great mathematicians are from Central Europe. Lots of Germans. It all started with Gauss at Göttingen."

"They're fond of G's, too, I guess."

"Hmm, 'Frequency of Letter G in Topics Related to the Math Profession.' Don't get me thinking thoughts like that. I need to sleep tonight."

"Mick, I owe you."

McGregor smiled at her and said, "Really?"

"You have my card. Thanks for this. And sorry to hear about your job. You'll land somewhere better."

"Give the Herr Professor my regards. A nondescript from the hinterland sends his respects." He turned back to his computer, clicking furiously.

"See you, Mick."

"High probability of that."

Nina felt so excited she almost ran the red light at Al Tahoe and Lake Tahoe Boulevard. Back at the office, Sandy had laid her brown-bag lunch out on the desk. "Looks yummy," Nina said. Tossing her jacket on the chair, she revved up her Mac and went straight to MIT, or the simulacrum thereof on the Web.

Sandy came in and deposited a sandwich wrapped in waxed paper and a can of cola on her desk. "Mangia," she said.

"I've got the Brown," Nina said. "Maybe."

"If you don't eat lunch you'll starve, drop to the floor, and never find out anything else."

Nina tore open the sandwich. Liverwurst and mayonnaise. Worse things had been turned into sandwiches, although she couldn't think what they were offhand. She ate, clicking and navigating with her free hand. Sandy sat down with a legal pad. "Well?"

"Braun's in Room 2-181 at MIT. Write down this phone number and E-mail. Here's a photo of him. Pale blue suit jacket, red tie, black hair, specs. It's his birthday. His sixteenth, to go by his looks. He's very young for a professor, isn't he? Mud-colored birthday cake, most pathetic-looking cake I have ever seen. Take a look at those sprinkles, the festive arrangement of yellows on brown."

"You're forgetting the one you made for Bob's twelfth birthday. Remember?"

Nina remembered. "The great thing was, he thought I did it intentionally."

"It took guts, serving that thing to friends."

"Yeah, I've got guts all right. Guts enough to put up with you and him both. Okay, back to our picture. There are students in the photo. No boys from India, no girls. Dreadful lighting that washes the blood out of everybody."

"Keep going."

"Braun was a finalist for the Abel Prize. I think that's like the Nobel, only it's given for math. He's a big shot, a full professor, even though he's young. Okay, the math department: fifty-two faculty members, thirty instructors, one hundred twenty-five grad students, and they graduate about one hundred forty undergraduates a year."

"Let's check more photos." Sandy edged around so that she could look with Nina. Additional pictures of student-faculty gatherings documented an unfortunate reliance on those rectangular brown cakes, which must have been a local caterer's specialty. A couple of girls here and there joined the company, but didn't seem to match the description of their witness.

The boys caught milling around in the photos looked conventional, except that a few were shaky on style, wearing short-sleeved oxford and plaid flannel shirts, the kind of thing that might have been sold at the Harvard Coop circa 1951. Hair ran the gamut from slickly modern to huge frizz to fifties executive. Chalked-up blackboards tended to dominate the backgrounds.

"They're so pale, like slugs slithering out from under a rock," Sandy said, disapproving. "I bet they never go outside."

"They eat cake and trade fashion tips instead. But let's not be unkind," Nina said. "So what if they don't sweat the small stuff?"

"Yes, but bad cake?"

"The real brain food. And to think my doc always told me to take fish oil for brainpower."

"Supposedly, these kids will rule the world."

Nina laughed. "Hardly, Sandy. They're mathematicians. It's not like they study law or anything useful." She bit into a gusher of grease. "Let's start with the Herr Professor." Drinking the last of her cola, she repressed a burp, consulted her watch, picked up the phone, and punched a number. "The direct method. *A* times *B* equals *MIT.*" Nina pressed the speaker button so that Sandy could listen to the ringing.

A brusque voice answered. "Braun."

"How do you do? My name is Nina Reilly. I'm a lawyer, calling from California on an important matter." She was grinning, feeling cocky. It must be the liverwurst.

"Oh? What can I do for you, ma'am?" Herr Professor didn't have a trace of an accent.

"I'm looking for some witnesses in a legal case here. One or more of the witnesses may be students of yours. May I give you some descriptions, and ask you if any of them sound familiar?"

"What kind of legal case?"

"A wrongful-death case. A woman was shot two years ago here at Lake Tahoe, and the students were witnesses."

"Information about our students is confidential."

"Of course. But perhaps you could confirm the existence of such students, as a matter of public duty. I'm not asking for anything else. The first one is an Indian. Of East Indian heritage, that is. He has thick black hair and a nice smile, and his eyebrows grow together in the middle." She went on with the description of the most memorable of the three witnesses, sounding perfectly calm. Sandy sat next to her, her bracelets jangling slightly as she wrote on the pad.

"You think he's one of my students?" Braun said when she had finished.

"That is my information. He's interested in, er, the Riemann Hypothesis, I believe. Possibly."

"And what would you do with him if you found him?"

"Ask him to come back to California for a deposition. All expenses paid."

"And if he didn't want to come?"

"That would be a problem," Nina said. "The witness-subpoena power does not extend beyond the state boundary."

"So he could refuse and you would not bother him anymore?"

"I would have no power to compel him to come here as a witness," Nina said. Sandy frowned at this circumlocution, and Nina winked at her. "Rest assured, Professor Braun, that I would not bother him if this were not necessary to right an injustice."

"Who did you say you were?"

"Nina Reilly. A California attorney."

"Give me your state bar number." She gave it to him. She wasn't grinning anymore.

"I'll look into it," the professor said.

"A woman was killed," Nina said. "This young man needs to step up and tell what he knows about it."

"I have your number in the memory. Good-bye, ma'am." He hung up.

"Is he gonna help us or not?" Sandy asked.

Nina tapped her temple. "Even great minds may err, Sandy. He's cautious, and that may outweigh his sense of civic duty."

"So are you gonna wait to hear back?"

"Book me on United to Boston for tonight out of Reno, would you?"

"Done."

"What have we got this afternoon?"

"The DMV. The lady whose boat dropped off the trailer onto the freeway. Roberta. You ought to be finished by four."

"Then I'll run home and get Bob over to his uncle's house and pack a bag. And please call Chelsi Freeman. I can't make the massage appointment this afternoon."

"What else should I do? When are you coming back?"

"After I have talked to those witnesses."

"I'm not even going to ask who is going to pay for this trip."

"What are credit cards for?" Nina said.

Chapter 14

HER OPTIMISTIC MOOD LASTED THROUGHOUT THE flight from Reno. She loved red-eye flights anyway, sitting in the window seat, watching dawn suffuse the sky, her beam of light trained on the material she was reading while the other passengers dozed uneasily beneath their inadequate blankets and the flight attendants gossiped in the back.

She was coasting on a strong sense of determination, of being on the hunt. She'd never need to sleep again. She would find her witnesses. She was sure of it.

She had brought piles of printouts Sandy had pulled off the Web concerning the two hypotheses, the state of mathematics these days, and MIT information. Packed in her carry-on were also the police reports on Sarah Hanna's death, a small tape recorder, and her laptop. There had been just enough remaining room for two pairs of underwear and her curling iron.

Nina read, making notes with her right hand, doodling, generating lists and plans.

By 9:00 A.M. on Friday morning Nina was washing her face in her room at the Charles River Inn. Outside, sloping uphill from the muddy river, spread the curiously European village of Cambridge, Massachusetts. The iviest of the ivy-covered brick campuses of the Northeast, which Mick called the Big H, was six blocks up the street, past Harvard Square and the Red Line subway station. MIT was a few miles' drive along the river, or a stop or two on the Red Line.

She took a taxi up Memorial Drive. On this winter's morn, sculls skidded through the icy water and boys and girls rushed along the banks as they had for about four hundred years. Bright sun blessed the bridges with golden light, sweetly disguising decades of gray grime. The venerable brown city of Boston loomed on the other side of the river, dry air sharpening the skyline, but even a clean hint of coming frost in the air couldn't entirely subdue the reeking diesel and industrial smells.

Lake Tahoe Community College had a serene woodland setting, with low California buildings. At MIT, islands of grass, brown at this time of year, were pitifully dwarfed by many-storied concrete stacks engineered by maniacal purists. One did not major in phys ed or English literature at MIT, as one might choose to do at Tahoe. One majored in science, any science. The older Greco-Roman style buildings, nods to classical academia, had in the last century given way to functional beige buildings that housed sharp minds who found beauty in things less evanescent than mere aesthetics.

Lack of sleep and her ongoing self-assured mood had made Nina bold. "I need Professor Braun," she told the male receptionist at the math department. "Room 2-181."

The boy, who appeared to be just a few years older than Bob, said, "Professor Braun's already gone for the weekend. Sorry."

"Oh, no! I really hoped to tell him some exciting results I have—this work I've been doing using Fourier inversions. I met him in Palo Alto at the American Institute of Mathematics a couple of years ago, and he was very interested in my work."

"The Riemann seminar?"

"Right! I'm from Stanford. Had to come to the East Coast for a wedding and stopped off here. I really need to talk to him." She clutched her briefcase to her chest and allowed herself to look slightly desperate, as though the nonexistent equations might be unraveling as they spoke.

"I'm sorry, but he's home in Newton. I can't give out his address."

It was a blow, but Nina had fallbacks ready.

"How about his student? You know, the guy who was going out with that pretty German girl, or was she Norwegian? He was Indian... I forgot his name..."

"Raj attended that seminar?" His voice was mildly curious. "I didn't know he had the interest."

A little thrill went down her back. "Raj. Yes, that's him. Any idea how I could get hold of him?"

"He's probably drinking coffee at the student center right about now. With the lovely Silke sitting devotedly by his side, lucky man."

Hot ziggety dog, Nina told herself. "Silke. That's his girlfriend, right? He talked about her."

He nodded. "You know, I applied to Stanford but couldn't turn down MIT. Man, I regret it every single time I have to put on a coat, hat, boots, and gloves just to go outside to pick up the newspaper off the front step. So you're a number theorist? An instructor there?"

Ouch. She couldn't pass for a student anymore. On the other hand, she had worn a suit and shiny high heels to impress the professor, and an expensive black wool coat she had borrowed from Andrea. Probably it was the clothes that had him thinking that. "Post-doc," she said. "I do assist in a couple of grad courses."

"Do you want to leave a message for Dr. Braun?" He pushed a pad of paper her way.

"You can't even give me a phone number?"

"It's against the rules."

"I'll run and catch Raj and come back to leave a message later."

"Suit yourself." He pointed toward the direction she had just come from. "Can you find your way back to Building Eight?" He looked dubious. "We're way over here, almost to Mem Drive. Can you get back there?"

She thought she could, so she nodded.

"Good. Then go back down—hey, you going to be around at sunset today?"

"I don't think so. Why?"

"The sun sets down this hallway everybody calls 'infinite' even though it's just long. It's a beautiful sight. People hang around all along the edges to watch it. The hall turns red. Glows. It's truly mysterious."

"I won't be here that late."

"Too bad," he said. "Okay, so go all the way out of that building, and down the steps in front. Then cross Mass Ave. The student center's that big building on the right, up steps with a glass front. You can't miss it."

Incredibly, the first thing she saw as she walked into the large, noisy, glass-fronted room was a couple who fit the description from Tahoe. They sat at a table against the windows overlooking busy Massachusetts Avenue. The boy, dark-haired and much better-looking than his description, studied *The Boston Globe*. He wore fashionable glasses and, in a well-fitted golf shirt and slacks, seemed an exception to Professor Braun's oxford-collar club.

The girl huddled in a big chair, trim legs crossed, a laptop computer propped on her knees. She raised and tipped a coffee mug, sucking thirstily, all the while fastening her eyes on her monitor. Attractive in an Italian-film-star way, full-lipped, healthy-cheeked, tousle-haired, she wore a long-sleeved white sweater over jeans, with thick socks and incongruous flip-flops on her feet. A chair next to her held their winter coats. At her feet, long leather boots lay akimbo, like a pair of abandoned legs.

They seemed to be here for the duration. Nina went to the counter to order a super-sized vanilla soy latte and a muffin. She needed them. Removing her coat, she looped it over the arm carrying her tray and walked back to her prey. She set the tray down on a low table in front of a cluster of chairs near them and tossed her coat over the chair back. "Hello. Are you Raj?"

The boy put down his newspaper. A wary expression spread over his face. He said nothing.

"My name is Nina Reilly. I've been looking for you. And you must be Silke!" She smiled and nodded at the girl. "Glad to meet you. Nina Reilly." She sat down across from them, broke a piece of muffin off, and ate it, following up with a long wash of coffee. "No breakfast," she said apologetically. "Just got off a plane." Not true, but while they considered the information she had time to take another bite and another swallow. As the caffeine rushed to warm her chilled extremities, she began to feel very happy to be in Cambridge sitting with these two kid fugitives, making progress at last.

"A plane?"

"From California. My card." She found one in her pocket and handed it to Raj, who scrutinized it and handed it to Silke.

"You're a lawyer," Silke said. Her clipped delivery suggested to Nina that English wasn't her first language. "Professor Braun told us a lawyer called him."

"That was me. I'm here to discuss that trip you guys and your friend took to Tahoe two years ago. No doubt you remember it."

Their young faces showed they did and weren't pleased at the memory, although they tried to hide it.

"When you got robbed. Not an easy moment to forget, I bet."

Silke looked at Raj, who lowered his eyelids.

"The woman who died that night was named Sarah Hanna. She was pregnant. Her husband watched her die. I represent him." Nina took guilty pleasure in watching the girl wince. She *ought* to feel lousy, running away.

"How did you find us?" Raj said.

"Why did you run away? Why didn't you stay and talk to the police?"

"Maybe we shouldn't talk to her," Silke said to Raj.

"What's the harm?" Nina asked. "You were just witnesses, right?"

"We can't be involved," Raj said.

"Oh, but you are. I have involved you," Nina said. "That mode won't work anymore." She drank some more coffee, reflecting that her excitement was turning to anger at these cavalier kids who had left Dave Hanna to sink into his misery. Taking a deep breath, she tried for calm, and failing that, decided why shouldn't they see how upset and mad she was? She flipped open her briefcase and touched a button on the hidden recorder.

"We don't have anything to say to you," Silke said, fright leaking into her voice, her accent more pronounced.

"Please, don't give me a hard time about this. I don't need much of your time, and considering the circumstances, talking to me is the absolute least you can do to make up for fleeing the scene."

"Did we break any laws by leaving?" Raj asked. Unlike Silke, he seemed relatively composed. "I don't believe we did."

"Are the police here going to—what does this mean, you coming here after us?" Silke asked.

"I have a few questions, that's all. The police here aren't involved. Not yet." Thus implying they would have first shot, if the two didn't cooperate.

"I never felt right about leaving," Silke said. She put her laptop on the low table, closing it gently. "But we were so scared."

"What's your last name, Silke?"

The boy and girl looked at each other.

Nina drank latte, settled in.

"Kilmer."

"You're from Germany?"

"Yes. Heddesheim."

"A math student here at MIT?"

"I'm a Ph.D. student with about two and a half years left until I finish my thesis. If all goes well, that is."

"How about you, Raj? What's your full name?"

"Sumaraj Das." He answered pleasantly enough, but she could tell now that he had been deeply shocked by her precipitous arrival. Nina wondered how long her air of authority and their astonishment at being found would keep them talking.

"And where are you from?"

"Silver Spring, Maryland." Raj had already had enough. "What do you want from us?"

"I need to know what happened."

"Look, I followed the news reports online. We don't know anything the papers don't know. We have nothing to add. Why did you come all this way?"

"The woman's husband needs to know who killed his wife. Wouldn't you want to know?"

Silke put her hand over Raj's. "We should talk to her," she said. "It's wrong to stay silent."

Nina observed as Raj sat back in his chair and relaxed, allowing Silke to decide for them both. A complicated man, she could see that. Strong but flexible. Unpredictable, Nina thought.

Silke turned to Nina. "We were there. We were robbed, as you said."

"With your friend. His name?"

"You must mean Elliott. Elliott Wakefield."

"Where is he right now?"

"He doesn't go to MIT anymore." She'd obviously just had second thoughts about giving him up after the name had slipped out. "We don't know where he is."

But Nina had his name. The third witness was as good as bagged. "Why were you at Tahoe?"

"Vacationing," Raj said. "De-stressing. You can only stuff your brain so full. Once in a while you need to get blank, do you know what I mean?"

"We gambled," Silke said simply. "We won a lot of money that night. I had it in my purse. The robber must have followed us from the casino. We were happy, you know, in a celebratory mood. Not noticing him."

"What's your game?" Nina asked.

"Blackjack."

Of course. The game of the smart, or wannabe smart. "Go on."

"We got to the motel—the Ace High—late, after midnight. There's a flight of stairs by the vending machines around a corner of the building, but it's very dark there, and there are dark corners where you can't see anything. Before we could climb the stairs to get to our rooms, a man jumped out in front of us."

"Pointing a big, fat gun in our faces," Raj added.

"*Ja*, a gun," Silke said. "He wore a ski mask, dark clothes. He told us to empty our pockets. Well, what are you going to do? Get shot for money? I laid my purse on the ground."

"But then our friend got too brave," Raj said.

"Elliott rushed toward the man, trying to knock him over or

something. The gun went off." Silke's white skin whitened further at the thought. "Oh my God. The sound of that shot."

"Your friend hit him and the gun went off?"

"I think he came into contact with him," Raj said. "The gunman fired one warning shot, and I think the second happened about when Elliott reached him. We always thought he wasn't aiming, because if he had been, we'd be dead. We were so close, only about ten feet from him, and Elliott was even closer."

"Elliott's a genius, perhaps," Silke said softly, "but one of those who is not well-adapted to normal life. You can't depend on him to behave logically—at least, not according to your logic or mine."

"When he heard the shot, Elliott let him go, but the gunman fired another shot. It went high, too," Raj said.

"Do you think he was trying to kill us or just trying to scare us?" Silke asked Raj.

He shrugged. "It's been two years. I've thought about that night so many times, and I can't figure it out."

"Did you see a couple on the balcony on the second floor behind you?" Nina asked.

"No. We never saw them. We read about it the next day, when we got back to Boston, and found out someone died. I guess when he fired those wild shots . . ." Silke said. "A random death, like a lightning strike or a car crash. So sudden. So awful."

"Then what happened?" Nina asked.

Silke said, "Elliott jumped away. He yelled at us to run. Raj and I ran around the corner. Our room was right there on the ground floor. We were very scared. We grabbed our stuff and about a minute later Elliott was pounding on the door, saying the gunman had run away. We went into his room and got his stuff. We ran back to Harveys. From there caught a cab to the Reno airport. We took the next flight east."

"Do you believe the robber followed you from Harveys?"

"Nobody would mistake us for rich people." Silke pulled at the few frayed threads around the hem on her wrist. "We look like poor students. We were staying at that cheap motel. No, he knew we had money somehow. He followed us and got all of our winnings."

"How much was that?"

"A lot," the girl said.

"Hundreds?" Nina asked.

Silke shook her head.

"Thousands?"

She evaded that. "We didn't count exactly."

"Okay, describe this man who accosted you," Nina said.

"He wore a mask," Silke repeated. "It was dark. His voice was soft. He was American. And he stepped forward toward us, and there was something strange about his walk. Something wrong with his leg, I think. His foot turned out. Are you all right?"

A hot iron burned inside her temple, and a brand-new headache began to pulse. Nina put down her cardboard cup. "Jet lag," she said. She had fallen back in her mind to the man in the floppy hat, with the funny walk, at Zephyr Cove. Dave Hanna hadn't mentioned that the shooter had a bad leg, probably because he hadn't seen the shooter moving in the dark.

The man in the parking lot who rigged their Bronco with an explosive had to have been the shooter, had to have been watching them in the rain. Why?

Because he was afraid she'd find these people, who could identify him? Silke still watched her speculatively. Nina struggled to regain her confidence.

"Now you describe him," she said to Raj. "Maybe you noticed something different."

"Fairly tall, medium weight, wearing sweatpants, just like every second person at Tahoe. I think he said it just exactly like this: 'Empty out your pockets,' the whole time, using the gun to gesture. I can't tell you about the gun except to me it looked big. I've never been so close to one before."

"If you saw him again, could you identify him?"

Again they looked at each other.

"I don't know," Silke said. "Probably not."

"What about the third shot?" Nina said. "The final shot?"

"Yes, we heard one more shot while we were running away," Silke said.

"As fast as we could. I've spent a lot of time on the treadmill since that night," Raj said, "trotting, cantering, galloping. I plan to run faster if there's ever a next time."

Nina didn't like him making light of the situation. " 'We' meaning..."

"Raj and me. Elliott was a few seconds behind us," Silke answered.

"Why didn't you stay, talk to the police, and make a report?"

"Personal reasons," Raj said.

"Which means that we were utterly freaked," Silke said in her precise speech.

Nina sat back in her chair, fighting the headache.

"You don't look well," Silke said.

"I need you to come back with me," Nina said, "for a deposition and to talk to the police. We have to locate this guy. I think he may still be in the Tahoe area, keeping an eye on the case."

Raj smiled. "I knew you would suggest that. A few minutes of our time multiplied many times over."

"Will you come?"

"Please, no," Silke said. "Can't we do something here?"

"We need you in California. Your expenses will be paid—" She squinted up through eyes that rebelled at focusing and saw two men standing at the table.

"Professor Braun!" Silke said, her voice shaking. "Hello."

"Don't bother to get up, Ms. Reilly, because I don't want

to shake hands with you. Let me introduce Mr. John Branson, my attorney." He rubbed Silke's shoulder avuncularly. "Did you know she is a lawyer? Has she been bothering you?"

"She's no problem," Silke said. "She had a few questions, that's all."

"She's trying to enmesh you in a major court case on the other side of the country under false pretenses," Branson said. "The professor is very concerned for you and asked me to assist if I can."

"Great," Raj said. "Here's a legal question for you. Do we have to go to California for a deposition just because she wants us to?"

Nina stood up. "Mr. Branson? You don't understand the situation. These people are witnesses—"

"Professor Braun filled me in," the short, small, angry lawyer with him said.

"You don't represent these people," Nina said. "You don't need to jump all over this. So back off."

"You want my help?" Branson said to Raj and Silke. Although Silke hesitated at first, she took her cue from Raj this time. They nodded. "Okay, I'm advising you to leave right now. This lady can't stop you and she can't force you to go to California, either."

"Keep my card, Silke," Nina said, rubbing her temple.

"Go," Branson told the students. "We can touch base later."

Rising immediately, Raj said, "Come on." Silke picked up their coats and took his hand.

"I've told you how meaningful your evidence could be to the family of Sarah Hanna. I can only hope that, now you know your importance, you'll do the right thing. You can call me at the Charles River Inn until two-thirty," Nina said.

"Good-bye," Silke said. Raj and Silke gathered their things and left.

Silke had good manners. Her new lawyer, John Branson, did not. "What the fuck do you think you're doing?"

"Interviewing crucial witnesses. As you apparently know," Nina said.

"What did they tell you?"

"Ask them."

"I will." Branson's distinguished head was held up by a bandy-legged body, like a pumpkin propped on sticks, but the suit was Italian and did a good job disguising it. "I'll also tell them they don't have to talk to anyone in a California civil case, or go there, whatever lies you may have told them."

"They can talk to the police, then."

"The police here have bigger worries than a two-year-old case from California, which by the way, doesn't even involve a criminal accusation."

"Well, it's been delightful, gentlemen, but I have to run along. A pleasure meeting you, Professor." Braun didn't reply. His hard eyes went well with his black hair, the winter outside, and his general demeanor of one who has had one put over on him, and resents it.

"Run along and don't come back," Branson said.

Due to the high-octane dose of caffeine she had just imbibed, Nina didn't sleep when she got back to the hotel, but the headache put her in bed for an hour until the full impact of the ibuprofen kicked in. Then she had a hot bath, went downstairs, and had lunch.

Then she felt better.

She made calls. She asked Wish to start searching for Elliott Wakefield electronically. He wasn't listed in the Boston or Cambridge directories. Sandy was checking out the lawyer named Branson, as Nina thought she might hear from him again.

At two-thirty Nina checked out of the hotel and went to the main police station in Boston to discuss her situation with someone in charge. She didn't expect the cops to rush out and arrest the two students as material witnesses in a murder, but she expected respectful attention and for them to fill out a report that might come in handy. The detective she spoke with listened to her tape and asked her what she was supposed to do about it.

"It's not our case," she told Nina. "Have your local police contact us. We have to work through them. That tape you made can't come in as evidence in a court case, you know. No consent. I'm a second-year law student at BU."

"Evidence, shmevidence," Nina said. "They're witnesses, and the right people will hear this tape and agree they're witnesses. The people I taped will come in person to make their statements if I have to dog them all day."

The detective said, "Well, I admire your persistence. By the way, a shame, Branson's involvement."

"Why?"

"He's a tight-ass who never gives an inch."

"I gathered that."

"And Braun is not just some nobody math professor. He married into a Boston Brahmin family, has more money than Wells Fargo Bank. They live with their two kids, a boy and a girl, straight-A students, no doubt, in a mansion in Newton bigger than Faneuil Hall, and are active fund-raisers for the local pols. He also consults for one of the big research outfits on Route 128. If you could persuade him to help you, he could do you a lot of good."

"We got off on the wrong foot," Nina said. "The detective in charge of the Hanna case at Tahoe is Sergeant Fred Cheney. I'll talk to him tomorrow and see what we can do about getting these witnesses to make formal statements. I have more questions myself."

"Can you subpoena them for the civil case?"

"Not if they're outside California. Not as witnesses. I have to rely on the police."

"Okay. We'll wait to hear from Cheney."

She taxied back to MIT, pulling her carry-on along the street, briefcase slung over her shoulder. She intended to try to collar Silke and Raj again, but they had left for the day and the new kid now manning the math department desk gave her the stink-eye. She was persona non grata at a great university, but such is the life of a lawyer.

Still, she wanted to try what she could to find Silke's and Raj's home addresses, or address, as the case might be. Phone information had no listing. The MIT directory wasn't available to nonstudents, but she wooed a bored office worker in administration and took a look anyway, without finding them. She tried talking to a few fellows in faded sweatshirts who were lounging around in the lobby of Building 8, but they turned out to be electrical engineers, busy bees, willing but unhelpful.

Her work in Boston was done. She took a short walk over the Harvard Bridge, enjoying the windy afternoon, then snagged a cab to Logan.

The flight was delayed an hour and she felt exhausted. She finally fell into her window seat, opened her *Vanity Fair*, sniffed as a new celebrity scent unfolded from the magazine, and began reading every word of the bilious interviews, self-aggrandizing columnists, and tales of aged billionaires. The case melted away. The magazine lasted all the way back to California.

Chapter 15

As dusk fell over the Sierra, the Great Tahoe Weekend got going. Winding her way up Spooner Pass from the Reno airport, Nina approached the California state line. The big casino-hotels hove into view, attended by their happy throngs, whose happiness would evaporate bit by bit over the next two days in direct proportion to their stashes of cash.

She turned onto Pioneer Trail with relief, leaving the fortune-seekers behind, and turned left onto the uphill cul-de-sac of Pony Express, where her brother Matt lived, and where she had left Bob twenty-odd hours before.

The house at the end of the block abutted some nice trails and good rock climbing. Although it wasn't quite dark yet, a full moon peeped over the hill behind Matt and Andrea's rooftop. She parked and walked up the path to the front door. Light spilled from the windows and she heard within the anxious cry of Matt and Andrea's baby, June.

"Come on in," Matt said. "How was your trip?"

"Breathless. How'd it go with Bob?"

"Follow me," he said. "Stuff to report on that front." He went to the fridge and pulled out a couple of diet root beers, offering her one, which she took.

"Hungry? Want some leftover spaghetti?"

"No thanks. Where's Andrea?" Nina asked.

"At a Women's Center meeting. I've got the kids. Bob and Troy are in Troy's room playing video games."

"Should we get June? I heard her crying when I came in."

"She's asleep now." They both listened with the exquisite attention of people who have experienced parenthood. No sound came from June's crib.

"Bob and Troy have gotten out of hand."

Matt had had a long day towing vehicles with flat tires around the shoreline. He was thinner these days, and so was his hair. He was only thirty-four, but age and three kids to support already marked him. He ran a parasailing business during the summer months, which made up for the slim pickings in the winter, when he rescued tourists with his tow truck. These days, he and Nina talked a lot about his businesses, his tax problems, employee problems, contract problems. The old carefree Matt still came out now and then, but the adult emerging lately was harassed, unable to be expansive and light.

"What did they do?" Nina said, setting her can down on the table, not wanting to hear the lecture apparently pending. Why couldn't she collect Bob and head home? Why did every single day have to be so fraught?

"They hung bolos on telephone lines all over town."

"Bolos?"

"They collect rocks and attach them to a couple of feet of electrical tape, then they skateboard around town until they find an accessible telephone line. They toss the bolo until it falls over the line, with the rocks dangling over either side. Yesterday they spent most of the evening throwing these things."

"Where in the world did they get an idea like that?" Nina said.

"Ask your son. Troy's his minion. He follows the plan."

"Oh, Matt. Like Troy has no say in the matter. As if he doesn't love every minute of it."

"I'm not excusing him, but Bob's older. He should act his age."

She thought about that, his age, fourteen, and what that meant.

"You look amused. It's not amusing," Matt said.

"Remember yourself at fourteen? The time you crawled through your bedroom window absolutely bubbling from beer, and Mom heard you, but thought you were a burglar and called the police?"

He grimaced. "Don't remind me. You know we expect better from our kids. And by the way, you could have told her but you didn't. You let the cops come and hassle me. I don't think I'll ever forgive you for that. And all the other stuff." Matt was upset. He didn't like it when Bob egged Troy on into trouble. Sometimes Nina thought that he was especially sensitive because when she and Matt were kids, she had done the same thing to Matt, persuaded him into all kinds of harebrained schemes.

Of course, Matt in his early adulthood had found much more trouble all on his own, but no need to get into that any further. He had turned into a strict parent who grounded his kids. He might be right, she sure couldn't judge, but it still struck her as a harmless prank.

She laughed. "I was sixteen and so superior. I thought you deserved a kick in the rear end."

"Mean older sister."

"Matt, it's not like they beat up a senior citizen," Nina said.

"Troy's grounded," Matt told her. "They had one of these

things slung over the line right outside. I made them get it down. It took a long time, because it isn't easy. Nina, quit laughing. Add some heavy snow during the winter and that line could come down. And it interferes with utility lines. They could get a ticket or something. Plus, they climb fences and go into people's yards without permission. Of course, most people don't care, but some of them are pretty protective of their space. They came here for some peace and privacy. They don't need a couple of wild kids rioting through their yards."

"Okay, you're right," Nina said.

"Make Bob understand he can't do things like that," Matt said, "not when he's staying with us, anyway."

"I will."

"He's out of control."

"I said I will!" But Matt didn't seem to believe her. Now she was upset, too. Bob wasn't a troublemaker. He was a high-spirited kid, and . . .

"Sometimes I think . . ." Matt started, then stopped.

"You think what?"

"Never mind."

"No, Matt. Spill it. What's on your mind?"

He scratched the back of his neck. He needed a haircut. His blond hair almost touched his shoulders. He looked fitter than a man in his early thirties, tall and muscular, but his face was as careworn as that of a man in his fifties. "I think he misses Paul. He's staying busy because he's dealing with a loss, too. Did that ever occur to you?"

"They never got along that well."

"I suspect they were closer than you imagined. And Paul—well, he's tougher than you."

"You mean because Paul's a guy? You think I can't manage my son on my own?"

"Nina, no," Matt said, shocked. "I never said that! It's just easier with two people playing off each other, bad cop, good cop. Gives them perspective."

"Hey, Mom." Unfortunately, Bob chose this moment to appear at the kitchen door, accompanied by Hitchcock, who rushed toward Nina.

"Hey, kiddo." She held Hitchcock off. "Good boy. How's my big boy? Down! Down!"

"I'll get my stuff. Meet you at the truck," Bob said.

"Thank your uncle for letting you stay over last night."

"Thanks, Uncle Matt," Bob said. "I love coming here."

Matt's expression softened. He said, "So long, buddy."

The three Reillys, human and canine, drove home. Nina felt disgraced. "I heard about the bolos."

"Aw, we were just havin' fun."

"You're out of control." This echo of Matt forced itself unbidden out of her mouth.

"I couldn't do my hazardous-waste work with Taylor 'cause I wasn't at home. There's nothing to do around here! Troy and I were just goofing around."

"Well, you upset Uncle Matt. You showed bad judgment. Tomorrow we'll drive around and you'll knock down all those bolos."

"Oh, for Pete's sake."

On Saturday morning after breakfast, they cruised around the area of Bob and Troy's bolo-tossing. The boys had restrained their mischief-making to streets near Pioneer Trail. Bolos swung from telephone wires all up and down the neighborhood. Nina parked at each one and Bob got out, found a rock, and started throwing. Some of the bolos wound themselves tighter. Only one cooperated by falling to the ground.

"Can we give it up, Mom?"

"What the—what's going on?" They had come to an unusual-looking bolo, strung conspicuously on a line on Jicarilla, only blocks from their house. "Those aren't rocks. Hey! My shoes!"

"Remember how you complained they were old and you needed a new pair of running shoes that would inspire you to run once in a while?"

"I never said throw them up for the neighbors to hate!"

"They made a perfect bolo. Sorry, Mom."

"My dirty old shoes! You get out there and knock them down."

But all Bob's throwing efforts only resulted in an extra loop of electrical tape wrapping around the line. It appeared that Nina's wretched sneakers would dangle forever above the street, symbols of anarchy and of the essential weirdness of the world.

Nina could not stand it. "Bob, you are grounded until you get those sneakers down. And you are not allowed to climb on the telephone poles or do anything dangerous to get them down."

"But Taylor and me have to go collect waste this afternoon!"

"How much money have you made with your work?"

"Why do you ask?"

"How much?"

"Sixty-two dollars."

"That should cover the cost of a good tall ladder. I'll help you finish this project. We'll get your money and go to the hardware store."

"I worked hard for that money! I have plans for it!"

"That's life in the city," Nina said heartlessly.

"Wait. Give us a chance first." Bob held his hands up. "Taylor's coming over. He'll help me."

"You can't leave the house except to buy a ladder and get my shoes down."

"I'll take care of it, Mom."

"Yes, you will." They drove back home in silence. Bob went to his room and got on the phone.

A short time later Taylor Nordholm, Bob's homie, showed up. Taylor hadn't had his growth spurt yet and was physically awkward, except in his weight-lifting arms, but he had an insouciant maturity in his manners. He went to find her and greet her.

"It's good to have you and Bob back in town," he said. "How are you, Mrs. Reilly?" He carried a brown paper bag.

"Fine," Nina said, plumping the pillows on the bed she had just made.

"Well, see you later."

"Don't do anything unsafe." The boys left and she completed a disaster-prevention pickup of the cabin. When she had folded the laundry, she collapsed on the couch, letting Hitchcock crawl beside her, letting the worry flow back in.

The man who had tried to hurt them was probably the shooter. She had talked to Cheney the minute she got back from Massachusetts, but the police hadn't found him yet.

She had to assume Sarah's killer knew her home address. She had apparently done what she never wanted to do: drawn attention to herself, and by extension, to her family.

She got up and walked to the entry closet, opened the door, and checked the lights on the keypad inside to see that all the doors and windows were properly secured, and the alarm was ready to be armed for the night. In the bedroom, she lifted the mattress. Yes, there it was, the knife in a leather sheath—crazy, but it made her feel better. Then she took down from its hook on the wall the shillelagh her dad had given her once upon a time. A heavy cudgel made of some extremely hard wood, it had a big knob on one end and a hole drilled through the other end for a leather cord. A leprechaun smoking a pipe had been carved into the base.

She swung it, first a little, then as if bringing it down on someone's head. Her blood rose, not in fear, but in anger. Uncivilized, these feelings. After tucking it into the cabinet by the front door, she checked the lock on the door itself. Secure. Midday sun poured down on the porch. She stepped outside to sit on the steps.

Bob and Taylor strolled around the corner into view, carrying her sneakers, Hitchcock rambling behind.

Smiling, Nina said, "How'd you do it?" She accepted the sneakers, which bore traces of electrical tape.

Bob said, "Taylor brought over his dad's shaver. It operates on batteries. We attached it with tape to a long stick we found in the meadow. Then I turned it on and held it up and shaved right through the tape, and the shoes fell down."

"Good move, kids," Nina said. "What an idea. I doubt I would have thought of using a shaver on a stick."

"You have to think outside the lines," Bob said, repeating an old line they often used with each other. "Am I still grounded?"

"Until you wash the truck," she said.

The boys were extremely pleased with themselves. Bob got the hose from the yard and they gave the truck a rinse, if not a wash, then Bob turned the hose on Taylor, who grabbed it away. They kept it up until they were screaming and almost blue from the cold. Then they went inside, dried off, and helped themselves to microwaved popcorn, leaving a good portion on the kitchen floor for Hitchcock to clean. Soon Taylor's dad drove up and collected them for their waste-disposal rounds.

You had to hand it to Bob. He had a way about him.

★   ★   ★

The afternoon passed in a blur of errands. Finally Nina was back on her couch, a freshly bathed dog at her feet, a crystal glass full to the brim with Clos du Bois—the sauvignon blanc, not the chardonnay—in her hand, and the news on TV.

The phone rang. The call was from the land of men.

"Hi. It's Mick." Mick the math teacher.

"Hello," Nina said.

"I hope you don't mind me calling you at home. You gave me your personal card. I hope it wasn't by accident. Hey, guess what day it is."

"Saturday."

"That's right. And Saturday night is date night. I heard around town that you might actually be free for a change."

"For a date?"

"That's right. A harmless sort of thing. Dinner, wherever you want. I know it's late notice. But we're grown-ups and we can break the rules."

"What about your wife?"

"I told you, she left me."

"What about the student?"

"She came to her senses and left me, too. It was a disastrous peccadillo. She was twenty-one, by the way. I don't want you to get the wrong idea."

"Mick, I can't go out with you. I'm very flattered. But I'm your lawyer. It would be unethical."

"You put up some major obstacles, Nina, but I am a mathematician and I anticipated that one. I am resigning as your client. I'll find some other lawyer. We have nothing pending anyway. I hadn't consulted you yet. Nina?"

"I don't think so, Mick."

"What are your plans for tonight?"

She planned to take a walk in the neighborhood with Hitchcock. On the other hand, it would be nice to sit across a table from a well-spoken man. Neither of them had a thing to do on this particular night. Why not?

Who cares? she thought. Mick, or Bova, or the next guy.

Quickies. Then the thought came: When did I give up all hope?

"Nothing too special," she said.

"No expectations," Mick said. "No strings. You have to eat dinner anyway."

"True."

"I enjoyed our conversation at my office."

"You have to be kidding. About Braun?"

"Don't you have some other math questions for me?"

Now, that was some invitation. "Well, all right. Sounds like a plan." She gave him her address.

"Bob!"

"Yeah?" He was in his room, up to no good, no doubt.

"I'm going out tonight. There's a Hungry Man in the freezer. Is that okay?"

"Yum."

"I'll set the alarm when I go. Don't forget it's on."

"Uh-huh."

Upstairs, she pulled out her low-cut red sweater and brushed her long hair. Let Mick's eyes bug out. She hoped he would have enough wits left to answer a couple more questions. Hitchcock followed her around, his tail wagging hopefully.

"Sorry, boy," she told him.

That ol' mountain moon shone down through the twilight as Mick's car pulled into the driveway. Nina watched from upstairs as he disembarked from the driver's side, carrying a bouquet of cranberry and gold.

Flowers! How long had it been since anyone had given her flowers?

"Greetings," he said at the door. "You look superb."

"Thank you." Demurely she took the flowers and invited him to come in to see the cabin, the orange Swedish stove in the corner, the big windows onto the backyard, the thick rug.

"Cozy," he said. She arranged the flowers in a jar and set them on the table. Bob came out in his sweats and was duly introduced. Mick, in jeans and a pin-striped shirt, but no pen in the shirt pocket, looked pretty harmless, like the boys at high school who always hold up their hands to answer the teacher's questions, the ones who seldom get drunk and always shower in the morning. Away from his office, he seemed more subdued, even nervous.

She suggested Passaretti's, only a few miles away on Highway 50 heading out of town toward Echo Summit.

She hugged Bob good-bye, gave Hitchcock a pat, and set the alarm on her way out, slamming the door tightly behind her, pulling on the handle once to make sure it had latched.

"Feels good to get out," Mick said, opening the car door for her. He drove a VW Jetta. All in all, there was a comforting normality and modesty about him. "My apartment is the repository of too many memories right now. Wait, I didn't mean to start out like that."

"It's okay."

"Right now is what matters," he said. "Tonight." Mick drove with one hand, fast. The trees on both sides of the road seemed to lean in on them.

At Passaretti's they found a private booth. The roadhouse twinkled with tiny lights and smelled like a garlic field. Nina ordered a glass of Chianti and Mick had a beer.

She guessed that he was about thirty, maybe six years younger than she was. Once they loosened up, they started talking like old friends, and the conversation quickly rose to an intimate level of honesty. Nina enjoyed herself. She wished Paul away. He had another woman. She had the right to other men.

After a while Mick leaned back against the wall of the booth and said, "You're intimidating."

"So are you. You're smart."

"Book-smart, you must mean? Surely you don't refer to how I conduct my life."

"What's going to happen with the student and the wife?"

"They'll leave my sphere quietly, I think. None of us wants trouble."

Nina said, hesitating, "Do you want to talk about it?"

"I'd rather have dinner with you, and talk about life and the world to come, and not talk about my everyday problems."

What a relief. She didn't want to talk about her everyday problems, either. "So, how long have you been at Tahoe?"

"Three years. I'm thinking of taking a teaching job in L.A. Living at the beach."

"Do you like teaching mathematics?"

"I love it. I love showing kids the beauty and elegance of math, how certain and satisfying the equations can be. I like undressing Nature. Seeing beauty bare. Do you like practicing law?"

"Yes," Nina said. "Although I fuss about the hours and the stress all the time."

Mick waited, but Nina didn't go on. She had said what she usually said, and seldom did anyone want her to go farther. But Mick seemed genuinely curious, in a pedagogical sort of way.

"That's all you have to say about it? Why work so hard? Why put yourself on the line for strangers?"

Nina said, laughing, "No boundaries, I guess."

"Be serious."

"Okay. This case I'm working on: I want to catch a man and make him see what he's done to a family. All the law can do is take his money and liberty. I want to make sure he understands what he did."

"You want more than what's required. Or even humanly possible. You're setting yourself up."

"I can handle it."

"But if this bad guy came to you and asked you to defend him, you would?"

"I might. To make sure the punishment is proportionate to the crime. To make sure he gets due process. What if he's mentally ill? What if there are mitigating circumstances?"

"You take on conflicting roles, avenging angel, bleeding heart."

"Sounds like the name of a great Chinese movie. Zhang Ziyi would be in it."

Mick said softly, "What's wrong, Nina?"

He had asked, in that disinterested tone of his, as if she were an equation with an unknown variable he wanted to investigate. She decided, just like that, to tell him.

She said slowly, looking down at her glass, "The problem is that sometimes my work attracts violent people."

"You can't mean Gottlieb Braun."

"No."

"Who, then?"

"You know, I don't want to talk about it, Mick. I want you to stay outside all that."

"I understand."

A long, comfortable silence ensued. Nina heaved a sigh.

"So here you are."

"Trying to be useful."

"You don't look like a lawyer tonight."

"Glad I can still surprise people now and then."

"Lots of people?"

"What do you mean?"

"Do you go out a lot?"

"Given my son and a twenty-four-hour job, I barely make it to the grocery store."

"Who's Bob's father?"

"Bob's father? Oh, a musician who lives in Germany."

"Still married?"

Nina said, "We never married. But I have been married twice. And I just left a two-year relationship."

Mick said, smiling, "I was intimidated before, but now I'm terrified. What happened with the marriages?"

"My first husband took up with a divorce lawyer. My second husband died." Talking about Kurt, and Jack, and Collier, and Paul in this way made her uncomfortable. It didn't seem dignified. Or maybe it was her complicated love life that sounded undignified. Since Mick's love life was even more undignified, it didn't matter as much.

They ate and talked on. Mick told her about his downfall at UC Berkeley, another student-teacher affair. He might be a hound for women, but he was funny and charming and understanding. She reflected that these qualities of Mick's might have been exactly what had gotten him into his trouble.

During the tiramisu, Nina said, "I found two of the witnesses. You helped a lot."

"Gottlieb Braun came through? You saw him?"

"I went to Boston."

"Wow. I'm impressed. What's he like?"

"Judging from the short time I spent with him, like something that makes a loud cracking noise and chips off the Antarctic Shelf."

"That's what I figured. Nothing personal, I'm sure, but a lot of mathematicians don't understand why other people need to take up space on their plane. Erdös called nonmathematicians 'trivials.' And he was considered sociable for a mathematician. So you nailed your witnesses?"

"I managed two taps of the hammer. But I still have one more for the hammer, and I think he may be the most important one."

"Another math student?"

"He dropped out of MIT in his first year of the Ph.D. program," Nina said. "He was listed as a candidate two years ago. I can't pick him up on the Web for the last two years."

"He's not publishing, then. Most of the papers are at least indexed on the Web."

Nina said, "Excuse my ignorance, but what exactly are all those papers about? There seemed to be hundreds of thousands in all sorts of journals."

"They're proofs," Mick said. "Proofs of hypotheses, extensions of specialty fields, refinements. There are about two hundred fifty thousand published each year."

"What exactly is going on in math?" Nina said. "Are all kinds of developments occurring that I won't hear about for five years?"

"You'll never hear about them," Mick said. "The profession wanders in the wilderness. Nobody's had a new idea in number theory since Selberg years ago. The heyday of math was the seventeenth through the nineteenth centuries. Look at Riemann. He came up with his hypothesis about the primes in 1854. We desperately need a new Euler or Riemann to burst on the scene."

"Are you being honest, or bitter?"

"Both. I haven't got the skill or dedication to write a paper. But that's okay. I'd rather see a student's mouth drop open when she finally gets Pascal's Triangle. I have to say, I'd be as happy as Gottlieb if somebody came up with a new idea."

"What about computers?"

"Yeah. Computers. Well, the kiddies are on top of base two now, but the real impact is a new emphasis on experimentation in math rather than developing algorithms. Like the prime numbers. Computers meaninglessly spin them out, one by one. I think we have a couple billion listed now. What good is a random list? Machines waste time. They don't prove anything. They create shopping lists. Am I boring you?"

"Not at all," Nina said. "This ex-student . . ."

"Care to give me a name?"

"I can't do that."

"I might know the little slacker."

"Maybe you can help me indirectly. Why would a young man who has been accepted into a Ph.D. program at MIT drop out?"

"Probably not money problems. MIT takes care of you at that point. Problems at home? Psych problems?" Mick stroked his chin reflectively. "By definition, he's a whiz kid. Have you looked at the list of high-school national prize winners? Maybe he won something before college. Like the National Merit, or Westinghouse Science Talent Search Award. The runners-up will be listed on the Web. You think he's the one who bought the books?"

"One chance out of three."

"The American Institute of Mathematics had a Riemann seminar a couple of years ago. And there are summer institutes just for young scholars. The Ross Program at Ohio State. MIT has something, the, uh, Research Science Institute I think it's called. Look up the teams in the USA Mathematical Olympiad. It's like *Jeopardy!* for high schoolers, only harder. Here's a napkin to write on."

As he rattled off names, Nina wrote them down. "You mentioned psych issues," she said. "What do you mean? Stress-induced problems?"

"Sure. It's a rough time, the late teens. That's when schizophrenia breaks out, especially in boys. I don't know where to go with that. Medical records will be confidential, won't they?"

"I wonder about this boy," Nina said. "Maybe I can locate him through the other two, but they have an obstructive, odious lawyer all of a sudden."

"Can I help? I'd like to know more about this," Mick said.

"I wish I could talk more about it," Nina said. "But . . ." The waiter brought the bill. Mick paid. They walked out under the stars, the forest looming.

"Late movie?" Mick said.

"I don't think so."

"Drink?"

"I'm sleepy already."

"Drive up Echo Summit and neck on the lookout? Or Mount Rose, if you're feeling particularly brave?"

Nina laughed. "Not tonight."

"We sadly settle for an after-dinner mint, then." He produced one.

"I think I should be getting back." She was thinking about Bob, home alone, feeling panicky.

"Is it me?"

"Of course not. You know you're attractive," Nina said.

"Okay." At her cabin, he jumped out, opened the door, and helped her out. They stood in the driveway.

Nina wondered if Bob was peeking out the window. "Thanks, Mick."

"Any time. Let's have a hug, okay?"

They embraced. Mick's strong arms wrapped her tightly. His mouth sought hers and they kissed. His lips were soft, not demanding. Unfamiliar.

Fine. Unfamiliar was just fine.

Chapter 16

Elliott's psychiatrist told him the dream precipitated his psychosis. He wasn't supposed to think about it: It would hinder his recovery. He spent more than a month in the psych hospital in Seattle, missing so much of spring semester of his junior year that he had to make it all up in the summer.

In a way, he enjoyed his stay. They let him wear earplugs so he wouldn't have to hear the TV. They made sure he slept and ate a lot. He wasn't allowed to do math, but the meds made that cool, too.

He gave up on six years of work. He decided that Riemann's work had been stupendous, but not supernatural. His talks with Silke about physics returned to him again and again.

A rest cure, his father called it. Elliott had allowed the breakdown to happen, gone exploring in the zeta landscape with full knowledge of the danger, and had taken a tumble, breaking something.

He had also brought something away with him, which no

meds could make him forget. Scrawled in his black notebook, his function filled several pages, in handwriting that didn't even look like his. He had his idea, but no proof yet.

That summer, he returned to MIT. Raj was in Madras, Silke in Germany. He rowed on the Charles during the hot hazy afternoons.

In the evenings, he worked on the prime numbers, taking care to knock off by eleven and sleep at least seven hours.

He now took life slowly, but there was never any question of turning his back on the primes. A very few people are granted knowledge of their destinies at an early age—gymnasts, musicians, great beauties, scientists, and many mathematicians. He had been blessed with a certain future. He knew his fate, but he also knew now that he wasn't God; he couldn't run rampant toward his goal; he would have to approach it stealthily, the painstaking calculations on the infinite sequence he had discovered, the endless checking and rechecking of the algebraic expressions.

He tried to explain it to his father over the phone, but Pop couldn't follow anymore. "The only actual numbers are primes," Elliott said. "The composite numbers are just junk in the road, piling up, slowing down the primes."

"Are you sleeping?" his father said.

"Each prime is a cloud of probabilities, like quanta."

"Come home as soon as classes are over."

"I'm back to the li line. I have finished the first phase of my work. If you give me any number up to three hundred digits, I can tell you egg-zackly how many primes there are to that point. Do you know what that means, Pop?"

"No, I don't, son."

"It's big."

"I'm worried about you."

"I'm fine. I'm sleeping. I'm eating. It's linked with physics. This correction we're looking for—there is information loss from the more fundamental structure behind what we see as primes. I'm moving into phase two."

He had traveled beyond Riemann. Keeping his excitement in check, he stayed on the safe side of the precipice. He corralled his imagination and worked on debugging his proof, which would be a long and arduous process.

The angel did not come to him again.

When the first year of their graduate programs began a year and half later, Elliott and Raj and Silke resumed their gambling jaunts. Elliott and Silke did it for the money. Raj did it for the kick. Even Carleen came along a time or two. She had decided against grad school and taken a job with a company on Route 128 that made security software.

Not wanting to see pity in them, Elliott avoided Silke's eyes. She and Raj were never apart. Fiercely entwined and forbidding to outsiders, they were as tight as barbed wire.

After a Fourth of July trip, the team was barred from the casinos in Atlantic City. Their photos were circulated. They dressed differently, changed their signals, and concentrated on Nevada, where they were still uncaught.

November came. They picked a weekend.

They chose Tahoe.

Something was wrong between Raj and Silke on the flight west. Even Elliott, who didn't pay much attention to silence and surly expressions, could feel it. Silke stared out the window, arms crossed, face shuttered. She ignored Raj. He didn't seem to care. He teased the attendant and drank some of the wine they served, which was very unusual for him.

Elliott sat behind them. He slept most of the way.

They took a cab to some motel by the state line, paying cash as always from the stash in Silke's purse. It was a Saturday morning, cool, dry, bright, airless from the altitude.

Later, inside Harveys, Elliott played desultorily, waiting for Carleen or Silke to signal him to move to a hot table. Silke suddenly came to him, tears in her eyes.

"I can't do this anymore," she said. "Can we go outside?"

"Let me tell Raj . . ."

"Don't tell him." They wound through the banks of slots and went through the revolving doors. At 6:00 P.M. or so the evening shift of tourists had just begun.

"Shall we go back to the motel?"

"No. Let's go toward the mountains." They crossed the busy highway and walked through Caesars' acre-wide parking lot. Then they were really in the mountains, walking uphill on a dirt path, alone.

"Did you hear? Raj is getting married." Silke walked ahead of him, wearing those high-heeled boots that seemed so silly away from a city.

"Oh."

"Is that all you can say? His parents found him a wife. A Wellesley girl whose family is from Madras. Tower Court, that's her dorm address. Sounds grand, doesn't it?"

"I'm sorry."

"He loves me, but he'll marry her. Wait, though. He won't marry her right away. He's checked his calendar and squeezed us both into his future! First, he and I continue to live together while we get our doctorates, he, a man with two foolish females to keep happy; I, the doormat; she the ignorant, innocent dupe. She'll finish grad school, marry him, and become a banker, he says, at least until the four children come. I, at that point, well, he forgot to say what I will be doing right then. But doesn't his life sound wonderful?"

She was really messed up, Elliott could tell by the perfection of her grammar, but she had always known this day would come. To tell the truth, he was glad Raj was finally leaving her. The old passion rose in him again, with the thought that she would be alone and lonely and perhaps turn to him.

Then he chastised himself for his unquenchable egotism, which converted her pain into a potential advantage for himself.

"He thinks he's another Ramanujan," Silke said as they walked. "But he has never had an original thought. Except in bed. He's very original. When we make love, he—can I say this?"

"Say whatever you want."

"He says, 'I—am—Ram!' over and over. You know. In rhythm."

"Who is Ram?"

"A Hindu god."

"Does it make things more interesting?"

"It's funny! I'm making fun of him! What would it be like with you, Wakefield? 'I have the proof!' Climaxes all around."

"Silke, you are savage."

"Only because—I do feel savage."

Elliott puffed now as the trail became steeper and rockier, petering out. He could hear the sound of a stream to his left. "Let's go this way." Silke followed him as he picked his way across the rocks. "Let's sit down," he said. "We'll figure it out." Bushes clustered along the bank of the streamlet he had found. He reached down, letting the cold pure water run over his hand.

"He gave her an engagement ring." Tears choked her voice.

"His family is wealthy," Elliott said practically. "Conservative. So is he. You always knew that."

"He loves me!"

"He does."

"He can't leave me."

"How do you mean? What are you thinking?"

"I'm not thinking," Silke said. She let out a bitter laugh, then said, "Do you still love me?"

"I'll always love you."

"I'll always love Raj."

"Stay with him, then, for as long as you can."

"But—" She brushed away her hair and looked at him dubiously. "I'm too good to be second best. I deserve—"

Elliott said, "What use is pride? What does it do besides keep you away from the one you love? I never let it stop me."

"I'd start to hate him."

"I haven't started to hate you."

"You're an idiot, that's why. You should hate me."

"Why are you so harsh to me, Silke? Why do you say things like that?"

Her face contorted. She reached over and put her arms around him. "Maybe you're right...maybe if he stays with me...he won't be able to go through with it," she said into his shoulder. He held her tight and pretended she was crying over him.

Finally, when she let go and wiped her face with her sleeve, he said, "I'll never get married." Then he added shyly, "I managed to find a function that seems to predict the primes. It implies an easy way to factor large numbers, too."

Silke became all business. "Are you sleeping?"

"Brother John, Brother John," Elliott sang. "Not another breakdown, not another breakdown—"

"Ding dang dong. Stop singing. Tell me."

"There are some flaws. But—"

She gave him a long look. She had sat down on the rock opposite, one knee pulled up in what Elliott remembered was called the Royal Pose in Asia. She looked like a small and perfect statue, her face immobile, a wet streak still evident on one cheek, like a stone goddess who has been left out in the rain. The wind-less air and shadows where they sat seemed to calm her.

"You found it through your work on the Riemann Hypothesis?" she said.

"No. I'm following up on some work by Connes and Berry in physics. I went back to the li line and started over, where Riemann started. Before he went down his blind alley. It's a correction to the Prime Number Theorem."

"You can prove it?"

"Not yet."

"You confuse me," Silke said. "Do you have a proof or not?"

"Not yet. But give me any number up to three hundred digits and I think I can tell you if it's a prime in about fifteen minutes. If it's a composite number up to about five hundred digits, I can factor it with my Mac G5 in about twenty minutes. The point is, it seems to work case by case. Now I need to figure out why."

"That's—those are huge numbers. Colossal."

"I may be able to go bigger. It's just that my computer doesn't have the capability."

"Let's say I believe you. Show me."

"I can't. I'm not ready. Even for you."

"I might find an error and save you some work."

"I gave Professor Braun some of my results. He'll review them."

"Who else knows?"

"I told Carleen. She called on my cell phone to see how we were doing."

"Idiot," Silke said. The way she said it, it sounded like "idy-ote." "Then the whole world knows. You know where Carleen works?"

"No."

"For an encryption company in Web security."

"I knew it was some kind of security software. So what?"

"They'll want to buy it."

"Why?"

"To suppress it. Public-key encryption is built around not being able to factor large numbers, Wakefield. The Web depends on this encryption. Banks, government, big corporations, they depend on it. Where have you been living?"

"In a zeta landscape," Elliott said. "I wouldn't let it be suppressed. It needs to be written up and published."

Silke put her hand to her mouth and smiled, her eyes widening. "You'll win the Clay prize! A million dollars! And they will call it the Wakefield Theorem! You will be immortal!"

"But first I have to finish the proof, and I have a long way to go. I probably need a couple more years."

"You know, Wakefield, my darling, I think I believe you." She looked at him with a sort of awe, which stirred him deeply. He had dreamed of receiving a look from her for so long, but this look wasn't mixed with the desire for possession she felt for Raj.

It's hopeless, he thought. But he knew that.

"Anyway. What are you going to do?" he asked her, and let her talk. Let her cry some more. Let her threaten Raj, then let her hold him and say what a good friend he was.

He had just offered her all he had, emptied out his life, his work, for her, but he could not awaken in her a desire for him. He would continue approaching her forever, never reaching her. It was another aspect of his destiny. He would be solitary. How odd to know such a thing at his age.

Chapter 17

Wish called on Sunday morning. "Elliott Wakefield," he said. "I found him, Nina. He lives on an island about fifteen minutes by ferry from Seattle. He owns a home there."

"Wonderful!" Nina said, yawning.

"His father just transferred title to him."

"Are we sure it's Elliott Wakefield the math guy?"

"The Vashon Island newspaper has a small article about his graduation with a B.S. in mathematics from MIT. I also finally located a paper he wrote while he was still enrolled there. I think it's his senior thesis."

"What's the topic?"

"'Conformal Mapping on Riemann Surfaces.'" The *Riemann* word again. "He's ours," Wish went on. "What do you want me to do?"

"Give me the home address." She wrote it down. "Wish, can you drop off a copy of that thesis at the community college

tomorrow? Professor Mick McGregor in the math department.
I'll call and tell him it's coming."

"Ten-four. I have Silke Kilmer's resume, too. I'll drop it off at
the office."

"How'd you get that?"

"She posted it on the Web. She's looking for a position for
next summer. She's an expert on something called Hermitian
matrices."

"Ugh. I hope I don't have to learn about this stuff," Nina
said. "But I really want to try to get to know these witnesses."

"They sound like they're from another planet."

"I've heard that theory."

"Do you like math, Nina?"

"No," Nina said. "I have to say, one reason I went to law
school was because I'd never have to see an equation again. That's
why this is so unfair. I have a book right here on prime numbers.
Somehow this Riemann guy is mixed up with them."

"Have fun. See you tomorrow."

It was still morning out on the deck. Bob had bicycled over
to Taylor's house. Nina had already devoured the Tahoe paper.

The prime-numbers book turned out to have medicinal
properties. She was asleep in the pale sun within five minutes of
opening it.

Even on a Sunday afternoon, the police are all business, including the naturally mellow ones, like Sergeant Cheney of the
South Lake Tahoe Police Department. He came to the counter
and escorted Nina down the claustrophobic hall to his office
without much greeting.

Paul and Cheney had gotten along well. Perhaps that explained Cheney's slightly unfriendly attitude. If so, he would have
to get used to the new regime, Nina thought.

Or perhaps she was the one thinking about Paul, and that disturbed her, making her attribute emotions to Cheney that didn't exist. She could try to psych out the large middle-aged African American police officer sitting across from her with his hands folded across his belly forever, or she could get down to it.

"I have something on the Sarah Hanna case," she said without preamble.

"I'm listening."

"You're the officer assigned to the case?"

"I am."

"You remember the three witnesses?"

"I sure do."

"I found two of them." She ran it down concisely for him. The sergeant's eyes never left hers.

"Let's have the tape you made," he said when she had finished. She pulled it out of her briefcase and he took it, handling it gingerly, as though it were a bird's nest, or a forged check.

"Now we'll tape you on a separate tape, and this time I'll ask questions," he said. She nodded and they started again. When she had repeated what she knew about Raj Das and Silke Kilmer, he switched it off.

"You want me to bring them back here," he said. "You can't bring them back yourself."

"That's right."

"I will be talking to them, but I can't promise how that's going to happen. I might have to go to Boston."

"That wouldn't work for me. I need to get them to California or the civil case goes bye-bye."

Cheney spread his hands. Nina said, "Do what you can."

"I'll do that."

"You'll let me know how it goes?"

"You'll be the first to know."

He opened the door to the reception area for her. "Thanks for the break," he said. "I appreciate it. How's my friend Paul?"

"Fine. He has plenty of business down in Carmel."

"Give him my best."

It was three-thirty when Nina left the police station on Johnson Boulevard. She would remember that later, that and everything else, with the same crisp clarity the day displayed as she drove down the boulevard. The deep blue of high altitude reflecting off the enormous hidden body of water close by shaded the mountains. Few people were about. They were watching football, hiking, gambling, picnicking by the water, anything except driving through town.

The trees that stood everywhere, even right here in the heart of town, seemed to float in this blue air, scented with resin.

She would remember the trees, too.

Chelsi's tiny studio, sandwiched between a closed watch-repair store and a beauty parlor called Hair 'n Now in the strip mall just before Al Tahoe Boulevard, had an open door with a sign that read Therapeutic Massage Only above it. Nina knocked at the entry and entered the front room with its enthusiastic ferns and posters of acupuncture points and scoliotic backs.

"Hey, Nina." Chelsi wore red running shorts and running shoes. She was in amazing shape. She had a rolltop desk tucked in the corner, where she was writing out bills. Her fine blond hair had been pulled into one of those negligent buns that manage to look both efficient and chic on the right person.

"Hi."

"I'm not going to talk about Aunt Sarah today, I just wanted you to know that, because this is your time, you know? Except, I just wanted to say, sorry about Uncle Dave and my dad. They get into it sometimes. I hope you got the information you needed."

"No worries," Nina said. "We are making progress. I'll be updating your uncle in a day or two." She went into the massage room and took off her clothes and lay down on the table with her towel.

"Ready?" Chelsi called from the other room. She came in and the soft music began drifting through the room as she rubbed oil onto her hands. "I'm generating energy," she said. "Have you had more headaches?"

"A couple." The hands began making long movements up and down her back.

"What were you doing just before it started?" She had asked that question before.

"I've been thinking about that. One of the headaches was definitely caused by fatigue and stress. The other one—you know, they often come right when I'm ready to go to sleep. You know what I do before I sleep?"

"Make love?" Chelsi giggled.

"I read."

"We're zeroing in on it now," Chelsi said. "You mentioned reading a few times. I'm ready to make my diagnosis now. This move here, you might hear or feel some cracking. Just ride with it."

Deep within the skeleton, some ancient sorrow protested, then disentangled itself reluctantly from Nina's spine and dissolved forever. "You haven't been swimming this week," Chelsi said.

"Is that the reason for my headaches?"

"No. But if you don't swim, your back will start going out from all the sitting."

"I'll swim. But what's the diagnosis?"

"Maybe you need glasses."

"Hmm. But my vision is perfect."

"Maybe just reading glasses."

"I have those."

"But you said your vision is perfect."

"You know. Reading glasses don't count."

"Maybe you need stronger ones. Don't buy them from the drugstore."

"Those are for old people, not me!" Nina wailed.

"That's what they all say." Chelsi giggled once more.

"Okay. I'll get my eyes checked out. There's someone I'd like to introduce you to, Chelsi. That feels really good, right there."

Chelsi didn't have any difficulty following this massage-table train of thought. "Like who?"

"A young man. My investigator. His name is Wish."

"You mean, like a blind date? Because I don't do things like that. This muscle between your shoulder and neck is called the trapezius."

"He's such a nice guy," Nina said. "I know you'd have fun. I just—I see the two of you meeting."

"Yeah, you're an old lady of thirty-six, better start match-making for other people," Chelsi said. "What about you?"

"I'm open," Nina said. "Even in my advanced state of decrepitude."

"Interesting that you should talk about this Wish boy. I've been thinking about guys I know, wondering who I could fix *you* up with."

"No need. I'm doing fine through the Internet," Nina said, and they both laughed. Chelsi massaged her legs thoroughly, using the light oil that she had warmed as she rubbed her hands. Nina turned over and Chelsi began on her jaw, which did not want to unclench. Eventually the jaw fell open obediently, though, and hung down toward her chest, doofus-style. The eye muscles said thank you and surrendered. Nina reached the Zen zone.

"That darn buzzer," Chelsi said. She gave Nina a final set of kneading strokes on her shoulders and polished them off with a pat on the hand. "See you outside," she said.

Nina didn't get up right away. She let herself float in this state of well-being, not thinking, not planning, not even feeling guilty about doing nothing.

Finally she opened her eyes to that peculiar luminousness coming through the open window, got off the table, and went to the hook where her jeans and polo shirt hung. Her underwear was on the chair and she stepped into her underpants, noting how supple she felt, how easily her back bent, swearing to herself to exercise more and maybe take up yoga.

She remembered later that she saw a movement from the corner of her eye. Her senses were very acute at that moment, and she noted that the movement came from the screened open window. With an intuition born of this unusual acuity she dove under the massage table, hearing the two knocks at the door that announced Chelsi was coming in at the same time.

A movement. Under the table. Knock knock. It went like that.

Chelsi opened the inner door and came in in her red shorts. Nina was facing her, wearing nothing but lace panties from Victoria's Secret, crouched on the linoleum floor under the table like some half-naked precursor of a human, and their eyes locked. Chelsi's eyebrows began to draw together in puzzlement and her lips parted.

There was a bang, sharp, enormous. A large red hole appeared in Chelsi's right cheek and her expression began to turn from bewilderment to agony. Another bang. Chelsi fell backward against the door, a red stain on her blue shirt, her eyes still open and still puzzled. She looked down at her shirt, tried to raise her hand to her face, but the hand lifted only briefly.

She slid to the ground.

Nina let out a shriek of horror and pain. It echoed around her brain and she thought, Now he'll come in and finish me off too. She saw Chelsi on the floor a few feet away, watching her, her eyes so surprised, so disbelieving, shaking her head slightly even as the blood ran down her face, down her shirt.

Nothing happened during the ensuing longest minute of Nina's life. Just maybe, she heard some slight noise in the parking lot that she translated as the shooter leaving.

Nina crawled the few feet across the floor and grabbed Chelsi by the arm. She dragged her under the table. One eye open now, not two. Chelsi wasn't conscious anymore. She was gasping, leaking blood too fast to survive.

Nina weighed her chances. It seemed to her that if the shooter wanted her enough, he'd come and get her and there was little she could do.

Or he was already gone. Meantime, Chelsi fluttered one eyelid and lay on the floor, legs akimbo.

Nina scooted through the door, duckwalking. Slammed it, leaving poor Chelsi in there. Ran to the front door, slammed it shut, locked it. Ran to the phone. 9-1-1. She had hoped never to dial this number again. She was crying, blubbering, looking around frantically as the dispatcher asked the questions.

She would always remember the tears sending scalding trails down her cheeks, her jaw clenched tight again, where she would always keep it from now on.

Chapter 18

CHELSI'S FUNERAL WAS HELD AT THE Bible Baptist Church just outside Placerville on Mother Lode Drive three days later, in the morning.

The death of a young person defeats some important plan. Babies are thrown into the world with every possibility ahead of them, and gradually their world narrows as they grow and experience and begin to express and produce. Someone very old may die, and it is sad, but the thought comes, They had their time. They had their chance. We saw, they saw, what they became.

But for a young girl to die shockingly, without her chance, without anyone knowing what she might have become, is an injustice as well as a tragedy.

Nina was still fresh and hurting from the assault at Chelsi's office. Throughout the long police questioning that had followed, the reporters' questions, the phone constantly ringing at the house, and the awful talk with Chelsi's father, she kept a grim calm. She accepted Wish's offer to move in for a few days and sleep on the couch at the cabin. He and Bob talked in under-tones while she made sandwiches, lay down on her bed, sat on the deck in the backyard, and watched the trees.

Half the town came to Chelsi's funeral. She had been popular in high school, a basketball player, a star in her drama classes. Many of her friends spoke about her life. Her mother came from Arizona and stood with her father, looking so much like her that Nina could hardly talk to her. Dave Hanna came, sober, shaved, head hanging.

Sergeant Cheney said, "There's some thinking around here that you might have been the intended victim. Placerville PD isn't turning up a scintilla of a motive to kill the young lady. She was very well-liked. Not even a boyfriend for us to take apart."

Nina had just returned to the office. Somehow, Sandy had kept order during her absence, though the pileup of court appearances the following week would be a problem. She had never felt so angry, so grim. These feelings left little room for personal fear.

"I'm protected," she said. "My son is protected."

"It's odd, though. He probably—"

"He or she."

"He or she probably saw you through the window before you dove under the table. If he knew what you looked like, he would have seen that the girl was younger with a different hair color. So maybe he didn't know what you looked like."

"Or maybe he was an amateur, and let off a shot when I took a dive out of panic. If he knew Chelsi wasn't me, why didn't he come in and shoot me?"

Cheney shrugged. "You tell me."

"He must have followed me to the massage place," Nina said. "He must have known what I looked like."

"You say she and her father were the prime movers on the

Hanna wrongful-death action. They pushed the hardest, provided the funding. That's my thinking right now."

"Mine, too," Nina said. "The shooter is keeping track of this case. He waited for it to be dismissed, but then I came in at Chelsi's urging and the case started to open up. He's watching. Here's a list of all the ways he might be watching." She handed Cheney the list he had stopped by to pick up. "Maybe he checked on the file at the clerk's office. Maybe he was in court the day of the dismissal. Maybe James Bova is sharing everything with some murderous significant other. Maybe it's one of the witnesses."

"Why would you think that?" Cheney said. He had one of those heavy-lidded gazes, mostly caused by the way he slumped in her chair and kept his hands folded on his stomach, that gives the false impression of somnolence. Behind him, Sandy leaned against the door.

"They didn't want to be involved."

"But they were victims, too. You think one of those Boston kids would care that much about having to come back here and do some talking?" Then he nodded slowly. "Okay. The robbery wasn't simple, that's what you're thinking."

"You know how often the robber knows the victim in some way, or there's a hassle between them. I'm thinking it's at least possible that one or more of those kids has some idea why they were being ripped off, and you have to talk to them. I already gave you the third witness's address. The one named Wakefield, who lives in Washington State."

"It's getting complicated," Cheney said.

"What do you mean, complicated?"

"The Boston kids' lawyer went to the Boston PD and offered to make a statement there. They're not willing to come to California. Sorry."

"Are you going there?"

"Someone is," Cheney said. "This has to be coordinated with

Placerville PD." The door to the outer office opened and Sandy disappeared, checking on whoever had come in.

"They're material witnesses! Why can't you have them arrested and—"

"We don't have enough to do that," Cheney said softly. "We don't have any real idea if they know anything at all. According to your tape, they don't. And you taped them without their knowledge anyway."

"They do," Nina said, her jaw set. "They have a lot more to say. This is how I see it, Sergeant. Either Chelsi was killed so that the case would go away, or the attempt was made on my life for the same reason. It's about the Hanna case, it has to be."

"What does your client want to do? He's the girl's uncle, right?"

"I don't know what my client wants to do."

"You haven't—"

"He was arrested for his third DUI on the road last night, after the funeral. He had gone to a bar and got drunk. He's in the Placerville jail. He's an alcoholic. He's going to have a public defender on that charge, and in the meantime he doesn't call me and I'm not going to call him. Because he hasn't got the guts to fight."

"Better hurry up with your case, then."

"What about your case?" Nina said. "What forensic evidence has turned up in Chelsi's death? Even on a drive-by, somebody must have seen something."

"We're working on it."

"No sign of the gun?"

"All we have are the two bullets," Cheney said. "Because the killer couldn't go in and dig them out of that poor little girl's body. And they're valuable bullets. Preliminary tests on them show they are not from the same gun that killed Sarah Hanna."

"It has to be the same person!"

"We'll ask him why he needed two guns, when we find him," Cheney said. "Maybe he threw away the gun he used to kill Sarah Hanna two years ago, and bought another one recently. We'll look into that."

Sandy said, "Sorry to interrupt. Your eight o'clock is here. And your eight-thirty is, too."

"I'll be right out."

"Good luck," Cheney said, nodding a couple of times and then hauling himself up. "Keep in touch."

Lunch hour. Nina closeted herself in the conference room with the computer and the law books. How could she force the witnesses to come to California to testify at a trial?

She started with Out-of-State Witnesses, Civil Subpoenas.

The Code of Civil Procedure was clear. Witnesses in a civil case can't be subpoenaed to appear at a trial from outside the jurisdiction.

Material Witnesses. Nothing in the books that would help anyone but the police, and the police weren't ready to use that power yet.

Flight from Jurisdiction. Those precedents only applied to defendants. Apparently witnesses can flee as far as they want. No problem, she thought angrily, just split and leave all that chaos behind.

She could go take their depositions in their states, but it would require a court commission. And that wouldn't bring them to California for trial.

If only the witnesses were defendants. She leaned back, put her arms behind her head, thought of the Ace High Lodge, a defendant because of the long reach of the legal concept of negligence.

Negligence means you owe somebody a duty of care, even if

it only amounts to a duty to act like a reasonable person around them. Negligence means that your act or omission results in unintended harm to that somebody. In the case of Ace High, the creative interpretation of negligence said you had a duty to keep your premises secure, and if you omitted to do that, and somebody got hurt, you were negligent.

What if the witnesses had been negligent in some sense? No, they had been victims. But what if—

Now she was thinking furiously, flipping through Witkin and looking for—

Yes. A robbery. The victim, defending himself. The assailant, shooting an innocent bystander during the struggle. What if the victim used unnecessary force on the assailant, or did something so rash in the course of self-defense that the victim could legally be said to have acted negligently when a bystander got hurt?

There were California cases, rare. A case in which the victim wrested the gun from the assailant and accidentally shot a bystander. That hadn't happened here.

Though how did she know it hadn't happened here? She went into her office, came back with her copy of the tape of Silke and Raj, and played it.

Wakefield had rushed the guy. Silke said so. There were shots, and Silke and Raj ran. The gun was missing, so who would know who actually shot Sarah Hanna?

"Could have been Wakefield," she thought aloud. She listened to the tape again. Even if Wakefield hadn't shot Sarah Hanna himself, had he been negligent in rushing an assailant with a gun?

You could allege that he was negligent. You could allege a lot of things, and at this stage of Dave Hanna's decrepit case, at this time when a beautiful young woman had been killed for some obscure gratification, you might as well get creative.

What about Silke and Raj? How could she allege that they

were negligent, too? That was tougher—they hadn't done anything but get robbed, and run.

On the other hand, you can allege anything. Let the other side come in and defend, in a California court.

I'm going to force the issue, she thought, bring them back. Excitement lodged next to the sorrow and rage in her heart. Force the law to behave the way she needed it to behave. Stretch the negligence idea like the biggest piece of chewing gum ever, all the way to Boston and Washington State. Bring the kids back kicking and screaming, and find the shooter through them.

Sandy knocked.

"Coming."

"Find anything?" she asked as Nina passed her.

"Could you find an order shortening time request, and model points and authorities? I'll give you some facts and cases and you plug it in. I need to get it to Flaherty today for signing. And call Betty Jo Puckett. Say I'll meet her at the courthouse at four-thirty. Tell her it's an emergency motion relating to the witnesses in the Hanna case."

"Can't it wait until tomorrow?"

"What else do I have today?"

"Interrogatories to answer. Demurrer to a complaint. Four big phone messages."

"How many of those can wait until morning?"

Sandy tugged at her lower lip and said, "If you don't make two of those phone calls, you're going to lose two cases."

"It's a deal. I'll make those calls." She went to her desk, sat down, made the calls and made them stick, and felt a hot rush of an emotion so foreign to her that at first she couldn't give it a name.

Ah. Vengefulness!

So this was what it felt like to be vengeful. Hard, fevered, superhumanly focused, like the skull is grinning inside the head, anticipating what it's about to do . . . how interesting that personal fear had no place.

It's a matter of honor, and behind that is the fact of humiliation. You don't kill a human being in front of me and not deal with me, you son of a bitch, she told the shooter in her mind.

Sandy buzzed. "Okay, I have the Petition for Order Shortening Time, and I have a draft order here, and I have model points and authorities. But what's the motion going to be? I need a title."

"It's a Motion to Amend the Complaint," Nina said. "I'm going to add three new defendants after Shooter Doe I."

There was a pause while Sandy digested this.

"And pull out three subpoenas for deposing defendants. I'm going to ask Flaherty to personally sign them."

Nina opened the file and looked at the complaint in the case of *Hanna v. Ace High Lodge and Does I–X.* Doe I would be changed to the shooter's name, when they found the shooter. She considered once more what she was about to do, suing three people who were going to be rather perturbed about it. And they had Braun and Branson to object.

So what? They had dodged involvement too long. They had no right to complain that she was getting dodgy, too.

She wrote on her legal pad, "Plaintiff David Hanna hereby substitutes for John Does II, III, and IV in the complaint, the following-named defendants."

"Silke Kilmer." A Jane Doe, actually.

"Sumaraj Das."

"Elliott Wakefield."

She looked out her window, at the black and lowering sky. November now ruled in the mountains, harsh and cold.

They were in for it.

Chapter 19

THE LEGAL SYSTEM HAD ALWAYS VEERED toward the person with the strongest conviction. If a lawyer believed in a case very strongly, the usual obstacles fell away. That made it a good system, so long as the lawyer's purpose was honorable, and that quality of honor would shine through, or it wouldn't. Nina's conviction overrode both Betty Jo and Judge Flaherty.

"All we want is out," Betty Jo told the judge. "We are willing to pay the price. We are bystanders as much as the lady who was shot. Your Honor, please, just approve our settlement agreement and let Ms. Reilly pursue the real malfeasors."

Great word, *malfeasors*. Nina wouldn't have thought Betty Jo was up to a word like that.

Flaherty was about fifty. Nina knew that he worried about his heart, and how long he could continue dealing with all the stressful bullshit he was exposed to all day, every day. He didn't like dodgy legal moves. He flipped through the file, finding no solutions there, then looked out the window, where rain fell. The enclosed paneled courtroom felt cozy after the drive through the dark afternoon.

"This ought to be a criminal matter," he told Nina. "This court, and you and Ms. Puckett, shouldn't be the ones trying to pursue this."

"But here we are, Your Honor."

"Two murders," Flaherty said, shaking his head. "A civil case. Wrongful-death cases aren't meant for this sort of thing. A senior citizen develops septicemia in her nursing home from bad care, and dies. That's a wrongful-death case."

"But here we are."

"I don't understand why the police aren't taking a more active role."

"Me neither," Nina said. "But they aren't."

"Maybe I should at least let the motel out."

"Maybe the motel's involved."

"You haven't presented any facts in that regard," Betty Jo protested.

"But two people are dead. The plaintiff needs, and the plaintiff deserves, every latitude the law permits. Let this case proceed, Your Honor. Let the motel remain as defendant. Allow me to bring the witnesses back to California to be deposed."

"They have a lawyer. You didn't serve him. You could have faxed him. I'm not sure about this ex parte stuff." Flaherty appeared uncertain, but ready to blow the way the strongest wind blew.

"Technically, he's not retained to represent them as defendants, to my knowledge," Nina said. "Naturally I will cooperate fully with him when I'm notified that he will be involved in that capacity." She turned back to her main point, adding urgently, "We have to find out who did this. The murder of Chelsi Freeman is an affront to the court. It's an attempt to intimidate us into not pursuing the complaint. It's the one thing, the one thing, Judge, we can never permit. Our justice system can't flee from intimidation."

Betty Jo said, "Your Honor, we see the steamroller and we would like to step to the side in time. Please. Let us out. We're just a building, a series of room numbers. We don't want to go two-dimensional during whatever attack Ms. Reilly has in mind."

"Two-dimensional?" Flaherty said. "Oh, flattened."

"That's tough," Nina said. "You could almost feel sorry for the Ace High clerk, E-mailing her boyfriend while a mother-to-be lost her life. She should have been at her desk. She should have called 911 sooner. Or how about that cul-de-sac, that tight vending-machine space, isolated and unsafe, set up by the Ace High. Or the three robberies in the past year on the premises."

"Whatever our culpability," Betty Jo said, "it's not worth more than the settlement we have already offered. A failure to accept the settlement at this late date will amount to bad faith."

"Then bad faith it is," Nina said. "The case has changed. It's about two deaths now, and nobody skates."

"We're good for fifty thousand, Your Honor. I thought Mr. Hanna took our offer. Where is Mr. Hanna, by the way? Hmm?" She turned toward Nina, her eyes narrow. Betty Jo was as aggravated as hell, and Nina didn't blame her.

"Tell me again. What's the problem with letting this party out of the case?" Flaherty asked Nina.

"We don't know enough yet. We don't know if someone from the Lodge might be involved somehow," Nina said. "Mr. Hanna told me on the phone this morning that he understands we cannot go forward with a settlement right now."

Betty Jo folded her arms and looked over the top of her specs at the judge. In a hard tone that Nina hadn't heard before, she said, "Well, then, the settlement offer's withdrawn, Your Honor.

It's off. It's as off as three-day-old chicken left in a hot car trunk. We'll stay in and request our attorney's fees at the right time." She didn't look at Nina.

"Then there's nothing before the court with regard to the settlement," Nina said.

"I can still dismiss the case next week based on the court's discretion, since two years will have passed," Flaherty said.

"And let the whole world know this court bows to a killer?" Nina asked. Her words seemed to resound through the courtroom. The clerk looked scandalized and the lawyers lounging in their chairs, waiting for their own arguments to be heard, shifted and whispered.

"No need to grandstand, Counsel," Flaherty said. "You still have another week. The court will consider any additional documents filed during that time that tend to show progress in bringing the matter to trial."

"Very well," Nina said. "Then I assume the court will execute the subpoenas requiring the newly named defendants to be deposed pursuant to our papers?"

"Any objection?" Flaherty asked Betty Jo.

"We're just the sacrificial lamb on the side altar, Your Honor," Betty Jo said. "Let's get on with the immolation."

"Immolation?" Flaherty said. "Do you object or not?"

"No objection. Bring 'em on."

"Then it is so ordered. The signed papers will be available from the clerk's office in an hour or so, Ms. Reilly."

"Thank you, Your Honor."

"Ms. Reilly—"

"Yes, Your Honor?"

"Be careful."

"Thank you, Your Honor."

Nina went out to the hall, Betty Jo at her heels. She tapped Nina on the shoulder. "Wait," she said. "I have a question for you."

"You should have raised it in front of the judge."

"I thought about it. Thought about asking if your own client approved you throwing away fifty grand. Then I realized, no way did he approve this. You're here blowin' off the settlement, and your client's in jail, 'cause he's a sick alcoholic. Who's backin' you? That's the question. Well, it's none of my business. Bottom line, you're never going to get a dime out of the Ace High now. I warned you."

"It's worth it, to have everybody still sitting together in the pot."

"And you're the little cannibal, stirrin' it all up with a big wood spoon."

"Sorry, Betty Jo."

Betty Jo shrugged. "I'll just tell Jimmy you've gone crazy. He'll understand."

Nina felt a rush of anger. She said, "A friend was shot to death three feet away from me. I am going to find and take down the shooter. I want you and your client with me on this. We can find the shooter and deal with him together. He's caused you as much harm as he has me."

"You want to ride piggyback on the Lodge," Betty Jo said, unmoved. "That's not an option. I won't let Jimmy crouch down so you can take a ride on his money and his business. You're on your own."

"I would think you'd like to find the guy who shot up the Lodge."

"You'd think wrong. The best strategy for the Lodge is to end all this. Every time you make a move, the *Tribune* reports it and Jimmy gets cancellations."

"I thought you were—" Nina turned away.

"What? Your mama?" This stung.

"No. An honorable . . . an honorable lawyer."

"You're a funny one," Betty Jo said. "Look, nothing personal.

You're causin' me a lot of trouble, but I forgive you because you can still use the word *honor* in a court of law. I'm startin' to figure you out. You're an idealist, and you're a romantic, and you have some ideas about lawyers being gentlemen champions on white horses."

"I do not," Nina said.

"White horses with gold stirrups, and a world just beggin' to be saved."

"I'm starting to figure you out, too," Nina said, "and it's too bad. A bright mind, a lot of life experience, and a strong desire not to rock the *Good Ship Lollipop* you find yourself sailing on. I was thinking you and I might become friends. It's too bad, it really is."

Betty Jo gave her a measured look. "No, I don't think we'd ever be friends. You take things too personally." She gave her umbrella a firm shake and opened it as they reached the portico.

"Yeah. And you don't take them personally enough. I'll let you know when I depose the three kids, so you can attend."

"Do that." They had reached the parking area. Rain fell straight down, mercifully free from wind. Betty Jo drove a Porsche Cayenne SUV, burgundy, water beading on its expensive hood. It let out a discreet burp as she used the remote to unlock it, and she swung into it. "Well, fuck you and the horse you rode in on," she said with a trace of her former joviality. She closed the umbrella and tossed it into the back seat, then slammed the door.

Nina went to her beat-up white Bronco a few stalls away and got in. Betty Jo purred past her onto Johnson Boulevard, her profile vague behind the water-smeared driver's-side window. But it seemed to Nina that on her way past, she gave Nina the finger.

Thus ended a beautiful friendship, which had barely begun, immolated, as Betty Jo might have said, on an altar to a blind Greek goddess who holds a set of scales. At least Flaherty had given her what she needed. Nina drove off, depressed because she liked Betty Jo, thinking about her unexpectedly rich vocabulary.

She had said Nina was trying to "ride piggyback."

That word again. Nina remembered the dream of a couple of weeks before, when the case was just starting up. How had it gone? A scary old lady trying to climb on Nina's back. All she wanted was a piggyback ride.

Some of her most important cases began with dreams, dreams that somehow meshed later with the case. They didn't exactly provide clues—she didn't believe in premonitions or any of that other New Age magic—but they sometimes did seem to pull something from her subconscious about the dynamics of the case.

She passed the small shopping center near her office, her wipers whapping across the windshield as the rain fell faster. The Starlake Building looked solid and warmly lit as she pulled into the lot. The *Titanic* had also looked solid and warmly lit. A killer was hiding somewhere, maybe still at Tahoe. It wouldn't be wise to relax her guard . . .

What did it mean, to ride piggyback? To use another's strength. To oppress someone, sit on them. To be an opportunist.

She shrugged mentally. If the dream meant something, it was something still in the future.

The Bronco door swung open and she struggled with her umbrella. What, really, was going on? Good thing the shooter couldn't read her mind right now, rife with speculation, unreined and vulnerable.

Several long days went by. Two things happened in the Hanna case: The new defendants were served with the Amended Complaint and Notices of Deposition, in Boston and Seattle; and

Dave Hanna was released from jail, not without having pled guilty and having his driver's license taken away, among other punishments.

Chelsi's father called as she worked through a stack of phone messages late in the morning. Rain still fell at lake level, with a blizzard above seven thousand feet on the cloud-concealed peaks ringing the lake. The radio in Sandy's office was predicting the ski resorts would open in a couple of weeks. Winter was lowering itself like a hearty lover upon the town.

"Dave won't answer his phone," Roger Freeman said. "I went over there, but he'd gone somewhere. A bar, probably."

"How are you?" Nina asked.

"Not too good. Chelsi's mom called me last night from Arizona. She was thinking about her and started feeling like it's all my fault. She wanted to take Chelsi to live with her when she left with her boyfriend years ago, but I fought her and got custody. If I hadn't, Chelsi would be sunbathing in Tucson right now. My beautiful little girl. Excuse me." He set the phone down and she heard snuffling and nose-blowing. Nina steeled herself not to fall into her own grief about Chelsi. She could grieve later, after she went to bed.

"She's very sad right now, Roger, and not thinking clearly," Nina said in a matter-of-fact tone when he picked up again. "You mustn't take it personally. It's not your fault."

"I have to ask—are you going to stay with the case? I couldn't blame you—you almost got killed yourself."

"I'll stay with it as long as Dave can stand me," Nina said.

"I'm glad to hear it. It would seem like this monster got his way, if we stopped now. But I'm worried that Dave doesn't understand that. He had already spent that settlement money in his mind. He's not too happy with you."

"I have to keep the motel in, until the case solidifies a little more. That's the way it is. That's my professional opinion."

"Fine, just fine, but I don't think Dave agrees."

"I'll come down there and talk to him."

"Don't come. If he sees you, he'll fire you. He needs money to pay his DUI fine and a bunch of back bills, Nina. He gets his disability, but he spends it on booze in the first week. I keep thinking he's not responsible anymore, can't take care of himself. I keep thinking—about what I told you, that he needs, you know..."

"A conservator?" Nina said. "I think that's what you mean. Someone to take care of his money for him."

"I would be willing to do that."

"Just thinking aloud, and this shouldn't be construed to be a piece of legal advice, but a conservator would take care of his legal affairs, too."

"Like deciding whether or not to stay with this case," Rog said.

"But I can't advise you about that."

"Why not? Aren't you supposed to be looking out for his best interests?"

"I suggest you consult another lawyer down there."

"I will. Right away. Nina?"

"Yes?"

"Could we let Dave out and bring me in as the plaintiff? I'd be a much better plaintiff."

"Believe me, I've thought about it, Roger," Nina said. "You have a cause of action for the loss of your sister, but it's not very strong, not like Dave's legal position. And it's too late in the game."

"Could I sue for Chelsi's death?"

"Sue who?"

"I don't know. The John Does."

"It's all wrapped up in Dave's case," Nina said. "He has to hang on."

"Okay. I'll do what I can to help you. You need another check?"

"I'm afraid the bill's in the mail."

"Don't worry, I'll pay it. This is my daughter and my sister we're talking about." He hung up. Nina walked out to Sandy's office. Fresh coffee was brewing in the espresso maker through the half-open door of the conference room. Sandy and Wish sat at the table in there.

"I was just about to call you," Sandy said.

"I never smelled anything so good." Nina went to the coffee and started steaming some milk. "You know, it's odd how allies turn into enemies and how new allies appear just when you need them."

"If you say so," Wish said. He was so soaked that rivulets of water were coursing onto the rug from his pants. His hair was plastered to his head, and his eyes were wild.

"Why, what is it, Wish?"

"I just heard from Ed Vasquez in Boston. He served the couple yesterday, then watched to see what they would do. They made a trip to the law offices of John Branson a couple of hours ago, about two P.M. Boston time—that's eleven A.M. here—"

"Too bad," Nina said. "I was hoping they would retain some charming, reasonable Harvard lady lawyer. I've already met that guy."

"Listen," Wish said. "They came out of the law offices, which are located on Boylston Street near Boston Common, at 2:35 Boston time. They walked to the side street where they had parked the car, a blue 2001 Corvette. The guy—Raj—got in the driver's seat and the girl got in the other side. Ed was watching from across the street in his car. After about ten seconds they jumped out and ran into a bank right there on the street."

Nina was still standing, her cup in her hand. "I'm getting a headache," she said. "I just know I am. Go on."

"The 'Vette blew up. That's what Ed said."

"It blew up?" Sandy said. "Ed said it blew up?"

"Exploded. Some people passing by got hit by glass. The bank windows were blown in. The car jumped about ten feet in the air and landed on its roof in the middle of the street."

"The couple?" Nina said.

"Unharmed."

Sandy and Nina looked at each other. Nina said, "Thank God."

"They came out a minute later, looked around, then left. They flagged down a taxi and—"

"Their car blew up, you say?" Sandy said. "Is this a joke?"

"I am not kidding, Mom."

"Someone went all the way to Boston to kill them," Nina said. "Right after they got served." She burned her tongue on the coffee, needed it too much to care, and drank some down, destroying a few taste buds in the process. "Because they got served. Someone knows exactly what's going on in this case, minute by minute."

"You make it sound like we have a mole here at the firm," Sandy said. "Which consists of you and me and Willis, so I don't think so."

Wish was nodding fast. "It was the next morning after they were served, Nina! It has to be about our case! Anyway, so then they got in a taxi and Ed followed them. They went directly to the airport in Boston—Logan—and they went to the Lufthansa counter and bought tickets for a flight to Frankfurt, Germany, leaving in four hours. Ed called as soon as he could. They're still in the waiting room, but they're about to board—he couldn't call right away—"

"They're going a long, long way away," Nina said. "Maybe they should."

"Shall we call the police in Boston? Try to stop them?"

Nina said, "My thought exactly."

"Have Ed tell them everything?"

"Sure. Have him call right away and report that the owners of that Corvette are fleeing the country."

While they waited for Ed Vasquez to call back, Sandy made Wish take off his sweater and shirt and gave him a sweatshirt she had tucked in the drawer. They all drank espresso. Cars sloshed through the traffic light on the boulevard outside. Although it was barely past noon, night seemed to be falling, the day so dark the streetlights began to sputter on.

Nina went to the ladies' bathroom at the end of the hall and took two ibuprofen, washed her face, forced a yawn or two.

When she came back, Wish's long face told her all she needed to know.

"The police didn't make it, Nina. Red tape. Ed doesn't really know why. He couldn't do anything to stop them himself. They're at thirty thousand feet by now. I'm sorry."

Sandy said, "How bad is it?"

Nina said, "I'm going into my office now. And I'm going to think about things. I'll be back out in fifteen minutes with assignments." She closed her door, gravitating as always to the window. Mist overspread the marsh leading toward the lake and she could hear rain pouring down the drainpipes, like Raj Das and Silke Kilmer, down the pipes and out.

Chapter 20

A MAN RANG THE DOORBELL AT ELLIOTT'S house on Vashon Island.
Elliott rushed downstairs. His father was coming from the
kitchen, walking slowly, having a good day. He held a finger to his
lips and his father said, "What's gotten into you?" but in a whisper.

Peering through the peephole, he saw a stranger in a black
windbreaker and jeans on the porch, carrying a clipboard, looking at his father's roses.

"Yes?" he had opened the door a crack.

"Oh, hi. Mr. Elliott Wakefield?" The man smiled and held
out his hand to shake hands, and Elliott said "Uh-huh," and
opened the door wider, automatically polite. Instead of a hand, a
manila envelope full of papers came through the door.

"You'vebeenservedwithlegalpapersandyoushouldconsult-
anattorneyrightaway." The smile never left his face. He turned and
jogged back down the path.

Elliott closed the door.

"Why, El, you're as white as a sheet," his father said.

"It's all right, Pop."

"Who was that?"

"Just someone bringing me some papers on a consulting job. Pop, listen to me. You have to let me open the door. Don't answer when I'm not home."

His father looked stricken. "What is happening?"

"Just—someone is trying to find me. It's a business thing. We have to be careful."

"Who was it that called you last night and got you so upset?"

"An associate." Silke, calling from Germany.

"Are you in trouble with the law? The IRS or something?"

"No."

"Well? What is it, then? Don't try to protect me."

"I have to go to a meeting today," Elliott said. "In the city. Please. Don't answer the door when I'm away."

"Take the ferry to Seattle?" He was tiring. A smell of burning bacon came from the kitchen.

"We'll have breakfast first." Pop nodded and went back to his cooking. Elliott showered and shaved, and when he came back down, dressed in a heavy sweater and jeans, he managed to deflect his father's questions pretty well. He made sure his father was tucked into his favorite chair by the fireplace and that Gloria was on her way before leaving.

He hadn't even opened the envelope. On the ferry he pulled it out of his backpack. It came from the Law Offices of Nina F. Reilly, Esq. When he read the contents, he groaned.

Now what? Wasn't it enough that the shooter had tried to kill Silke and Raj, was probably looking for him, and he had to go talk to these corporate honchos today when he wasn't feeling well?

At the ferry landing he pulled out his Seattle map. The building he needed was right downtown, only a few blocks away, and the day looked clear and cool. He could see the snowcap of Mount Rainier floating in the eastern sky. He walked past the Market and up the hill, turning right at the light. He felt frightened, but he really wanted to hear what these people had to say to him, so he trudged inside and went up to the fourteenth floor, to a law firm.

Oriental rugs. Mahogany reception desk, and a smart-looking receptionist who took his name. Uneasily, knowing he was out of his depth, he sat on the edge of one of the upholstered chairs and stared at the law books crawling up the walls all around. The place could have been empty for all the sound he heard. The receptionist murmured something into her phone, and a few minutes later two men and a woman strolled down the hall toward him.

"Elliott! It's great to see you again," Professor Braun said. He had lost weight, and it felt wrong to see him in this setting, but his handshake was firm. "Let me introduce the gentleman who let us borrow his office today, Mr. Phelps."

"Nice to meet you." Mr. Phelps had a shiny watch and white cuffs. He was middle-aged and corpulent, his handshake friendly, his eyes guarded.

"And this is Patty Hightower, executive vice president of the firm I consult with, as I mentioned on the phone, Elliott." Patty Hightower shook his hand. She was awfully young to be a VP, very blond and very slim, wearing pointed high heels. In fact, she was extremely good-looking, and the way she was looking at him made Elliott plunge his hands into his pockets and look away.

"Nice of you to come over today, Elliott," she said with a smile that showed she understood his thoughts.

"Let's go in, eh?" They all followed Phelps into a private office with a wall-sized view of the San Juan Islands, boats and ferries dotting dark blue Puget Sound.

"How have you been?" the professor asked when they were seated in the leather chairs surrounding the polished table. "Miss the campus?"

"Uh, I'm fine. Thank you. How are you?"

"Getting along." The professor had never been a big talker and without a blackboard didn't seem to know what to do with his hands. Elliott thought with a start, He's nervous! Which made Elliott more nervous, which made him wonder why he had ever let the professor talk him into coming over here when so much else was going on. "I've told Patty here what a fine student you were, your areas of interest, and XYC is looking for someone like you."

"So this is—this is a job interview?"

"Not for a job where you'd ever have to leave home, Elliott," Patty Hightower said. "Not that you wouldn't be welcome on Route 128 anytime." She sat down next to him, crossing her legs, which were encased in sheer black stockings. "We're looking for consultants. Part-time, and you never have to go anywhere."

"I'm not really looking—"

"People as accomplished as you rarely are. We have to talk to knowledgeable people, like the professor, and find you rather than the other way around."

"What kind of business is this?"

"Internet security," Patty Hightower said.

"Like RSA?" RSA was a well-known Internet-security firm.

"Right. We handle financial encryption for some customers you have definitely heard of."

"What does the name 'XYC' come from?"

Patty smiled. "From the x,y axis. Plus 'Corporation.' We thought the abbreviation XYC would look good when the stock went public."

"I mentioned your work regarding factoring large numbers

to Patty," Professor Braun said. "Not in any detail, Elliott. Just the general direction you're heading in."

Patty Hightower said, "We'd like to hire you to help us keep the Web safe for credit transactions, Elliott. And for many other purposes."

"I don't know a thing about that stuff," Elliott said. "I do pure math. Combinatorics. Analysis. Number theory. I don't even have a doctorate."

"But you have some very promising results, don't you? An algorithm that efficiently factors large numbers? That predicts the primes? I can hardly believe I'm saying this. It's been a Holy Grail for mathematics for so long—my field is information technology. But my B.S. is in math. Princeton. I have to congratulate you, Elliott."

"I haven't even published any of my work. How do you know so much about it? Professor, what have you said about my work?"

"Just that I think it's going to be ground-breaking, and that XYC would be smart to help you find the means to continue."

"And we have a friend of yours consulting for us. She mentioned you independently of the professor. Carleen Flint."

Carleen knew a lot about Elliott's work, unlike the professor. She knew all about the blackjack, about Silke, about the function. She also knew about Elliott's notebook. Elliott's fright was increasing.

"I feel like you've been watching me," he said. "Strange things have been happening lately."

Patty looked at the lawyer, at the professor. "I'm not sure what you mean. You've come to our attention and we'd like to have you on board along with the many other very talented mathematicians who work for us. I'm not trying to overwhelm you, Elliott. As a matter of fact, I wish we hadn't met in a big office, in such a formal way. Would you like to go down to the Market and have a little lunch? Just you and me? My treat."

The professor was nodding, but Elliott said, "I'm sorry, but I have to get back across the bay soon. My father's not well. Why don't you finish saying whatever you came to say right here." Patty looked disappointed for a moment, but she leaned forward so she was very close to Elliott and he felt suddenly hot.

"A million dollars for signing with us, Elliott," she breathed. "And a million dollars per year salary for the next three years. Work under our umbrella, that's all we ask."

Elliott, stunned, said, "That's a lot of money. I don't understand." Then he said, "You mean you would own my work?" He remembered Silke talking to him the afternoon of the shooting two years before. What had she said? That companies like XYC would want to suppress his work.

He recoiled, and Patty saw it; a pearly tooth bit into her glossy lower lip.

"Would I still be able to publish?" he asked.

"After our legal department has had a look. Perhaps not everything."

"Would you want all my work to date?"

"That would be part of the signing bonus, yes. Payment for your work to date on prime number theory."

"Your company would own my work? Have control over my work?"

"In a manner of speaking. And you would be free, in just a few years, financially secure, able to spend your life working without worries, your father taken care of . . ."

"Professor, you know I'm not worth that kind of money."

"But you are, Elliott. You are working in precisely the most crucial field of applied mathematics right now. You are ahead of everyone else. I believe in you. I want you to succeed. Your work will be of enormous importance in keeping the Internet safe. The use of large primes for encryption is the basis of the whole emerging global economic system. There is no mathematician in the world today who has come as close to you to being able to decrypt our system by factoring the products of enormous primes. Frankly, I'm in awe. The Internet has come to depend on—"

"On keeping my work a secret," Elliott blurted.

"Not at all. The focus of your work would change for a few years, to preventing attacks on public-key code systems. It's a very laudable way of using your expertise. I'd enjoy working with you, and Carleen is looking forward to a collegial relationship. You'd have every resource imaginable. You'll love being a part of XYC. Many MIT graduates have decided to join us. You're a very lucky young man. And a very gifted one. We'd be proud to have you."

It was a heck of a speech. Elliott looked at the professor, at the ascetic face with the high cheekbones and the long fingers that he had watched, mesmerized, through several seminars, performing magic with chalk. Braun was the only professor at MIT who had shown any interest in his work. He had tried to help Elliott when he was sick.

He imagined it, working through some of the problems he was having with the help of Professor Braun, having his full attention. He believed in Elliott, and had arranged for him to join him.

"I am grateful," he said. "Professor, your interest means a lot to me."

The professor breathed out and said, "You had me worried there for a minute."

"I'm grateful, but I can't join you, Professor."

Braun said, frowning, "I don't quite know how to respond to that, Elliott. Are you sure you appreciate what Patty has come all this way to offer you?"

"All she's offering is money," Elliott said. "I want to expand human knowledge. So this would include buying up all my mathematical work to date?"

"Only work related to prime numbers. The work summarized in the notebook you keep. Carleen mentioned it."

Now he was fighting full panic. His notebook! Years of his blood!

"N-no way," Elliott said.

"I beg your pardon?" Patty Hightower said.

"I'm going home. Please don't contact me again."

Patty Hightower held up a hand, and the professor sat back in his chair. She said, "Nobody else will make you a better offer, if that's what you're thinking. We could actually go higher. A two-million-dollar signing bonus. How's that sound?" The atmosphere of the room had changed. Now Elliott saw the three of them very differently, as though they were shape-shifters who had suddenly become predatory, malign. He jumped up and grabbed his backpack.

"So I'm Hippasus," he said.

"Hippasus?" Professor Braun looked startled. Then he let out an incredulous laugh.

"Your days as a card counter are numbered. How are you going to take care of your father?" Phelps said from the door, which he was blocking.

Red fog clouded Elliott's eyes. He said, "Did you arrange the robbery? The one at Tahoe? Was it to get my notebook? Did you hire the man with the gun? He's looking for me." A new flood of images made him shout, "Did you kill that girl at Tahoe last week? Try to kill my friends?"

"Take it easy!" Professor Braun said. "What are all these accusations? This isn't the Mafia! We're a business!"

"You didn't answer my questions. Did you? Did you?"

"Of course not," Patty Hightower said. "Wait! Don't go yet. We have to . . . Stop him!"

But when he pushed Phelps, the lawyer shrugged and stepped aside, and no one ran after him, no burly security guard chased him down the fourteen flights of stairs, no one stopped him as he rushed breathless from the building into the rational coffee-scented Seattle morning.

Leaning one hand against the granite wall of a building to support himself, he reached inside his jacket and felt the reassuring bulk of his notebook over his heart. He felt shaky. The people walking by on the street paid no attention to him.

Was he thinking straight, though? Confusion overwhelmed him.

Hippasus. The Pythagoreans had murdered Hippasus for telling a secret that undermined their system.

He covered his eyes with his hands and rocked a little. The professor must know how many nights Elliott had lain awake in bed, imagining the joy, the acclaim, when his proof was finished. His work didn't just belong to him, it was a permanent advance in human understanding. Knowing all this had allowed Elliott to work endlessly, to give it everything. How many times had he fantasized about Professor Braun reading his proof in the *Journal of Mathematics*, appreciating it, thrilled that his student had come so far!

His work was all he had. What trick was the universe playing on him now, that such a hard-won discovery had become such a threat to the powerful?

Silke would never love him, and his work would be stolen and destroyed. His father was dying. Wherever he looked, he saw failure and disappointment.

He was rocking a little as he stood against the building, getting some glances now.

Have to get out of here, he thought. Can't go home. But—Pop! He started walking blindly up the busy street.

As he turned a corner, he pulled out his cell phone to call Silke and tell her everything, get her advice.

No answer. She was in some tiny town on the Rhine more than six thousand miles away. She couldn't help.

I'll hide it, he thought. The notebook came first. Silke had told him the night before that he should stay home and keep his guard up. Was it all he could do, stay home knowing they would have to come for him, like Hippasus?

"Hallo?"

"Hello? Is this Silke Kilmer?"

"Who's calling?" the voice responded in English.

"Ms. Kilmer, this is Nina Reilly, calling from California."

A pause. "Sorry, I don't want to talk to you."

"Are you represented by counsel?"

"A lawyer? Not anymore, since we came here."

"Then please, give me a moment of your time."

"How did you get my number?"

"You told me you came from Heddesheim. You're staying with your parents, I take it." It was eleven at night, and Nina lay on her bed in her kimono, practicing law. Germany was nine hours ahead.

Silke Kilmer said in a voice so low Nina almost couldn't catch it over the transatlantic static, "Do you know what happened to us? Why we left the U.S.?"

"Yes. An explosion. You weren't hurt?"

"A miracle. The car smelled wrong. Like a bad aftershave. I don't know. I said, 'Raj, someone's been in here.' He panicked, thank God, and dragged me out and we went running. It must have been set off with a remote trigger. The man was waiting not far away. I suppose he watched us get in and he was looking down or something, and didn't see us run from the passenger side, and set it off. We shouldn't be alive."

"I'm very glad you're all right."

"So. You can understand, this lawsuit of yours—so long as the man is at large, we cannot help."

"He'll stay at large unless you do help. Another person has died. One of the people who helped bring this lawsuit."

"Why are you pushing this?" Silke said. "I don't understand people like you. This thing is ruining my life. I had to leave school."

Nina said, "You don't have to understand. There is a court order requiring your presence at a deposition in ten days here at Lake Tahoe. I am calling to offer you and Mr. Das traveling funds."

"You make me laugh. We're not going anywhere. We'll be killed. Your police are letting this man run amok."

"Then help us get him."

"You have the head of a mule, Miss Reilly. I admire you for staying there yourself. But I'm not brave like that."

"Elliott's been served too," Nina said. "Are you going to let him travel here all alone?"

"He won't come."

"Then I'll get a judgment against him and you and Raj that will compromise your futures for years to come," Nina said. She wasn't too sure she could do that, but it wasn't completely impossible.

Another pause. The faint crackling continued. Nina imagined phone cables laid across the still, freezing floor of the Atlantic, her words flung like pellets toward the woman in Germany.

It was probably all done by satellite anyway. Who could keep up with technology?

"Elliott isn't well," Silke said finally. "He has had some psychiatric problems. He doesn't deal with stress very well. Please don't harass him."

"What's wrong with him?"

"I'd rather not go into it."

"If you don't come, what can I do?"

"We aren't coming! Our lives are in danger!" Yet she was still talking. Nina thought, She's torn, she's looking for a way to help.

She thought, What if I do drag them here and something happens? For a moment, the whole effort of overcoming the obstacles in the case seemed insuperable. ·

"I'm getting off the line now," Silke said.

"What if I come to you?" Nina said. "I might be able to persuade the court to allow me to take your depositions in Germany, where you feel safer. Don't say no without thinking, Ms. Kilmer. This may be the only way out for both of us."

"You would come to Heddesheim?"

"If I can work out the legal details." It would be expensive. Nina tried not to think about that. It was, in fact, highly irregular. But it had been done, in cases where people were too sick to travel, for instance.

"What about Elliott?"

"I have to depose him, too. He may have seen something you and Raj didn't see."

"What if Elliott comes to Germany, too? Could you take all of our statements the same day?"

"It's a possibility," Nina said.

"He's in danger in the States."

"What do you all know that is causing you to live in fear? The sooner it's known to everyone, the sooner you'll be safe."

"I don't know what we know! We had money, he wanted it. What else is there to say? He killed a bystander, now he has to kill us so we can't testify about him."

Nina said, "You were very close to him. You saw some identifying feature."

"Then come here and help us figure it out. I'm going to call Elliott and tell him not to say anything until he is with us."

"You seem to care a lot about him."

"He's my friend, okay? I watch out for him. You don't understand. Elliott is brilliant. Brilliant, but very fragile."

"You won't be safe in Germany, either, until you have been deposed. From that point forward, I can't see what use it would be to hurt you and your friends. The deposition transcript could still be used in court, if you were . . . unavailable."

"You make me feel so much better." Sarcasm, in one so young.

"Anyone can get on a plane to Europe. I'll call you tomorrow, Silke."

A sigh. "If you have to."

When Nina came downstairs, she found Bob sitting at the kitchen desk, text on his computer screen.

"I hope that's your homework," Nina said.

"Me and Dad are instant-messaging." Some new words popped up on the screen and Bob started typing back.

"Dad says hi," he reported shortly.

"You know, Bob, sometimes I think someone up there is rooting for us," Nina said. "Could I, uh, type to your dad for a couple of minutes?"

"Sure. It's easy." Bob showed her, then left for the kitchen.

Hi, Kurt. It's Nina.
Hey there! You!
Sorry to interrupt.
No problem. How are you?
Frazzled. You?

Hands still bad. Otherwise can't complain.

Sorry. How's the weather in central Germany?

Rainy. It'll be better when the snow comes in December.

Same here. Rainy.

So. Is this about Bob?

Actually no. It's about a case.

Okay.

I need to come to Germany.

No kidding! When?

Quickly. Some paperwork first. I have to do some depositions
     with witnesses in a place called Heddesheim.

That's not far from Heidelberg. It's only about an hour, hour and
     a half from here.

Problem is, I don't speak German and I'm worried about getting
     around.

Don't worry. They all speak English. Anyway—

It's just tha—

—you'll be with me.

Don't get that.

I'll help you, Nina.

I could use help.

Please bring Bob. Can you?

It's business.

I'd love to see him. Thanksgiving holiday for him soon?

Coming up.

It's a deal then? You'll love my car.

What is it?

A surprise.

He had added a smiley face. Nina stared at it, shook her head,
smiled back at it.

Now all she had to do was wade through red tape even Kafka
had never imagined.

Chapter 21

Sergeant Cheney now joined the small group of Nina's allies in the Hanna case: a select and counterintuitive group that did not, for instance, include her client. Cheney submitted a declaration to Judge Flaherty alleging that the new defendants had relevant information and that the interests of justice would be advanced. This impressed Flaherty more than all of Nina's other arguments.

Flaherty came through with the necessary orders for deposing witnesses in a foreign jurisdiction. He was interested in the case, and made no more reference to a discretionary dismissal. He, too, was becoming an ally.

Betty Jo, erstwhile ally, did not even attend the hearing. A hundred pages of pleading paper and many a phone call later, Nina had her orders, her appointments, and her tickets.

Roger, ally, attended to Dave, non-ally, who remained mostly incommunicado. Roger did not move forward on the conservatorship idea.

"I found another way to handle Dave," he told Nina. "We had a talk. To be honest, I let him have it. I told him I was disgusted with him. He told me he was disgusted with himself. He said he's barely hanging on right now, and he can't help, but he's not going to interfere with your work."

"Thanks. Great."

"It's the least I can do. That, and pay for your airline ticket."

"Much appreciated."

"How much more will you need?"

"I'll front the rest," Nina said. "The German official who sits in and the transcriber. We're staying with a friend who has a car, so it won't be too expensive."

"Good luck."

The case had become an intelligence war; the shooter in Nina's mind was like Bin Laden, hiding in a cave, making dark forays from time to time. His freedom hurt her. She thought about Chelsi every day, the flutter of her eyes as she lay on the floor so close to Nina, the little business she had built up all by herself, her beauty, her heart.

It felt almost like being shot again herself. She couldn't rest until the shooter was found; she imagined what it would be like to stand face-to-face with him.

It would happen soon. He was close, watching, unquiet himself. The Heddesheim depositions would break the case, she was sure of it.

Silke became an ally. Over the next few days, she persuaded Elliott Wakefield to fly to Germany from Seattle. She persuaded Raj not to allow Branson, the attorney from Boston, to represent them.

Bob was jubilant that he would be seeing Kurt over his holiday, but he kept giving Nina worried looks as she sat night after night in her bed, reading over the autopsy reports, working on her motions, making endless notes.

"Mom, you're getting obsessed," he told her one night. "You're not going to get him by staring into that math book."

"It's interesting."

"What has math got to do with it?"

"The new defendants are mathematicians."

"So?"

"So. I'm going to be questioning them. Their work might come up, be important in some way."

"I have the same brain as you, and I know obsessed. And you're getting obsessed."

Nina said, "Okay, it's true. I don't know why the mystery of the primes interests me so much. I don't know if this math stuff has anything at all to do with my case. It's one way to go, that's all." She kept her place with her finger and added, "I'm going to find this sucker, Bob."

"That's what I'm worried about. Or else he'll find you." Now she knew what was at the root of his worry.

"Come sit on the bed for a minute," she said. Bob came in and sat down on the edge. His baby picture on the dresser still matched up with this tall fellow, though a curious solidification and elongation had occurred over the years. He still had the mole on his earlobe, dark hair that fell forward, blunt fingers, narrow feet.

"I'm sorry," Nina said.

"You oughtta be." Bob said this with feeling.

"I can't help it."

"You need a life."

"I have a very full life."

"Books aren't a life."

"Don't you think my work is important?"

"I don't know. I guess it is. But you get into it too much, Mom."

Nina said lightly, "Do you think I'm going to lose my

marbles? Start mumbling to myself on the street? Bob, I'm sane as a post."

"Well, watch it. Anyways, what if this guy comes after you?"

She wanted to be flippant, say something like "Well, then you'll protect me." But he was so earnest, his brow knitted in the lineaments of worry.

"We're leaving in two days, Bob. Wish and the police are watching out for us. We have a really good security system here." She was still watching Bob, and she realized how much he wanted to help protect them. In a moment of maternal insight, she asked, "Is that why you've been practicing throwing rocks? The bolos?"

"I didn't think you'd let me buy a Luger."

Nina sighed. "That doesn't explain my sneakers on the line," she said. So he was practicing throwing rocks because he had no other way to protect them. She pulled him closer and put her arm around him. He let her do it. His shoulders were heartbreakingly bony. "Listen, bud, I promise you, we're going to be fine. Okay? Now go start the laundry or you won't be able to pack."

"Okay."

"Love you," she said lightly. She kissed him warmly on the cheek. It had been too long since she had done that.

On the day before the flight, at the office, Mick McGregor stopped by. He waited patiently while Nina saw her client out.

"Hi, Mick! What brings you here?"

"You," Mick said. Sandy let out a muffled "Hmph" from her desk ten feet away.

Mick had a burning look in his eye and a fistful of gladioli. He wore a corduroy sport coat with leather patches on the elbows hilariously reminiscent of the sixties.

"Look at the color of those flowers," Nina said. "Uh, Sandy . . ."

"I'll get the vase." Sandy went into the conference room and shut the door, mostly.

"Can I buy you dinner?" Mick said. "I need to buy you dinner."

"I really can't. I'm leaving tomorrow on a trip."

"You have to eat dinner."

"That line only works once," Nina said, and smiled. She appreciated his obvious interest in her, but he was hard to take seriously, what with the wife and the students.

"How about a quick drink after work? You have to drink after work."

"True."

"Don't you have any more questions for me? Please? Ever been to the top floor of Harrah's, to the bar there?"

"No."

"What time shall I pick you up?"

"Six. But I only have an hour."

Six came and went, but Mick waited for her. When she saw the bar, Nina wished she'd had time to change out of her work suit. The sixteenth floor at Harrah's consisted of a restaurant and a "view" bar: The view stretched west across the Tahoe valley to the mountains, and across the grassy slopes of Heavenly only a mile or so south of the casino-hotel. Taking a slow leave, the sun still left a gleaming trail across Lake Tahoe to the north, and several of the guests stood at the tall window looking out.

"Lucky time of day," Mick said. He held her arm and steered her toward a small vacant table in the back.

"I'll have a glass of white wine," she said.

"Live a little," Mick said. "Ever tried B & B?"

"Why not?" It was delicious, sweet. Mick had one, too. He drank it down in a gulp and that marvelously exciting look came back into his eyes. He put his palms together and held them to his face as though he was considering something important, still looking at her. His eyes were dark blue, she noticed.

"It is hard to extricate you for an hour," he said. "I get the feeling you have to be cajoled from point to point."

"Are you cajoling me somewhere?" She had to smile.

"To my lair, I hope. Someday," he added hastily. "I don't know how to act with you. Masterful, I think, but I'm not really the masterful type. I'm more of the puppy type, to be honest."

But you know the language of love, Nina thought to herself. "I would have said that you're the wolf type," she said.

"Predatory?"

"I do get this feeling of something with paws creeping up on me."

"Puppies do that too. Then they roll over and beg for it."

"Wolves call themselves puppies," Nina said. "Let's have another one of those."

"Okay, the puppy thing isn't going anywhere, I'm going to take another tack," Mick said. He ordered another set of drinks and said, "Wow, look at that sunset." They truly did have an angel's view of the spectacle from their tower in the sky. The lake was flaming now, a sheet of red shading to indigo above.

Nina let her spine loosen. She was enjoying sitting opposite a charming younger man in a comfortable place, listening to his stories. She even wanted to tell Mick that, but . . .

He wanted to be in love. Did he care who he was in love with tonight? Did it matter if the splash of his erotic fancy had only accidentally encountered her one day, as she sat on the bank of the river of life staring drily at a book?

Maybe Mick could help keep this grim angry feeling about Chelsi from overwhelming her. It would be such a relief to lie in the freckled arms of this, uh, math professor . . . what kind of sheets would he have? A grid pattern?

Mick put his hand on hers.

"What are you thinking?"

"About something I read. I'm still reading about prime numbers."

"The subject does tend to suck you in."

"Mick, let's talk about l-i-e-s." She spelled the word out because she was not sure how to pronounce it in this context.

He took his hand back. "Isn't it a little soon for that discussion? If I can momentarily adopt a masterful tack, well then I insist that topic will come up much later in our relationship. If ever."

She laughed at his expression. "I mean in the mathematical sense."

"Oh, good, 'cause it's such an alarming word in its plain English sense." He noted her glass was empty. Again. "Can I get you another one? No more for me. I'm driving."

"I shouldn't."

"These things are small and weak. Like me."

"Oh, well. Why not." Dinner would have to come from a cardboard box in the freezer, preformulated, but then, as Bob had mentioned, it usually did lately.

"You want to know about lies, eh? Well, all sorts of lies relate to math. There's a Chinese professor by the name of Li."

"Not him."

"There's also a Norwegian mathematician from the turn of the century, named Lie. He gave his name to some concepts called Lie Groups and Lie Transformations."

"Are they used in prime number theory?"

"Maybe. But if so, it's way over my head," Mick said. "So much genius has been wasted trying to figure out what the hell the primes are, and why they sit where they sit on the number line, that I'd have to look it up, and I might not know enough about that field to help.

"Here's the thing about number theory: Any fool can ask a simple question that no genius can solve. Is one a number? What's the square root of minus one? Why can't you divide by zero? And the question that has you hooked: How come the primes, the building blocks of all numbers, can't be located using some formula?"

"It's true," Nina said. "It seems so simple. There must be a pattern. I look at the list of numbers, and I think I see a pattern like a mist just behind the list. That there's some simple little adjustment to be made, and they would fall into a regular sequence—2, 3, 5, 7, 11 . . ."

"There's a very great mathematician named Grothendieck who said you have to come at things this difficult with the mind of an infant," Mick said. "Maybe the mystery will be solved someday by some retired postal worker who likes math puzzles. Meantime, let's talk about one more 'li.'"

"The li that comes close to predicting a pattern of prime distribution," Nina said.

"Right. Let's start with maybe the greatest mathematician who ever lived, the incomparable Gauss. Active in math in the late seventeen hundreds. A child prodigy. He kept notebooks, and he only published a small number of his discoveries. It's said that his failure to let the world into his brain set mathematics back a century.

"When he was fifteen, he wrote a stunning little function in his notebook. He wrote, 'N over the log of N.' This predicted approximately how many primes would be found as one went higher and higher on the number line. That teenage observation, with some refinement, became the Prime Number Theorem after about half a century of work by other mathematicians proving it. It's still the most important thing we know about the primes."

"You said 'log.' A logarithm is some kind of root, is that right?"

Mick scratched his head and said, "I don't think of it like that, but, yeah, it is a root. The natural log is the power a base number has to be raised to in order to equal the particular prime. Most people have had to study base 10 logs, but the scientific log is called the natural log, and . . ." He saw Nina's eyes glazing over and said, "Yeah, it's sort of a root," and laughed.

"But not exact?"

"No. Close, but no cigar. Still, close was an amazing leap of creativity. Tantalizing, how close he came."

"Are we getting closer to li yet?"

"Li. Hold on to your glass. Bring all brain cells into play. Grit your teeth. Ready?"

"Go for it."

"Li means 'logarithmic integral.' It's a refinement of the theorem that comes even closer to predicting the number of primes up to a certain number, and it gets more and more accurate as the numbers get larger. It still can't predict individual primes, it just comes closer. Gauss came up with it later. It's a root of a root, you might say. You make an x,y graph. Make a line representing the actual prime numbers, which of course we know up to a hundred digits or so. Make another adjusted line representing the lies of those numbers. The lines run extremely close to each other."

He drew a simple diagram on his napkin. A right triangle— "The vertical axis is y. The horizontal axis is x, the number line. Where they intersect is zero"—then added another line starting from the zero point and extending out with an arrow at about a forty-five-degree angle.

"That's the li line, which predicts how many primes there should be up to any point. But it only works approximately. Each prime is located at some random distance below the li line." He drew a jagged stepped line which ran under the li line like a narrow staircase. "See where the actual number of primes are located? It's as though the primes got pulled away from their line and have sunk at different rates." He spread his hands. "To find out how and why this force acts to distort the prime distribution, I would sell my soul. Now I'm getting romantic. It's because of those brown eyes of yours."

Lights were winking on all across the forest now, leaving the mountains and the lake in their mysterious darkness.

"Then Riemann found another pattern, somehow related to the li line, by working with a function called the Zeta Function. And his work still seems like the best approach to finding this force or differential or whatever you might call it. So prime theoreticians went looking in that direction. But so far, the Riemann Hypothesis hasn't been proved."

"I've been reading about that."

"I have a really good book about it at home I could lend you. So this is connected to your case?"

"I told you, one of the witnesses is very interested in prime number theory."

"Maybe he works for an Internet-security company," Mick said.

"What?"

"Well, really big numbers can't be factored—nobody can find the primes they're made of—even with today's computers. So a company called XYC invented a method of encoding financial and other information using that fact, so information couldn't be hacked as it traveled from one Web site to another. The code lets you type in your credit-card number for certain eyes only. Ever buy anything on eBay?"

"No."

"You will soon. Everybody will. Local markets can't really compete. Where was I? Oh, yes. Internet codes. I have a good book about that at home as well. Want to borrow it? We could stop by there."

Nina had been lulled into such a scholarly daze by Mick's disquisition that she almost didn't notice that he had made his move. Maybe she didn't want to notice, erect defenses, analyze, think it through. "I would," she said. "I could take it to read on the plane."

"Let's go, then. Maybe you should call your son and say you'll be a little late."

"Good idea." Nina called Bob and said she'd be a little late. She wasn't hungry. The B & B warmed in her stomach. She was on the trail of something intellectually challenging. Mick was a fount, a real fount. He was holding her hand as they emerged into the parking lot.

Okay, be honest, she was on a trail all right, but the trail had just forked, and his hand was confident.

He went on talking during the short trip to his place in the Tahoe Keys, and Nina leaned back in the passenger seat, allowing herself to be fed information as if he were spooning ice cream into her mouth. Up the stairs they went into his dark cabin. He didn't turn on the lights. He opened the door to his stove-fireplace and a blast of heat came out and flames flickered into action.

"Let me show you something," he said. He drew her to the window. Outside sparkled one of the canals that led to the lake. The stars shone down.

It didn't surprise her when he began to undress her. "Ssh, ssh," he said. "Let's get comfortable and I'll show you the books. It's getting hot in here."

She had heard that line in a bad rap song, but somehow she was in her slip, and his hands caressed her. "Right in here," he said, drawing her over the threshold into his bedroom, where a large bookcase took up half the wall. The bed took up the rest of

the room, though, and hardly had they entered when Mick engineered her to the bed and said, "Relax, I'll get it in a second."

She sat on the bed, tired all of a sudden and acutely aware of
Mick kneeling in front of her, sliding his hand up her thigh. In
the dark she only sensed his head below her. She took a handful
of his hair, ready for the ride.

"This'll only take a minute," he said. "You're really going to
like this book, sweetheart. It's full of details about logs that make
you want to be close to somebody who understands. Like I'm
close to you right now, touching you. Mmm, you are absolutely
luscious. You're hot, baby. And now I'm going to show you a log,
a natural log, you're gonna get this right away . . ."

He went on like that, and he did have some books, though
she didn't get back home with them for another hour and a half.

As for the sheets being in a grid pattern, she didn't have time
to look.

Chapter 22

HER SILVER-TONGUED MATHEMATICIAN DUMPED HER the next day, via a cell-phone call Nina missed on her way to the Reno airport. While she and Bob waited for the hop to San Francisco to be called, she found it after a last-minute message from Sandy.

> Hi. Maybe it's better this way. You know that job offer in L.A.? They need me right away, so I won't be here when you get back. I loved every minute and I think you're sweet. And please don't be mad—remember, I never lied to you. Bye, and good luck cracking the primes.

She didn't return the call—what would she say? Another watershed of single life spread before her—the hookup followed by the cheerful phone message. Apparently he hadn't "caught feelings," as the alternateens say. She glanced over at Bob, who read

Rolling Stone magazine in the seat beside her, and realized he was the wrong person to confide in.

She examined herself. Emotional trauma?

She felt ruffled, yes.

Damage to her vanity, then?

Some. Mick should have found her so irresistible that he changed his plans, changed his circumstances, changed his very personality now that she had lit up his life. Then she would have decided at her leisure what to do with him.

Regret? Some. Mick had been fun, but then again, the fun wouldn't have lasted. The main regret was that she had lost her math expert.

She hadn't caught feelings either, then. It seemed that she would survive handily. Mick would go on his way, a very lonely way, finding women at every stop, staying with none of them. He hadn't harmed her, and she was a big girl.

Well, then, could she just enjoy the memory, and not analyze it into smithereens?

No way; analysis was always necessary, at least after the fact.

What lesson had she learned?

Math is sexy, she thought. Who knew? Then she thought, like giving herself a slap, You're starting to sleep around. She would have to think about that.

The loudspeaker blared and she shrugged, slung her bag onto her shoulder, and said, "That's us, bud."

They flew to Frankfurt on a crowded Lufthansa flight from San Francisco.

On long flights, a devolution occurs in the passengers. They begin polite, tidy, and optimistic. Toward the end of the flight, it's like an aerial Animal House. Debris slops all over the cabin, the kids jump around, the bathrooms are not to be trusted, and the adults sprawl in their seats trying to achieve blottohood with liquor or sleep.

Bob slept all night, his head on her shoulder or parked at a strange angle against the seat, drooling a little, shifting, muttering incoherently. He woke up cranky but pulled the bags down from the overhead compartment with the energy of the well-rested.

Kurt waited just past the customs booth. He put a hand on Bob's shoulder and as Bob spun around, he smiled broadly, reaching out so that Bob was enveloped in a long tight hug.

"Hey," Bob said, and Nina thought with a start, Does he call him Dad, or what? He had spent much more time with Kurt than she had, and they had never all spent time together.

"How was your trip?" He turned to her and she found herself hugging him. He stepped back then, as though he was afraid he had come too near her too soon, but she really didn't care, she was tired and glad to see him.

"Long."

"All your baggage arrived?"

"Just what we're carrying."

"Good. Let's get out of here. It's raining, sorry. November in Germany isn't our prettiest season. Put on your jackets." He kept a hand on Bob's shoulder as he marshaled them to the next line. The doors to the street opened with a *whoosh,* leaving all the stale air inside.

Diesel fumes and shouts mingled in the narrow street they crossed on their way to the parking structure, which looked just like the one in San Francisco. The wind whipped under the stout black umbrella Kurt deployed to protect them, and they were all dripping and gasping as they walked into the dimness.

"Here we are." It was the smallest car Nina had ever sat in, a yellow Citroën from the seventies, a minicar that belonged in a cartoon.

"My baby," Kurt said. Getting older suited him; his smooth

face had some rugged lines now that she liked, and she even saw a smattering of gray at his temples. He wore a black sweater and jeans, just as he always had. He looked happy to see them, but unsure how to treat them.

"It's cute," Nina said.

"It's the future. Tiny cars and pedestrian malls. Like it, Bob?"

"Is there room for all our stuff?" Bob asked dubiously. He snaked into the back area and drew in his duffel. Nina sat up front, her bags tucked at her feet and on her lap. The car enclosed them like a neat yellow envelope. They drove out into a sky of blue overlaid by a dense gray cover above, rain still spattering now and then across the autobahn. Kurt stayed right as the Mercedes and BMWs zoomed past in the faster lanes. A silence fell upon them, the silence of adjustment to a new situation.

Nina hadn't known she'd be casting about for some conventional rule to guide her in talking to Kurt. He was really a stranger. Fifteen years before, she had known him for three weeks, and the intense feelings from that time were no longer relevant.

Though they had resulted in the boy sitting quietly behind them. Fifteen years, and then nothing, while she raised Bob alone, not wanting Kurt even to know about his son. Then a few more weeks at Tahoe in which she defended Kurt in a murder case. He was innocent, but in the process of proving that, Kurt and Bob had found each other. Now they exhibited the same shyness toward each other she was feeling, as though they hadn't formed their own warm relationship over the past two years.

Vineyards flowed by under the lowering clouds. Kurt drove with both hands firmly on the wheel, very differently from Paul, who merely kept a couple of fingers handy near the wheel in case something might come up on the road. Nina hadn't had time to think about what it would feel like to stay with Kurt.

They were friendly, linked; Bob would of course be staying with him; he'd offered to drive them to Heddesheim. Now she wondered if she should have stayed at a hotel. She thought of the tiny living environments she'd seen at the Ikea store one day, and wondered if he lived like that.

In a half hour or so they turned off the highway and drove into Wiesbaden, where the rain had given way to unequivocal sun as if in honor of their arrival. They cruised past an expensive row of stores and cafes, the waiters just now coming out with chairs to set up in this moment of warmth, and soon passed a graceful, long building with Roman columns all along the front.

"The Colonnade," Kurt said. "Couple thousand years old. The town was founded by Celts in around the third century B.C. Everybody came for the hot springs." Then they were in the main market square, dominated by a shining Gothic church. Kurt told them about it, and about the State Theater, where he often played. In front they saw an enormous statue of a nineteenth-century personage. "Schiller," Kurt said. And that was the tour.

Even so, Nina caught the spirit of the city on the Rhine: luxurious, wine-loving, musical, healthy, nestled in its forest away from the gray granite of Frankfurt. The shoppers and dog-walkers looked pleased with themselves, even with the puddles.

They came to a townhouse on one of the side streets and Kurt pulled his yellow cube into a minuscule garage. He shouldered some of the bags and they entered a hall with no windows facing a staircase, which they began to climb. On the third floor, as Nina admitted to herself that she wished she'd stayed at the Hyatt, Kurt brandished his key and entered one of the flats, Bob right behind him, Nina following with some trepidation.

But the ceilings were high, with ornate molding, and there were bay windows looking out at the market square. Kurt moved to the fireplace, causing an attack of déjà vu as Nina thought of

Mick doing the same thing, and said, "Sit down. I have good coffee. C'mere, Franz. Come on, say hi to Bob and Nina." He picked up the big orange cat and brought it to Bob.

Somehow, the room reflected that an American lived here, in spite of the antique furnishings, the white grand piano in the corner, the piles of books. Bright with blues and yellows, the Danish rug in front of the fireplace gave the room warmth. She could see Kurt through an open doorway under a strong light, moving around.

"Mind if I look around?" she said. She found the bathroom, another high-ceilinged cavernous room with a claw-foot tub and a tall fern in the window, then went down the hall to see the bedrooms. Kurt had already made a bed for Bob in his room. His own bed was a mahogany four-poster much like Nina's at Tahoe. Portraits in oil of musicians and dancers hung on the walls, painted as if by Rembrandt so that vivid faces and figures appeared to emerge from darkness. A stack of music lay on a stool by the bed.

Why, he's been living here all these years, carrying on a life, and I never really thought about him at all, she thought. While she struggled through law school, married, moved to San Francisco, made Bob's lunches, learned how to practice criminal law, divorced, moved to Tahoe, married briefly again—he, too, had been living a life, dealing with his own struggles and pains, celebrating his own successes. Their paths had crossed so briefly that it seemed a miracle that she should be here, meeting him now for the third time.

The Miracle himself sat down at the piano and opened it, running his hands over the keys. Bob hesitantly began to play the first movement of Satie's *Gymnopédie,* which he had practiced over and over on the electronic keyboard at home, and which had never sounded like this. Because of the hardwood floor and the height of the ceiling, the rich sound of the grand piano filled the room.

Nina came to her doorway from the hall to watch and saw Kurt do the same across the room, leaning at the doorsill to his kitchen, a white towel over his shoulder, nodding at each hesitation as if urging Bob on. Light came through the window onto the carpet and a fire burned in the grate. The music was calm, spare, and steady.

Bob, in profile, bulked up by his parka, looked all grown up. He frowned as he played, leaning into the keyboard, head low, engrossed. A lump came into Nina's throat. She looked at Kurt. He was grimacing as though he was in pain, and she was just about to go to him and ask what was wrong when he turned abruptly and went into the kitchen. It was emotion, she realized. Bob was playing for him, and he was proud of Bob.

She didn't feel part of this warm loop between them. In truth, she felt very odd standing there watching her son with another parent. She felt both happy for Bob, who seemed somehow more complete, as though he were the apex of a triangle that now had both legs under him, and angry at having to share him. She stayed and listened and clapped when he had finished. Then she went into the white-tiled kitchen and helped lay out the lunch on the coffee table, there being no dining table.

While they ate, talking became easier. "So when is this thing?" Kurt said.

"What time is it now?" Nina said.

"Twelve-thirty."

"We cut it close. Four this afternoon, and tomorrow morning."

"No problem. It'll take about ninety minutes. How about a nap before you go? Did you see your room?"

"It's fine." Her room seemed to be a music workroom, the table covered with sheet music, the walls full of books and music, a guitar leaning against the bed. The window opened and cool damp air entered with the light. "I like it."

"I'll clear a space on the table so you can work," Kurt said. "I've been doing some composing, now that my performing days seem to be over."

"Your hands seem—you don't wear a splint or anything?"

"They're fine for daily life. But as for the Rach Three concerto—they're shot."

"What are you composing?" Bob asked. He had maintained the same adult mood.

"Some things you could play, if you practice." Kurt smiled. "Anyway, let's go for a walk and let your mother rest a little."

The house fell still. Franz the cat didn't come in. The street noise, the scents, the light, were strange but not disturbing. Nina lay down on the creaky bed, but sleep—no, she would just lie here and think about Chelsi, and worry and wonder.

She needed a shower. Stripping off the clothes from the plane felt really good, and so did the hot shower, handheld in Kurt's enormous tub. She blew her hair dry, went back to her room, put on her black suit with her blue silk blouse, figured out the phone, confirmed that Herr Kraft would be present at the offices of the judicial commissioner at four, and was reviewing her notes when Bob and Kurt came bursting in, bringing a puff of moist air and smoky smells with them.

"Time?"

"We have about ten minutes."

"Bob, you better comb your hair. And change your clothes. We're going to a restaurant tonight." Kurt said this, and Bob went. No back talk.

Kurt sat down on the couch in front of the fire. "Can you sit down for a minute? I'd like to know a little more about your case. Do you have time?"

"Since I'm dragging you into this, I had better explain." She sat down at the other end of the couch. He smiled at her, right at home. He had always been one of those people who do the right thing, who discipline themselves, who are sure who they are. Personal strength comes from that inborn sureness. The glad feeling came back, and Nina realized that she needed his support.

"All right. It's a wrongful-death case. A civil case. An innocent bystander, a woman, was killed during a robbery, and I represent her husband."

He nodded. The cocked eyebrows and narrow jaw were the same, the long dark hair brushed straight back, the knitted brows and hollows under the cheekbone. He was as tall as Paul, but lighter. She saw the faint scar on his cheekbone. She had forgotten that he, too, had once been hit by a bullet. She remembered that they were the same age.

She said, "Long story short, I reactivated the case when it was about to be thrown out. I've been looking for the shooter, and to do that I needed to find the people who were robbed. They're here in Germany, and they've agreed to make statements."

"What do they know?"

"They saw him. He was wearing a ski mask, but they saw him. They know more than that. They know why he decided to rob them, and they have been reluctant to talk about it. But I'm going to get the full story now, and on the record."

"Good."

"So why am I jumpy? Why is this so sudden? Because the shooter seems to have reactivated, too. What he's trying to stop is the Hanna case."

"What has he done?"

"He killed a friend in front of me. At Tahoe. He shot her. I think he thought it was me."

Kurt leaned back, closed his eyes, and expelled a long breath. "What else?"

"He's been watching me. And Bob. I'm sorry, Kurt."

"Bob, huh?"

"That's why I have to end this fast. He's been prowling around Tahoe. He's mobile, though. He threatened two of the witnesses in Boston."

"He threatened them?"

"Tried to kill them. They went to Heddesheim because the girl's family lives there and they thought they'd be safer."

"Anything else?"

"That's all that matters."

"He could try to get at you through Bob."

Nina caught her breath. "You always had a way of cutting through facts. You could have been a . . ."

"Am I right?"

"Yes, you're right. That's one reason I wanted to get out of town and take Bob with me. I'm hoping the police will track him down while Bob is here."

"Could he have followed you here?"

"I just don't think . . . it's so far. The decision to take the trip was made so fast. But I have to say that the guy seems to know what I'm doing. I don't know how. Kurt, I have not given your address to anyone."

"My phone number?"

"Only Sandy has it."

He must have understood by the look on her face that Sandy would reveal nothing that might endanger them, not ever. "So we're safe here. But what about this office we're going to?"

"It's in the police department. I set it up that way." She waited for his verdict.

Bob came back in, presumably cleaned up, though it was impossible to tell from the parka and baseball cap. He looked at them and said in an accusatory tone, "What'm I missing?"

"I was just telling your dad about the case."

"I brought my camera. And my GameBoy."

"We'll find plenty to do while your mother is busy," Kurt said. "And then we'll eat."

"So it's okay?" Nina said.

"It is what it is," Kurt said. "Let's go." He locked up carefully.

Heddesheim had a lot of cars for a quaint village. In fact, Nina was figuring out something else about Germany: The facade was traditional, with half-timbered homes, geraniums, cobblestones; but the mostly-invisible technology was twenty-first century. Accompanying the respect for history was a very modern energy.

They wended their way through the town square and somehow Kurt found them a parking spot a couple of blocks from the police station. It was three-thirty in the afternoon, and seemed to be getting dark already. The yellow streetlights had begun to sputter and the shop lights were on. Christmas lights and wreaths hung in the pastry shop and the butcher's, and the street was full of shoppers and office workers with cell phones at their ears.

As they rounded the corner, they saw the imposing building where the depositions would take place across the boulevard, the red, black, and yellow German flag hanging limply from its tall pole in this early dusk in the light of a single lamp. On the steps Nina saw three young people, one a girl, standing uncertainly in a huddle, talking, all dressed similarly in dark jackets and pants.

"Those are my witnesses," she said. "I'll take it from here."

"Want us to go in with you?" Kurt asked her. His eyes scanned the street traffic. It was noisy and hard to hear.

"No, no, you guys go get something warm to drink. Take some pictures." She wished the weather were more welcoming, that they had more to do, but Bob was looking around with interest. "I'll break it off for the night at about six-thirty and call you."

"Be careful."

She stepped off the curb and crossed, looking back once to see Bob and Kurt still standing there, watching her. A moist breeze, the remnant of the rain, blew down the avenue.

"Hello."

The three turned to her. Three young, scared faces.

"We have come." The young Indian man, Sumaraj Das, shook her hand. He wore a red cashmere muffler and an overcoat.

"Hello, Silke."

Silke was pale but her expression was determined. "Yes, we are ready," she said. "And this is Elliott. Raj? What are you doing? Are you all right?"

Raj had closed his eyes and brought his hand up to his chest.

"Raj?" Silke Kilmer said again, panic in her eyes. Then she made another sound, a grunt, a sound that this young lady would never have made in company, except that she had just been shot. Nina knew this instantly.

"Uh." Silke fell with Raj.

Nina and Elliott tumbled against the short wall at the top of the stairs and fell behind it, entangled.

Nina's leg was still exposed. She pulled it quickly behind the shelter of the wall. Elliott was shouting something beside her, but she was feeling very quiet, paralyzed almost, praying, Please don't let him shoot me, too.

She heard screams. Nina opened her eyes. Elliott Wakefield crouched beside her, his glasses askew, peering around the wall toward the steps. He was about to jump out there. She pulled him back.

"But—my friends!"

"Someone else has to help them! He could be waiting for

you to show your face!" Elliott comprehended this. He fell back against the wall and reached in his jacket and felt for something.

"Do you have a gun?"

"No! How could I get a gun through customs?"

"Just sit tight," Nina said. "We're just going to sit here and not move."

"Did he kill them?" His eyes were wild.

"Just sit tight!" The tall double doors burst open and several uniformed police officers came running out.

After the ambulances left, after the police took them inside and questioned them at length; after Elliott had some sort of panic attack and had to be subdued and kept from running away; after the officer came in to tell them that Silke Kilmer and Raj Das hadn't made it; long after full darkness came upon the town and the traffic noises subsided outside; after the German police woke up Sergeant Cheney at his home at Tahoe and confirmed the details of Nina's story; after she gave them a false address for Kurt and said they'd be available for more questions the next day; after Elliott said to her in the cold waiting room, "What should I do?"; after all that, Nina and Elliott were released.

It was past ten. Kurt and Bob waited for them at the back door. The Citroën was running at the curb, its headlights bright. A police officer walked them down to the car. Nina kept her arm around Bob.

Kurt was waiting in the driver's seat. Nina sat beside him. Bob and Elliott Wakefield sat in back.

Nina realized he hadn't made a plan during the long hours he had been waiting. Elliott lapsed into a daze in back, gazing dully out the window at nothing.

"The first thing is, let's get out of here," Kurt said after a moment. He put the little car in gear and drove swiftly through the town.

"My stuff," Elliott said from the back seat. So he was still with them mentally. "At the hotel."

"We'll have it picked up tomorrow, okay?"

"But where am I going? To the airport?"

"We can't, not yet," Nina said. "We have to stay at least through tomorrow. The police—"

"Screw the police! It happened at the police station!"

"You can stay with us," Kurt said quietly, cutting through it again. "It'll be safe. No one knows my address."

"Maybe he's following us," Bob said.

"I'd know it." Kurt was right. The Citroën's humbleness provided a novel way to avoid a tail. They were on the autobahn, in the slow lane, moving so slowly the cars seemed to whiz past. Anybody following the Citroën would be obvious.

"Silke," Elliott said, and began sobbing.

PART THREE

We must know; we will know.

—David Hilbert

Chapter 23

NINA TOSSED IN THE BED AS if floating on a creaky ship in a storm. Yellow streetlight fanned through the blinds.

She was through sleeping. Maybe she could sneak by Elliott's couch and get a glass of milk. She threw back the covers and padded quietly toward the kitchen. But Elliott, dressed in Kurt's bathrobe, was poking at the fireplace. The living room was stuffy, almost hot. He had turned on a small lamp on the side table.

"Hello," he said. Red, swollen eyes turned her way.

"Sorry to bother you. I was just on my way to the kitchen. How are you doing?"

"I'm hungry," Elliott said. They never had gotten around to dinner. Elliott had cried all the way to Wiesbaden, then lay down on the couch, turning his back to them, and fell into a sniffly slumber while Nina, Kurt, and Bob tiptoed around him. Though she had tried to act calm around the others, Nina had been struggling with her own emotions, fright and outrage, and her own exhaustion from the trauma of the shooting and the hours of questioning overcame her early. But now, in the middle of the night, the event boiled up and pushed her back into wakeful consciousness with a new emotion. Guilt. She had initiated this sequence.

"Then we'll eat." She went into the kitchen, found a pan and melted some butter, and added a half-dozen eggs, moving quietly so as not to wake Bob and Kurt, although in the old apartment with its thick walls they might as well have been a block away.

Elliott followed her. "My father makes them with curry and tarragon," he said. He sounded pitiful. He was a complete stranger, but Nina felt she knew him well. She had been thinking about him, sought him, for some time, and the fact that he had been saved with her linked them.

"Will salt and pepper do? I could grate in some cheese."

"Sure. Anything. I'm starving."

"Do you want to talk?" she asked Elliott when the plates were set on the coffee table.

"This is good." He was already eating like someone famished. He had a doughy face, not unpleasant, rimless glasses, tousled sandy hair. A budding academic if she had ever seen one.

But few academics would say what Elliott said next. "I'll kill whoever did it," he said. Nina sat down next to the fireplace, which began baking her right side, wondering how to respond. "I'll do anything. What should I do?"

"Your life is in danger."

"So's yours."

"And my client's and maybe others."

"It's all about that stupid robbery. How many people has he murdered?"

"Four," Nina said. "Sarah Hanna, Chelsi Freeman. And your friends."

"My friends. I'll do the deposition. I'll lay out everything I know. I told the officer here—when he took me in the back room—I told him everything I could think of."

"That would be courageous of you, to do a deposition in my case now."

"Do we have to do it here, though? He's here."

"I'd feel more comfortable back at Tahoe. I have a friend there, a private investigator, who can help us both with protection."

"Is my father in danger? He's disabled. But we have an alarm system."

"I don't know. But you should alert him," Nina said honestly. "Let's do this. Let's go back to Tahoe and get you on the record as fast as possible. You can talk to the police there. Then go home to Seattle, and you and your father can decide what to do."

"I can't figure out if it was the money or my notebook," Elliott mumbled. "Do you have any whiskey?" Kurt had a table near the kitchen with bottles on it. Elliott brought back a glass for her.

When he had stretched out again on the couch and had a good slug of the stuff, Nina said carefully, "What's your guess? Was it the money?"

"You already know about it? The card counting?"

"Mm-hmm." She thought, What were these kids up to?

"We had about thirty-five thousand in winnings and about twenty for the original stake in Silke's purse."

"You had fifty-five thousand dollars on you the night of the robbery?"

"You get used to it. With three of us, we felt pretty safe. We took measures. We never flashed that much money. We stayed in cheap places and drove cheap cars. But I was winning some big hands that night, and somebody may have noticed and followed us."

"Where were you playing?"

"Harrah's first. Then Prize's. We had supper, then we gambled for about four hours. About average. Who told you about the card counting?"

"Silke, on the phone." Silke wouldn't have objected to Nina using her name to elicit the story, Nina felt sure. "She had the cash?"

"Oh, God. Silke."

"No offense, Elliott," Nina said gently, "but it sounds to me like you were in love with Silke."

"I'm still in love with her. I'll never love anybody else. Only her." He drank some more, but his voice stayed steady. "Let's have another one."

"Let's wait, Elliott. Talk to me a little more first."

"Okay."

"You had already crossed the street and you walked through the covered entry to the vending machines when it happened, right?"

"The three of us. Silke was thirsty. I gave her some change for a soda. She had just put the money in the vending machine when this guy comes in from the street with a ski mask on."

"What else do you remember about him?"

"I'm sure Silke told you this. He—something was wrong with his left leg. The foot turned outward. But he could still move fast."

"Yes. He moves very fast." So it had definitely been the shooter who followed Nina and Bob at Spooner Lake. Bob had told her about the limp. "He has been watching me and my son too," she said, her voice shaking. "He tried to kill us, too."

"God, I'm sorry."

"What happened then?"

"He came up behind us and said, 'Turn around slowly.' I couldn't see the gun very well, but I couldn't take my eyes off it.

I had never seen a real gun before. There wasn't much light. The window to the office was right behind us and I was hoping the clerk was dialing 911. Raj said, 'Everyone please be cool.' Silke pressed up against him. Her bag was hanging off her shoulder.

"The man said to Silke, 'Give me your bag.' She took it off and laid it on the ground in front of her. Then he said, 'Empty out your pockets and take off your jackets and leave them, too.' I couldn't do that."

"Why not?" Nina said.

"Because my notebook was in the inside pocket of my jacket. I always carry it on me. I just couldn't let him have the notebook. I couldn't."

"What was in the notebook, Elliott?"

"The proof I'm working on. I've been working on it for a long time."

"Tell me about this proof."

"What's your math background?"

"Average."

"Let's just say, it's about predicting large primes and factoring large composite numbers."

"I found out that you were working on prime number theory from the bookstore at Tahoe."

"The Crandall-Pomerance book? I did buy it there."

"So I've been doing some reading myself."

"It's pretty abstruse," Elliott said. "You're not going to get much just diving in. You need a background in number theory and quantum mechanics."

"I'm a lawyer," Nina said. "That's what I do all day, make sense out of difficult sets of facts. Each case has its own realm of knowledge and I learn the basics fast."

Elliott shook his head. "Not this stuff," he said.

"It's just logic, a special vocabulary, processes," Nina said. "Go ahead, talk to me. Pretend I'm Leibniz or Fermat. They were both lawyers, weren't they? Are you working on the Riemann Hypothesis?"

Elliott closed his eyes and stretched his back. "Not anymore. I think it will never be proved or disproved. The Riemann Hypothesis is fun to play with, but it doesn't predict where the primes are."

"I thought that was how the mystery of the primes was going to be solved."

"I tried for a long time. If you look at an X ray of Riemann's Zeta Function, you see two curved lines overlapping in different ways around the zeros. The lines are out of phase with each other. Two phases are superimposed on each other within a very short interval. I was looking for the equations that would bring the phases back into coherence. I decided the Riemann function is too indirect to find an exact error term. Even using a quantum mechanics model."

It sounded like gobbledygook, but amazingly well-spoken gobbledygook, considering the state Elliott was in. He was staring into his empty glass as though it contained a secret. His face was slack and exhausted.

Nina persevered. The lawyer's tool is asking questions. "Then— how are you approaching it?"

"Well, quantum mechanics has a fatal flaw—it doesn't explain why individual events happen. Bohr said not to think about it. What a crock. I went back to early Einstein," Elliott said. "He always thought that the universe wasn't based on random events, as quantum theory says. He said God doesn't throw the dice. Elementary particles may seem to move randomly, but that's only because the real laws are behind the quantum veil. And they are deterministic, Newtonian laws.

"Classical physics, behind the quantum veil, can use all variables and is therefore continuous. But quanta are discrete information packets. As information passes through the quantum veil, some of it is lost because it becomes discrete. What is not random looks random."

Nina nodded. "We have a legal concept that is very similar. It's called the corporate veil. An individual incorporates, and the corporation becomes a protective veil between the individual and the rest of the world. If someone wants to sue the person, they can't. They can only sue the corporation, and the individual's money is protected."

"The real treasure is hidden behind the veil," Elliott said. He tried to grin, but his face just twitched a little. "Yeah. In the case of the quantum veil, the underlying pattern is hidden behind the veil."

"Sometimes you can pierce the veil in law. Get at the hidden assets."

"That's what I think I did. I pierced the quantum veil. I think I really may have done it. I don't know why it happened to be me who figured it out."

"Why does physics come into it?" Nina asked.

Elliott said, "What's a number? Ah, shit, this is what Silke and I used to talk about."

He got up and came back with another small tumbler of whiskey, and Nina realized that his expansiveness would soon turn to the snoring escape of deep drunkenness. In the meantime, though, this young man she had sought for so long was lying on a couch a few feet away, talking into the air, and the moment would never recur. She felt, as she had before, urgently and without much foundation, that Elliott's work had a profound relationship with Sarah Hanna's death. She intended to go wherever he wanted to go.

"What's a number?" she answered. "It's that thing you count with."

"One sheep, two sheep. What's a one?"

Nina held up a finger.

"No," Elliott said. "That's a finger. 'One' is an abstract piece of information. 'One' doesn't pick your nose. True?"

"True."

"What's a hydrogen atom?"

Nina said, "Let me guess. Another abstract piece of information?"

"Correct. It's the energy state of the atom, in terms of the forces that bind its electron to its nucleus, as described in Schrödinger's equation. That and other mathematical descriptions constitute an atom. The information about its behavior is all there is. There is no other 'there' there."

"You mean the hydrogen atom isn't a thing?"

"All we can know about it is the math, which completely describes it. There's nothing else to be said about it. It's real in the way you and I are real. We're made of atoms."

"Okay. But what has the hydrogen atom got to do with locating and factoring prime numbers?"

"Prime numbers are raw information. They have the same properties as fermions—the elementary particles that make up things like hydrogen atoms."

Nina said, "Are you telling me that you think numbers are real, like particles?"

"What does 'real' mean? I'm telling you they're the same thing. They have identical properties, so they're identical. The basic problem with both of them is the same: location, the exact location of each quantum and the exact location of each prime. The Riemann real part one-half corresponds precisely with the fermion spin of one-half. The symmetry of the Riemann zeros corresponds to fermion symmetry. And of course fermions contain odd numbers of subparticles, just as primes are odd-numbered, except for the number two, which is too close to the beginning of the number line to worry about. And the fermions behave randomly within a specific set of limits, just like the primes. The identities go on and on."

"Very interesting."

"And on and on," Elliott said very definitely. He had sat up straight and was now for some reason holding his glass so that he could see it in the mirror above Kurt's fireplace.

"I think I'll have a shot of that whiskey," Nina said. She poured herself a shot of Jim Beam. Maybe it would help her understand.

"I went back to the basics. To the li line. Let me think how to say this. The prime number line drags along forever below the li line, unless you believe Littlewood, which I don't. It's not really a line. It's a zigzag sequence. But"—he pointed his finger at her before continuing—"each prime point wants so much, so very much, to be in a close relationship with the li line."

"What do you mean, wants?" Nina said.

"Can you imagine what it would feel like to be able to see where you belong, but not be able to move toward it? She—she—it's too late. It is so sad. So—damn—sad."

"You should have a glass of water."

"I can have a glass of water when I'm dead." But he accepted the glass Nina brought him. "I really ought to be dead, too, after today. I wonder what it feels like to be dead. No, I don't wonder. It's too awful. I don't want to wonder. I don't want to think about Silke right now. Let's talk about math some more."

"Okay. I'll tell you how I see the li line. The li line is like law," Nina said. "Primes are like individuals in a society, unruly and unpredictable on their own, but society as a whole does follow the law. QED." She tipped her shot glass back.

"No."

"No?"

"Well, sort of." He waved his hand and went on. "I found a

damping coefficient—that's from quantum mechanics—that describes the amount of friction each prime has been subjected to. It's like a relative error term. My damping coefficient is built into a function based around the natural logarithm, which explains a lot of patterns in nature. As soon as I had that, I could factor really large non-prime numbers, too, as a simple corollary. Are you understanding any of this?"

"I'm not sure. But you sound authoritative. That's half the battle."

"Maybe for lawyers. You only have to be convincing. Not in math. In math you have to be right."

"So you know where the prime ought to be at any point on the li line and you know how far it has been pushed from the li line. It becomes simple to find where the prime actually is."

Elliott blinked. "Egg-zackly," he said. "The whole secret is that the continuum breaks into quanta as it passes through the quantum veil. It's an artifact of the definition of primes, insisting that they have to be integers. Integers! There's no such thing as integers! It's time for math to blast out of that particular childish fantasy! Like I said before, what is not random looks random after it passes through. Get it?"

"I'm trying."

"It's One getting broken into little twigs. All of math is really found between Zero and One. Real part one-half is in there. But Riemann—"

Nina smiled. "Okay. I give up."

Elliott said, "Oh, well." He sighed heavily.

"How long ago did you come up with this function?"

"Mostly after my breakdown. Junior year. Three years ago."

"Tell me the function," Nina said coaxingly. "Put it in words for me. I won't understand it or remember it. I'd just like to hear it."

"Why?"

"Because the way you love numbers, I love words."

"I'll tell you what I start with. The difference between pi of x and li of x is Big Oh of the square root of x over log x."

It sounded like a guy dancing in a pentagram naked and trying to invoke a spirit, magical and improbable.

"I like that. Big Oh," Nina said. She was sitting in a firelit cave with the shaggy Shaman of the Primes, hearing his incantations. She wished she could follow Elliott into his theories, appreciate the connections as he did.

"Oh, it is gorgeous," Elliott said. "That's the part everybody knows. Then—my function."

"Tell me the function. Just say it out loud, once. I bet you never have put it into words."

"Why do you really want to hear this? Are you taping this or something?"

This moment of paranoia on his part snapped Nina back to reality. A lawyer again, she said, "It's four o'clock in the morning, Elliott. The robbery might be based on your damping coefficient. People may have died because of it, I don't know. I guess I just want to hear the information that might be the cause of all this."

"Read it in the *Journal of Mathematics* in about a year." His voice had taken on a ragged edge. He obviously wasn't about to tell her his damping coefficient, not that she would have had a clue what it meant anyway. "So you think Silke and Raj died because of my discovery?"

Nina didn't answer.

"Fuck," Elliott said. "Maybe they did. You know the old Greek? Pythagoras?"

"The philosopher?"

"Yeah. The Pythagoreans worshiped integers. They killed

Hippasus when he let out the secret of the irrationals, like the square root of two, that can't be described using ratios of integers. I think they're going to kill me, too."

"Who?"

Elliott answered, "The Pythagoreans of Silicon Valley." He laughed into his glass.

"And are these people who want to kill you real, or just abstract bits of information?" Nina asked.

"That's a really stupid question." He seemed affronted. Nina didn't think it was so stupid, considering what he had been talking about.

"Okay, tell me about the Pythagoreans."

"Now you're just humoring me. But I'll tell you anyway. These Palo Alto Pythagoreans take meetings. They have a lot of money and power. They can pick their noses. I'd say they're real. The name of the company is XYC." He then launched into a story about a meeting in Seattle in which Professor Braun had tried to buy Elliott so that the function would be suppressed.

He was talking faster and faster, like a sparkler that flares up one last time before it goes out. It sounded like raving, but Nina wasn't going to challenge him on anything right now.

"But why try to rob you two years ago, and only a week ago try to buy you?" was all she said. "It's backwards."

"They offered me a lot of money. I bet I could have got them up to ten million," Elliott told her.

Nina took this in, her mouth open. "Your notebook is worth that much?"

"Guess so. It would be a lot cheaper just to steal it. I don't dare keep a copy, and I could never redo the work I have done on the proof."

"But you'd still know your function, wouldn't you?"

Elliott sloshed whiskey out of his glass as he sat up. "Now I get it! Now I get it! That's right!"

"What's right?"

"He was going to grab the notebook and then shoot me. I was supposed to die."

"Where is it now? The notebook?"

"Right here with me."

"Could I see it?"

Elliott said, "I don't show it to anyone. I'm neurotic about that."

"Is it real, Elliott?"

"Of course it's real. What do you mean, is it real?"

"Then let me see it."

"No." He made a protective motion with his hand. He apparently was carrying the damn thing inside Kurt's robe pocket.

"Put it into a safe-deposit box."

"I'm still working on it. I thought about doing that, but I worry about it when it's not on me."

"Publish your results. That might make you safe."

"Not until the proof is finished." He drank the last of the whiskey and gathered the bedding around him. "It's your fault. If you hadn't talked Silke into doing this deposition here, they would have let her go. Oh, I shouldn't say that, I know. Sorry."

"Maybe you're right," Nina said. "Maybe I took it too far. But after my friend was killed, I was going to pursue it to the ends of the earth. Maybe I should have thought more about the human consequences."

"Well," Elliott said with a shrug, "you're a lawyer. Maybe I should have thought more about human consequences too."

"Well, you're a mathematician."

"Yeah. I'm going to sleep now. Here I go." He laid his brain-heavy head onto Kurt's couch pillow. And that was that.

Chapter 24

A SOFT KNOCK AT THE BEDROOM DOOR. Kitchen smells. "Happy Thanksgiving, Mom," Bob's voice said. "Dad's cooking a turkey, and the police are here."

"*Guten Tag.*" Two uniformed police officers, both men, sat with Elliott around the coffee table, papers spread in front of them. Elliott, wrapped in his comforter, nursed a mug of coffee.

"Excuse me." Nina went into the kitchen.

Bob chopped onions on a board on the counter. Kurt stood at the stove, stirring something, a white dishcloth tied around his waist over his jeans. The kitchen air was hot and moist, with an old-fashioned dishwasher sitting in the corner, all its hoses exposed. The stove had legs, as she had noticed while cooking the eggs. But the smells were familiar.

"Happy Thanksgiving. Sleep all right?" Kurt said.

"How long have they been questioning Elliott?"

"Just a few minutes. You haven't missed anything. They had some more details to go over. Here. Have some coffee."

"It is Thanksgiving, isn't it? I'd forgotten."

"And I had quite a time finding a big turkey. Had to get a friend to buy it for me at the Hainerberg PX. It's already in the oven. Turkey, chestnut stuffing, pumpkin pie. Home food. Nice job there, bud."

"How you doing, Mom?"

"Okay."

"The kitchen's taken care of."

"I see that." She made her coffee, letting her hair fall forward so they couldn't see how emotional she felt this morning.

"It's no big thing," Kurt said. "I always celebrate Thanksgiving. My sister came over last year."

"How did the police get your address?"

"They called," Kurt said. "I already had your plane tickets out tonight. I thought it would be okay. Is it okay? I don't think they'll be staying long."

"Sure." Nina went back into the living room and Elliott made room for her on the couch. The detective was taking him through the same story as yesterday, and Elliott seemed quite coherent for a guy who in the middle of the night had just about convinced her that nothing was real. The detective spoke very passable English. Nina sipped her coffee and listened.

When they finished with Elliott, he went in for a shower and they started on her. She had to repeat everything she could remember about the shooting. They looked disappointed when she had nothing new to add. At length the lead detective, a pale man with a shock of blond hair, gathered up his papers and said, "I knew Silke and her family."

"I'm sorry."

"An old family in Heddesheim. Her father was killed in a car accident when she was a baby. Her mother is a baker. Silke's brilliance was noticed from an early age. She will be greatly missed. She was the first person in her family to go to university, and such a university! You know how it is in a little town—we had a parade for her. A send-off, I think you say."

"It's so unfair," Nina said. "Such a waste." The full weight of Silke's death had finally fallen on her shoulders.

"Is there anything you can add to your description of this man with a gun who is wanted in the U.S.? He limped, he spoke American English, he moves around freely, he shoots well, medium height, medium weight—anything?"

"No."

"Do you have any questions for us?"

"Where did he shoot from?"

"Across the street. The upper floor of a furniture store, empty at the time."

"What did you find up there?" Nina was just doing her job, asking. She didn't expect an answer of any substance. The police are adept at not giving out information.

"A fresh fingerprint," the detective said. "At the window."

It struck like a brick in the face. Nina put down her mug. "You have a print?" She was covering her mouth, willing it not to cry out and willing her eyes not to water. Evidence! A print.

"We're running it through Interpol and your IAFIS right now."

"He's been so careful. It's hard to believe."

"A full impression. A thumbprint."

"A print." She blinked and lowered her head.

"Here." He handed her a handkerchief.

"I'm afraid I'm still pretty upset," Nina said.

"He took a cab to the airport. We have a partial description. But he wore a—"

"Ski mask?"

"A hat that covered much of his face."

"Did the driver notice if he had a limp?"

"He favored his left leg."

"It's the same man. He has killed four people."

"So it seems. We will track him down. He will pay."

"Thank you. I can help, after you know more. You have my card. A print!"

"We will let you know."

"Thank you," Nina said again.

"I'm not afraid of this jerk," Bob said, selecting a big piece of turkey breast from the platter. The police had left. The four of them were gathered around the coffee table, which Kurt had covered with a batik. A big fire burned. They were all starving.

"Hang on," Kurt said. "We're going to have a blessing."

"Oops."

"Who's going to do it?"

"You should, Kurt," Nina said. "We're just visitors."

"All right." He thought a moment, then said in his reverberant voice, "On this Thanksgiving Day we gather for a meal like the old pilgrims, grateful to be here together. We are grateful for this meal, and feel glad to share it. I am happy that my son is here along with his lovely mother. And that all here in this house are safe."

"I am grateful that you cooked," Bob said, sniffing, "and it smells so good. And I'm glad to be here, too."

Kurt smiled at him. "Thank you, Spirit of All, for this moment, for this fine food. In the midst of trouble and sadness, together we celebrate life."

"Think of my friends Silke and Raj," Elliott added quietly. "Remember our missing friends and family."

"Amen," they all said. It was the most heartfelt "amen" Nina had ever heard.

It was also the best turkey and stuffing she had ever eaten. A creative type who undoubtedly needed a lot of nurturing himself, Kurt was taking care of them. He had realized how close to chaos they had come, how battered they felt, and he had prepared a meal and a cocoon of warmth for them. Nina would always be grateful to him for that. They ate, and ate more. They clinked glasses. They even laughed.

After they had finished an entire pumpkin pie and pot of Earl Grey tea, Kurt stood up, rubbed his stomach, and stretched. "You guys clean up." He nodded toward Bob and Elliott. "I'll direct you on the dishwasher."

"What about me?" Nina asked.

"We're going for a walk around town, of course. It's traditional on a holiday."

"But is it safe?"

"You yourself said nobody but the police knew we were in Wiesbaden."

"Right."

"And I'll keep you safe, Nina." He pulled her coat out of the closet and held it out for her.

She put her arm through the sleeve, trembling slightly at his touch. "I guess we could. Bob, don't you want to come?"

"You go ahead, Mom."

Kurt held open the door. "See you in a while," he called to Bob and Elliott.

"Later," Bob called from the kitchen.

The light was fading. "Let's go toward the park," Kurt said. "You're not too cold?"

"Me? No." They walked down the street, the stores still open, matrons choosing fruits and vegetables for dinner. At the end of the street was a green park full of tall trees. Old fellows in overcoats behind tightly leashed and well-behaved little dogs walked among the lindens.

"Do you often come here?" Nina asked.

"All the time. I'd like to have a dog, but the landlady's afraid of them. Franz keeps me busy, though, always trying to get out. He's a hunter. You don't want to know some of the funky prey he's brought me."

"This whole morning he lolled innocently on the windowsill."

"His eyes narrowed, secretly on the alert for danger," Kurt insisted. They both laughed at the idea of his slumbering cat on the lookout. "Is this really your first trip to Europe?"

" 'Fraid so. I always wanted to go to Paris to see the Picabias at the Musée d'Orsay. I took French in high school and I love French wine, so I meet the minimum qualifications, I believe."

"You should go." He closed his eyes. "I see it all. Your pretty hair hanging down your back, bugging you because it's come loose; drinking too much St. Emilon in a cafe on the Ile de la Cité, inside to hide from the rain, a good man holding your hand, confessing his love across the table while you flirt with the Moroccan waiter."

"Don't forget the part where I'm making a fool of myself ordering frog legs in aspic when all I really wanted was a turkey on rye."

"You're many things, Nina, but never foolish."

What presumption, she thought. You don't know me anymore. Then she smiled to herself. Here she was being foolish, annoyed by what amounted to a compliment. "Oh, you've forgotten."

"I haven't forgotten anything," he said seriously. "I haven't forgotten we talked about Paris before, and that I promised to take you there."

They walked on in silence as a soft mist fell between the trees along the parkway.

"Do you have to go back right away?" They had reached an

allée of trees, the path civilized and crunchy beneath their feet. The twilight lingered.

"I'd like to stay," Nina said. "But I have to help take out this asshole. This has to stop."

"Nina, I have no right to say this, but I feel compelled. Don't go back to Tahoe. You've almost been killed twice. This killer's on a rampage, trying to eliminate everyone, witnesses, lawyers. You can't tell what he might do."

"I'm a big girl," Nina said.

But Kurt didn't accept that. "You're a young woman and you are a mother. You don't belong in the line of fire. Is this how it always is for you? This stress? This worry?"

"No, of course not. We have a life," Nina said. "We have a dog, a big one. He could teach Franz a few things about bringing down funky prey. My brother and sister-in-law—I'm crazy about them. Bob loves his cousins."

"You know, Bob's very protective of you." He said this as though it had great significance.

"He's fourteen, just a kid. I watch out for him. What are you getting at, Kurt?"

"He doesn't want to let you out of his sight."

"He has so much heart. He doesn't get incredible grades— he's not like Silke Kilmer, you know? He's a complete, perfect, normal human being. He goes to school. He plays ball. He loves his dog..."

"You don't have to tell me. I wonder if you have any idea how well I know him and how intensely I love him."

"Stop. Kurt. Please, stop. You make me feel guilty." She stopped and faced him.

"He has your focus and pragmatism, Nina. Your depths of emotion."

"He has your musical talent."

"Keep after him with lessons."

"He looks like you."

"He reminds me of you. He reminds me of us."

An earthquake of feelings shook through her. She touched the scar on his cheek. He flinched.

"Sorry."

"I try to forget it's there."

"Did I ever tell you," she said, wishing she could bring him up to date on who she was now but afraid they had lived too many years apart ever to make up for the lapses, "that I was shot a few years ago, before you came back into Bob's life? It happened during my first murder case, when I had just set up my practice at Tahoe. A bullet brushed my lung. I hate the scar."

"Poor Nina," Kurt said. He appeared angry, but after a minute or so, during which he put his hands in and out of his pockets a few times, balling them up and releasing them, he finally said, "When you're young, you can't foresee the amount of tragedy, how much baggage you'll carry into adulthood. No wonder we all seem so serious and burdened to the young."

"It's true." The girl she was saw sweet things ahead. The hardships, like car crashes, struck so suddenly there was no preparing.

"I try to remember the alternative and appreciate that all I received was a scar," Kurt said. "But I don't like being marked."

"That's it. You never forget. You just don't get over it. I'm really feeling bad about involving you in this violence. I put you at risk. I didn't realize—"

"It's everywhere," Kurt said. "Don't worry, I can handle it. It's you and Bob I'm concerned about." He put his arm around her.

"Don't," she said, shrugging it off. "You watch out," she went on. "I've been through a lot lately. I'm not myself."

They came to a pond where swans glided, bordered by a grassy yard with a carousel. They sat down on an iron bench and watched a few kids go round and round. A few feet away she saw a gaily decorated cart selling hot dogs. It was just another November weekday in Germany, not a holiday for them, not many people about.

Cold, she held her arms around her chest. Kurt had picked up a stick from somewhere and begun to draw lines on the gravel.

"So this is Germany."

"It's the Kurpark. We have a casino here in Wiesbaden, pretty famous. I'd take you under other circumstances."

"What time is the flight?"

"Eight-forty. Listen, Nina, about the flight. I have to tell you something. It's hard to say."

"Well? What could be so difficult after—"

"I only bought two tickets."

Puzzled, Nina said, "What about Elliott? He's coming back with us."

"He's going back with you. Bob isn't."

Nina shook her head. "No, no, no," she said. "This is crazy. You can't take Bob away from me."

"He asked me how he could get a gun when he goes back."

"What?"

"He said he would protect you that way."

"Oh, no." But she thought about the bolos, Bob's relentless rock-throwing. "No."

"You've put yourself in a line of fire twice in the past month," Kurt said. "What if Bob's beside you next time, sick with worry about you, immature. Trying to be the man in your life."

"It's not like that with us. I'm the parent. He knows that I'd do anything to keep him safe. He's fine!"

"Anything?" Kurt sounded almost, not quite, casual as he asked what amounted to a piercing question. "I called the high school and talked to the vice principal. She faxed me a permission form to allow Bob to take a leave until after Christmas vacation. She'll work with his teachers. They can send him lesson plans so he won't fall behind."

"You can't do this! I need him with me."

"You have to sign the form."

"I won't."

"Do you remember that time you wouldn't leave the cabin at Fallen Leaf? The local squirrels infected with plague. Signs all around. Signs hammered into trees. Danger. Hints of an ugly death. Still you wouldn't leave."

"Of course I do. Note, please that I didn't catch anything."

"Then you were alone. You risked only your own life. I believe," he said, "individuals should control their destinies, right down to choosing death, if they must. I admired your left-brained willfulness. You said the odds favored your survival."

"Is that why you parked yourself out front and made me your mission?"

"My destiny was different. Mine involved—" He sighed. "Shall we walk some more? There's a path around the lake." His voice stayed calm.

They walked for a while along the gravel path. A pale setting sun broke through the cloud cover and more children came out. She couldn't take her eyes off one particular chubby-cheeked toddler running back and forth across the grass, bundled into a sphere in his red coat.

"Look, Kurt, what I admire about myself is that I can admit it when I'm—occasionally—wrong," Nina said, feeling pain with every breath. "Bob stays with you."

He took her by the shoulders and turned her so she faced him, appearing entirely unsurprised at her change of heart.

"Did you already tell him?" Nina asked.

"No. We'll tell him together. This will be a good time to consolidate our power. Two parents can prevail when one might not."

"This murdering animal is ruining my life," Nina said, unleashing only a little of the anger that burned in her. "The minute he's caught, Bob comes home."

"Of course. You could stay, too. Reconsider. Paris is only eight hours away by car."

"No. I do my job. I always do."

His head tilted as he considered that, as he considered her, in her wholeness.

Paul would be mad. Kurt wasn't. What did it all mean?

"Sweet of you to offer," she said.

"Once you would have followed me anywhere." He was smiling now, looking at her with Bob's deep-set bluish-green eyes. "We didn't follow up very well after the trial."

"How do you mean?" Nina said. "You and Bob got to know each other. He spent a whole summer with you in Sweden."

"You were with Paul."

"And you? Were you alone?"

"A girl from Uppsala. An artist."

"Ah. The paintings in your room?" He nodded. "So . . ."

"So. When my contract ended in Sweden, I decided to come back to Wiesbaden. We met for a few weekends, once in Copenhagen. But it petered out." He pondered this, then added, "Franz never accepted her. She sneezed when he merely rubbed demandingly against her leg."

"You're alone now?" Nina prodded.

"I'm used to it."

"Well, just don't get used to having Bob around."

He offered her a wry smile. "I guess we should be getting back. How did you like the pie? Homemade. Momma Scott's old family recipe."

"Magnificent," Nina said. "I didn't know you could cook."

"I remember you couldn't, back when I knew every freckle on you."

She felt a blush creeping up her neck, which she tried to stop by thinking of cool things, green trees, the ocean, the Truckee River splashing. "When Bob came along I had to learn. I'm good with macaroni and cheese. Someday, when this is all over, I'll cook for you."

"Or maybe I'll cook for you. Frog legs in aspic. Something yummy like that. Sans noodles."

"Or we'll order food from people who know their food."

"From a Moroccan waiter. And if you flirt with him, I'll follow him into the kitchen and kick his butt."

Chapter 25

NIGHT ON THE PACIFIC, MOONLIGHT ON cloud-tops. A painted torpedo toy streaking through the vault of sky, stuffed with human beings ignoring their precarious situation.

Most people were sleeping. Elliott had purchased an airplane pillow at the airport. He slouched in his seat, pulled the inadequate blanket to his chest, leaned his head back, and let his mouth fall with gravity. His breath was sour with the wine he had drunk, and shaving had not been on the agenda.

Nina, in the window seat, waited until he had not moved for almost an hour. Then she carefully lifted the blanket away from his chest. He wore his parka, unzipped, over a striped shirt, the top buttons undone. His naked Adam's apple moved regularly up and down and she could see scanty chest hair.

She inserted a hand inside the parka, just above his heart. He seemed to heave a sigh as she slowly removed the notebook, as though his heart noticed and regretted the theft. No jerky movements, she told herself as the hand snaked back home with its prize.

The seat light sent its focused beam onto a thick black leather-covered notebook, about four inches square, held shut with a laughable silver lock like the one on the pink diary Nina had kept in seventh grade.

The toothpick from the dinner plate worked, though she had several other possible tools ready. She wondered how this thing that Elliott protected like a dragon could have been locked so flimsily.

But it wasn't the lock, of course, it was where he kept it, right next to his heart. She squeezed the ends of the lock and it clicked open. Reading glasses! They were gone, no, they were on her head. Don't get excited, she told herself. If he woke up, she would calmly hand it back and admit it.

The inside of Elliott's universe was as neat as the toothpick that had opened it, no loose scraps of paper, no cross-outs and scrawls. Obviously this was where he kept results, not work in progress. Flipping through it, she estimated that there were three hundred pages of neatly written notes and calculations and beautiful graphs. Each page was dated.

She turned back to the beginning. The cover page said, "Elliott Wakefield's Theory of Everything. Do Not Enter. Or you are Cursed." There was also a boy's drawing of a skull and crossbones, and a curlicued "EW." On the next page, the first date showed that Elliott had been keeping this same mathematical diary for ten years. He must have been in about eighth grade when he started it.

She flipped through it again. A doodle or two, no blank pages interspersed. Elliott had been rigorous with himself, amazingly so for the boy who had begun this venture. She glanced at him, at the boy in the man this time, and realized that she really, really wanted it all to be true—that he had solved the mystery of the prime numbers.

If it was true, what she held in her sneaky hands would be

immortality. Prizes and honors would only be the beginning. This book would go to a museum.

She turned back to the first pages, where the writing was bigger. He had used a fine-tipped mechanical pencil throughout. The pages had gold edges. Water had stained the tops of some of them. The notebook itself was pliant, the cover soft.

The book began with the harmonic series, in some form she could barely recognize. Even at thirteen, Elliott was ahead of her. She saw signs she recognized as calculus, and some infinity symbols and ellipses, and knew he was working with series of numbers and their limits. That pi sign meant "prime number." "Let something be the something of something something."

If only Mick were on this flight. If only a copy machine were back there with the chatting flight attendants, right next to the microwave. Could she copy any of it on her napkin? What should she copy? She turned to the last page and did copy the equations as well as she could, though most of the symbols were new to her. The folded napkin went down her blouse, near her own heart.

Yet she couldn't bring herself to give it back yet. She was touching the dragon's jewel, running her fingers over the leather, feasting her eyes on page after page of the dragon's magic formulae. Elliott's universe.

She wanted to keep it. But he would miss it immediately, and this was no cave she could flee.

Please be true. She wished it passionately for him, because his grief for his friends was real and deep and she might have had a hand in causing their deaths.

After a while she lifted the blue blanket again and opened the parka, slipping the book home again. Elliott dreamed on while Nina watched and wondered. Thirty thousand feet down within the still ocean, whales swam through the night, singular, extraordinary.

Chapter 26

FIRST SNOW FELL OUTSIDE THE WINDOW. Betty Jo Puckett, Elliott, Sandy, Nina, and a transcriber sat around Nina's conference table. The espresso machine coughed on the counter nearest the door, and the lamp was lit in honor of winter's arrival.

Elliott had already told his story, changing nothing from his talk with Nina in Germany.

Betty Jo had caused no trouble about the lack of notice regarding the changed deposition. Nina suspected that she had had second thoughts about not attending and was relieved to be able to do so at Tahoe. She wasn't her flippant self, though; she said little and listened carefully, making occasional notes.

Elliott stared at the table in front of him. He had been asked about the Heddesheim shooting, but Nina had made it as merciful as possible. Getting him out of bed this morning had been difficult. She was afraid that jet lag and grief were turning into depression.

But he did his duty, and at last an eyewitness account of Sarah Hanna's death had been given.

"Do you have any questions to ask the witness?" she asked Betty Jo. Though it was Nina's show, Betty Jo had every right to go over whatever she wanted. She had taken notes throughout Nina's questioning, and as the story poured out, the card counting, the money, the shooting, the primes, XYC, she never blinked. She was on a mission and she had her own theory, that was obvious.

She regarded Elliott with her head cocked as if taking his measure. She had worn a tweed suit and UGG boots to the deposition, which did not make her look ridiculous, as she had long toned legs, and her fluff of silver hair was set off by the silver of the suit. With her steady eyes and dark eyebrows, the slight shadow of a mustache, she was formidable behind the down-home facade.

"Well, Elliott, you've been avoiding having to do this for a long time, haven't you? I mean, you could have contacted Mr. Hanna a long time ago and shared this information with him, couldn't you?"

"As I said, I was afraid. I didn't see how I could help."

"You were afraid to tell the truth?"

"I didn't say that."

"Do you agree with Ms. Reilly here that the motel should have done more to protect you?"

"I—I—don't know."

"Ms. Reilly must have explained to you that you're a straw defendant, that she used a legal trick that required callin' you a defendant. You know that, don't you?"

"She said she had to do it to get my testimony."

"And she's not trying to get any money from you regarding this incident, is she?"

"Not that I know of."

"You and she are good buddies?"

"I like her all right."

"Stayin' at her house, aren't you?"

"Yes."

"You're workin' together to get some money from the Ace High Lodge?"

Elliott looked surprised. "No, I don't want any money."

"But you're helping her, to get her off your back so you can go home?"

"It's about my friends at this point."

"Feel guilty about them dying, don't you?"

"Yes."

"Why?"

"Because it was probably my notebook he was after. Like I said."

"You feel guilty about rushing the robber, don't you?"

"Not really. Maybe a little."

"Sure you do," Betty Jo said. "I would." She paused and took a sip of water.

"Did you at any time see the motel clerk, Meredith Assawaroj, during this incident?" she went on.

"No, ma'am."

"Did you at any time see the owner of the motel, James Bova, during this incident?"

"No, ma'am, unless he was the man in the mask."

Betty Jo showed him an eight-by-ten photograph. "Defendant's Three," she said. "Now, I will represent that this is a recent photograph of James Bova."

She passed another print to Nina.

"I'll stipulate that this is Mr. Bova," Nina said.

"Did you ever see this man? Have you ever seen this man?"

"Not unless he was the man in the mask. As I said."

"I will represent to you that Mr. Bova is just over six feet tall. Counsel?"

"We can verify that later," Nina said.

"I believe you said that the man in the ski mask was of medium height, is that correct?"

"It was dark. I would say he wasn't unusually tall or short."

"In your mind, is someone over six feet tall medium or tall in height?"

"I guess tall," Elliott said. "I'm five-eleven and I consider myself tall."

"So this man was not tall?"

"I didn't notice that he was unusually tall."

"How much did this man weigh? The robber in the mask?"

"I would say he was on the skinny side."

"Skinny?"

"I guess so."

"You don't have to guess," Nina said.

"I didn't notice anything unusual about his weight."

"I will represent to you that Mr. Bova weighs two hundred and twelve pounds. Do you consider that skinny?"

"Not really."

"You grappled with this man?"

"I bumped him and hit at his arm, and the gun went flying."

"So you had physical contact with him?"

"Yes. He was hard—he worked out. That's about all I could say."

"Come on," Betty Jo said. "You can do better than that. When you came into contact with him, was he taller than you?"

"I had my head down."

"Did he weigh more than you? What do you weigh?"

"One seventy-four."

"Did he weigh more than you?"

"I'd say so. Yeah, I was wrong. He wasn't really skinny."

Betty Jo didn't like that answer. She moved on.

"After the shots, how much time elapsed before you heard the screaming of the motel clerk?"

"Does he know if it was the motel clerk screaming?" Nina interrupted.

"How long before you heard a woman screaming?" Betty Jo went on.

"Seconds."

"How many seconds?"

"I had time to run almost all the way to my room. Approximately forty seconds, forty-five seconds."

"She must have been very close, right?"

"Pretty close. I heard later she was at the Internet cafe next door."

"Never mind what you heard. So you had attracted a lot of attention at Prize's, winning all that money?"

"The pit boss was getting too interested."

"You had made thirty-five thousand dollars at one five-dollar-minimum table?"

"At two tables."

"Other people were watching you? Guests of the casino?"

"Sure. It was time to leave."

"Did you ask for any security to carry this large amount of cash?"

"No, we were staying just across the street."

"Did you make any efforts to avoid being followed?"

"He didn't have a duty to do that," Nina said.

Betty Jo said, "He might have. He was a pro in a dangerous business. If you can sue him to bring him here, I may as well sue him, too." Elliott didn't look too happy at this.

"Did you? What did you do to protect yourself from robbery?"

"There were three of us."

"Anything else?"

"Tried to keep a low profile."

"That didn't work out, though, did it?" Without waiting for an answer, Betty Jo said, "You were standing right at the vending machine when this man appeared?"

"Yes. We were. Silke had just put in the money."

"Defendant's Four. Photo of the area around the vending machine." The transcriber pasted an identification label on the photo and returned it to Betty Jo, who passed it to Elliott.

"How many ways in and out are there from this area?"

"Two. The street side, and the parking-lot side."

"Three actually, aren't there? Look again."

"Oh, the staircase."

"You weren't boxed in, were you? If he came one way, you could run another way? You did run another way? And got away safely?"

"Yes."

"The two people on the balcony—you saw them?"

"Just for a second."

"You didn't see the woman get shot?"

"No, I was running for my room when I heard the third shot."

"The police report doesn't mention any third shot. Where were you for the first two shots?"

"Going toward him."

"And you say he shot in the air? Think he was trying to scare you?"

"You don't have to guess," Nina said again, but Elliott answered, "Yes."

"And when you heard the third shot your friends were ahead of you, and had already run into their rooms? You were almost at your ground-floor room?"

"Yes."

"So why would he fire a warning shot?"

Elliott stared at the table. "I've wondered about that, how it happened. He must have noticed them after he picked up the gun again. He must have just shot straight at them."

"Excuse me," Nina said. "Just to clarify the record, you're speculating, right?"

"It just seems logical. We weren't there anymore."

"Okay," Betty Jo said, "I want to suggest something to you. And I want you to search your heart and remember you're under penalty of perjury, even if you're not in court today. Understand?"

"Yes."

"I suggest that there were a total of two shots, as Meredith Assawaroj told the police. Wait just a minute. I suggest that you were struggling with this bad guy, this robber with a gun, and you lifted his arm up, trying to get the gun, and the gun went off and hit the lady."

"There were three shots, I know that much. I don't care what the police reports say. And after the second shot, I saw them crouched up on their balcony."

"Were you facing the robber?"

"Yes."

"So he had his back to that balcony?"

"Yes."

"You're the one facing the balcony, struggling over a gun." Betty Jo raised her arm and said, "I've got the gun and you're going for it. You push my arm back and it goes off."

"Objection," Nina said. "Lack of foundation, calls for speculation, misstates the testimony. Counsel is testifying. Just for the record."

Betty Jo said, "You want to get at the truth or not? Let's end this here. This boy made a mad rush at an armed robber, and in the struggle an innocent bystander was accidentally killed, and it's hard for him to admit." She turned back to Elliott. "You seem like a nice boy."

"Objection," Nina said. In depositions, alas, there was no judge to rule on objections and make the lawyers behave; one could only object for the record. It would have to be sorted out later.

"Is it my turn?" Elliott said. "I looked her in the eyes as I turned and ran, and she was alive, crouching in a corner, watching."

"How do you know she wasn't hit?" Betty Jo said. She had a loud clear voice and she talked like a school principal. Elliott had a hangdog look. A guilty look, even, but so would anybody subjected to Betty Jo. Nina was worried at the beating Elliott was taking, but she couldn't help appreciating the other lawyer's style. "Well? She could have just been shot, couldn't she? Crouching there in the corner, poor little thing, while you macho boys slugged it out and the shots went a-flyin'. How far away was she?"

"Fifty to sixty feet. Forty feet on the horizontal, ten feet up. The square root of two hundred and sixty." He took out his calculator. "Fifty-two point zero-zero-six feet. That's an estimate."

"Can you swear to me under penalty of perjury that she wasn't hit when you looked at her for that split second?"

Elliott shook his head.

"Speak up!"

"I can't be positive."

"There wasn't any third shot. Nobody else heard it but you, Elliott. All you have to do is admit it and you can spare us all a world of misery. Haven't you had enough misery already?"

"Objection," Nina said. "That question is irrelevant, incompetent, and immaterial, and the rest is just badgering." Her objection went into the record, but Betty Jo could ignore it here, and that's exactly what she did. Silke had heard a third shot, but Silke couldn't attest to that anymore. Dave couldn't remember, and Raj was dead, too.

Elliott placed his hands on the table, palms down, and looked at them. "I don't know anything anymore," he mumbled. "I can't go on. I don't feel well."

Betty Jo had the audacity to lean across the table and pat his hand. "Just tell us the truth, now, honey." She gave Nina such a glare that Nina didn't pipe up with another objection. Her suspicion was fair. She was trying to get at the truth. Elliott wasn't Nina's client, after all.

Maybe Betty Jo was right. Maybe Elliott had done just what she said. Nina couldn't prove differently. Hard to believe Elliott could lie, though.

Elliott wasn't lying now. He wasn't saying anything.

"Two shots or three shots?" Betty Jo said, waiting expectantly.

"Three shots."

Betty Jo threw down her tablet, stood up, and said, "I won't sit here and listen to this bucketful of lies any longer." She picked up her Hermès briefcase and walked out.

"Whew," Sandy said. The transcriber raised her eyebrows and said to Nina, "Now what?"

"We're finished," Nina said.

Wish was waiting in the outer office to take Elliott back to the house. He didn't mind being the babysitter as long as he had access to Nina's computer and phone at the cabin. But Elliott said, "I'm slept out. I have to do something."

"It's better for you not to go out until your flight tomorrow," Wish told him. "Nina?"

"What do you have in mind?" Nina said.

"I want to play some cards. Wish can come."

"I can't protect you in a casino," Wish said, but he added again, "Nina?"

"There's no safer place on earth than a casino," Nina said. "But how about getting there and getting back?"

"We could take my van. It's pretty discreet," Wish said. Nina was acutely aware that Elliott was not in her custody and that he would not fare well staring at the wall of Bob's bedroom. She said, "Be careful. Both of you." Elliott brightened a little.

"Did I do all right?" he asked. "The thing is, that lawyer almost made me believe it was a straight robbery. I could almost see me lifting the man's arm, when she lifted her arm. But I don't think I did. I hit his arm, and the gun went flying. And there were three shots."

"You did fine," Nina said. "Thanks."

But as he pulled on his parka, Elliott said, "Maybe it was a robbery and she was in the wrong place at the wrong time. Maybe I'm trying to find some sense in this when it's all random. Some criminal saw me win some money and all this other stuff happened."

"Go play some cards," Nina said. "Rest your mind."

When the door closed behind them, Nina said to Sandy, "She's so good she has me half-convinced it was all Elliott's fault. Did you call Sergeant Cheney?"

"He's got a call in to the Heddesheim police. He said he'd phone when he hears anything." Sandy had returned to her desk and was looking at something on the Net. "Wish wants you to check this out. Come around here."

It was a porn site, the writing, whatever there was of it, in a foreign script. The site had a .thailand html.

"Thailand?"

"Brittney" posed in red leather underpants. She had red lips and spiky black hair, a slight body that didn't seem right for the togs. She smiled for the camera. She was riding a large gray mutt, canine species, and swung some sort of spiked ball on a chain in the air, like an elf-queen going into battle. The background colors were comic-book. There were several stills, all involving the dog.

"That's Meredith Assawaroj! The clerk at the Ace High! I saw her photo in one of the newspaper accounts of the shooting!"

"She's a naughty girl," Sandy said. "Not to mention, we had to pay twenty bucks to get this site up, and I'll be getting porn spam for the next year on this computer. I hope it's worth it."

"It's disgusting. Look at that!"

"I wish Willis hadn't."

"Did Wish say anything else?"

"He just said to have a look. He interviewed her and he was following up." Meredith had her hands full with the dog.

"She still works at the Ace High," Sandy said. "You have court at three."

"What's the weather prediction?"

"Eighteen inches of snow."

"I wish Bob were home. He'd be excited. Did you send the copies of the tape and the napkin to Mick?"

"He wants five hundred dollars to grant you his wisdom."

"Grr. Fine. I'll make out the check."

The plows were out, but the boulevard still had several inches of fresh powder and the snow kept coming, straight down on this windless dark day. Though it was only noon, Christmas lights strung merry colors along the way. Few cars were out.

Meredith sat in the overheated motel office, reading a Thai newspaper. The lipstick was still red. She had a complicated ar-rangement of piercings in her ears and a pointed chin. She jumped to her feet and said, "Welcome to the Ace High. How may we serve you?"

Nina gave her a business card. Her face closed.

"I can't talk now. I'm on duty."

"When someone comes in, I'll stop."

"I already talked to your boy." She meant Wish. "I don't know anything."

"Are you still posing for porn photos?" Nina said. Meredith's eyes veiled and her expression hardened.

"So what?" she said. "You want to buy one? You can't black-mail me. It's totally legal. My lawyer said so."

"Does Mr. Bova know about it?"

Meredith laughed. "He loves them. Why are you here, bugging me? Go away."

Nina stood her ground. She was five feet three, but Meredith was at least three inches shorter and quite a bit younger. It was nice to have a physical advantage for once, but Meredith wasn't the kind of girl who responds well to pressure. "Okay," Nina said, "I can't put any pressure on you. I didn't mean to sound accusatory."

"Brittney" folded her arms. "You're damn straight."

"How about if I buy you lunch?"

"Why? You don't care about me. Nobody does."

"I won't ask you any questions. Let's just have lunch."

"You'll just hassle me."

Nina shrugged. "I'm hungry, and I want to eat well, and I don't have anyone to eat with." Meredith didn't buy that, but she seemed to like the idea of having lunch bought for her.

"Where?" she said.

"You pick."

"It's snowing."

"The heater in my truck works fine. I'll drop you back here."

"You're buying?"

"Damn straight," Nina said with a smile.

Meredith said, "You want to buy me lunch at the Summit restaurant, I'll go."

"Why not?" Nina said.

"I have to set up the answering service." She did that, and put on a furry coat. She wore black leggings and ankle boots. She kept casting sideways glances at Nina that said, You're a fool.

It was a long shot, a whim really, but Nina had a feeling.

"I don't really have a lawyer," Meredith said over her halibut. She drank some wine and dabbed at her lips. "I always wanted to come to this place."

"Mind if I ask how old you are?" Nina said.

"Twenty-six."

"Were you raised in the mountains?"

"You know I wasn't. You know I still have an accent. I was born in Chiang Mai, Thailand."

"Oh," Nina said. "I've heard it's a beautiful place."

"No snow there. I can't believe how hard it's snowing. It scares me. But we'll have so much business from the snowboarders. We get a lot of people from England and France and Germany."

Nina added some olive oil to her salad.

"What are those little green balls on your salad?"

"Capers. They're—you know, I'm not sure what they are."

"So do you despise me? Because of the photos on the Web? You don't think I really gave permission for those things to be in every bedroom in America, do you?"

"Is that why you're eating lunch with me?" Nina said. "Because you need a lawyer to help you get those photos off the Web?"

"What are my chances? The creep is my ex-boyfriend, of course. He's in Bangkok."

"Did he take the photos?" Nina asked.

"Every one. He set it up. He brought the dog. My boss—Mr. Bova—doesn't really know."

"Did you sign anything?"

"It wasn't like that. It was a joke at the time."

"When did he post the photos?"

"Over a year ago."

"Did he use your real name anywhere?"

"No, he used the Brittney name."

"We found the site by Googling your real name."

"God damn it!" For such a small girl, she spoke with a lot of force.

Nina stabbed a small tomato and said, "I'm sorry, Meredith. If he were in California, even somewhere in the U.S., maybe I could do something."

Meredith finished her wine. "I think I'll tell my cousin back home. I'm mad enough to confess to him. My cousin will take care of it. This is good food. Could I see a dessert menu?"

She chose crème brûlée with a drizzle of raspberry syrup. "It upsets my stomach, but so what." Nina watched her eat, drank her coffee, and let her talk. Snow fell from the sky, and another day in her life was passing. Meredith wasn't going to solve the case for her. She relaxed and started thinking about the two cords of wood due to be delivered on Saturday, and that it would take her days to stack it without Bob.

"I have to get back."

Nina got out her credit card.

"I still don't know why you did this," Meredith said when they were back in the Bronco with the heater on, compacting snow with the studded snow tires as they moved slowly down the street on their way back to the Ace High. "I told you I wouldn't say anything."

"It's all right," Nina said. "You already told the truth. No need to make you tell it over and over."

Meredith pulled down the visor and applied lipstick. "I like my job. I need it."

Nina kept her eyes on the road, nodded.

"You're making me feel bad."

"Why?"

"There is something I didn't tell, because I'll lose my job."

Nina stopped the Bronco right in front of the office.

"Don't you want to know what it is?"

Nina said, "Yes. But I have no way of finding out, except if you decide to tell me."

Meredith grabbed her purse. "Well, I can't!"

"Suit yourself. Door's unlocked."

The girl flung it open and snow immediately drifted in. Jumping down, she said, "Bye."

And then she paused.

"I owe you now. You were nice to me. I'm really not what you think I am."

"It's all right."

Meredith leaned her head back into the cab and said, "When I heard the shots, I ran out of the cafe, across the lot, and around the corner to the vending machine by the office. The husband was halfway down the stairs, yelling. I didn't see the robber. But I did pick up something. Stay here."

She ran into the office and a minute later came out with a plastic grocery bag. The Bronco door on her side was still wide open. She set the bag on Nina's seat and said, "So look. I didn't know the lady had been shot or I never would have taken it. I couldn't sell it when I learned she was dead."

Nina opened the bag and saw a blue-steel revolver.

"No lecture," Meredith said with a warning tone in her voice. She had the sullen, frightened look of a child about to be spanked.

"Why now?"

"You have brought back the whole thing for me. After your boy talked to me I can't sleep. I was broke and I was going to go to Reno to pawn it. Then—I realized I couldn't do that. I almost threw it in a trash can, but I kept thinking about her. Maybe the gun was important. So I said to myself, Okay, let's see if they find the killer without this. I'll just keep it. And they haven't found him, and I have this thing which is like a tool of a demon, like it's on fire in the secret place where I kept it. And you come. That's all."

Nina couldn't quite believe this story. "Who has handled this gun?"

"No one but me. Oh well, I can always go to Vegas. Even if Mr. Bova—"

"You think Mr. Bova will fire you? Why would he?"

She brought her face close and hissed, "You really want to know? You want to know why I kept the gun?"

"Tell me."

"What if he shot the lady? What if he was the robber?"

"He was in Sparks that night," Nina said.

"That's what he said."

"His girlfriend agrees. So do several neighbors who saw him there that night."

She got very still. "Really? He really didn't do it?"

"So you thought you were protecting him?" Nina said. "Weren't you afraid if he found out he would hurt you, if you thought that?"

"How would he find out?" Meredith said. "I wasn't going to say anything. I wasn't protecting him. I was protecting my job. And now I look stupid. Oh well. I took the gun and I kept it. I thought I could sell it someday, and I thought maybe my boss did the shooting. If he went to jail, he would have had to sell the motel."

"His alibi is as solid as Hoover Dam," Nina said.

"Okay, you see? I'm stupid. I'm mixed up. I have been very, very poor in my life. And now I'm very, very cold."

"Thanks," Nina said.

Meredith said, "You're welcome."

Chapter 27

NINA DROVE TO THE COURTHOUSE COMPLEX on Johnson Boulevard. Snow lay heavy on the fir boughs. The sky had turned iron-hued. It was disorienting, this sudden change from blue and green to whites and grays. Traffic was building on the highway as the skiers poured out of their knotholes in the valleys below the Sierra, drawn to the mountains like carpenter ants to fine wood-work. The snow came over the tops of her heels and her feet froze.

The police department was right next door. Sergeant Cheney came out and escorted her to his office. Still standing, she placed the bag carefully on his desk and said, "I haven't touched it. It's the gun that killed Sarah Hanna."

Cheney looked at the bag as though it contained scorpions, then, gingerly, pulled it open at the top and peeked inside. He picked up the phone and said, "Is the forensics tech still around? Send him in. Tell him to bring an evidence kit."

While they were waiting, he said, "Where'd you get it?"

"The clerk at the Ace High Lodge picked it up off the ground right after the shooting."

"She's been hiding it all this time?"

"She didn't want to get into trouble."

"She made her trouble worse." He made another call.

He gave her a speculative look. "You know, we're going to have to make you an honorary member of the police department if you keep this up. 'Course, there are a few officers you've crushed on the witness stand who might differ with me."

"It is an interesting change from criminal-defense work," Nina said.

"You're as persistent as a horsefly on a hot day. It's been a bitch of a case. If you hadn't come charging in, I don't know where we'd be."

The tech knocked and came in, carrying rubber gloves, a digital camera slung around his neck, and a small case.

"It's the weapon. Hanna case. Or so we have heard."

"Fantastic," the man said. He took a picture of the white plastic grocery bag on the desk and said, "Why not bring it down to the evidence room?"

"Because I think it has been enough places already, and I'm not going to join the chain of custody. You take charge of it. I haven't even opened the bag. Let me know when you're finished."

"I hear you, brother." He asked questions, put on the gloves, took the gun out, and took more pictures.

"It's a good old Saturday night special," Cheney said.

"Six-shooter. Thirty-eight caliber."

"How many left in the chamber?"

The tech picked up the gun with a latex-gloved hand and examined it. "Three."

"So if it was fully loaded, three shots," Cheney said.

"I bet you got A's in arithmetic. Okay, I'm gonna tag it." He made Nina sign the tag with the date, time, and place, and left with the gun. As soon as it left the room, she felt better.

"I'll call this the Tahoe gun," Cheney said. "Two guns down, this gun and the one that killed Chelsi Freeman, one still to find, the Heddesheim gun. The German police have it. They tell me that it was probably a Sig, a target pistol, a single-action semi-auto. This guy must spend half his time at gun stores."

"Now we know why he had to buy another one," Nina said. "He left the Tahoe gun at the scene of the robbery, and Meredith grabbed it."

"And he couldn't bet on getting the second gun through customs, so he bought the Sig under the table over there. How about a cup of water?" Cheney said. "I'm taking your statement now."

"I have court in"—she consulted her watch—"twenty minutes."

"We'll call the judge's clerk."

"Twenty minutes," Nina said. "Flaherty waits for no one. My client needs me there. I'll finish up later if I have to."

It took less time than that.

When she was finished, Cheney turned off the tape and said, "I'm going to bust her ass. For withholding this evidence. For touching that gun. For sitting two miles away with this thing for two years. For keeping me out late tonight when my wife is making gumbo in honor of the season."

"She makes gumbo?"

"Every year, at the first snowfall. I love winter. I'm so happy it's here."

"Why?" Nina asked.

"Because it buries everything until spring. Everything but this case. This case is hereby pried wide open." He gave Nina a hard look. "Aren't you going to plead for the girl? Show mercy, et cetera et cetera, tell me how she came through in the end?"

"No," Nina said. "Nail her. Three more people have died."
She got up. "Next case," she said. "See you later."

"I'll walk you out. Oh, by the way." He walked down the hall
with its awful lighting and ushered her into the lobby. "Germany
got a hit on the fingerprint in Heddesheim."

It was like being hit in the head. "Ohh," Nina moaned.

"What's the matter?"

"Headache."

"I'm sorry. I really am. I couldn't help wanting to spring it on
you. My wife says I have a little sadistic streak. We have a name.
Leland Moss Flint. Aka Lee. He attended Annapolis and graduated in 1984. If we're lucky, we'll have another print of his on
this gun."

"Lee Flint," Nina said. It was such a short, sweet name to give
her such a sharp pain in the head. "Where is he?"

"We'll know soon. You all right?"

"I'm having an existential moment. Lee Flint killed so many
people, Sergeant. It's almost frightening to hear his name."

"We'll find him now."

"You won't have to look far," Nina said. "He's here at Tahoe."

"How do you know that?"

"I just know. And he's desperate."

She called Dave Hanna after court. It was Roger she wanted
to call, but she reminded herself that you don't pick your clients
and went ahead.

He sounded slightly, but not dispositively, blitzed. "Yeah?"

"It's Nina."

"Wait, let me sit down. Okay. What do you want?"

"I don't want anything. I want to post you on the progress in
your case."

"How bad is the blizzard?"

"We're going to get more than the prediction. The whole town's celebrating."

"That's good. Jobs. It's only raining down here." Placerville was only at four thousand feet, while Lake Tahoe lay at sixty-two hundred feet.

"Your time will come," Nina said. She was relieved that he was willing to make small talk. He seemed almost friendly.

"Roger says you've been working hard for me. I can't believe you went all the way to Germany. Too bad about the witnesses. I haven't been feeling good lately. I guess Roger told you."

"We have developments. We have the gun, we have a fingerprint, and we have an ID." She summarized what she knew.

"Unbelievable," Dave said. "I'd like to come up there and really talk this through, but Echo Summit is closed and I'm kind of a mess." Echo Summit, the pass into Tahoe from Placerville, was even higher, at seventy-four hundred feet.

"Dave? You need to be careful. We are cornering Leland Flint."

"Never heard of him. Who is he?"

"We don't know yet. But we're going to get him, Dave."

"I can't cope with all this pressure."

"Talk to the police down there. Get some help. Maybe Roger will come and stay with you."

"Not Roger. He's always on me. Ragging and nagging. We're not getting along."

"Then the police."

"Why would he come after me, anyway?" The news was sinking in, and his tone was uneasy.

"It's your case. It's where the heat is coming from."

"Not really. It's your case. It's always been your case. You took it against my will. If anything happens to me, it's on you." She heard the familiar resentment against the world coming through.

"That's not fair, Dave."

"None of this will get Sarah back. She's dead. You can't fix that, and the rest is crap."

A surge of anger overtook Nina. "Your wife, your niece—they were murdered," she said. "Stop fighting me."

"He'll go after you first," Dave said. "You're the source of the noise. You watch your own back." He hung up.

She drove home in the early dark. KTHO said Tahoe was expected to have a couple hundred thousand visitors over the weekend. The motels along the way all had No Vacancy signs. The big ski resorts—Heavenly, Alpine, Northstar—were booked solid. On Kulow Street, every house but hers had its lights to keep away the winter ghosts. The lights weren't about Christmas in the mountains, not really. They were about the dark, keeping it away. Not having Bob with her took away her daily life, her sense of well-being.

She thought about getting out of the Hanna case, because she was so angry at Dave Hanna. Then she thought about Chelsi, and how close they were to finding her killer. Her eyes—so innocent and bewildered in those last moments—

Wish's van was in the driveway. She pulled in behind it, and struggled through the snow up the icy stairs.

Wish answered the door. He helped her take off her coat, took her briefcase from her, led her to the couch in front of the fire, handed her a glass of wine.

"Stop," he said. "For a few hours. Lie down there. I'm cooking. We'll eat soon."

"Elliott?"

"He won twelve thousand dollars. We stopped at the Raley's and bought eggs and coffee and milk."

"All right."

"Lie down."

"Just for a minute."

They met at the dinner table: Elliott, in a funk, his hands shaking; Wish, spooning out mashed potatoes like a lady in a hair net in the asylum cafeteria; and Nina, three-quarters of the way down her second glass of wine. Nina could feel a draft at her feet, probably from the old windows next to the table, which led to the backyard deck, which, she noticed, would have to be shoveled soon, in case the snow kept falling all night. She didn't have a garage for the Bronco, either, which meant that after supper she'd have to open the ski closet and find shovels and brushes and scrapers.

On the other hand, Wish and Elliott were just right for outdoor tasks, and Elliott especially could benefit from exercise. Yes, it would be for their own good. She had some turkey loaf and complimented Wish on the cuisine, then told them both about Meredith and the gun.

"So you're vindicated, sort of," she concluded, as Elliott embarked on his second serving of everything. "Three bullets gone."

"But was it the third shot that killed her?" Wish asked, breaking the encouraging spell Nina was trying to weave.

But Elliott finally spoke up. "I saw the first two. He aimed high."

"She was high, on a balcony," Wish said.

"She was behind him. He shot toward the street entrance at about an eighty-degree angle."

"Too bad the police couldn't find the third bullet," Wish said. "Anyway, I hear you. You saw the first two shots aimed high and in the opposite direction from the woman."

"Yes. I've been thinking about it all afternoon. He didn't fire when I struggled with him. I couldn't have leaned his arm back like the lawyer said."

"Good, that's clear, then." Nina went into the kitchen and put on the teapot and thought, I hope.

"He must have seen the Hannas on the balcony after the students ran, and panicked and shot at them," Wish offered.

The kitchen and the dining room of the cabin were essentially one room, so she could continue the conversation without a beat. "Why?" she asked. "He wore a mask. They couldn't identify him."

"I surprised him," Elliott said. "He lost his bearings. He couldn't think straight anymore."

"Right after dinner I'm getting on the Web and see what I can find on the name," Wish said. "What did you say his name was?"

"Guess I forgot to say," Nina said. "He was ID'd as a man named Leland Moss Flint."

Elliott got up from the table, clumsily. He made fists with his hands and started rhythmically beating them against his head from either side, walking around the living room.

"Elliott, what are you doing?" Nina asked.

"Thinking. Thinking. Am I making this all up? Is this my fantasy? Are you people real?" Nina and Wish exchanged glances.

"It can't be. She wouldn't. But I remember she had one. Or maybe I'm making all this up to look important. Maybe the notebook's full of shit. I knew I should burn it. It's driven me crazy, like Cantor. I'm crazy, that's right, that's the problem."

Nina went to him and said, "Put your arms down. Please. Come on, sit down again."

"You better call the loony bin." But he sat back down, wearing an anguished expression. He looked from Wish to Nina and said, "Is it really because of me? Four deaths? I can't take that. All I wanted was to figure out the problem. Such a fascinating problem, and I didn't want to be famous, exactly, I mean posthumous fame would have been fine, it was good enough for Cantor. I wanted people to know and appreciate that I solved it, that's all."

The teapot began to whistle, and he jumped. "I never met him, but she had one."

"One what?" Nina said.

"A brother."

"Who had a brother?"

"Carleen."

Somewhere she had heard that name. Oh yes, Carleen had been a card counter with the other three, but left the group months before the shooting. "What about Carleen?" she said.

"Carleen. Carleen Flint. She had a brother. A Flint like her, I'm sure. So she must have told him and he tried to steal my book. Carleen. I suppose I hurt her feelings. She was jealous of Silke."

Wish leaned forward. "Hey, what was the brother's first name? Think back."

"I never knew. But isn't it clear enough? Carleen knew we were going to Tahoe. She and Silke still talked. Carleen works with Professor Braun at XYC."

"Now we're gettin' someplace," Wish said. "Nina, I have to go get on the computer. Excuse me."

"Am I making this up?" Elliott watched him go. "I know that paranoids—they always think their friends have turned against them. They always think they have some great discovery they're going to give the world. Am I—are you going to have me admitted? Because I want to be in Washington State if I'm going to be in the hospital."

"Listen to me, Elliott," Nina said. "I don't think you're crazy. But unfortunately, I'm afraid it is about you. There is really a man named Lee Flint who robbed you. If he is Carleen Flint's brother, that's real and we'll establish it quickly."

"I'm the cause?" His face was screwed up like a child's and his eyes welled up.

Nina wondered if he might try to commit suicide. The idea that he was responsible for the deaths seemed to have sunk serrated teeth into him.

"Have a cup of tea," she said. "Will you do me a favor, Elliott?"

"What?"

"The snow's so heavy out there, it's going to knock down my old deck if it doesn't get shoveled. I can't manage it and Bob isn't here. Would you shovel it for me?"

Elliott followed her like a zombie to the closet and she found him a hat, gloves, and the big aluminum snow shovel. "Go on," she said. "I'm really worried about that snow."

"Yeah, why not, snow." Nina pulled open the sliding door and snow drifted onto the floor. She turned on the floodlight and saw it coming down more heavily than ever. Fine, she thought, let him work out there until he falls down from exhaustion. Then let him sleep, and tomorrow's another day. She had used the same tactics on Bob now and then when he got into truly terrible moods.

Elliott stomped out there, making deep holes with his boots, and started wielding the shovel with an energy born of all his doubts about himself. He seemed occupied for the moment.

"Nina," Wish called from the kitchen. He was gulping tea and staring at the computer screen.

"What have you got?"

"Leland M. Flint," Wish said. "XYC Security. No resume or photo, but look, there's the name."

Flint was apparently low on the totem pole, not even a supervisor. The name was listed with many others as "XYC support staff" on the Web site. He had been as easy to locate as a bunion on a small foot, once they had the name and reference.

"They have a killer on their staff," Nina said. "Maybe they put him up to it, the robbery. As for the other killings, maybe he was on his own, trying to cover up, maybe not."

"What are you going to do now?"

"Call Cheney. And first thing in the morning—"

Wish waited.

"I'm going to sue the bastards," Nina said. "I always wanted to say that."

Chapter 28

SANDY SAID, "HERE YOU GO." THE complaints and summonses made a very satisfying package. The agent for service for XYC, Inc. was a law firm in Palo Alto, California, home of Stanford University and countless start-up computer-technology firms.

But XYC was no start-up. The company stock traded on NASDAQ and had split recently, capitalized at over $550 million, its value all in a couple of business parks and a couple of patents. The *Wall Street Journal* article Nina read said that XYC had been the brainchild of two math grad students at Stanford, who had found a way to use prime numbers to develop a hackproof encryption system for Net commerce. The system was incredibly successful and used by just about everybody now.

"Did Wish get Elliott to the airport?" It had stopped snowing, but flights had been delayed even down the hill in Reno.

"He called in and said the plane took off on time. Elliott had the eyes of a cornered squirrel, he said."

"And that ain't good," Nina said, stealing one of Bob's

favorite phrases. "But he's told his story now. He'll feel better barricaded at home."

"Is he crazy?"

"A little. Speaking unscientifically," Nina said. "But man, can he throw snow off a deck. He was out there again when I got up this morning. He knew he needed the distraction. He and Wish cleared the driveway and stacked my wood."

"They work it off," Sandy said.

"It beats headaches. Okay, the pleadings look good. Let's serve 'em. Have Wish drive them to Palo Alto as soon as he gets back from the Reno airport."

"Palo Alto's four hours away. And Echo Summit just re-opened, so it'll be slower than usual. Five hours."

"Which means he can get them there by five o'clock, easily." An elderly couple walked in and Nina brought them into her office. The will consultation took almost an hour, and when she was free again, Sandy said, "He's been and gone. I made sure he had the money to stay at a motel if he can't get home."

"I wish I could see their faces," Nina said. "Professor Braun and the gang."

"If you're wrong about any of this, they're going to pulverize us," Sandy said. "We can't fight a big company like that."

"Watch me."

"Your judgment is shot. You're taking this personally," Sandy said, impassive.

Nina started to speak, to defend herself, but Sandy held up a hand.

"That's the only reason we got this far," she said. "Bullhead-edness. Don't stop now. There's a phone message from the college teacher on your desk."

Nina nodded and went back into her office. Mick wanted to talk to her.

"Hard feelings?" he asked.

"No."

"It's rare to meet a mature woman."

"Don't push your luck," Nina said.

"Right. Well, I read the page you copied of Wakefield's work. The physics were too hard for me, so I called a physicist friend of mine. The math was too hard for him."

"So you can't evaluate it?"

"You need some topflight guy in the field."

"The field of what?"

"Well, mathematical physics. Michael Berry is your man. He's a Brit. Bristol."

"Just tell me what it's about, Mick."

"Oh, sure. Write this down. Tell the world. Wakefield claims the primes are eigenvalues of a Hermitian quantum operator associated with a classical Hamiltonian."

Elliott wasn't the crazy one for pursuing this, she was, but she made Mick spell the words and wrote everything down. "Is there an English translation?"

"He's trying to predict prime numbers using properties of real matter. Atoms and their components."

"Did he succeed?"

"My friend can't say. We'd need the complete notebook plus a few months."

"So—we don't know what he's doing?"

"Word is he was in a psychiatric hospital. Is that true?"

"I don't know," Nina said. "Maybe."

"Too bad for him, but just about all the greats spent some time weaving baskets in an institution. André Weil did some excellent work on Riemann's theories while in prison during World War II. Incarceration in general has inspired some astonishing leaps forward in human knowledge. Anyway, we have contemplated licking Elliott Wakefield's feet, Nina. But we're not sure if he deserves it or not."

"You're no help, Mick."

"Look, he treats prime numbers as if they were real. As if numbers were matter. As if—following this, Nina? As if the actual universe we live and laugh and cry in is nothing but a stream of mathematical information. All for the purpose of finding the error term between the actual distribution of the prime numbers and the li line."

"He calls it a damping coefficient. The error term. I guess the question is, is he succeeding?" Nina asked.

"Give me more."

"I don't have more."

"He has three hundred more pages, you say?"

"Just about."

"What do you expect from a single page? The math is hard. Hard like diamonds are hard."

Mick wouldn't commit himself to anything more. "So—I didn't break your heart?"

"My heart?"

"You do have one, don't you? It's a physiological necessity, I believe."

"Oh, that heart. No."

"I could have gotten pretty passionate about you, but I knew I'd be moving."

"I hope you stop someday," Nina said. "For your sake."

"Don't judge me, Nina."

"I just don't see how anyone on the move all the time can be happy."

"I don't see how anyone standing still can be happy."

"Try having a child," Nina said. "You put down a root. You feel the wet earth. You don't want to skitter along the surface anymore."

"Very poetic," Mick said. "However, no offense, you move plenty yourself, from man to man and place to place, and I might even hypothesize that your heat on this subject has to do with your own lifestyle. I'm not feeling this rootedness from you that you talk about."

Nina did not like hearing this. He was turning her judgment back on her. And it was stingingly accurate.

"Touché," she said.

"Furthermore, there is a hot babe waiting for me at a certain Mexican restaurant. Still friends?"

"Enjoy your dinner."

"I'll send you a bill."

So dinner was on her. She drove to Matt's with her comforter and pillow, drank a glass of wine in front of a big fire with him and Andrea, and fielded their questions, and really, she wanted to be depressed about Mick and men in general, but she nodded off early and didn't get around to it.

December 15 rolled around. Christmas shoppers had joined the skiers along Lake Tahoe Boulevard. There was art of the carved-grizzly-bear variety, turquoise jewelry, sporting goods including the new snowshoes that left your heels free, denim jackets with sequins for the slot-machine players, snowmobile rentals. The casinos brought in heavy hitters for the season and vacancy signs disappeared. The concrete pools of summer held three-foot drifts and the white walls along the road were higher. Every inch of snow was a million-dollar windfall for the resorts, and it looked like a heavy winter.

The lawyers took their cut in traffic accidents, divorces, and business disputes. Sandy tried to fit in the new business. She knew that the courthouse would go as dark as a playless Broadway theater around the twentieth.

"If I were a serial killer, this would be the time," she remarked to Nina the next morning.

Nina said, "I sent Bob's presents to Germany this morning. Some clothes, a book, and a stuffed bear. Like he was still three years old."

"This case'll be over by Christmas."

"If it isn't, I'll be separated from him."

"You'll come to Markleeville and eat with Joseph and me and the family."

"That would be nice."

"We do spaghetti on Christmas Eve. You'll like it."

"That's nice. Thanks."

The phone rang, and Sandy answered.

"Just a moment." She wagged her head toward Nina's office, and Nina went in, shut the door, and picked up.

"Ms. Reilly?"

"Yes?"

"The name is Branson. We met in Boston."

Oh, no, not Branson. She had hoped Branson would not flap his leathery wings so far west.

"I am of counsel to the firm in Palo Alto that will be handling your suit against XYC. We would like to meet with you before this goes any farther."

"Come on up."

"We realize you are a busy lady. Could we fly you down tomorrow for a meeting?"

"Fly me down?"

"A private plane will be waiting at the Tahoe airport at eleven. I believe that's only a few miles from your office."

"True." The Tahoe airport served only private pilots these days.

"We could have you back by four at the latest. It's just a jaunt. I guarantee you a good lunch."

"What is the purpose of this meeting?"

"To get to know each other. And see if something can be worked out."

It was ear candy to a lawyer. Nina said, "I'm looking at my schedule now. It does appear that I could clear my calendar."

"Very good. Just go out onto the landing strip at eleven and look for the blue-and-white Cessna."

"Okay."

"See you then." Branson's manner had been completely proper. Nina thought to herself: Ally? Or enemy?

Now, why in the world would she even begin to think of him as an ally? Cockeyed Irish optimism was the only way to explain it. She would gird her loins firmly on the morrow, assuming for purposes of argument that women have loins, and that girding would not involve tight spandex.

Tonight she was back home, Wish playing video games on her computer in the kitchen. Wish didn't seem to mind acting as her shadow, and she was glad to have him. She had her couch to sit on, he had the yellow office chair by the refrigerator, and they were getting used to each other.

The phone rang. "I'll get it," Wish said, and picked up. "It's a lawyer."

"Nina?"

"Betty Jo?"

"We need to talk to you. Me and Jimmy. Right away."

"It's late, and I'd like to know how you got my home phone number," Nina said.

"Everybody has your phone number. Jimmy got it off PrivateEye.com. And I know it's late."

"What is it?"

"Jimmy was attacked tonight. He wants to tell you about it.

He was in the Ace High office taking over for Meredith, who by the way is in jail for obstructing justice, thank you very much. A man in a mask. It's bizarre. You have to hear this."

"I appreciate your call, but I'm confused. We're on opposite sides, and—"

"Pish-tosh. You have to hear this."

"Has he called the police?"

"They came and went already. I'm here in the office with him. Can you come down?"

"I'm on my way." She hung up and said, "Wish, would you come with me? The Ace High had an incident today."

"Let me lace up my boots." He was already shutting down the computer. Nina pulled her parka and boots on over her jeans and they piled into the Bronco.

Adrenaline moved through her veins. She found herself talking to the shooter again. You're here, all right, she thought. You won't get me or mine. I'll get you.

The No Vacancy sign lit up the frosty night. Someone, probably Meredith, had set out plastic reindeer on either side of the entry to the Ace High office. Their noses flashed on and off. The door moved heavily with its jingling wreath as Betty Jo let them in. She looked behind them, left and right, ready to slam it in their faces if anything moved.

And that ain't good, Nina thought to herself.

Locking and testing the door, Betty Jo said, "I thought you might be able to help me figure this out."

"How is he?" James Bova lay on a couch in the dark on his back, a pillow under his head. He held something to his nose.

"Broke it," Betty Jo said. "Got kicked in the belly, too. I just spent two hours at Boulder Hospital with him. Nothing got kicked out of him, he'll recover, but he wanted to talk to you right away." Betty Jo turned on a low lamp and Wish checked the windows to make sure the blinds were fully shut. He hadn't said a word. He took up a position in the corner and Nina was aware that her back was covered.

"Mr. Bova?"

Nina moved closer. Bova's eyes opened. They were swollen above the bandages and he would have twin shiners in the morning. "It's all your fault," he said, moving his mouth with difficulty.

"That's what they all say," Nina said. "How do you feel?"

"Vicodin. I'm going to sleep pretty soon." He moved a little and grimaced, but the drug was keeping him comfortable.

"He's goin' home with me," Betty Jo said. "Hector borrowed the neighbor's Rottweiler just in case we're followed. That makes three animals in the house. Nobody'll get through. Let's make this quick. Jimmy just met Mr. Lee Flint."

"He waltzed into the office," Bova said. "Ski mask. Brown with yellow around the eyes. I knew right away it had to be the same guy. I tried to call 911, but he pushed me against the wall and started beating me. Not talking, just hitting. He broke my nose and blood was spurting all over him. I thought he was going to beat me to death. I've got two kids in Sparks. I didn't want to die."

Nina had arrived with the usual suspicions—maybe Bova had faked an attack, maybe Betty Jo was pulling something—but seeing Bova now, hearing him, it was plain that someone had set out to hurt him.

"He wasn't huge, but he knew how to punch and kick. He pushed me onto my knees and started talking to me in this eerie voice, low and harsh, asking me questions. He was mad with fury. That's the only way I can describe it." Bova sniffed and grimaced again and Betty Jo adjusted the pillow. "I'm going to sell this place. I can't stand this."

Nina sat down on the scuffed floor beside him. "Take your time," she said gently.

"The only reason I'm alive is that he believed me when I told him. He knew every word was God's truth."

"What did he say, Mr. Bova?"

"He said nobody rides piggyback on him. He made it sound—I don't know, sexual. 'Nobody rides piggyback on me.' Then he hit me hard and I lost a tooth. 'It had to be you,' he says, like the old song.

"I said, 'What? What did I do? Whatever it is, I'll make it right.' I just made him madder. 'You know damn well,' he says. 'Stop that fucking bleeding. I'm talking to you.' He made me take off my shirt and hold it over my face, and he says, 'You killed that woman and you're trying to bust me.'

"I said, 'No! I never killed anybody! I swear!' He said again, 'It had to be you. You were in the office, you saw me with the kids. You ran out when I dropped the gun and shot the woman. Why?' Then I got it. He was talking about the robbery. The Hanna case. I told him—told him I was home in bed with my girlfriend when that happened. The cops called me. I live in Sparks. That's an hour away. I couldn't have got home fast enough to take that call.

"I said, 'I'll prove it to you! I'll prove it! I'll give you the phone records. Just leave me alone, let me catch my breath, we'll talk.'

"He went over it and over it. He got my girlfriend's name. He stopped beating me and he was just pushing me, still really mad, but he was starting to believe me. Cussing. He pushed me back on the floor and he stomped around. 'Then who?' he says.

"'I don't know who,' I said, and I said he could have the cash-register money if he wanted it. He let me get up and give him the money. I was afraid the whole time he would change his mind and kill me after all. He kept his fists balled and he shoved and pushed me the whole time.

"When the money was in his pocket, he pulled out a knife. 'That was for you,' he says, 'if you didn't convince me.'

" 'I swear to God,' I said, 'why would I kill that poor lady?' and I could see he believed me.

" 'All right,' he says. 'You give somebody a message for me.' I said, 'Anything.' He says, 'Tell Nina Reilly I didn't kill Hanna's wife.' I said, sure. He said, 'Some other fucker did her. Tell her. You going to tell her like I said?' I told him I would tell you.

"So here's your message," Bova said. He had lifted his head as the words rushed out. Now he lay back and a groan issued from his torn lips.

Nina bit her lip. She sat back on her heels. Betty Jo and Wish watched.

The clock on the wall ticked loudly. The ice machine next to the vending machine right through the wall made clunking sounds. From somewhere came faint laughter.

"You have any more questions, you can ask tomorrow," Betty Jo said. "Let's get you back to Incline," she told Bova. Wish helped Bova, who was still holding the towel with ice to his face, to his feet, and Betty Jo opened the door and looked around carefully. Her Porsche SUV was right out front.

"It looks safe," she said. "But then, we don't know anything anymore, do we?" All three of them got Bova into the passenger seat, lying almost flat and covered with a blanket.

Betty Jo shut the passenger door. "Well?" she said to Nina. "I'm not a criminal lawyer. I'm not used to this. I like Jimmy. You have any explanation for Flint's statements?"

"Sounds like he didn't shoot Mrs. Hanna," Wish said.

"That's what the man said," Betty Jo told him drily.

"You want us to caravan up to Incline with you? To make sure you get home all right? Would that be okay, Nina?"

"Yes, let's do that," Nina said. It took forty minutes, even so late, to drive the dark lake road to the North Shore and Betty Jo's mansion on Champagne Way. Wish scouted around and then they brought Bova into the house. Betty Jo's little old husband stood guard at the door, holding a big dog with a powerful head on a tight leash. He wasn't smiling anymore, but he didn't look frightened.

After Bova was safely in the house, Betty Jo came back out. She handed Nina a bottle of French wine. "Thanks for the guard duty," she said.

"You don't have to do that."

"It's also an apology. I realize our interests are different. I think I'd be taking the same steps you're taking if I were on your side. Which I am not. But when this case is over, let's have lunch. If you don't mind me sailing in on the *Good Ship Lollipop*."

Nina smiled.

"Drive safe." Betty Jo smacked the side of the Bronco like it was an old stallion.

Wish drove back, leaving the windows cracked so he wouldn't get drowsy. They were alone in a postcard winter wonderland. A brilliant half-moon duplicated itself in a water-moon on the vast lake. Snow clumps fell from the trees and he had to run the wipers now and then.

When they were almost home, Nina said, "Wish? Are you positive Elliott went back to Seattle?"

"Positive? He had his ticket. He was in the line inside."

"That's all you know?"

"You think it was him? Elliott—he couldn't hurt someone. He couldn't get that angry. It couldn't be him, Nina."

"There are some psychiatric conditions—"

"But why would he hurt James Bova?"

"I'm just asking," Nina said. "Wish, first thing in the morning, call Roger Freeman. Tell him about the attack. Tell him he needs protection and so does Dave. We need to get the Placerville police involved in this too."

"Who is this guy?"

"I hope to learn more about that tomorrow in Palo Alto."

Chapter 29

Nina strapped into the luxury leather seat and the Cessna took off. They flew due west and left the white Sierra range behind. She watched a cross-section of California unwind below as they flew from Tahoe to the San Francisco Peninsula: greening foothills, the still-dusty San Joaquin Valley with Sacramento and an endless maze of subdivisions and freeways surrounded by patchwork fields of almonds and tomatoes, then on to San Francisco Bay, the city itself shrouded in a fog bank to the north, a long flat bridge below that rode close to the quiet water, and finally the easy runway of the Palo Alto private airport.

A black Lincoln awaited. Nina thanked the pilot and said hello to the driver. She wore a blue silk suit and round-toed Jimmy Choos, and carried her new briefcase. She was deeply worried about the safety of just about everybody—Sandy, Dave, even Cheney, unable to predict Lee Flint's demented steps. She carried a hope within her that XYC, Inc. would have an answer or two.

*   *   *

Five men sat on the other side of a polished mahogany conference table. In a perfect illustration of Silicon Valley schizophrenia, one wore jeans and a wrinkled button-down shirt, and four wore expensive suits. The jeans guy had a beard going gray. He sat in the middle.

She had entered the penthouse of a five-story building that seemed to be owned entirely by XYC's outside law firm. The plate-glass window had a view of the clock tower and terra-cotta buildings of Stanford University.

"Gentlemen," she said, nodding, and set her briefcase firmly onto the table. "Hello, Professor Braun. Mr. Branson." Braun nodded back. Nobody got up. Branson said, "This is Greg Foster, a senior partner here." Three of the suits were now accounted for.

"How do you do." Foster, a pale man with distinguished white hair, gave her a curt nod. No handshaking with this crew.

"Tom Elias, executive vice president for administration at XYC, sitting in with us today."

"Hello." Elias wore the jeans and the facial hair. He gave her a relaxed and curious smile. He had been part of the start-up. The XYC legend had to do with Stanford students and garages and the famous IPO that had made Elias and his friends multimillionaires overnight.

"And Special Agent Aaron Dietz, from the NSA."

"The National Security Agency?"

Dietz nodded slowly, taking her measure. He had on the stiffest suit of all. The shoulder pads put him in the linebacker class. Nina waited for an invitation to sit down, but all she was getting was stares, so she pulled out a chair and helped herself.

"Water?"

"Yes, thank you." Each had his own glass and carafe of water, the carafes half-full to empty, which meant this meeting had been preceded by a strategy session, of which she had undoubtedly been the focus.

"You have sued XYC," Branson began from across the table. His face had lost none of its pugnacity. "We'd like to know why."

"I'd be happy to lay it out for you. Your employee committed an armed robbery two years ago, in the course of which my client's wife was shot to death. He appears to have killed three more people since then, as well as attempting to kill me and another person. Last night he attacked the owner of the motel where the robbery took place. It's a no-brainer," Nina said. She folded her arms.

"Leland Flint has not been in XYC's employ for a long time," Foster said. Nina remembered that Flint had been noted on the XYC Web site.

"Well, if you want to get right to it, maybe you'd like to tell me the date he left XYC's employ," Nina said. "That is certainly important." She uncapped her new Mont Blanc pen and let it hang obligingly over her yellow legal pad.

"We didn't bring you here for a free discovery session," Foster said.

"Then he was in XYC's employ at the time of Sarah Hanna's death," Nina said.

"Nobody said that."

"It's clearly implied in your evasive answer."

Foster sighed. "Let's start again. Why have you sued XYC?"

"I thought I just explained it. The basis of corporate liability is the doctrine of *respondeat superior,* as you all know, and that's the fifth cause of action in the amended complaint served on you."

"You allege in that complaint that XYC authorized Flint's robbery attempt. But you don't have a shred of evidence of that, do you?"

So she was to be cross-examined. They expected her to be intimidated, but she was much too focused on finding and stopping Flint to get involved in a male-lawyer-dominance game. She would be straightforward, ignore the rudeness, and—

Oh, shucks. Live a little.

"Ask nicely, and I might tell you a thing or two," she said. She smiled, nicely, and clammed up.

They all looked at Elias, who still wore his own faint smile. He looked friendly and approachable, which was why he had surrounded himself with warriors. He's the only one who matters, Nina thought to herself. The others were just legal poundage, except for Dietz. Dietz was from a government security agency, not XYC. Nina had only the vaguest idea what the NSA did, but it was clear that a threat to XYC's encryption method was relevant here.

They were apparently less familiar with female-lawyer-domination games. Foster said, "Look here, Ms. Reilly. Forgive our exasperation. We understand that XYC's former employee has become a menace, and we intend to cooperate to find him as soon as possible. Here is the main piece of information we would like to convey to you today: XYC did not authorize that robbery attempt. Flint heard about Elliott Wakefield's work from his sister, Carleen—"

"Who is a consultant with XYC, I believe," Nina said.

"Here is what happened. XYC has been following Mr. Wakefield's work for years."

"Through the professor here, and through Carleen Flint," Nina said.

"Never with any intention of harming Elliott or stealing anything from him," Professor Braun interjected. "In fact, we met with him and offered to hire him."

"I heard about that," Nina said.

"He is difficult to deal with."

"Back to Flint," Foster said. "He is an ex–Navy operations officer who worked at XYC's headquarters in our security

division. He was not a supervisor. He was not a high-level employee. Obviously, we regret hiring him now. He had been with
XYC about a year when Carleen discussed Mr. Wakefield with
him. Carleen was a summer intern with us at that time, still at
MIT, and in fact Flint had persuaded her to apply for the internship. Anyway, Flint decided that Mr. Wakefield was a threat, and
he decided, unilaterally, without any authorization from XYC,
let me make that clear, that he would obtain Mr. Wakefield's
notebook."

So Elliott was right. Elliott was sane, and he was right. The
man in the mask had wanted the notebook. Nina mentally apol-
ogized to Elliott for doubting him.

"No one, including Carleen Flint, and I emphasize, no one, at
XYC knew of his intention."

"That's your position," Nina said.

"It's not just a position. It's the truth. You can litigate this case
for years if you want, depose every single XYC staffer, and you
will not learn anything different."

"Is that correct, Mr. Elias?" Nina asked.

Elias smiled and said, "Greg's doing the talking."

Foster went on. "Flint called his sister the day after the robbery and told her that he was going underground. She informed
management immediately. He was fired and XYC had no further
contact with him. Carleen stayed with us and became a valued
member of our team. Your client, Mr. Hanna, filed a lawsuit that
was about to die a natural death, and then you came along."

"Yes," Nina said. "It's all my fault. Where is Mr. Flint? You
know where he is, don't you?"

Another exchange of glances. Foster said, "I haven't said
that."

"Well, do you?"

"I wouldn't say that, not in so many words."

"He's still listed as an employee on your Web site."

"That's a mistake."

Nina turned to the NSA agent. "What is your interest?" Dietz did not respond. He was regarding her as Nabokov might have regarded a specimen butterfly just before impaling it on a pin.

"I'm getting to that," Foster said. "The point is, we may be able to help regarding Mr. Flint."

"Except that?"

"We still have an interest in Mr. Wakefield's work. An even stronger interest, at this point. And he won't talk to us. In fact, he told us you represent him."

"I see," Nina said. She would have to talk to Elliott, quickly. It put her in a pickle, because she didn't represent him. On the other hand, she couldn't pretend to represent him, that would be unethical.

Professor Braun had been listening quietly. Now he said, "I wonder if you have any idea how dangerous Elliott's work is."

"Well, it sure has been dangerous to him," Nina said.

"It's a danger to the whole world. It's a lethal bomb. It's the equivalent of Hiroshima."

"I won't let you get away with that, Professor. People won't die in the hundreds of thousands because of Mr. Wakefield's work."

"They will be homeless in the millions. Their national economies will be in ruins. The Internet will be down for the foreseeable future, Ms. Reilly. I don't think you have the slightest idea what that means in this day and age.

"Elliott doesn't understand. He doesn't care about large institutions and he thinks individuals will not suffer. He has to be made to understand that they will suffer. How will they pay their bills? How will they talk to each other? Do you have any idea how this will impact civil liberties? Ordinary people can now encrypt their E-mails to each other. They can talk to each other and there is some check on the government's technical ability to listen in. That check will be gone.

"He's young, his judgment is poor, and he has chosen you to be his representative. That's why we are talking with you today, Ms. Reilly. We need your help."

Aaron Dietz of the NSA cleared his throat and said, "The nation insists on your help."

"Civilization as we know it will disappear," Nina said.

"Don't take this lightly, Ms. Reilly."

"This code has only been used for ten years, Professor. All codes are broken eventually. Isn't the real problem that XYC is built around this encryption code? Your corporate world may be in danger, but I think the rest of the world can adjust in due course."

"You simply don't understand. The impact—"

Nina interrupted. "When did you talk to Mr. Wakefield?"

"His home was searched yesterday in the early-morning hours," Dietz said. "He was present at that time. On NSA's affidavit and pursuant to court order."

"I haven't spoken with him about that," Nina said.

"No? Well, he didn't resist. He didn't ask to talk to his lawyer, if that's what you want to know."

"And the notebook?"

"Still wherever he hid it," Dietz said. He gave his red silk tie an angry yank.

"The worst thing is that he won't show anyone his results," Professor Braun said. "There is probably a mistake somewhere. It could all be a mistake, which would explain why it's taking him so long to provide a proof. But we have to proceed as though he has found a way to break the XYC encryption system. What have you seen of his work, Ms. Reilly?"

He had asked nicely. "Oh, nothing, really," Nina said. "We

talked about it a little. I'm no mathematician. Generally, he shows that the primes are strictly analogous to eigenvalues of a Hermitian quantum operator associated with a classical Hamiltonian."

Braun's face paled. He gripped the table. "What Hamiltonian is that? Is he using Alain Connes's p-adelic Hermitians?"

"I'm sorry, Professor. You understand." Nina smoothed her skirt, had a sip of water.

The men looked at one another. Braun muttered, "Connes. Incredible." Foster nodded at Branson and the atmosphere in the room electrified.

Nina straightened her back and prepared herself.

"Ten million and a confidentiality agreement for Wakefield, two million for you, properly sheltered from income tax, and a million for your client Mr. Hanna," Branson said. "And Mr. Flint's ass, encased in a sling and delivered in a white limo."

Nina wrote down those lovely round numbers. It gave her a second to think.

"And in exchange?"

"Confidentiality agreements all around. The notebook. Mr. Wakefield's cooperation. Dismissal of your causes of action against XYC."

"Is this severable?" Nina asked. "Because Mr. Hanna and Mr. Wakefield don't have the same interests. In fact, there's a conflict. For example, what if Mr. Hanna agreed to drop the suit against XYC in exchange for a million dollars and Flint?"

"And Wakefield?"

"Let's say his side of things would have to be negotiated independently."

Branson said, "You already know the answer to that one. Nobody gives a shit about Hanna's lawsuit. You want Flint, you bring Wakefield to the table. You want to handle the Wakefield part without Hanna, that's fine with us, though we'd like to take care of everything at once. Am I being nice enough?"

"I'm afraid not," Nina said. "I want to talk to Carleen Flint before any decisions are made." There was a stir around the table. They were all looking at Elias again. "Mr. Elias?" Nina said. "Is she available?"

Tom Elias scratched his cheek. "Mr. Branson?"

"What do we get in return?" Branson said.

Nina said evenly, "Mr. Elias? She's here, isn't she?"

Elias shrugged and said, "Five minutes."

Branson brought Carleen Flint in and made a place for her. Nina barely had time to reflect that her loyalty to the company was crucial to them. Carleen was small and slight, wearing a nice gray suit. She wasn't a pretty woman, and she was very nervous right now, trembling like a greyhound.

"This lady has a few questions for you," Branson told her. "As we discussed."

"May I?" Nina asked Branson.

"Five minutes," he reminded her.

"You know who I am?" she asked Carleen.

"They told me."

"You are Leland Flint's sister?"

"Yes."

"You are willing to talk to me today? No one is forcing you to talk to me?"

"No."

"It's all right, Carleen," Tom Elias said. "Be frank."

"How long have you been employed at XYC?"

"Two years full-time. Before that I was a student intern for a summer."

"How did your brother come to work there?"

"He had just been discharged from the Navy. He was in an operation in the Indian Ocean and there was an accident. He was injured. His leg. His face was scarred. He decided to get into security work, and there were openings at XYC. After he started working there, he told me he liked it there and he encouraged me to apply for an internship."

"What was your relationship with your brother?"

"What do you mean?"

"Did you get along?"

"Yes. He was very protective of me, but he was the one who needed help. He was always athletic—he was physical—but after he got hurt he changed a lot. I worried about him being able to work. Our parents are dead. We had to make it on our own."

"What do you mean, he changed a lot?" Nina said.

"Well, he felt like a pariah. His leg—the corrective surgery only made it worse. He was very angry."

"Did he find out about Elliott Wakefield from you, Carleen?" Nina asked gently.

"Yes. After I started working at XYC I realized that Wakefield's work could be extremely valuable. I told Lee about the notebook and how much XYC might pay to have it. He knew I—I was mad at Wakefield. He decided to steal the notebook. But I didn't know! I didn't know, Mr. Elias! I swear it! He did it to make money for himself, not because I was angry or— he never told me his plan, and as soon as he told me what happened, I went straight to you, and—"

"And I believed you, Carleen," Tom Elias said. "Or you wouldn't still be with us."

"So you had no idea he might try to steal the notebook from Mr. Wakefield?" Nina said.

"None at all. He only told me afterward, when he got back

to Boston. I was horrified. I did some research and found out about Sarah Hanna and confronted him. He swore he didn't shoot her. I couldn't get him to admit it. It was all a nightmare. I went to Mr. Elias and told him everything, and my brother disappeared. He knew how to hide, how to fake IDs. I didn't have one word from him for over a year. Then he called me from Nevada. He was living there, in Reno. He asked me not to tell on him a second time. I saw him a few times. I'd fly out to Nevada and do some gambling and see him. I was worried about him. He just kept obsessing about how his life was ruined and that shooting."

"Until a few weeks ago?"

"Yes. You were fighting the motion to throw out the case. It was in the local paper. Lee kept close track of the Tahoe paper. I decided to fly back and help him figure out what to do, and the first night I was at Tahoe, we saw Wakefield wander into Caesars. I was working a blackjack table and I let him find me, and Lee was watching. After Wakefield left, I had a minute to talk to Lee, and we decided I would go back to Wakefield's place with him and make sure he wasn't planning to do anything reckless. But we got into an argument instead. Lee's impossible. I flew back, but I kept getting his phone calls. He didn't have anyone else on earth to talk to. I couldn't give him away again."

"And Lee didn't quit," Nina said.

"He was afraid. The police seemed to have reopened their investigation, too. He has a thing about small places. A jail would kill him. And—I don't know." She had finally begun to cry. "He went back to Tahoe and tried to stop you. I told him—I couldn't make him see. After—after the girl died—Chelsi Freeman—I told Lee he was on his own. I told him to stay away from me, not to call. I'm the only one—Lee's my family—but I couldn't stand it. I went to Mr. Elias again. I told him everything."

"And what did you do about it, Mr. Elias?" Nina asked. Branson started to speak, but Elias held up a hand.

"Nothing," he said. "We had fired Flint two years before," he said, "but we were still worried about liability."

"Be quiet, Mr. Elias," Branson said.

"Shut up, Mr. Branson, your advice got us into the state we're in today." The lawyer sat back in his chair.

"I didn't bring in the police," Elias said. "That will always be on my conscience."

"You could have prevented the deaths of two more people, Mr. Elias."

"That's why I'm trying to be generous to those who remain."

"It isn't always about money. Sometimes it's about justice," Nina said.

"Mr. Elias," Branson said, "we have to cut this off. This isn't advisable." The other heads nodded. Dietz, the tough guy, was gnawing on his fingernails.

"Please take the offer, Ms. Reilly," Elias said, keeping his eyes on hers. "We're all doing the best we can." Carleen had lapsed into quiet weeping.

"You're still not going to the police."

"We have stockholders. We are innocent bystanders in all this. There is no need for police involvement," Branson said.

"Mr. Elias?"

Elias shrugged.

"Carleen? Where is your brother?" Nina asked.

"Don't answer that," Branson told her. She was still on the payroll. She closed her mouth. One last tear blinked out of her eye. She was miserable, but not so miserable as to ignore Branson.

Nina stood up and said, "I need to get back and unfortunately won't be able to stay for lunch. I'll talk to Mr. Wakefield and Mr. Hanna."

"Talk to them in the hall. You need a cell phone? Use mine," Branson said. They evidently thought the deal was in the bag.

Nina said, "Mr. Branson, gentlemen, thank you for inviting me here. I will get back to you. I believe the car's still waiting downstairs."

This time they all shook hands. Elias said, "Nice meeting you, Nina."

Branson said, "I'll take you back down."

In the elevator, he stood across from her, staring at her, sweating. It's hard work, wanting to lay waste to somebody and having to restrain yourself. "How's it going to go?" he asked as they walked across the polished floor toward the front door of the building.

Oh, shucks. Live a little. "Badly," Nina said. It was perhaps an ill-advised word choice. Perhaps she had an overwhelming desire to tie Branson's balls to a string and toss them onto a telephone wire. It was precisely the wrong thing to say, and she knew it.

"Look," Branson said. He grabbed her arm and made her face him.

"Let go of me!"

"We had our meeting. Now here's a message from me. You faked your way this far and we're willing to let you nick us for the money. But no little bitch is going to stop the flow of events as planned by XYC. You have the wrong lawyer and the wrong company. Flint will go down and we won't get touched on the way. Wakefield is a psycho and he'll be stopped one way or the other. Your client Hanna is a lying dickhead trying to make a buck off his dead wife. Take the offer and talk them into it or you're going to get hurt and your client is gonna wish he was as dead as his wife.

"Have a good flight," he said. He squeezed her arm hard and pushed her toward the door.

Chapter 30

THEY FLEW BACK TOWARD THE MOUNTAINS. The pilot was occupied with his radio and his instruments. Nina watched
California rise toward the snow and ate her peanut-butter sandwich.

She had behaved badly, not shown cur-like respect for the
amount of money arrayed across the table from her in Palo Alto,
and she had a bruise on her left upper arm to show for it. She was
lucky Branson hadn't sunk sharp incisors into her neck. She was
lucky they hadn't pulled the plane and made her take a Greyhound
bus home. It was probably just an oversight that she was returning in style.

Or maybe Elias, the billionaire, had lifted a pinky and said,
"Leave her alone."

They knew where Flint was, but she knew things about Flint,
too—that he was probably at Tahoe. It was too cold to camp, so
he was staying at a hotel or motel.

Sergeant Cheney would catch up with him soon, without

XYC. The only question was whether he could catch Flint before Flint hurt someone else.

She sighed. In a way Branson was right. She had gone as far as she could with the case, spent all the money she could spare for expenses, sacrificed Bob's stability. . . . Is it really my fault? she thought. Chelsi? Silke and Raj? This thought affected her deeply and she felt helpless. What should she do now?

First and foremost, she had a duty to the client to find the person responsible for his wife's death and to try to recompense him for his loss in the only way the legal system could recompense him, with money. Perhaps there would be moral satisfaction and closure for Dave Hanna, too, when Flint was caught. Perhaps there would even be redemption and rehabilitation, but that would be up to Hanna.

As for herself, she had a strong need for Flint to be caught to avoid further harm and because of Chelsi.

So—help catch Flint. The course was still clear.

Her thoughts turned to Elliott. He hid the notebook, she thought, good for him, he let it out of his sight. She hoped he hadn't buried it in his garden just before a rainstorm. Elliott, she thought, you're going to have to give it up, the pressure's too intense, these Pythagoreans are going to drown you if you don't let them suppress your discovery.

This mad insistence on finishing the proof—Nina was more familiar now with the math culture, how mathematicians hid in their garrets for years working alone to finish their proofs. A mathematician named Wiles had kept up this solitary secrecy for seven years while working on his proof of Fermat's Last Theorem, so others could not piggyback on his work, finish the proof first, and have their names linked with his work forever.

In the end, mathematicians seemed to be artists of form and number as surely as Picasso was an artist of form and color. They were sensitive and jealous of their work like artists, too. Pure mathematicians didn't have much to do with the eventual applications of their work. Look at peaceable Einstein, whose work had helped to split the atom.

What would Elliott do? Elliott with his damping coefficient, his hidden variable behind the veil . . .

Resting in that comfortable seat with the drone of the plane and the secure presence of the pilot in his headphones beside her, Nina felt the fatigue of the last month. She closed her eyes and, as happens sometimes, remembered the piggyback dream, allowed it to come to life within her. Yes, the scary old lady approaching her in the lurid half-light of dreams, scary because she was very ugly, smiling toothlessly. Unstoppable, that was what made her so frightening. She hunched her way toward Nina, who in the way of dreams stood petrified. As she came closer, she began to gesture and Nina tried desperately to understand. She wanted something. What? What?

A piggyback ride. This time Nina bent down in her dream and let the old lady climb on her back. She was heavy and her arms clung tightly. Nina began crawling on all fours. She felt fine now, like she was getting somewhere. . . .

Her cell phone vibrated in her pocket and she jumped back into wakefulness. She took it out and saw that Sandy was calling, but the pilot had spotted the phone and shook his head and motioned for her to turn it off, so she couldn't take the call.

Ahead she saw the peaks of the ten-thousand-footers that ringed Tahoe. She would visit Sergeant Cheney and spill her guts again. She would call Betty Jo, see how Jimmy Bova was doing. Had she gone with Wish to the Ace High only the night before? It seemed like a century ago.

They had begun their descent. The great lake shimmered in its bowl.

What had Bova tried to tell her? Flint wanted him to tell Nina that he didn't kill that woman. He must have meant Sarah

Hanna. Flint had beaten Bova and accused him of killing Sarah Hanna. Just how demented was Flint?

Flint had said, "Nobody rides piggyback on me." That was how Nina's dream had returned to her; the phrase was sitting in the back of her mind, waiting to be processed.

She let it all turn to a mishmash in her mind and watched the mountains, and two phrases kept going round and round.

Hidden variable. Ride piggyback.

The case has a hidden variable, she thought. Can't figure it out the way I've been thinking. Look behind the veil. Ride piggyback.

Somebody's piggybacking. The hidden variable is piggybacking. On something.

"Nobody rides piggyback on me."

Meaning... meaning... he had done the robbery, no question of that. Did he mean that someone had piggybacked on the robbery?

Shot Sarah Hanna, with Flint's gun? Elliott had been alone with Flint. But why would Elliott shoot Sarah Hanna?

Someone else? The timing had been so quick.

The chill spread downward and rooted in hell. If Flint hadn't shot Sarah, had run, and someone had picked up the gun, then who had killed Chelsi, and Silke, and Raj?

Who was the hidden variable?

Chapter 31

SANDY AND WISH WAITED AT THE runway. The cold dry air of the mountains filled Nina's lungs.

"Sergeant Cheney called. Flint is at Dave Hanna's house in Placerville."

"What?"

"He's got Mr. Hanna."

No one acted as fast as Flint. Nina blinked back tears. "I can't stand to lose him, Sandy. Not another death."

"He's still alive, we think. The Placerville police got a 911 from Roger Freeman and surrounded the house. We figured you'd want to get down there."

Wish took her briefcase. "I'm driving."

They tore over Echo Summit, careened down the winding Highway 50. Nina sat in the back, holding the oh-shit strap in the ceiling, numbly watching the snowbanks turn to patchy white.

She descended for the second time that day, from winter back to autumn. Sandy had brought the running shoes Nina had kept at the office. Nina pulled off her stockings, put on the shoes, and tossed her jacket to the side.

A parked police car and a yellow tape across the entry to Hanna's neighborhood greeted them. "I'm Hanna's lawyer," Nina said. The officer made a call and let them through.

There were a dozen police and sheriff's-department cars a few hundred feet down, past two empty houses. An ambulance idled in back. Hanna's picket-fence gate hung crookedly on its hinges. The windows were shut, the blinds drawn.

Roger Freeman stood with Sergeant Cheney. He was shouting something, gesticulating. "Stay here," Nina said to Sandy and Wish. Sandy nodded.

"Roger," Nina said.

Roger's arm came down. "Dave's a hostage," he said. "I couldn't protect him after all."

Sergeant Cheney said, "I thought you'd be along."

"What happened?" she asked Roger.

"I came over at two to check on Dave. He usually starts drinking at noon, but he promised me he'd stay sober. He said he could take care of himself. Dave's got a rifle. We used to hunt together. I thought he'd be okay during the daylight hours. What could I do? He wouldn't come stay with me."

"I should have tried to have him put into protective custody. But Flint moves so fast. I worried, but I didn't really know he'd go after Dave," Nina said.

"The gate was like that, and I knew something was wrong. I called to him from outside. Flint shot at me. I heard Dave shout for help, and that's the last I've heard from him."

"I don't think he meant to hit Roger," Cheney said. "The shot went wide."

"Are you sure there's nobody else in there?" Nina said.

"Doesn't seem to be," Cheney said.

"What's happening now?"

Cheney said, "Placerville police are trying to make contact. He won't answer the phone, so they're going to try a bullhorn."

"He'll kill Dave if he wants to," Nina said. "He's a security expert. He'll know whatever hostage-rescue protocol you use."

"If we hear a shot, we'll rush the house. That's all we plan to do now. When night comes we can do more. Aerosols and so on. Meantime, he has to see that if he shoots again we'll rush the house."

"You talked to Jimmy Bova last night, Sergeant."

"Yes. Flint again."

"He—Flint—was trying to communicate with me. Did Bova tell you that?"

"It was just junk talk."

"I think he believes he didn't kill Sarah Hanna. Maybe he's crazy, but that's how I understand what he told Bova." She explained her thinking, but Cheney didn't look impressed.

"Then he's a liar," he said. "Or delusional."

His radio crackled and he stepped away from them.

Roger slumped against a police car. It was five in the afternoon and the shadows lengthened, leaving the house dark. "I'm going to tell you something. The truth is, I never liked Dave. Not from the first day I met him, hanging on Sarah at the Sacramento County Fair. Now I'm wondering if he wouldn't stay with me because he knew it all along. Because he's proud. Then Flint wouldn't have found him at home."

"Stop it, Roger. Flint might have come to your house. You might be a hostage, too."

"Dave said he had his rifle. He's a good shot. We've hunted wild boar, wild turkeys, deer together. But he's a drunk."

"You couldn't prevent it."

"What did Flint think he could gain?"

"It's a surefire way to end a lawsuit," Nina said. "Dispose of the plaintiff. It's no way to end a murder investigation, though. Flint is very violent, Roger. Thank you for checking on Dave and calling the police. I believe he would have been dead hours ago if you hadn't. Flint would have come and gone."

"I don't know if Dave is alive or dead," Roger said. He breathed out heavily. "I don't feel well at all. It's too much. My daughter." He slipped to the ground. "I'm so tired," he said.

"Do you need a doctor?"

"Just tired."

"I'll be right back." Nina ran to the van and asked Wish for help. Together they brought Roger back and laid him down in the back seat, covering him with Wish's parka. "Rest there," Nina said. "If you don't feel better soon, we'll get you to an ER."

Sandy had been standing by. She said, "What now?"

"It'll get dark, and they'll make a move."

They heard an amplified bullhorn. Nina could see a uniformed man holding it. "Mr. Flint, please pick up the phone. That's all we ask. We are not interfering with you. Please pick up the phone so we can talk. We need to find out what you need right now." He lowered it and waited. Nothing happened.

"He doesn't need a gun to kill Hanna," Wish said, voicing the thought that was also in Nina's mind.

"Maybe he'd like to talk to me," she said. "He sent me a message last night. Maybe he wants to know how I reacted."

"Let the cops handle it," Sandy advised.

"I'm going to ask Cheney." The sergeant was huddled with a group of Placerville deputies on a neighboring property. Nina steeled herself and went to him. "He might talk to me," she said. "He has said that he wants to talk to me."

One of the deputies said, "He's not talking to anybody." But Cheney puffed out his cheeks and considered her.

"Better to let trained people try," he said eventually.

"They've been trying."

"You'd be out of range. You'd be safe."

"I'm willing."

"I don't know. You're not known for your soothing qualities. What makes you think you can sweet-talk him?"

"I'll just ask if there's anything he wants to tell me," Nina said. "If he doesn't respond, I'll get out of the way. I'm very worried about my client, Sergeant. His brother-in-law has collapsed and his wife and his niece have been killed by this asshole. I'm all he has out here. Just knowing that I'm here might help Dave."

"I'll go talk to the guy in charge."

She went back to the car. Roger was sitting up in back, drinking from a bottle of water. Sandy and Wish sat in fold-out beach chairs behind the car.

"Better?" she said.

"I think I had an anxiety attack," he said. "I felt dizzy, but I'm better now."

"Good." She went around the car.

"How's it going?" Sandy asked. She was just sitting there, under an oak tree that hung over the street, looking comfortable with her legs up on the fender, a thermos on the ground and a cup in her hand. Wish read the Placerville want ads.

"No change. You look all right."

"As long as it takes," Sandy said.

"You should go home. I can get a lift with Sergeant Cheney later."

"Listen to her," Sandy said to Wish, shaking her head. "Thinks we're going home."

"He's our client," Wish said to Nina. "We can't go home until he's okay."

"There's nothing you can do."

"We're sitting with him," Sandy said. "He's in there, we're out here, but we're with him. He needs us."

"You need us," Wish said. He got up and made her sit in his chair. "Coffee," he said. "Long night ahead, maybe."

At the bottom of the hill where the police had stopped traffic, Nina could see many more lights and people. "Reporters," she said. "I wonder what they know." She drank the coffee gratefully.

Nothing happened for over an hour, except that the sun did a lot of things that must go on every evening, which she didn't often notice: It sent sharp rays through the trees, it sparkled in the west on a neighbor's chimney, it withdrew its warmth, it disappeared, leaving its radiant trail. The police grouped and regrouped, talked on their radios, moved their cars around. Now and then the officer with the bullhorn repeated his request that Flint pick up the phone. The Hanna house with its unkempt yard and old fruit tree became the focus of her world.

At seven Wish braved the reporters to bring back pizza. Roger huddled in a blanket in the car, and Nina and Sandy continued their vigil from the plastic chairs. It reminded Nina of a Fourth of July at Tahoe when she and Bob had sat on the beach at North Shore with a crowd of people waiting endlessly for the first burst of fireworks in the sky, but the mood was very different now.

They were waiting, helplessly, for a tragedy.

Cheney found them a few minutes later. He ambled up and leaned against the van. "It's full dark now," he said. "The talk is of trying tear gas. I mentioned your offer to the Crisis Negotiation Team. The officer in charge wasn't interested an hour ago, but he just told me if you want to talk through the horn, just to ask if Flint wants to talk to you, he'll allow that. He'll be beside you to coach you if Flint responds. If nothing happens, things are going to get rough."

"Right now?" Nina said.

"Right now." He extended a hand and Nina took it.

"Hold the fort," she told Sandy, an old joke between them.

"Good luck," Wish said. Nina and Cheney moved carefully from car to car, until they came to two uniformed police directly across the street from the house, standing in the dirt of a neighbor's flower bed. One of them held the bullhorn. "Officer Christian. Nina Reilly," Cheney said.

"You're the hostage's lawyer?" Officer Christian said. He was a tired, square-jawed young man who barely looked at her.

"That's right."

"You say Flint has attempted to communicate with you?"

Nina explained.

"There has been zero action inside ever since our arrival. We're about to quit this attempt. My concern is that you might say something that will set off an incident."

"I know. I understand."

"Here's what you'll say." They rehearsed for a couple of minutes. Christian warned her about her tone, which he said would be more crucial than her words. The gravity of what she was about to do made her throat feel tight. All around her were silent police officers standing amid flashing red lights.

"Go." He showed her how to hold the horn. A cord ran from it to the nearby police car. It was heavy and awkward and rusty. She held it up with both hands.

"Mr. Flint? Mr. Flint, are you there?" She waited a moment to allow the fact of her female voice to sink in inside the house, and to recover from the shock of hearing her voice amplified from, it seemed, Sacramento to Reno. "Mr. Flint, I'm Nina Reilly. I'd like to help. If you'd like to talk to me, all you have to do is pick up the phone. I'm calling you right now." A uniformed woman nodded and dialed the Hanna number.

"Do you need anything? I'm right outside, and I can help."

"It's ringing," the officer said.

"It won't hurt just to talk for a minute," Nina said through the horn.

The officer passed her the phone. Just like that. Nina dropped the horn and it made a loud protest. "Hello? Hello?"

"He says, nobody try anything."

"Dave?" The voice was ragged, gasping, but recognizable. "It's Hanna!" she mouthed, hand over the phone. They could all hear Dave's voice on the monitor in the police car. Officer Christian was breathing fast, trying to tell her what to say, but it was hard, they were both so shocked that it was Hanna on the line, not Flint.

"Dave, are you all right?"

"Did you hear? Nobody try anything."

"Nobody will try anything. Nobody."

"He says he wants a helicopter and pilot. Two hundred fifty thousand in cash in the passenger seat. One hour."

We can talk about that, Officer Christian mouthed. Nina said, "We can talk about that. Are you injured, Dave?"

"He says, shut up. He says listen. One hour."

"Okay, there is discussion out here, Dave. Arrangements are being made." Christian had nodded and told her to run with the demand.

"He says he'll let me go. Please don't let them try anything for a while, Nina." This sounded like Dave's own words, like he was very frightened that the police were about to enter the house forcibly.

"While they talk, Dave, do you or Mr. Flint need anything? Some food or water?"

A pause. "He says, shut up and listen. He says he wants you to know he killed Sarah. Shot her because she was watching." This bald statement sent shock waves all through the assembled group. Nina thought of Roger.

"Okay," she said. "I understand. He killed Sarah."

"He says he killed Chelsi and the others to stop the lawsuit."

"Okay."

"He says you started it and made him finish it. He says it's all your fault."

Tears started up in Nina's eyes. Hearing this was like being gouged by sharp beaks. I'm quitting law, she thought. I'm getting out.

"He says, time's up. Do we have a deal?" Dave said.

She was swallowing, trying to control herself, but she couldn't. She shook her head. Christian took the phone. Helpful hands supported her.

Sandy and Wish put her in the front passenger seat of the van. She was crying uncontrollably. Roger had disappeared. "It's all right, all right," Sandy said, patting her shoulders. Wish made her drink some water. "I think we should take her home now," he told Sandy.

"He said I caused it."

Sandy said grimly, "He caused all of it. If I get my hands on him—"

They heard a shot.

For a moment, the whole forest was quiet. Then the police sprang into action, taking up positions, guns drawn, yelling. From several hundred feet away Nina could see Officer Christian holding up his arm, raising it up and down as though to quiet them.

"Oh, God," she said. "He shot Dave."

A new, uneasy quiet descended. The police were close to storming the house, but Christian was making the signal No, no to them. He grabbed the bullhorn and said, "Don't shoot! Don't shoot!" The door to the house was opening.

A man came rushing out, looking wildly around and yelling something. He was tackled instantly, made to lie supine on the ground while two officers cuffed him. He struggled for only a minute, then lay on the ground quietly. Other officers rushed into the house.

Nina, Wish, and Sandy moved toward the house. No one stopped them.

A policeman came back to the front door and made a sign. The man inside was dead and it was safe to come in. "Oh, no," Nina said. "No!" It was impossible, Dave Hanna gunned down in his own home while she watched the whole thing—there was Roger, running up the steps onto the porch. He rushed inside.

Then he came back out, waving his arms. He looked around and saw the cuffed man on the ground.

"Dave?" he said. The police officers pulled the man to his feet.

It was Dave Hanna, disheveled and bloody but alive. "I got him, Rog!" he cried.

Chapter 32

"I GOT HIM"

PLACERVILLE, Cal. (AP)—

A man held hostage at gunpoint in his own home by a serial killer managed to turn the tables on his attacker yesterday, wresting the gun away and shooting the attacker fatally.

Dave Hanna, a former firefighter from Placerville, California, was resting at home today after the violent face-off with Leland Moss Flint of Palo Alto, California, the man who killed Hanna's wife and niece. Flint allegedly shot Hanna's wife, a bystander, during an armed robbery at Lake Tahoe two years ago. When Hanna filed a wrongful-death lawsuit that developed leads to Flint, Flint allegedly killed Hanna's niece and two witnesses to the robbery.

Yesterday, Flint crawled through a basement window in Hanna's house. When Hanna came home, he was beaten and tied up. Police arrived after a 911 call by Hanna's brother-in-law, Roger Freeman, and they surrounded the house.

Five hours into the grueling standoff, Flint demanded a

pilot, helicopter, and large sum of money in return for Hanna's life—but while the killer was talking to the police, Hanna loosened his bonds and jumped Flint. In the ensuing struggle Flint was fatally shot.

"It's miraculous that he got the gun away from Flint," said Sergeant Fred Cheney of the South Lake Tahoe Police Department, one of the multidistrict police forces called in.

"He's a hero," said Rosetta Williams, a next-door neighbor of Hanna's who was evacuated during the hostage situation. "We all knew and loved his wife. It's fitting that Dave caught the killer."

"No quote from you," Sandy observed, handing Nina the front page of the *San Francisco Chronicle* when she came in the next morning. "How'd you sleep?"

"Sleep? What sleep?"

"The schools are closed. The prediction is two feet."

It was snowing, large, dry flakes, the temperature in the thirties. The cabin on Kulow had been warm and silent, and all Nina had wanted that morning was to stay in her bed under the Hudson Bay blanket, watching it fall and covering all the horror of the Hanna case.

In the end, she hadn't wanted to be alone. And Sandy would need her. So she threw on corduroy pants and a ski sweater and let her hair hang loose. It was the first day of the rest of her life, the one in which she quit, because it was her fault.

"You have a lot of mop-up on the Hanna lawsuit today. Mr. Hanna already called. He's actually not at home, he's staying with Roger. I thought you'd be in at nine."

"Sorry. You and Wish were great yesterday, Sandy. Thanks again."

"I hope we never have anything like that again. The waiting was bad. I never thought he'd get out alive." Sandy looked tired, too. "Why are you looking at me like that?"

"I'm happy you're here, Sandy. Where's Wish?"

"Sergeant Cheney called and Wish said he'd go see him. Are you sure you're okay?"

"I'll be in my office."

"Don't you want some coffee?"

"Give me a minute." Nina went into her office and shut the door. She went behind her desk, kicked her shoes off, put up her feet, and closed her eyes. She had spent the night alternately pacing the floor and sitting on the couch in front of the fire, trying to understand what she had done.

Flint's words, that it was her fault, damned her. The guilt was overwhelming. Even with Dave's miraculous survival, she had it from the killer's mouth that she had set him off on a murder spree.

And for what? What good had come of her legal machinations, her travels, her theories? Three murders and several attempted murders. She was tapped out on the expenses, Dave would get little besides scars and traumatic memories, and Chelsi was dead.

Tapped out. Yes, that was it. In a way, she had tried to play God with a devil. And this was the result.

She didn't think she could go on. She would quit practicing law, teach or something. She didn't have the hide for it anymore. Representing a client meant being personally responsible, and she was responsible.

Flint himself had said she had set him off.

She picked up the receiver and called Roger's house.

"How are you both this morning?" she asked when Roger picked up.

"Dave is holding court. He looks pretty banged up with the bandages on his face, but he's in a great mood. The docs say he'll be fine in a couple of weeks. He slept last night and this morning the reporters found us, so he's been doing interviews. I threw out all the booze in the house."

"Can I talk to him?"

"Sure. Hang on."

Hanna's voice sounded weak. "Hi."

"Hi. I called to see how you were."

"Fine. My rib hurts but I have some pills. There are people here. I can't talk long."

"I'm glad you made it," Nina said. "I wanted to apologize. For getting you into it. I guess I really did get Flint going."

"Yeah, he blamed you for everything. Not that he wasn't about to kill me, when the cops came."

"I'm sorry. For what you went through."

"That's what I get, for letting Roger and Chelsi talk me into hiring you. It was them, too, pushing, pushing. Flint went crazy."

"Did he say anything to you—anything strange?"

"Like what?"

"That he didn't kill Sarah?"

"The opposite. He was real clear about it. He did it." She heard someone talking in the background. "There's a guy here who wants to buy the rights to my story. Do you know a lawyer who handles stuff like that?"

"I'm afraid not."

"Listen, I'm gonna go. Nina, start dismantling whatever you've been up to, okay? Roger and I have talked about it and we feel we've suffered enough. Just throw the case out or whatever you do."

"How about if we talk tomorrow about it?" Nina said.

"If you want. Bye."

Nina hung up. She felt sick. It was the whole Hanna case making her sick. At least Dave made it through, she thought.

Wish burst through the door, Sandy right behind him. "Have to talk to you right now," he said breathlessly.

Nina held her hand to her chest. "Not another murder!"

He dropped into a chair. Sandy had locked up outside. She took the other client chair. "Stop scaring us, Willis," she said. "What is it?"

"I talked to Cheney. He says the coroner gave him a preliminary report this morning. The coroner told him that Lee Flint had bruising on his arms and legs and cheeks."

"So? Dave struggled with him."

"It's not like that, Nina," Wish said slowly.

"Well, out with it," Sandy told him.

"These are specific marks of being tied up. You know, in the chair at the Hanna house."

"The chair Dave was tied in?"

"Sergeant Cheney had just talked to the hospital. Mr. Hanna didn't have any marks like that."

"Flint was tied up? Not Dave?" Nina said. "You're confusing me, Wish."

"No, you have it exactly right. Flint was tied up, not Mr. Hanna. We're sitting in the sergeant's office and he's telling me this. He wants to have you brought in for a discussion. Then he gets a phone call from the police forensics lab in Sacramento. I was right there, Nina. He almost fell off his chair."

"Why?"

"It's about our client, Nina. Are you ready?"

"Go ahead," Nina said.

"The fingerprint report came in on the gun Meredith gave you. The one used in the robbery."

"And?"

"There was a surprise."

"Which was?"

"Mr. Hanna's fingerprint was on the barrel. Along with Flint's and Meredith's."

Nina said, puzzled, "Dave handled the gun? When could he have done that?"

"Yes, when?" Wish said. "You see?"

"Slow down," Sandy said. "I'm still thinking about bruises."

Nina swung her legs down. She put her hands on the desk. "Dave touched the gun."

"Yes."

"He came running down after his wife was shot and touched the gun."

Sandy objected, "But Meredith saw him coming down. That's when she picked up the gun, when she saw him on the staircase, yelling."

"If she's telling the truth, he couldn't have touched it—"

Wish said, "You see? Unless he had already been down there—"

"And he was going back up the stairs?"

"Not coming down to get help?" Sandy said.

"Going back up, after he touched the gun," Nina said. "I don't like what I'm thinking." The shock made it hard to think clearly. "No possible mistake about the fingerprint?" she said.

"No. It was from his hunting license."

"He saw the attempted robbery from the balcony, with his wife," Nina said. "He saw Elliott rush Flint and knock the gun out of his hand. There was an interval between the first two shots and the third shot."

"The students and Flint—they must have all run away after the second shot," Wish said.

"What are you saying, Willis?" Sandy demanded. "You're not saying our client fired the third shot?"

"What do you think, Mom?"

"I don't know."

"Nina?" Wish said.

"Let's say he came running down the stairs and saw the gun on the ground. He picked it up and saw his wife. He shot her. He might have heard Meredith coming. He only had seconds, Wish! He should have wiped the gun, or kept it."

"But he didn't have time to think. He only had time to run halfway up again and pretend he was coming down for the first time when she saw him."

"He just didn't have time to deal with the gun," Nina said.

"There you go," Wish said.

"I don't believe it," Sandy said. "Why would he kill his wife? She was pregnant!"

"Yes. She was thirty-eight and she taught school and she was going to have a baby," Nina said. "His baby."

"I just don't believe it."

"Hang on." Nina held up a hand. She struggled with a feeling so intense she couldn't speak for a minute.

Betrayal. To be betrayed like this by her own client hurt. She breathed in and out, trying to think.

Sandy was still saying it couldn't be true, but Wish just stared at Nina as she tried to encompass the enormity of Hanna's lies.

Finally she said, "Remember what Jimmy Bova told me at the Ace High? Flint attacked him because he thought Bova might have shot Sarah. But Bova convinced him he didn't."

Sandy's eyes narrowed into an expression Nina didn't recognize. Her face changed. Her nose stood out prominently, nostrils wide. Her lips became a thin line.

"I'm starting to believe it," she said. "Because the next man Flint went to see, the very next day, was—"

"Our client," Wish said. "He started in on Mr. Hanna, but then the police came after Roger Freeman called 911 and Mr. Hanna must have gotten the gun away from him. Mr. Hanna tied Flint up, not the other way around."

"But Flint was making Mr. Hanna talk on the phone," Sandy said, "wasn't he?" and an expression Nina did recognize, of horror and rage, came into her face. Nina felt it, too. The hidden variable had revealed itself like some cold demon riding through a dark sky, trailing misery and bloodshed.

"Hanna had good luck and bad luck," Nina said. "He did struggle with Flint, and he got the gun away from him. I imagine the police were just arriving. He didn't know what to do at first, so he did nothing."

"And outside, everyone believed it was a hostage situation," Wish said.

Sandy said, "He was safe that whole time? I don't want to believe it, because then that man is so cruel. Cruel!"

"Letting Roger and everyone worry," Wish said. "And he was fine, he was just trying to figure out how to keep Flint from talking."

"Cruel," Sandy repeated, shaking her head. Nina closed her eyes and thought back to the awful moments in Placerville when Dave was talking to her on the phone, pretending to relay Flint's statements.

It was Dave, cruel Dave, who had told her it was all her fault.

When it was really Dave's fault, Dave who killed his wife and tried to hide his secret, Dave who obstructed Nina's efforts to find Sarah's killer.

But Dave couldn't know then that the robber whose gun he picked up and used wasn't a random robber, wasn't some punk off the streets of downtown Reno.

Lee Flint didn't know who had killed the woman whose death he was being blamed for. He watched and waited for two years while the police investigation fizzled and the civil case wheezed toward dismissal. Then, when Nina came in, he started his own investigation. And he started covering his tracks, eliminating witnesses.

"Hanna piggybacked on Lee Flint's robbery," Nina said.

"Flint got blamed for Sarah's murder. He hadn't killed her. But he couldn't afford to be caught. To stop the investigation from leading to his robbery, he decided to kill Silke and Raj—"

"And you, too, and Elliott. Flint thought Chelsi was you," Wish said. "We're lucky you're still with us."

"So Dave Hanna killed his wife," Sandy said. "I'm gonna believe it. I'm gonna go down to Placerville and kill him myself for killing his wife and lying to us and making you feel like you pulled the trigger on those people." Her face had turned purple. She stood up.

"Mom?"

"Break his scrawny little neck." She went into the outer office and Nina and Wish started to follow her. "Feed him to my horses. Don't try to stop me." She was putting on her coat.

Nina said, "Sandy, take your coat off, please. Dave's incredibly dangerous. Do you guys realize he must have shot Flint there at the end, while Flint was tied up and probably gagged?"

"It's sickening," Wish said. "He's sickening. Cheney told me not to talk to Hanna. I think he'll be arrested within a few hours. What do we do, Nina?"

"He's still our client, even though he's a lying, murdering sack," Nina said. She was trembling with rage.

"Do we warn him?" Wish asked. "Should I go down to Placerville and try to help him?"

"You mean kill him," Sandy said. "Don't you?"

She still stood at the door in her coat. Nina thought of all the hours Sandy had put in to help Hanna, the deadlines, the phone calls, the hours in Placerville worrying for him. She and Wish had also been betrayed. Wish walked over to her and put his arm around her and said gently, "Mom, come on back here and sit down."

Nina said, "Wish, call Roger Freeman and ask him to come

up here. Use some pretext. I don't want him in Hanna's house when the arrest goes down. Sandy, draw up a Withdrawal of Attorney in the Hanna case. Make copies and date it today."

"We're abandoning him?" Wish said.

"We signed on to help him sue the man who killed his wife," Nina said. "He had to sue, or it would seem as though he didn't care. But the whole case is a lie. There is no case."

"Where are you going?" Nina was pulling her hiking boots on.

"For a walk. The trail down to the lake. I want to feel some clean snow on my face."

"It wasn't your fault, you know," Sandy said. "You do know that?"

"All I know is that Bob can come home now," Nina said.

She went to the morgue. She had to see Flint.

He was on a gurney, post-autopsy, covered with a sheet. She pulled it back and stared at his scarred face. He looked younger than she had thought. In the way of the dead, he gave nothing back except the empty calm of eternity.

Bastard! she told him. He didn't answer. She had never seen him alive. She would never fully understand him. Unknowable, he had escaped her by dying before she could tell it to his face, tell him, Got you, got you.

Got you. Selfish and doomed, he rested in peace.

She had one more call to make. Four hours later, in the evening, after Cheney called to tell her that the arrest had gone down quietly, she went to see Dave Hanna at the Placerville jail. The drive down the hill went slowly because of the drifts and she welcomed the chance to think some things through.

★   ★   ★

"You took your time," Dave Hanna told Nina through the glass in the visitors' room at the Placerville jail. His ruddy face showed fright. "I only got to make my phone call an hour ago. The cops said I was under arrest for Sarah's murder. That's all they would tell me. It's all a big—"

"Let me bring you up to date, Dave," Nina said.

She told him about the gun, the fingerprint, the bruises on Flint's body.

Hanna began to cave in as she talked. He slumped and said, "Oh, shit," several times. When she finished, he started to cry. Nina watched him do that.

After a few minutes, when the sobbing and hiccuping had died down, Nina said, "Why did you do it, Dave?"

"I don't like the way you're looking at me. This is—still confidential, right?"

"I'm still your attorney. It's confidential."

"Why'd you have to open up the whole thing?"

"Why'd you kill her?" Something in her voice must have shaken him.

"It just happened," he said. "I snapped, I guess."

"What does that mean?"

"We saw the robbery from the balcony, then the man in the mask ran one way and the kids took off toward their rooms. I told Sarah to stay put and I ran down the stairs."

"Why?"

"I saw the gun lying on the concrete. I don't know why, I just wanted it. I picked it up. It was hot, alive. I wanted to use it on something. I looked up and Sarah was standing on the balcony looking down at me. And she knew."

"Knew what?"

"That I was thinking, I'd like to shoot her."

"Oh?"

"She already knew. So I pulled the trigger and made it real. I was surprised myself. I heard a noise and I thought, Drop it and run back up and yell. So I did that and I had just made it a few steps up when the motel clerk came around the corner, and I stopped." He grimaced. "Later, I felt really bad about it."

"About what?"

"Leaving the gun. But I didn't have enough time to think. You have to understand, Nina, it was like somebody else did it."

Nina was silent for a long moment. Then she said, "But why? Why did you kill her?"

"Why? Why? How should I know? She was just putting up with me. She ragged on me about money, about me having a few beers at night, about brushing my fucking teeth before I went to bed. She was going to have a baby and there wasn't going to be any room at all for me after that. The gun was in my hand. It happened."

Nina leaned back and closed her eyes.

"I was tired of her. Everybody gets that way sometimes. I had a gun in my hand. It's like an accident."

"An accident," Nina repeated.

"The whole thing. A series of random events that put the gun in my hand. I haven't told a soul," Hanna went on, "except my attorney. How strong is that evidence, Nina? What's going to happen to me? If she hadn't given me that look, like I was an ass-hole, when I looked up at her on that balcony, it wouldn't have happened."

"What about Flint?" Nina said. "Was he gagged and bound when you shot him?"

"Flint? Why are you talking about him? That was no crime, not really, he had come there to kill me. It was self-defense."

"You shot him in cold blood!"

"So what? He deserved it, didn't he? Fool. He didn't dream I could take him."

Nina said nothing. Dave went back to his wife.

"It's not my fault. I never did anything wrong my whole life. I walked her to church, I folded the clothes, I went and got the paper for her in the morning. For years. Years. Something snapped. I wasn't myself. I'd had a few. Whatever."

"Did you kill Chelsi? Did you follow me to Germany?"

"No! It was Flint. I wouldn't have done that to little Chelsi. Poor little girl. I was so scared while all that was going on, Nina. It was very hard to keep it together."

"Flint only finished what you started," Nina said.

"Not at all. You don't understand. Flint had nothing to do with me."

"I'm afraid the difference escapes me."

Hanna's face drooped. "I appreciate your coming down, Nina. I was afraid you might walk out. It's good to know that at least you're going to do your duty and help me in my hour of need. Lucky for me you're a criminal lawyer, too. I'll sell the house. You'll be paid."

"Don't put up the For Sale sign on my account," Nina said. She opened her briefcase and pulled out the legal pleading, never taking her eyes off Hanna. Then she plastered the paper against the glass. "Read it," she said. He read it.

"You can't do that!" he shouted. "You're my lawyer and you have a duty!"

"This is a new matter."

"I told you I'd pay you. Don't leave me, please, Nina. You have to help me. I don't want to go through this with a stranger."

Nina said slowly, "You know, Dave, I never really knew what evil was until I met you. I could find some excuse for every one of my guilty clients. But you taught me. Now I know."

"But—"

"Evil is a man who kills his wife and thinks he deserves pity. You make me sick. Listen. Remember this one thing from our conversation."

"Wait—"

"Remember this through all the years to come, Dave. It *was* your fault. All of it." She spat the words out.

"Don't do this!" He was shouting again. He kept it up while the guard came in and dragged him back into the secure area. Nina sat, her head bowed, until the guard came to fetch her.

Epilogue

THE PRE-CHRISTMAS SNOWSTORM TURNED INTO A whopper. Three feet of snow plumped up the street with mounds of marshmallows. Four feet packed the higher ski resorts. When bright, dry conditions returned, Tahoe went wild. Tourist SUVs clogged the roads in and out, ski racks piled high on their roofs. The Heavenly Gondola sagged with the weight of the people going up and down from the lodge. The lake that never froze, rimmed by its white peaks, gleamed under a cloudless, deep sky. The casinos rocked into the night and Christmas carols jingled across the mountains.

Nina Reilly's law offices closed, leaving behind a Happy Holidays sign to swing on the door, reminding unobservant clients that the world had shut down. For this short time, all the running hamsters in the town lumbered down from their wheels, ate too much, drank too much, and fell into luxurious stupors. Nobody worked. Even Sandy and Wish went home to Markleeville, Wish's brown van stuffed full of presents and feed for the animals.

On Vashon Island in Washington State, at his scratched old desk, Elliott Wakefield set down his mechanical pencil and cocked his head at the result. He had checked the equations over and over, and the results never varied. He couldn't find an error. Starting with any integer on Gauss's li line, he could first determine precisely how many primes there were up to that point, and then generate the nearest prime by plugging that number into his function. Factoring any-size composite number followed as a necessary corollary of the function.

He had finished his proof, twenty-three pages of closely reasoned math and physics condensed down from two hundred pages.

He got up and wandered around his room, looking at the books, picking up the loose papers on the floor, leaving his notebook displayed on the center of his desk like a black square-cut diamond.

Now what? Ask some colleagues to read it before daring to submit it to a journal? He really should.

He had wanted Silke to read and appreciate it. Now he wasn't sure what he wanted from it.

"El?" his father called up from the foot of the stairs. "Dinner."

"Two minutes," he answered.

The Net was open to one of the XYC bank-account sites inside Bank of America. XYC was cheating with several other Cayman accounts, which Elliott had recently also accessed, but there was still plenty in the B of A checking account he was looking at.

He transferred $1,739,197 to his proxy account. Always a reasonable amount.

Always a prime number.

But that would be theft. He transferred the money back. Aw, I'm only playin' witcha, he thought.

For fun, he punched in the primary URL for Russia's military accounts. The Russians, too, were being bad boys. For now, he was just enjoying himself, educating himself on how the world really runs.

You know, El, the fame and immortality thing can wait a while, he thought, beginning a conversation with himself. You're only twenty-three, you can always publish in ten years. Meantime . . .

"El?"

. . . you have changed. Learned a lot.

He twisted back and forth in the chair, thinking.

The money thing wasn't important either, not really.

But the revenge thing—the revenge thing was important. XYC should have stopped Flint. There would never be another Silke on this earth, and not only were people dead, but he, Elliott Wakefield, would never love another woman.

He thought for another moment, then went to his E-mail server and typed in messages to Professor Braun and to Branson, the lawyer.

To the professor, he wrote:

Forming new company using unbreakable encryption formula. Would like to have you on board. Interested? Will double your fee.

To Branson, he wrote:

Are you available to serve as my counsel on a start-up here in Seattle? My encryption formula is unbreakable. I'll need some patent work.

He thought, I'll ask Nina to handle some of the lawsuits. He sent the E-mails and leaned back. Did he want to cannibalize anybody else from XYC? Patty Hightower?

No. Leave the phonies. Keep the competent hard-asses and hit XYC where it would hurt. They thought he was a naive fool. They would find out what it means to take on a mathematician.

Numbers, quanta; they're shifty. Yesterday's off-ramp is today's cinder-block wall. Sometimes the cosmos does seem to dissolve and re-form with certain subtle differences. He should know. It had happened to him. He had hardened, grown up.

"El!"

"Coming." He shut down and walked downstairs. Pop couldn't get to the second floor anymore, so his research could remain private, if he wanted. As for the NSA searchers, they could come back, but they would never find out how he accessed his sites and he'd just slip the notebook under Pop's behind again. Nobody would pull Pop out of his wheelchair to search.

His father shook the old snow dome of Santa in his sleigh and placed it in the middle of the kitchen table. White flakes landed on Santa's shoulders, then drifted down to the ground. "Merry Christmas Eve," he said, holding his glass of wine high, admiring the candlelight glowing through the red.

"I have news," Elliott said.

"Oh?"

"It's finished. You know what I mean?"

His father's glass stopped and hovered in the air.

"I can't find an error."

"You really finished?" his father asked. "All that work came to something, eh? All that concentration." His voice quivered slightly.

"It took a long time. I doubted myself, Pop. I told everyone I could, but I didn't believe it."

"I always said, you're a bright one."

"Merry Christmas, Pop." They clinked glasses and drank. His father had grilled steaks. Elliott poured on the A1 sauce.

"I read a good article in the *International Journal of American Linguistics* today," his father said. "I might write up a little note on it and submit it."

"I'll input it for you," Elliott said. He took a big bite, savoring the flavors. Nobody could grill a steak like Pop.

Outside the cabin windows, last whispers of the old year's snow murmured around the trees of the Tahoe basin. Inside, the Christmas tree cast its blurred colors across the shadowy ceiling. Presents lay under the tree. Unable to keep his eyes open, Bob had gone to bed after midnight, just after Christmas Day arrived. Hitchcock lay at Nina's feet on the couch, paws crossed, eyes fluttering as he dreamed.

Sitting in the armchair nearest the fire, Kurt relaxed, wearing the same sweater and jeans he had worn when she picked him and Bob up at the airport. His boots were propped by the front door, his suitcases and backpack next to them. They had all eaten out and talked about the trip and the Hanna case. Then, when Kurt and Nina were alone, they had shared their histories, really talked.

Now a silence dropped between them. Nina could hear the big fir bending in the dark front yard, the heat turning on, the wood spitting and crackling in the grate. She got up and went over to Kurt, sitting down at his feet, her back to him, watching the fire. She stretched.

"Tired?" he asked.

"Only a little. Kurt?"

"Mm-hmm?"

She leaned back, touching his leg. "Come to bed with me."

He stroked her hair.

"It's been so long," she said.

"You are something."

"I'm glad you still think so." She turned to face him and took his hand. "It's late. Bob will be up early."

"It's Christmas, and you offer gifts to your old lover."

"Not so old," she teased. "You're in your thirties, last I looked." She put her fingers between his and enjoyed the softness of his large and long-fingered, artistic hands. "You're so warm."

"And you're so inviting."

A moment passed.

"Yet you sit there," she said, slightly peeved.

He had been looking at her hand, reacting to its movements between his fingers, but he fixed his eyes on hers and she could read what she saw in them as easily as she could read the casinos' neon billboards down on Lake Tahoe Boulevard, through blizzards, rain, whiteouts. He wanted her as much as she wanted him. In his unguarded eyes she saw the same need, caring, and lust she was feeling.

"Come upstairs with me," she said.

"I can't do that."

She took her hand back. She wanted to couple mindlessly with him, and this interruption in what should be a flowing thing bothered her. "Why not?"

"I'm not them."

"Who?"

"The others."

She knew who he meant. So what about them?

"All of them. Men you're no longer with. Jack. Collier. Paul. Others I don't know about."

Nina looked back through the years, at the flaming and burning out in between. She considered Mick. Had she really loved Jack? She had caused the divorce as much as he had. Would her love for Collier have lasted? They had never gone beyond the first glory of romance.

And Paul—pain lacerated her—had she known all along that he was wrong for her? Strung him along?

"You don't trust yourself with men."

"You ought to know why." The heat of her reaction surprised her.

Kurt said slowly, looking down, "I disappeared from your life when we were in love. That disrupted both our lives. But Nina, I had no choice. You know that. I suffered, too."

Although she tried to stop it, the image rose in her mind of a young girl wearing a short flowered dress on a bench overlooking Lover's Point in Pacific Grove. That girl looked out at the holiday revelers, now eternally frozen in place in her mind, getting soaked by salt spray, waiting for hours for a man she trusted totally. It was the memory, the one she had returned to again and again, cried over, puzzled over. She had clung to this memory, kept it strong in her mind, and allowed it to structure her life. The memory seemed tattered around the edges now, though, no longer lit with an awful radiance. It felt like a disaster that had happened to two young people she had once known.

Still, from the remnant of her pain, she said, "But I didn't know why for twelve long years. Even though I understand why now, the scar will always be there."

"Where?"

What a silly question. That scar wasn't real. "Well, there's this," she said instead. "The one I told you about." Her finger traced along her chest. Shot, survived. Knocked down, got up. Deserted, continued alone. She had gone on without him.

He reached for her, wrapping his fingers around her chilled ones. Under her own fingers she felt her pulse quicken.

"There?" he asked.

"Everywhere." You wounded me more than any gun ever could, she thought. "I'm not the girl you knew. I got tough. I had to. I don't believe—"

"In me?" His hand tightened over hers. "Or you don't believe in love, is that what you're saying?"

"Let's not talk. I've said everything I want to say." She had been exposed under that thin cotton dress, her heart steady, right at the surface, beating for him, ready to make any sacrifice. She had never felt entirely happy since. That much she admitted, but silently, only to herself. She took her hand out from under his and moved it so that it pressed against her breast. A wash of feeling splashed through her body like an ocean wave. "I still want you. That never changed. Take me to bed."

He took his hand away and, seemingly absentmindedly, put his finger in the center of her neck, to a hollow nobody else had ever noticed or touched specially, only him. "You haven't changed. You're still the woman I loved, chasing squirrels off the porch at Fallen Leaf, swatting at mosquitoes with your flip-flop. Falling asleep while I played Bach in that ratty cabin of yours."

"No, I'm not." She closed her eyes for an instant and recalled him making incredible sounds come from a beat-up piano as shadows spread over the lake.

He stroked her arm. Her body rippled under his touch. "We can begin at the end," he said.

Mesmerized by the power of his touch, she felt unable to make sense of the jumble of sensations. She had trouble tracking what was old business, what was new, and what was happening right now. She urgently needed to get it over with, get him out of her system so he—so he—she got up and took off her sweater, unbuttoned her jeans.

"Stop, Nina," he said.

"I need someone right now. Not tomorrow or someday."

"You have me, okay?"

"I don't want to be alone upstairs. I don't understand what's going on." She looked at him, at his calm face and the warmth in it. He wasn't exactly rejecting her—or was he?

"No, I'll sleep on this charming couch." He punched its gnarly cushions. "Tomorrow I'll move to a hotel, look for a permanent place."

"And where am I in this?"

"Nearby. Taking hikes with me and Bob. Teaching me to live in the mountains. Taking it slow with me." He turned away and gazed out into the black night.

She came up behind him and circled him with her arms, pressing her body against his back. "Kurt, what is all this you're saying? Don't you want me?" His shirt scratched against her bare skin.

"Don't you see what I'm offering you?"

"I only know that we're here tonight, and . . ."

"We have a child together." He turned to face her and smiled, that amiable grin of his, eyes trying to tell her—what? He brushed her face lightly, as if brushing past a veil. "A chance together. It's late, but it's not over for the three of us. Don't you see?"

A thought took shape in her mind, too big, too much to ask for in this shifting world. Could he mean . . .

We have a child together, she thought. A child, a sacred tie. That's what he's saying. He's talking about—he's talking about uniting a family. He wanted real love.

"I . . ."

"Don't be afraid," he said. He put his hands on her arms and faced her. "I never loved anybody but you." Then he pulled her closer until she could feel the hairs on her skin touching his face, and then closer, until she felt the light steam of his breath on her mouth and she bent back in his arms. His body smelled like pine on a hot day. He kissed her, but gently.

"Nina," he whispered.

"Yes, Kurt?"

"Good night."

"Sleep well." Nina picked up her sweater, shook her head, smiling, and went upstairs to bed.

Acknowledgments

Our late brother, Patrick R. O'Shaughnessy, advised, supported, and contributed jokes, fun, and wisdom to this book, as he has with all our books. He was part of Perri and his death is an overwhelming loss. His friends John Kunkle, Andrew McKenna, Emmett O'Boyle, and Kathleen Roberts made his loss more bearable.

As always, Nancy Yost of Lowenstein Morel Yost and Associates acted as much more than an agent in the writing of this book. She was a friend, an editor, and an enthusiastic support.

Danielle Perez, senior editor at the Bantam Dell Publishing Group, knows just how much to change in a manuscript to make it better without changing its flavor. She stayed with us through-out the writing of this book as a constant and reliable resource. Irwyn Applebaum, our publisher, has given us the freedom to write. He has always given us the feeling that he would go as far as necessary to give our books the widest possible audience. We are very grateful to Irwyn. We would also like to thank Nita

Taublib, deputy publisher of Bantam Dell, who has worked hard behind the scenes for our books. Besides these wonderful people, many others at Bantam Dell have helped us. We would like to offer thanks to Robin Foster, our copy editor, Susan Corcoran, our publicist, Shannon Jamieson, the artists, the sales force, the binders, the distributors, all who have shown such professionalism.

We thank Patrick Morriss of Foothill College, Los Altos Hills, California, for consulting with us on the mathematics in this book. We also thank our families, Brad, Meg, Sylvia and Frank, Andy, June, Connor, and Corianna, and so many more in our extended family: always with us, in happiness and sadness. And we thank good friends and associates for all they have done for us in a hard year: Nita Piper and June Snedecor, who have worked so hard on the perrio.com Web site, and Ardyth Brock, Elizabeth Blair, and Dawn Marie.

For a list of fascinating books and materials used as background material for the mathematics and gambling scenes in this book, please check our Web site at perrio.com. All mistakes and speculations are our own.

At the moment, though there is talk of using other encryption methods for the Net, such as quantum encryption, prime number encryption is the best method we have. Thus one of the seemingly most arcane mathematical mysteries has suddenly become immensely important to the mundane world of commerce and politics. No one today can predict exact prime numbers using a formula.

But that day will come. And, in addition to its immediate practical significance, it will have an even greater scientific significance: It will brush aside one of the darkest veils of the mysterious and magnificent universe we live in.